ACCL

The Headmistress of Rosemere

"This book has it all: shining prose, heart-wrenching emotion, vivid and engaging characters, a well-paced plot and a sigh-worthy happy ending that might cause some readers to reach for the tissue box. In only her second novel, Ladd has established herself as Regency writing royalty."

—*RT Book Reviews*, 4 1/2 stars, TOP PICK!

"Sarah Ladd has written a story sure to warm your heart even on the coldest day."

—Laurie Alice Eakes, author of *A Lady's Honor*

"[E]ngaging scenes of the times keep the pages turning as this historical romance . . . swirls energetically through angst and disclosure."

—*Publishers Weekly*

"Readers will cheer for the determined heroine and the flawed hero in this engaging story of redemption, set in the lush English countryside. Sarah E. Ladd is quickly establishing herself as a rising star in Regency romance."

—Dorothy Love, author of Carolina Gold

The Heiress of Winterwood

"If you are a fan of Jane Austen and *Jane Eyre*, you will love Sarah E. Ladd's debut."

—USAToday.com

"My kind of book! The premise grabbed my attention from the first lines and I eagerly returned to its pages. I think my readers will enjoy *The Heiress of Winterwood*."

—Julie Klassen, bestselling, award-winning author

"This debut novel hits all the right notes with a skillful and delicate touch, breathing fresh new life into standard romance tropes."

—*RT Book Reviews*, 4 stars

"Oh my, what an exquisite tale! With clarity and grace, Sarah E. Ladd has penned a timeless regency that rises to the ranks of Heyer and Klassen, a breathless foray into the world of Jane Austen with very little effort . . . and very little sleep."

—Julie Lessman, award-winning author of The Daughters of Boston and Winds of Change series

"This adventure is fashioned to encourage love, trust, and faith especially in the Lord and to pray continually, especially in times of strife."

—*CBA Retailers + Resources*

"Captivated from the very first page! *The Heiress of Winterwood* marks Sarah E. Ladd as a rising Regency star sure to win readers' hearts!"

—Laura Frantz, author of *The Colonel's Lady* and *Love's Reckoning*

"Ladd's charming Regency debut is enhanced with rich detail and well-defined characters. It should be enjoyed by fans of Gilbert Morris."

—*Library Journal*

"A delight from beginning to end, *The Heiress of Winterwood* is a one-of-a-kind regency that kept me sighing with joy, laughing, crying, and even biting my nails when the occasion called for it!"

—MaryLu Tyndall, bestselling author of *Veil of Pearls* and the Surrender to Destiny series

A LADY at WILLOWGROVE HALL

Also by Sarah E. Ladd

The Houses of Yorkshire Novels

The Letter from Briarton Park

In the Shelter of Hollythorne House

The Cornwall Novels

The Governess of Penwythe Hall

The Thief of Lanwyn Manor

The Light at Wyndcliff

The Treasures of Surrey Novels

The Curiosity Keeper

Dawn at Emberwilde

A Stranger at Fellsworth

The Whispers on the Moors Novels

The Heiress of Winterwood

The Headmistress of Rosemere

A Lady at Willowgrove Hall

Stand-alone Novels

The Weaver's Daughter

A LADY at WILLOWGROVE HALL

Whispers on the Moors Book Three

SARAH E. LADD

THOMAS NELSON
Since 1798

Published in Nashville, Tennessee, by Thomas Nelson. Thomas Nelson is a registered trademark of HarperCollins Christian Publishing, Inc.

Thomas Nelson, Inc., titles may be purchased in bulk for educational, business, fund-raising, or sales promotional use. For information, please e-mail SpecialMarkets@ThomasNelson.com.

Scripture quotations are taken from the King James Version of the Bible.

Publisher's Note: This novel is a work of fiction. Names, characters, places, and incidents are either products of the author's imagination or used fictitiously. All characters are fictional, and any similarity to people living or dead is purely coincidental.

ISBN 978-1-4016-5827-4 (custom)

Library of Congress Cataloging-in-Publication Data

Ladd, Sarah E.
A Lady at Willowgrove Hall / Sarah E. Ladd.
pages cm — (Whispers on the moors ; book 3)
ISBN 978-1-4016-8837-0 (paperback)
1. Women—Fiction. 2. England—Social life and customs—19th century—Fiction. I. Title.
PS3612.A3565L33 2014
813'.6—dc23

2014015399

Printed in the United States of America

23 24 25 26 27 LBC 5 4 3 2 1

I lovingly dedicate this novel to
my grandmother, Colleen.

Thank you for inspiring—and sharing—
my lifelong love of literature.

1

Blacksmith's Cottage at Aradelle Park
Detham, England, 1814

Is it always a sin to tell a lie?

Sixteen-year-old Cecily Faire rolled over to glance at Leah, who slumbered in the narrow bed they shared. A worn, wool blanket was tucked tightly under her sister's chin, and her long, auburn braid lay limply against the pillow.

For weeks she had kept a secret from her sister. Her dearest friend. Her closest confidante.

Cecily swallowed the emotion that welled within her.

Each little lie that she had told haunted her.

But had there been any alternative? Secrecy was imperative.

Cecily relaxed her head against her own pillow and stared at the rough, wooden beams running the length of their bedchamber and struggled to make out their uneven shape in the night's shifting darkness. Outside their room's only window, unremitting rain battered her family's modest cottage, clattering against the thatched roof and disturbing the shutters.

Normally, she did not mind a rainy night. The weather changed without warning on the moors. She had grown accustomed to the peculiar groans and whispering creaks conjured by harsh winds. But tonight, the uneven cadence made it difficult for her to hear the single sound that mattered above all.

The chime of her father's clock.

How clearly her mind's eye could recall the timepiece's ivory face, golden hands, and intricate carvings of vines and leaves. It was by far the most elegant piece in their home. It sat in the parlor, just one floor below, marking each passing hour.

Unable to remain still another moment, Cecily clamped her teeth over her lower lip, held her breath as she pushed the thin covers away, and sat up, careful not to wake Leah.

Even as Cecily's heart trembled in anticipation, Leah's prior warning echoed like a boisterous raven, screeching its unpleasant song from the brush. Only two days past, Leah had discovered Cecily and Andrew arm in arm under the lacy shadows of the apple trees in Aradelle's south orchard.

You would be wise to stay away from Andrew Moreton. Her sister's stern voice had quivered with anger as she grabbed Cecily by her work-worn hand and dragged her back to their cottage. *He is not good for you. People in his position are not what they seem. Any relationship with him will only bring about your ruin.*

Cecily swiped her unruly hair away from her face, the very memory of the words igniting agitation.

What did Leah know of love? Of passion?

Cecily may only be sixteen years of age, but she knew well her heart.

Andrew Moreton loved her. He wanted to marry her. Had he not said those very words? And he would be waiting for her at the midnight hour, just down the lane from their cottage gate, where the road bent and the copse of hawthorn trees gave way to open moorland.

A wave of excitement pulsed through her at the very thought of Andrew's broad shoulders. His dark-brown eyes. The manner in which his cheek dimpled with his carefree, impulsive smiles and the affectionate warmth in his expression when he looked at her.

Perhaps Leah would feel differently if she knew what it was like to be in love.

Tonight she and Andrew would travel by carriage northward to Scotland where they would marry. She knew no other details, but Andrew had assured her that he had made the necessary arrangements. Even though he was only seventeen, he knew people. Powerful people.

Her hands shook so that she could barely pull her nightdress over her head. She had remained fully clothed beneath in her best gown of straw-colored muslin in anticipation of her journey. She inched her way over to the chair next to the casement window. As she slipped on her half boots and tugged at the laces, she glanced to the garden below. The shrubbery bowed and swayed in a dance with the wind and raindrops. Cecily's hold on the laces slacked as she thought of how her mother, dead seven years now, would disapprove of the garden's wild state. Cecily had tried to tend it in a manner in which her mother would have been pleased, but with all of her other chores, time had slipped by.

But once she was Mrs. Andrew Moreton, she would have no chores. No cares.

She snapped the laces tight.

Andrew had promised her as much.

He had whispered in her ear the promise of love and security, of freedom from worry and want.

She turned back to Leah. The moon's intermittent light now

slanted over her twin's slight figure, glinting on the long, red hair. Only twelve minutes her senior, they were identical in so many ways. Looking at her was like beholding a living, breathing looking glass, from her straight nose to the smattering of freckles on her cheeks.

But whereas Leah was far too cautious to follow the demands of her heart, Cecily was not.

One day Leah would forgive her for stealing away in the dark of night. Once she married the heir of Aradelle Park, their worries would cease. No longer would she be merely the daughter of the man who worked the estate's forge and did odd jobs in the village. For when Cecily returned from Scotland, she would be a lady. The scandal would pass, and Andrew's family would accept her as one of their own. Then she would send for Leah. And the nightmare they lived would end.

The chime.

The familiar melody was soft at first, but it seemed to grow louder, like a beacon summoning her. Imploring her to move quickly. It taunted her, urging that if she did not hurry, she might awaken, and her cherished fairy tale would be no more than a tragic dream of what might have been.

Lightning flashed in the tiny room, and at the brightness, Leah stirred. If Cecily was going to leave, now was the time.

With her boots now secured, she stood, crossed the room, and pulled her packed valise from the corner where she had hidden it behind a chest. She opened a small box on the dresser and pulled out a folded piece of paper. At the top she had carefully written her sister's name in her finest handwriting.

Everyone would wonder where she had gone. Someone needed to know.

She propped the folded letter on the bureau where Leah would be sure to see it.

A thrill surged through her, and she paused to look around the room that had been hers all her life. Even in the dark she could make out the low bed. The leaning wardrobe in the corner. The battered, painted chest beneath the window.

She turned to leave but stopped as her eye caught on a simple coral necklace next to where she had placed the letter. It had been their mother's, and it was the only piece of jewelry that remained in their possession. Their father had sold everything else, but somehow this trinket had escaped his greedy eye. At the sight of it, her throat tightened and her vision grew misty.

Their mother had always wanted more for them. More than they would receive as the daughters of a blacksmith.

Would her mother approve of her decision to run away from everything for a chance at a better life?

Cecily had no one to turn to for guidance.

She had to trust her instincts.

She snatched the piece of jewelry, tucked it in her bodice, glanced back at her sleeping sister, and quitted the room.

The corridor was quiet, save for the steady fall of rain. It was too quiet—normally, their father's snores would fill the modest cottage. She tried not to let that fact dissuade her as she descended the steps, avoiding the spaces that would groan under her weight.

With every step she should be feeling freer. Lighter.

But at the foot of the staircase, doubt washed over her. The tiny hairs on the back of her neck prickled.

Cecily fought the ominous suspicion and strained to hear the night sounds, but the erratic beating of her heart drowned out all other noises. Another flash of lightning sliced through the darkness, lancing her already taut nerves. The sooner she was free of this cottage, and the memories it held captive, the better she would be.

She hurried through the kitchen and out the door to the overgrown garden. She hastened amid the neglected lavender, roses, and foxglove. The hedges of overrun hawthorn and elderberry, which once had been a place of play, now seemed dangerous and foreboding. Ahead of her was the wooden gate. Only a few more steps.

Cecily stopped.

Was that thunder?

No. She took another step.

Voices.

A shout. One heavy with Irish brogue, rough and gritty like a growl.

Father.

It was alarm, pure and violent, that pushed her farther into the unkempt garden. The blood raced through her ears, and try as she might to make out words, the wind muddled them. She dropped her valise and ran toward the gate. The overgrown shrubbery grabbed at her skirt, and she struggled to maintain her balance as her boots sank in the thick mud. It was as if the very ground were trying to keep her captive.

Her father had discovered their plan.

It could be the only explanation.

She skidded to a stop by the gate and rounded the corner. There stood her father, towering over Andrew and appearing more like a hulking monster than a mortal man.

"Stop, Father!" Cecily squealed, lunging forward and grabbing his thick arm. "Stop!"

But with one swoop of his forearm, Joseph Faire knocked Cecily to the side, nearly sending her to the soggy ground. When she gained her balance, she swiped her drenched hair from her face. The weak light from the lantern at her father's feet flickered in hard angles on his wet face, his eyes mere slits.

Fearing more for Andrew's safety than her own, she scrambled back to her father in an attempt to distract him, but he would not be deterred. His massive hands were fixed on Andrew's fine coat.

"Stealing in like a thief in the night!" her father bellowed. "How many times did I warn ye? Tell y'ta stay away from 'er?"

Andrew's eyes were wide and his chest heaved. Cecily had never seen him frightened before.

Andrew's shoulders looked narrow in her father's grip as he pressed the young man against the stone wall. His Adam's apple bobbed. He glanced over at Cecily and then back to her father. "I love Miss Faire, sir. I intend to marry her."

"Ha!" Her father's voice held vicious sarcasm. "You'll ne'er marry a daughter o' mine." The familiar scent of ale and rum wafted around her.

She knew what her father was capable of.

She was unsure if Andrew did.

For so long she had tried to hide the truth of her father's rages. Now there could be no denying.

Cecily's dreams were dissolving right before her, like a tallow candle left too close to the fire. Summoning every ounce of bravery in her small frame, she lunged forward, attempting one last time to divert her father's attention enough for Andrew to break free.

The muscles in her father's exposed forearms corded, and his hands shook with intense pressure. He bunched his fists around the lapels of Andrew's coat. His words came out in a hiss. "Stay away from my daughter. If I see ye 'round her again, 'twill be the last time."

He then shoved Andrew to the ground. He turned as if to leave, but then pointed a shaking finger back toward Andrew. "Your father may pay me wages, but dunna go thinkin' you can take what's mine. You dunna own me. You are a snake. You are all alike. The lot o' you."

Her father stumbled toward him, and fear for Andrew's safety trumped Cecily's own desires. "Go, Andrew. Run!"

With that, the youth scrambled to his feet and took off.

Her father turned his angry eyes on her.

"Get down, girl. Be smart about it."

Cecily winced at the harshness in her father's tone, but fear kept her lips pressed together. After the five-hour cart ride in the rain, in the dead of night, it was the first time he had spoken to her.

This was the gamble she had made, for she had known if her father ever discovered her plans, there would be no reprieve from his fury. She'd been so careful to conceal them. Although rough, her father was a cunning man, his shrewdness—and his contempt—sharpened by a lifetime of striking blows. It didn't take long for him to notice that she was fully dressed in the black of night and to find her discarded valise. She confessed her plan in the hope that he would forgive her. But instead of finding redemption, she incited his anger further.

Cecily clutched the side of the cart's bench and stared at the ground as if it were a pit of fire instead of dirt and gravel.

"I'll be glad to be free of ye, y'romp." He spat. "I said get down!"

Cecily jumped from her seat and scrambled down, propelled by the fear of bringing his wrath on her once more. She didn't dare look at him. She knew what she would find in his expression.

Dishonor.

Disgust.

Drunkenness.

Instead, she glanced up at the building, trying to figure out where they were.

Somewhere in the misty distance, a wren broke into a morning song, and the gray light of an early spring dawn cast long shadows on the manicured landscape. Morning dew clung to the grass and evergreens, and in the light, it shone like diamonds.

And then she saw the brass marker nearly hidden by shrubbery.

Rosemere School for Young Ladies.

As the words registered, Cecily's heart thudded, threatening to burst free from her chest. How many times had he threatened this? To send her away to a girls' school. To separate her from her sister.

As if moving by some unseen force, she rounded the front of the cart. The donkey poked his nose against her arm, no doubt seeking a stub of a carrot or a lump of sugar. Hot tears stung her eyes. Would this really be the last time she saw the animal that had been her companion for as long as she could remember?

She did not have time to contemplate it, for in two large steps, Joseph Faire reached around and snatched her up by her arm. A cry escaped her lips. His grip tightened around her arm, and he all but dragged her to the door.

Struggling to maintain balance, she glanced up at the building—a formidable building of gray stone and latticed windows. A movement above caught her eye, and through the wavy glass, curtains parted and the faces of two girls appeared.

Cecily bit her lower lip.

Her father pounded against the heavy, wooden door, the volume of which disrupted the silence and set a dog barking. He adjusted the grip on her arm and muttered under his breath before pummeling the door once more.

Shame forced her to look at the worn toes of her black half boots, and she tried to stay calm.

Stupid, foolish girl!

Her father continued to beat on the door until movement and muted voices stirred within. After several moments it swung open, revealing a tall, sinewy man in haphazard dress, his rumpled linen shirt hanging over his trousers, his frock coat askew on his shoulder, and his feet in stockings. Sleep marks creased his wrinkled face, and his graying hair pressed against his head.

"What is the meaning of this?" the man hissed in an obvious attempt to keep his voice low. "It's barely dawn!"

Her father, on the other hand, made little effort for discretion. "I have a new pupil for you." He shoved Cecily forward. She stumbled at the sudden jolt.

The man shook his head, the crisp morning breeze whipping around the building's corner and disrupting his hair. He pushed his crooked spectacles up on his nose and assessed Cecily before speaking. "Return at a more suitable hour and we will discuss—"

"I'll not return at another hour." Joseph Faire's tone darkened. "We'll speak now."

Cecily was familiar with her father's brash ways, but the rise of the man's bushy eyebrows suggested he was not accustomed to being spoken to in such a manner.

The man finally blinked at her, then back to her father. "This is most unusual, you understand."

"What's unusual 'bout it?" Joseph Faire barked. "I've a girl, you've a school, and I've money to see her through 'til she's o' age—no more, no less."

The distance and the nonchalance in his tone shouldn't have shocked her, but they did. He spoke as if he were bartering for services or trading animals. Their relationship had always been strained, but did she mean so little to him?

A younger woman with a long, black braid appeared, dressed in a wrapper and hugging her waist. She placed a hand on the man's arm, her face drawn in pointed concern. "But we haven't the room. It will be at least another month before we can even consider—"

"Well, she'll not come home with me," spat her father, interrupting their conversation. "So 'tis up to ye, either she stays here, or she is on her own."

Her father pushed Cecily forward . . . again. She stumbled.

What a pitiful sight she must be. Her hair hung in stringy clumps about her face, and mud clung to the hem of her gown and books. And while she had not seen a mirror, she could feel the effect of her father's hand on her cheek.

Tears burned hot in Cecily's eyes, a sharp contrast to the cool spring morning. Feeling emboldened by the piteous stares, she looked directly at her father for the first time in hours. "Father, please. This is a misunderstanding."

"Nay!" he shouted, his rough Irish brogue echoing from the stone walls and the canopy of birch trees flanking the entrance. "Ye've been naught but trouble for me since the day ye were born. Maybe they can make you mind your wild ways."

Her father extended his hand, a leather pouch clutched in his rough fingers. "This will cover her expenses. When it's gone, she's on her own."

At this, both the man and woman looked at her, speechless. Cecily began to tremble. It started in her legs and moved up to her stomach.

And then with a quick motion, Joseph Faire turned to the cart. For a moment, nobody else moved, but when his intention to depart became clear, the older gentleman pushed past her. "But, sir! Your name? Where can we contact you?"

Her father looked at Cecily from the cart's bench with hard eyes, the iciness of which froze her every limb. With a shout and a slap of the reins, he urged the fat donkey into motion, never looking back. Cecily jerked free from the woman and sprinted toward the cart, but her feet shifted and she skidded across the loose gravel. "Father!" she shrieked. "Father, please don't leave me!"

But her words were carried away by the wind. "What about Leah? Please, Father!"

She stood fixed to the ground, staring at the empty space around the bend where her father's cart had disappeared.

The woman approached her and touched her shoulder. "Come inside. No doubt you are chilled through."

Cecily cast one last glance up the road, but it was not to look for her father. How her heart ached to see Andrew rushing up the lane, her valiant knight coming to rescue her. To whisk her away from the madness, just as he had promised. He was the one person who knew her heart. He said he would always love and cherish her, and she'd willingly given herself to him, heart, mind, and body.

But now, the sickening realization that she had made a mistake pressed on her. She'd sacrificed too much for a chance at a better life, and now she was ruined, destined for a life of shame.

She had seen the fear in his eyes. The disdain.

He would not be coming . . . and she would have to abide with the consequences of her actions.

2

Laurel Cottage at Willowgrove Hall
Wiltonshire, England, 1814

Nathaniel refused to cry. He was a grown man of four and twenty. He should be able to control his emotions.

And yet, his quivering chin betrayed him.

He adjusted his position in the Windsor chair and gripped and ungripped the chair's arms before finally clasping his hands before him.

His father's thin voice cracked the silence. "Look at me, Nathaniel."

He could not deny his father such a simple request. But when Nathaniel finally mustered the strength to comply, what he saw threatened to undo him.

Before him, his father, Thomas Stanton, lay abed. The candle lamp's flicker cast odd shadows over his glistening brow and straight nose. His long, gray hair had escaped his queue and clung to his clammy cheeks and neck.

His father was dying.

At the thought, a bolt of terror ripped through Nathaniel's core.

He wanted to jump from his seat and wrestle to the ground the unseen force stealing his father's final moments forcing it to release its hold. But he sat still, unmoving.

"Son, I must speak with you—without the women present." The older man struggled to sit up against the pillows, the linen shirt he wore plastered to his skin and his gaunt face twisting in pain. "'Tis important now, and we haven't much time. Draw nearer."

Nathaniel inched closer, dreading—fearing—what might pass his father's lips.

"I am proud of you, lad. Proud of the man you have become. But all is not as it seems." His father drew a deep breath, his chapped lips trembling at the movement. His weak tone grew pensive, his words slow and barely above a whisper.

"There is something you must know. Something you should have been told long ago."

"Whatever it is, we can discuss this at another time," Nathaniel protested. "You must rest now."

"No!" His father's voice rang with surprising emphasis. "If I fail to share this with you, it shall haunt me as I pass from this life to the next. You must hear it."

Alarm ran down Nathaniel's back.

"When I am dead, you will take my position as steward of Willowgrove Hall, just as I took my father's position upon his death. It is a proud legacy and one with great responsibility, Nathaniel. Do not doubt it."

Nathaniel only shook his head. Was his father failing? They'd had this discussion before. Numerous times. It was the reason he had worked for so long beside his father, learning the intricacies of the profession.

"But hear me. Hear me well." He fixed his eyes on Nathaniel with such intensity that Nathaniel suspended his breath. "You are bound to this land by a far stronger thread than being the steward's son."

Nathaniel blinked. "I do not understand."

Thomas Stanton lowered his eyes. "Your mother and I have kept a secret from you. From everyone. At first I convinced myself it was my duty. And now I realize what a selfish fool I have been.

"This news will not be easy to hear, I fear, and it pains me for you. There were times I thought you might have suspected it, but . . ."

When his father's words trailed off, Nathaniel's throat constricted, making it a struggle to breathe. Nathaniel cocked his head. The room grew warm. The air too thin. "Suspect what?"

"I am not your father. Not in the biological sense."

Surely this was delirium talking. "Father, you are ill. You know not what you speak of."

But the old man, in a sudden burst of strength, reached out and grasped the wool of Nathaniel's sleeve in his frail fingers and yanked it tight. His face distorted in agony, and his voice faltered as he forced words through clenched teeth. "Hear me, boy! I know what I am saying."

Nathaniel shook his head and wanted to escape the moment, but he was bound—out of respect—to listen. "Who is it, then?"

His father relaxed the grip on Nathaniel's sleeve and let his head fall back against the pillow. "Mr. Trent."

The deceased master of Willowgrove Hall.

The master of the estate where his father had labored his entire life. Where he himself would be steward upon his father's death.

It could not be possible.

His father's words came in a rush. "There is much you don't know, Nathaniel. Your mother was a lady's maid to Mrs. Trent, twenty-five years ago now. This is likely a shock, given their interactions. Katherine entered into a relationship with Mr. Trent and became with child. You."

His father was outlining an impossible scenario. Everything within Nathaniel wanted to deny it, but the strangest sensation coursed through him, prickling the hairs on his neck.

His father paused to draw an unsteady breath. "You are well acquainted with Mrs. Trent's temperament. At one time, she and your mother were very close. But time and circumstances have a tendency to uproot even the strongest of alliances. When Mrs. Trent learned of your mother's betrayal, she became quite violent. Katherine was facing ruin. The Trents faced humiliation. I had always been fond of your mother, pretty lass that she was, and when Mr. Trent proposed that I take her as my wife and raise you as my own to prevent scandal and secure my future, I accepted."

Nathaniel could not comprehend what he was hearing. This was a fever-induced rant of a sick man on his deathbed. And yet the expression in his father's eyes was lucid.

But as a tear, the first tear he had ever seen from his father, slipped down the withered cheeks, the sobering reality hit him. He had spoken the truth.

As the fog of confusion lifted, anger—hot and red—fused with the blood flowing through him. He ripped his hand away and stood, the force of which nearly knocked the chair to the ground. He stomped over to the room's single window, the thud of his heavy boots echoing from the planked floor.

"There is more." His father's voice, which moments ago had seemed soft and weak, now was too loud to bear. "In exchange for discretion on the matter, Mr. Trent guaranteed me, and you after me, the position of steward of Willowgrove Hall. That is to say, upon Mr. Trent's passing, Mrs. Trent would not be permitted to terminate my role as steward, nor you thereafter. As an illegitimate son, you will not inherit Willowgrove. 'Twould be impossible. But he has provided for you in his will. After his wife dies, you shall inherit Lockbourne House in Northumberland."

At the window, tendrils of cool, predawn air seeped through the cracked pane. Nathaniel fixed his eyes on the shadowed ground below him, which was blanketed with an early spring frost. He and his father had traveled to Lockbourne House once as a boy. He recalled with indifference the ancient house with dark rooms and crumbling plaster. What did Nathaniel want with such a dilapidated, unkempt place? More significantly, how could a mere house excuse a lifetime of lies?

Nathaniel whirled from the window, his neckcloth now feeling tight. "How could he live so close to me? Watch me grow, and never speak a word?" He narrowed his eyes. "How could *you* not tell me?"

"Consider your mother. If this news was ever made public, her reputation would be tarnished beyond repair. Your sisters would be ruined. No dowry I could provide could make up for such a blemish."

The room grew warmer.

Stifling.

The overcoming scent of death, sickness, and betrayal clung to Nathaniel, threatening to pull him down.

Everything he knew was a lie.

And what was worse, *he* was a lie.

Nathaniel's breath came in huffs now.

His father raised his hand. "This news is a shock, but you must control yourself. Despite it all, you will very soon be the head of this family. You are still your mother's son. Brother to your sisters. It will be you they depend on. You will provide for them. Protect them. But upon my honor, I could not take this to my grave."

The sickening realization that his own mother took part in

this betrayal and never told him settled on his shoulders like a load too heavy to bear. "Does Mother know you are telling me this?"

"Not yet, but I will inform her. You must continue to keep this secret. Give me your word."

Nathaniel stared at him. "This changes everything."

"I asked you a question, lad. Do I have your word?"

Nathaniel set his lips in a firm line. Without looking at his father, he gave a rigid nod.

"I must hear you promise this!" His father was trembling now. Perspiration raced down his stubbled cheek. "Say it."

Nathaniel drew a sharp intake of air through his nose and focused on a faded painting hanging just above his father's head. How could he not promise? This man, whether or not by blood, was his father. "You have my word."

Thomas Stanton eased back onto the pillow. "This has been my greatest regret. But life is not easy. Not for anyone. I am trusting you, Nathaniel, to do what is honorable. Your time for redemption will come."

3

Rosemere School for Young Ladies
Darbury, England, 1819

A voice broke the late-afternoon silence. "Mrs. Sterling asked to speak with you."

Cecily jerked her head up from her copy of *The Castles of Athlin and Dunbayne* and let the novel fall to the side. Mary, the housemaid at Rosemere School for Young Ladies, stood in the bedchamber threshold, a pressed linen apron hugging her wiry form and a mobcap sitting atop her chestnut hair.

"Mrs. Sterling wants to see *me*?" Cecily said.

Mary nodded. "Said to fetch you right away, miss. She's in the study."

Cecily sat up straighter on her bed. "Thank you, Mary."

Cecily waited for the door to close before letting her shoulders roll forward and giving a little sigh.

What had she done *this* time?

Cecily stood and shook out the folds of her pale-blue muslin skirt, ran a hand over the sash under the bodice to smooth it, and pivoted to face the cracked looking glass fixed to the plaster wall. The sun slanted in the room through leaded windows, highlighting the wrinkles in her gown. She frowned and brushed her hand over the fabric, the color of which always reminded Cecily of the bluebells that had grown in her mother's garden. There was little she could do about the wrinkles now. She leaned closer to assess her hair, patted a few wayward curls back into her chignon, and then straightened.

When Cecily first arrived at the school, she found it difficult to adhere to the strict rules and rigid routines. In her early days at Rosemere, she was often tardy for meals or would talk during lessons. Her obstinate temperament—fueled by her unsettled emotions—had, at times, exposed her to judgment. But she endeavored to tame her impulsive—if not unobservant—ways, and it had been months since Mrs. Sterling, the headmistress of Rosemere, had last requested to speak with her alone. Even then, it had only been to discuss the terms of Cecily's position as a teacher at the school. Of course, she saw Mrs. Sterling nearly every day, but being summoned to her study was another matter entirely.

Now a woman of twenty-one, Cecily had graduated from the schoolroom several years prior. With no connections outside of the school, she taught needlework and literature in exchange for room and board. She was satisfied with the direction of her life and, not having heard otherwise, assumed that Mrs. Sterling agreed. True, her tendency to speak too loudly and her propensity to excitement did raise an eyebrow a time or two, but as of late, her behavior had been pristine. Her students were doing well and growing in the skills she taught them.

Cecily quitted her bedchamber, descended the broad staircase, and paused at the footing. A wide fireplace at the end of the foyer filled the dark, paneled room with warm light. She fussed with the lacy chemisette at her throat and turned toward the study, where the door stood ajar.

She drew a deep breath before tapping on the door and pushing it open. "You wanted to see me, Mrs. Sterling?"

Patience Sterling looked up from the desk, her black hair pinned smoothly atop her head. Mrs. Sterling was one of the most beautiful women Cecily had ever seen, but there was something beyond her pleasant smile and bright eyes that made her so. The headmistress had taken great care to ensure Cecily felt comfortable and welcome. "Miss Faire! Yes, please, do come in and be seated."

Cecily sat in a chair opposite the desk and folded her hands in her lap. As her nerves tightened, she could barely keep her toe from tapping against the chair's leg. "I do hope all is well."

"Of course it is. I called you here because I have news that I think will please you very much." Mrs. Sterling pushed aside a book she had been reading and focused her attention more fully on Cecily. "I recall the day you came to us, Miss Faire, five years ago now."

Cecily looked down at her hands. She remembered the day with poignant detail.

"You were brought here early that spring morning, those many years ago, when the sun had not even yet begun its ascent over the moors."

With every word Mrs. Sterling said about that day, Cecily's heartbeat quickened. Heat crept up her neck and blood rushed to her face.

Cecily could feel Mrs. Sterling's eyes on her. She drew a deep breath. "That seems so very long ago."

"Perhaps to you it seems like a long time, but to me it feels as though only a day or two have passed." Mrs. Sterling rose and moved to the window to look toward a copse of elms, where budding leaves hinted that they were waking up from winter's long slumber. "You have blossomed into such a lovely young woman."

The words warmed her, yet they seemed to carry with them the breath of change.

Mrs. Sterling retrieved a letter from a stack on her desk. "I have just this morning received a letter that made me think of you."

Cecily leaned forward and looked more closely at the letter in Mrs. Sterling's hand. Her insides twisted. It could be from anyone. Her father. Her sister.

"Before your arrival at Rosemere, one of our students, Miss Lucinda Vale, left our school for a position as a lady's companion at Willowgrove Hall in Wiltonshire. Miss Vale has since married, leaving her position vacant, and Mrs. Trent, the lady she stayed with, is seeking a replacement." Mrs. Sterling tapped the letter in her hand. "Mrs. Trent was vastly satisfied with Miss Vale, and since she is not acquainted with any other young ladies of suitable age to be a companion, she wrote me and inquired if I might recommend someone. I thought of you."

Shocked hardly seemed the word to describe Cecily's reaction. She could not deny the disappointment that the letter was not from her family, but the subject of the letter intrigued her.

"A lady's companion?" Cecily possessed dozens of preconceived notions about what the position would entail—and she was suitable for none of them. She was not elegant. She was far from fashionable. What did she have to offer in the way of companionship? "But I would not know what to do! I would surely disappoint. I have no—"

"Now, Miss Faire," interrupted Mrs. Sterling in a kind voice. "I would not have brought this to your attention if I were not confident it suited you." She crossed the room and sat in the chair next to Cecily's, her enthusiasm evident in her bright expression. "Of course, I adore having you here at Rosemere. You are a part of this school, a member of this family. But your life is just beginning. It saddens me, but we cannot pay you to teach here, and this opportunity brings with it a handsome allowance, far beyond what you would receive as a governess or teacher elsewhere. Not to mention it would provide you the opportunity to forge connections with people outside of Darbury. You will be free to make your way in the world."

So this was it. This was her proverbial push from the nest, like a nightingale urged to leave the shelter of its mother's wing. Cecily had known this day was forthcoming. She could hardly stay at Rosemere forever.

She shifted in the chair, recognizing that a glimmer of enthusiasm twinkled within her. Isn't this what she had desired since the day she arrived at Rosemere? To be free of expectations and scrutiny and to find her own way? Perhaps even find her sister? And now that the opportunity presented itself, fear seized her. For beyond the walls of Rosemere, she knew no one. Time had severed all connections.

But if Mrs. Sterling regarded this position as ideal for her, how could she argue? Cecily looked from Mrs. Sterling's face to her own hands clasped in her lap.

As if sensing her reserve, Mrs. Sterling patted Cecily's shoulder. "All will be well. You shall see."

Cecily nodded. She was in no position to argue. She had exhausted the money that her father had left for her years ago. She was at the mercy of the school and should be grateful for the opportunity being presented. Some young ladies were not so fortunate.

"Please remind me. Where is the position?" Cecily tried to sound eager.

"It is at a rather large estate, Willowgrove Hall, in Wiltonshire, an idyllic town not too terribly far from Manchester. Mrs. Trent is the lady in search of a companion, and based on her letter, as well as the letters I've received from Miss Vale, I believe Mrs. Trent to be in poor health. At one time she and Miss Vale traveled extensively, but as of late, they have been resigned to either Bath or Willowgrove Hall."

Cecily chewed her lower lip. She knew how rare this type of an offer was. She had expected that if she were ever to leave Rosemere, it would be for a governess position or to teach at another school. The idea of being a lady's companion had never occurred to her. "I am flattered you thought of me."

Mrs. Sterling smiled. "You are destined for things beyond our quiet Rosemere, Miss Faire. Now, for a few more specifics, are you aware of the responsibilities of a companion?"

Cecily shook her head.

"It is quite a lovely situation, really. It is imperative you understand that you are not a servant. You will be a friend to Mrs. Trent and keep her company. It can be lonely for a widow on such an estate, especially if her health is failing. I am of the impression that she does not have a great deal of family or friends in Wiltonshire. You will be at her disposal. Instead of wages, you will receive a handsome allowance, one that, if saved, could give you a bit of independence in the future."

The tone of Mrs. Sterling's voice was definite. The headmistress clearly expected her to accept the position. And Cecily could devise no valid reason why she should refuse. A cold chill swept over Cecily, and she rubbed her hand over her arm. "When would I leave?"

"The letter says that Mrs. Trent will be returning to Willowgrove Hall at the end of this week and would need a young lady at that time." As if sensing Cecily's hesitation, she hastened to add, "I know it is rather sudden."

Cecily looked at the face of the person who had been like a mother to her since her arrival. Mrs. Sterling had her best interest at heart. "I trust your judgment, Mrs. Sterling."

A smile creased Mrs. Sterling's face, and she stood. "Then all is settled." She turned to the table behind her and lifted a stack of folded fabric. "Since this journey is unexpected and we have little time to prepare, I thought you might like some attire that is better suited to travel than your regular gowns. I wish this were new, but it should suffice."

Emotion tugged at Cecily. She had been given dresses as a school uniform, but she had never received a gift like this. She swallowed and unfolded the garment, shook out the folds, and held it at arm's length. It was a lovely gown of heavy wool, the color of the evening sky just before darkness claimed it, trimmed in darker velvet around the bodice and the sleeves, with a matching walking-length pelisse lined with cream sarcenet and a straw bonnet with matching blue ribbon.

"I hope it fits. You are a little smaller than I, but it shouldn't be too far of a stretch. Even though spring is upon us, it could get chilly while you are traveling, especially if it rains. I would like for you to have it."

Unsure of how to handle her feelings, Cecily looked down and folded the gown over her arm. She should refuse the gift, but the notion of having something to remember Mrs. Sterling by was too great. "Thank you."

"And there is one more thing." Mrs. Sterling returned to her desk, opened the drawer, and pulled out a small book bound in black leather. "I want you to take this with you."

Cecily accepted the book and turned it to read the cover. "The book of Proverbs."

As she read the words aloud, her heart sank. During her years at Rosemere, Mrs. Sterling had tried to strengthen Cecily's faith. But even as the trust between them deepened, Cecily never told the headmistress why her father sent her away. Mrs. Sterling believed Cecily's father's abandonment was unprompted. Surely if Mrs.

Sterling knew, she would agree: God would want nothing to do with Cecily. But to be polite, Cecily hugged the book, along with the gown, to her chest. "Thank you, Mrs. Sterling."

Mrs. Sterling stepped forward and embraced her. When the woman released her, she said, "You are a mystery to me, Miss Faire. I hope you have enjoyed your time here at Rosemere, for I know I have enjoyed your sense of humor and sweet nature. I sense you are searching for something, and I hope you find whatever it is. I know you will do well for yourself, but remember, you have family at Rosemere. If you need anything, anything at all, you can always come home."

Later that night, alone in the tiny attic room she shared with Martha Riddle, another teacher, Cecily gathered the treasures and trinkets she had amassed since her arrival. She did not have many. She had arrived with only the dress on her back, the worn half boots on her feet, and her mother's coral necklace she had hidden in her bodice that fateful night.

Her shoes and gown had been quickly replaced by the school gown of blue muslin and new black half boots. She folded each of her gowns—two blue, one lavender, and one pale yellow—and tucked them in a cast-off traveling trunk. On top of those she placed her extra stockings, nightdress, shawl, spencer, winter cloak, petticoat, and chemise. Once satisfied with the placement, she arranged her personal things, including her tooth powder, comb, and the small container of rosewater Mrs. Sterling had given her on her birthday. Her trunk was nearly full, and she looked at what remained: three worn books, a smaller chest with her embroidery things, and a single letter.

She picked up her embroidery box and ran her finger over the smooth wood. If she possessed any talent, it would be the art of embroidery. Many of the other girls were gifted at painting, singing, or playing the pianoforte. Cecily had learned some of those skills at

Rosemere, but her strength lay in her aptitude with a needle. She looked down at her sleeve and smoothed the tiny row of flowers she had embroidered along the hem. Not a single one of her gowns had escaped her alteration, and when she had embellished her own gowns as much as she could without having them appear overly ornate, she would adorn her friends' gowns with similar ornamentations.

Cecily's mother had worked as a dressmaker before she married Joseph Faire, and as such, she taught both Cecily and Leah how to work a needle by the time they were old enough to hold one. Cecily wiped a fingerprint from the embroidery box, tucked it inside, added her books, and then held the letter to the light.

It had been hidden in the bottom of a drawer for nearly two years. She had little need to read it for she had committed most of it to memory.

After her father had left her at Rosemere, she had written to her sister several times, hoping—pleading—for a response, which she never received. Cecily doubted her father would allow any letters, and after the physical violence her father displayed toward Andrew, his employer's son, it was improbable they were even still at Aradelle. But she wrote nonetheless. After a year of hearing nothing, she gathered her courage and wrote to a friend, Emma Sanders, who worked as an underhousemaid at Aradelle Park.

Two months later she received a letter.

Cecily drew a deep breath and opened it.

Dear Cecily,

How I wondered where you went, and to find that you are at a school for girls? How I envy you! You must be learning all kinds of wonderful things, but I am sorry to hear that you are separated from your family. I had no notion of it. To answer your questions, I wish I had different news. The day you left, your father was dismissed in a very public episode with Mr. Moreton. He left Detham in an awful fury! I have assumed all this time that you were with them. I did hear that your sister had accepted a position as a dressmaker with your aunt in Manchester, but I have no news of your father.

Cecily lowered the letter. The rest was comprised of accounts of the busy happenings of the life she used to possess. They were of little consequence to her now.

She drew a sharp breath. She had found a version of peace and accepted the fact that her father had abandoned her. And over time her tender heart had healed from the pain of being separated from Andrew Moreton. But it was her separation from Leah that brought her the most anguish. Even in the midst of dozens of girls, she missed the closeness they had shared. The memories. The secrets.

Cecily had never been close to her aunt. Indeed, she had never even met the woman. All she knew with certainty was her name and that she lived in Manchester—at one time. After receiving Emma's letter, she wrote to her aunt weekly, trying to locate her sister. After years with no response, she stopped. But now, perhaps if she earned enough money, one day she could travel to Manchester herself and look for her sister. It was her only lead—and she would cling to it, even from Willowgrove Hall.

4

Willowgrove Hall
Wiltonshire, England, 1819

Nathaniel Stanton stood on Grange Peak, the highest point on all of Willowgrove Hall property, and looked to the north at the main house. A filmy, late-afternoon fog hung in the air, layering the patchwork landscape in shades of pewter and blanketing the grounds with a chill. The spring rain had stopped, but the low clouds churned with ominous speed, and a grumbling to the east promised the arrival of more bad weather.

But it was not the weather that distracted him. Or the dampness in the air. He'd lived his entire life in such a climate. It was the standing water on the grounds below that held his focus.

Three days past he had awoken to news that the sluice at one of Willowgrove's ponds had given way and flooded the southern grounds and surrounding field. It had wreaked havoc on the carefully designed irrigation system that provided water to their tenants. But when Nathaniel had climbed up to Grange Peak, he was not prepared for the sight he beheld. Grazing land and gardens alike were beneath patches of water, and the water itself had made its way much too close to the main house and stables. The force of the water rushing from the pond down the Lennox River washed away the foundation of the bridge connecting Willowgrove's main drive to the road that led to the village. Now, days later, the water had not receded. Indeed, days of rain had compounded the predicament, and before him stretched a broken sea with water filling in the low-lying areas and encroaching on the farther gardens and fields.

Silas Yeatsman, Willowgrove's head gardener, stood beside Nathaniel, fists akimbo, surveying the landscape through hooded eyes. The hem of his threadbare coat and blue woolen work apron fluttered in the wind. Despite his pauper appearance, he was the most gifted gardener for miles, highly respected for his ability to make plants and trees thrive.

Nathaniel paused to pat Gus, his pointer puppy, before speaking to Silas, who was seeing the flooding from this angle for the first time. "What do you make of it?"

Silas whistled, long and low. "'Tis an ugly sight."

Even though he knew better, Nathaniel had hoped for a more optimistic response. "Has it ever been this dire?"

Silas shook his head and scratched his uneven beard with pudgy fingers. "Nay. The same pond flooded, oh, maybe thirty years since, but the sluice wasn't there then. Ne'er had a worry with it since."

The words sank into Nathaniel and reverberated. As the steward of Willowgrove Hall, it was his job—his duty—to ensure all ran smoothly. But flooding of this magnitude weighed heavily. He thought of the damage it had done—it had crumbled the bridge that led from the main road to Willowgrove's entrance and obliterated the early crops for the nearest tenants. And several of Willowgrove's famed gardens were affected.

The thought of rebuilding was heavy enough. But the thought of explaining the entire situation to the older woman was almost unendurable.

"Mrs. Trent will not be pleased that her gardens and grounds are beneath water." Normally, he would never speak freely of his employer in front of others, especially other servants beneath him. But Silas had known Nathaniel since he was a boy. He'd been his father's closest confidant, and now Nathaniel considered him a trusted friend.

Silas pulled his hat low over his forehead. "You can't control the weather any more than you can control the seasons. I'd wager Mrs. Trent no longer cares for such details, as ill as she's been. It's that nephew of hers what'll care."

Nathaniel crossed his arms over his chest, ignoring the manner in which the wind caught in the folds of his greatcoat and billowed it behind him. Silas was right. There was a time Mrs. Trent would have grown irate at such a crisis, but time had intervened. After her husband's death, she'd thrown all of her energy into learning the inner workings of the estate, but her vigor was now failing and, as a result, her days of such involvement.

But Mrs. Trent's nephew, the future heir to Willowgrove Hall, was another situation altogether. He was a silly man, full of unrealistic plans for the future of the estate, and he would no doubt have words. Nathaniel tugged his neckcloth. "I had a conversation with him last autumn about having the engineer out to assess the sluice when we first began having trouble with it, but he thought the expense unnecessary."

"He was a foolish boy, and he has grown to be a foolish man." Silas sniffed. "Mrs. Trent's not long for the earth, and then we will deal with him every day of our lives."

"I wouldn't be too sure." Nathaniel skimmed the horizon. "I'd say he will be here a few months out of the year and spend the majority of his time elsewhere. Mr. Trent might have preferred to have a hand in the day-by-day happenings at Willowgrove, but I daresay his replacement will have naught to do with it. At least such an arrangement will leave us to go about our business in peace."

"Days of peace are over, lad. Everything is changing." Silas adjusted his footing on the wet carpet beneath him. "'Tis a shame. All this hard work. And it could have ended so differently."

Nathaniel caught the look Silas flung in his direction before he turned to survey the land. As if intercepting Nathaniel's thoughts, Silas slapped him on the shoulder. "I am sure you will figure it out, lad. I will tend my gardens. You see to the rest."

Nathaniel could not resist one last question. "What do you think my father would have done in this instance?"

Silas huffed. "Which one?"

Nathaniel stiffened at the reference, for Silas had struck on the truth that he'd kept hidden from the world. Only four living souls knew the truth, and Nathaniel needed to keep it that way. Silas was a trusted man, but referring to it in such a lighthearted manner irked Nathaniel, especially when the weight of responsibility already pressed upon him.

Silas's withered face fell when Nathaniel did not join him in a chuckle. "My apologies. Did not mean to offend."

"You did not offend me," Nathaniel said, propping his foot on a nearby stump and then leaning on his knee and staring off to the distance. "Truths are truths."

"Most men only have one father. You were blessed with two."

Nathaniel grunted. He rarely spoke of this matter with anyone. "Blessed? I cannot see how." Nathaniel straightened. Silas was getting too close.

As if sensing Nathaniel's discomfort, Silas cleared his throat and returned to the topic at hand. "As for what your father, old Mr. Stanton, would have done, it is simple to say. He would have done what was best by those who depended upon him. And that is the farmers whose livelihoods rest on the grounds they tend. He would have fought to get the sluice fixed posthaste and do whatever necessary to see such an event did not repeat itself."

Nathaniel drew and held a deep breath. Silas was right. Nathaniel, and his father before him, were stewards, but without a separate land steward or bailiff to oversee the relationships with the tenants, the responsibilities of managing the house and the tenants fell to him. It was the part of his occupation that he found the most satisfying, but at times, seeing to the needs of the tenants could put him at odds with the mistress of the estate. He released his breath. "Well, there is nothing we can do by staring at this. We had best get to work."

Thunder growled, and Silas turned his pale eyes heavenward. "Don't think you'll make much progress 'til tomorrow."

Never one to back down from a challenge, Nathaniel scratched his puppy's ear again and turned to take the path back down Grange Peak. "Well, we'll not get anything done if we do not get started now."

And with that, he strode back down the hill.

Cecily gasped as the coachman tossed her trunk to the ground from atop the carriage.

"Do be careful!" she shouted, struggling to be heard above the howling winds and rustling branches.

But her words were carried away with the gusts, and her trunk fell to the soggy ground below with a thud, splashing up mud and bits of earth. She shrieked when the brass latch popped open, spilling two of her clean dresses onto the waterlogged road. She scrambled to save them from the puddle and as she did, hot tears blinded her eyes.

No, no, no!

The entire day of traveling from Rosemere to Willowgrove had been uncomfortable at best, and now, after hours of traveling on rutted roads, Cecily's nerves were as raw as the bitter spring wind.

She attempted to latch the trunk, but the leather strap had torn away from the side.

She looked up at the coachman, expecting assistance of some sort, but the driver adjusted his flapping, caped greatcoat, climbed back to his perch, and gathered the reins in his thick, gloved hands.

"Where are you going?" Cecily demanded, straightening her posture. "How am I supposed to get to Willowgrove Hall?"

The driver nodded his head toward a gate. "Willowgrove Hall is through that gate, down the lane, and you will curve through the woods. From there you will not be able to miss it."

She frowned as she assessed the gate he referred to. Beyond it, the dark, twisting road curved into a forest thick with a shifting evening fog.

She was not about to step a single foot into such a place.

Around her, rain started to fall in fine, misty waves. Cecily shielded her eyes and looked back up at the driver. "Then you must take me there."

"'Tis not possible. Bridge is washed away. I'd never get the horses through."

"What do you mean the bridge is washed away?" she asked, almost laughing at the ridiculous statement. "Then how am I to get across?"

The driver jerked the reins in apparent frustration and adjusted his collar.

When he did not respond, Cecily continued, "Well, surely there is another entrance. This cannot be the only one."

"This is not a private carriage, miss, and we have already gone off our main route. We're late as it is."

Cecily's chin began to quiver. Now was not the time to be demure. She was expected at Willowgrove Hall, and she needed to find a way to get there. In her most authoritative voice, she said, "This is not acceptable. I insist that you take me on to Willowgrove Hall immediately."

"Hear me." The driver spoke to her as an adult correcting a child. "That bridge is gone. I'm not about to take my horses for a swim. Now, either I can take you into Wiltonshire for the night, or you can walk on to Willowgrove Hall yourself. Makes little difference to me."

Cecily hesitated. Her money was limited. It would hardly be prudent to pay for a night's lodging. For what if she needed the money another time? She did not have time to give it another thought, for within the span of time it took for her to consider her response, the carriage groaned into motion. She looked up to see the driver flicking the reins on the horses' wet backs.

"Wait!" she cried. She tried to run after them, but the clingy folds of her skirt tangled around her legs, making it impossible to take another step without falling face-first to the muddy earth.

As the carriage disappeared around the bend, she wiped the rain away from her face and gave a little sob. This was not how it was supposed to be.

I will not cry.

She forced herself to look in the direction the man had pointed and blew out her breath. The gate, black and shiny from the rain, loomed before her. As she stood lamenting her situation, a clap of thunder echoed from the trees and a streak of spring lightning sliced the darkening sky. She clutched her skirt, lifting it above the mud.

She reassessed the open iron gate and sniffed. She could either stand here in the rain or commence walking.

Feeling rather resourceful, she removed one of the leather straps from her trunk and looped it through the handle, and with a sharp tug, angled it appropriately and began dragging it through the gate and behind her. Once she had walked a couple hundred feet down the road, she rounded a curve. As she did, a silhouette of a cupola appeared above the tree line, standing stark against the churning sky.

Willowgrove Hall.

She had no idea how long her walk would take, but the stirring clouds urged her to hasten her step. If she kept her eyes down, the brim of her traveling bonnet kept the rain from her face.

As she took another step, she caught a glimpse of her mud-caked hem. Her shoulders sank. This was no way to meet Mrs. Trent, damp and soiled, dragging a broken trunk. She was supposed to be a well-bred lady. Or at least, that was what she wanted Mrs. Trent to believe. At present, she feared her appearance resembled more a vagabond than a proper lady's companion.

Somewhere to her left an owl hooted, its clear call rising above the steady pound of rain. And then, as she was about to turn another bend, a small animal lunged from the tree line, howling, and circled her. She gave a short scream and hugged the leather strap to her heart with one hand and clutched her skirt in the other. "Shoo!" she cried. "Be gone!"

She didn't see the animal until it was quite upon her. It was small. And black. A fox? A small wolf? Heaven help her, with her frayed nerves and total exhaustion, her mind could run away with her.

She did the only thing she could think to do.

She screamed.

5

Nathaniel walked down the lane to his home, his leather satchel flung over his shoulder and his hat pulled as low as possible to keep the rain out of his eyes.

Mrs. Trent and her traveling companions would be arriving in the morning. He had written to her of the flooding to prepare her for the shock, but he doubted the letter would have reached her. Indeed, he doubted she would even read it if it had, such was her way in matters concerning Nathaniel.

The rain fell in sheets now, one belligerent wave after the other. In the distance, yellow light winked at him from the windows of Laurel Cottage, his family's home. Nathaniel quickened his pace.

Gus, his pointer, bounded ahead of him. Normally, Nathaniel would call the pup back by his side, teaching him to stay with his master, but after the day's troubles, he felt more lax than normal.

But then the animal stopped in the road and cocked his ear.

Nathaniel whistled low to call the dog back, but instead of obeying, Gus barked a series of high-pitched howls before abandoning their path and diving into a small copse of trees that separated the lane from the main road to Willowgrove Hall.

He cupped his hand around his mouth. "Gus! Come!"

Gus barked. Then barked again. No doubt the dog had tracked some unsuspecting hare or rodent. "Gus!"

But it was when he heard a shriek—a human, feminine scream—that he dropped his bag and raced through the thicket. The wet branches and leaves tugged at him as he forced his way through the thick brush.

Despite his wide-brimmed hat, raindrops latched onto his eyelashes, and he slid the rough sleeve of his woolen coat across his eyes. But in the split second it took to wipe the moisture away, he was through the brush. Standing before him was his dog . . . and a woman.

He stood, momentarily captivated, his movements slowed by the sheer shock of seeing her standing alone, in the road, at this late hour, and in this weather.

If anyone, he'd expected to see his sister, or perhaps one of the townspeople.

But this woman was a stranger.

Nathaniel stepped closer. His youngest sister's stories of enchanted woodland fairies catapulted to the forefront of his mind. Especially when she was younger, his sister would pretend to see them on their walks through the forest.

But no, this woman was very real.

The stranger was cloaked in a pelisse that was so wet it appeared black and a straw bonnet with a thick ribbon that sat askew on her head. He could only see her profile in the night's shadow, but her wet hair hung in clumps about her face and shoulders. She stood a few feet from the dog, hands at her chest, eyes fixed on Gus. When the dog moved closer, she scurried behind a tree trunk.

She had not yet noticed Nathaniel, but her shouts at Gus pulled him from his trance.

"Get away! Go!"

Nathaniel rushed to Gus and pulled the small dog back.

"I am sorry, miss," he said, kneeling to hold the dog by the collar. "Did he harm you?"

The woman drew several breaths. Her eyes flicked from the dog back to him. "Y-Yes. I mean . . . no. He caught me by surprise, is all."

Thunder rumbled in the distance, and a sharp gust of wind pelted them with more rain.

"He is harmless. Merely excited."

They stood silent for a few moments, each staring at the other. When he did speak, his words came out rougher than intended. "I do not believe we are acquainted."

She clutched her pelisse closer. "No, sir, we are not. I am traveling to Willowgrove Hall." She offered no additional information, only eyed the dog bouncing at its master's feet.

Nathaniel thought it odd that a woman should be traveling alone, but if she were a guest on the property, he needed to make sure she was safe. "I am Nathaniel Stanton, steward at Willowgrove Hall. May I be of assistance?"

She drew a deep breath and met his gaze directly. "I am Cecily Faire, and I thank you, sir, but I am quite well. If you would be so kind as to point me in the direction of Willowgrove Hall, I will continue on my way."

"Impossible." He had to raise his voice to be heard over the sound of the wind racing through the branches above them. "It is far too dark to walk in this weather. You've still about half a mile."

He thought he noticed her chin tremble. "If I may ask, how is it you came upon this road? Most do not travel it on foot."

She returned her gaze to the trunk by her feet. "The carriage delivered me at the gate, but the driver said he could not continue through to Willowgrove on account of an impassable bridge. He suggested I walk."

"His advice to continue on foot was misguided." Nathaniel nodded toward the main house. "What is your business at Willowgrove?"

"I am to be a lady's companion to Mrs. Trent."

At the moment, he was not sure which surprised him more—meeting a young woman on such a secluded road or the fact that Mrs. Trent had acquired yet another companion. She had an unusual habit of bringing guests and not informing him. Such details would be helpful at times like this, when unfamiliar young ladies showed up unannounced.

Nathaniel tilted his head to see around the curve in the road. The sky grew darker by the minute, and the road beneath him had turned to mud. He could neither allow her to stay here nor to continue on.

Unsure of how to proceed, he assessed her. She was not a common person, but rather a lady, sent to be the mistress's personal friend. Even her pelisse, albeit wet and dark, appeared elegantly trimmed and cut.

Inwardly, he groaned. The last thing he needed was to have any interaction with Mrs. Trent's companion. But she looked so young. So fragile on so rough a night. He was not about to leave her in the wind and rain.

"My home, Laurel Cottage, is through those trees. Would you consider accompanying me there? My mother and sisters are at home, I am certain, and once out of this weather we can decide the best course."

Miss Faire frowned and looked back over her shoulder, lifting a delicate, gloved hand to shield her eyes. "But Mrs. Trent will be expecting me. I've no wish to disappoint her."

"Mrs. Trent is away. She will be returning tomorrow. Besides, the driver was correct. The bridge is impassable; the supporting beams were washed away. There is a makeshift footbridge, but that is for the workers and the brick masons. I'd advise against crossing it with wet shoes and in this weather."

She looked back over her shoulder again and then turned her eyes toward him. In the gathering darkness, in the shadow of the elms lining the drive, her eyes shone green. Even with wet hair and a soggy cloak clinging to her narrow shoulders, she was very becoming.

Yet another reason he should have nothing to do with her.

He released Gus, paused to ensure the dog did not rush the new companion, and stepped forward to pick up her trunk. He spied the long strap she had tied and lifted it. "What's this?"

"My trunk was damaged when it was dropped from the carriage, I fear. I tied the strap so I could pull it."

Mud and mire caked the battered trunk. He was already soaked. What harm would a little mud do? He hefted the trunk onto his shoulder.

He whistled to Gus, who trotted over, tail wagging, and then turned to her. "Follow me. Mind your step, miss, and stay close."

Feeling more preposterous than ever, Cecily followed Mr. Stanton through the low-lying brush and thick branches. Mr. Stanton was but a black silhouette before her, outlined in the shifting shadows of the wind-tossed forest. She was unaccustomed to walking in such dense forestry. At Aradelle, she had spent many hours exploring the wooded lands around the estate, but those days were distant memories.

How she wanted to hesitate, to inspect where she was putting her feet to be sure the ground was solid. But Mr. Stanton was traveling at such a pace that she had to trust him, despite that every sensibility within her was screaming a warning.

Cecily tried to heed his caution and stay as close as possible, attempting to follow his footsteps to the letter, but she winced as she felt her foot sink into something soft. Her breath caught in her throat when she stepped too close to a branch and it caught on the straw of her bonnet. She paused to free herself.

When they finally emerged on the other side of the trees, she noticed yellow light spilling from two windows up ahead.

Mr. Stanton's voice was low, and he pointed toward the structure. "Laurel Cottage. There."

Cecily drew a deep breath and wiped the rain from her eyelashes. Nestled in a clearing stood a cottage, the white walls of which seemed to glow almost blue in the darkness. Upon closer inspection, the cottage was unlike any she had ever encountered. It was a large, symmetrical building, and the entrance was situated between two projecting wings with steep gables. The exterior appeared to be a mixture of stucco and weatherboarding. Dark timbers crossed the frame, and a steep, thatched roof gave way to stone chimneys jutting black into the night sky, the smoke puffing from them becoming one with the rainy haze. She paused to take in the sight, but Mr. Stanton continued ahead. Nerves danced within her. He had said he was the steward of Willowgrove Hall and that ladies were in the house. She should trust him, should she not?

The dog came running back from behind them and wove around his owner as he walked toward the cottage. She gathered her skirts and hurried to catch up.

Mr. Stanton called out to signal their arrival, and within moments the door swung open.

And then chaos ensued.

A young girl in pale green with blond hair gathered in a large, pink ribbon darted past her to the dog. A heavy woman in a white apron hurried to Mr. Stanton, and two young ladies clad in printed dresses stared at her for several moments before one reached forward and tugged on her arm, gently escorting her inside.

Once inside, the older lady stepped in front of Mr. Stanton in obvious assessment of Cecily. "Oh, my dear! What is the meaning of this?"

Mr. Stanton removed his coat, flicking water onto the clean wood floor, and handed it to the little girl bouncing beside him. "Allow me to present Miss Faire. We met on the road to Willowgrove. She is to be Mrs. Trent's new companion."

Not knowing what else to say, Cecily self-consciously ran her hand down her pelisse, dipped in a curtsey, and tried to recall every bit of the polite conversation skills she had been taught at Rosemere. "My apologies for the intrusion. I fear I must look a sight."

But the lines on the woman's face softened, and she motioned for Cecily to move closer. "Oh, you poor soul! You are soaked through! Come with me." She took Cecily by the arm and pulled her deeper into the house, which, with the heavy wool skirt, was quite a feat in itself. "Charlotte," she continued, "go tell Bessie to get some tea, and quickly."

Cecily allowed herself to be led into a room off the main hall, which she assumed to be the parlor. She scanned the room as discreetly as possible, trying to get a sense of her surroundings, for everything about her was in motion. The low-ceilinged room was centered around a large, stone chimneypiece with oak shelves stacked with tomes. A calico-covered sofa and two wingback chairs atop a woven rug formed a sitting area around the fire. Lobby chairs, a small table, and a long-case clock sat against the back wall.

The older woman's high voice recaptured her attention. "Well, who can believe this weather? A fine greeting for you, is it not? Here, permit me to take your bonnet, and we shall set about getting you dry."

Cecily had not realized she was trembling until she attempted to untie the soggy ribbon fixed beneath her chin. The knot felt too tight, her hands too weak. She looked around her. Two, no three females watched her with wide eyes.

Cecily tilted her head. The steward still stood in the hall, his broad back to them, and removed his hat, revealing wet black hair. The sight surprised her, for judging by the depth of his voice, she had expected him to be graying, like the woman who had answered the door.

One of the young women brought her back to the task. "Here, allow me." The tallest girl, with fair hair and skin, and eyes that reminded Cecily of the color of chocolate, stepped forward and within a matter of seconds had the satin ribbon hanging freely.

Cecily stole another glance at the steward. Thick, wet hair hung over his forehead, but it was when his brilliant blue eyes landed on her that her pulse quickened. It was the first time she'd been able to see his face. The start of a beard's shadow darkened his chin, highlighting a strong jaw and broad mouth. She grew self-conscious of how her own hair must be disheveled and the awkward manner in which her clothing hugged her form.

As if interpreting Cecily's timidity, the older woman stepped forward. "Introductions can wait until after you are dry and tea is made. Rebecca, take Miss Faire upstairs and get her into something dry, will you? It will be easier to assess the situation once everyone is comfortable."

Cecily motioned to her trunk. "I fear my belongings took quite a tumble."

"Yes, I can see that quite plainly." The older woman put a pudgy fist at her waist and turned her attention to the mud-caked trunk. "Well, fortunately you found your way to a houseful of ladies. Surely we have some garment that will fit you. Off with you, then. When you are done, come back down for some tea, and we will have proper introductions."

Cecily was eager for a dry gown and, at the mention of tea, realized she had not eaten since early afternoon when they stopped at Rhysbourne to switch the horses. Cecily felt she should object. This entire situation seemed one mishap after the other. It did not feel right to wear another's clothes, to intrude on a family's solitude. But moisture seeped through the layers of her pelisse and gown, and her skin began to feel chafed with the incessant rub of wet fabric, so she reluctantly complied.

Miss Stanton took her by the arm. "Follow me."

Cecily followed her hostess from the warmth of the parlor to the cool darkness of the hall. The young woman paused to retrieve a candle lamp from a sideboard and then proceeded to ascend a flight of steep stairs. Another hallway was off the square, cramped landing, and four closed, paneled doors lined the corridor. Cecily was led to the room at the end of the hallway. The soles of her shoes clicked on the bare plank floor, and with each step, the house seemed to grow colder. Her skin pricked in resistance to the chill. The door opened into a small, dark room.

This chamber was much draftier than the cozy parlor below. A low, single bed was against the far wall, and a painted dressing screen and wardrobe chest stood opposite. Two curtained windows rattled with the wind, and the icy air seemed to slice through the very fabric of her gown.

Cecily could not deny the appeal of a dry gown, a warm shawl. With shaking fingers she unbuttoned her pelisse.

The young woman who led her to the room placed the candle lamp on a nearby table. "We were not properly introduced. I am Rebecca Stanton."

Cecily gave a small curtsey to the pretty blonde. "It is a pleasure to meet you, Miss Stanton."

"No, no, 'Miss Stanton' will not do. You must call me Rebecca, for everyone here does. Oh, you poor dear, look. You are shivering. Here." She paused to pull some garments from the chest and then went to the wardrobe to select a dress. "I daresay they will be too big for you, but at least they are dry." She placed the items on the bed. "Is your chemise soaked?"

Cecily lifted her gown to assess the first layer of clothing. The wet fabric clung to her legs. "I fear so."

"Here is a dry one. You can change behind that screen."

Cecily obeyed, taking the garment in her hand and stepping behind a dressing screen. With the faint glow from the candle as her guide, Cecily managed the tie to her traveling frock. She felt much lighter when she finally shed the wet wool from her body. As quickly as she could, she peeled her cold things away and donned the dry chemise, then stepped back out.

"I will ask Nathaniel to bring up your things, but this flannel petticoat is the heaviest I have and should warm you until your own things are dry."

How strange it was to dress in another person's clothes, to wear their stockings and petticoats. But despite the awkwardness, Cecily found comfort for the warmth it brought. Her memory flashed back to her first cool dawn at Rosemere. Her simple dress had been muddy and damp with morning dew then too, and she'd shed it, along with her former life, for a Rosemere gown.

And now she was beginning afresh again.

"You are fortunate, Miss Faire, to have happened upon a household with so many women," Rebecca said, "for if Nathaniel lived alone in this house, you would have naught but his shirts and coats, which would not do."

Cecily slipped her arms through the borrowed petticoat and allowed the girl to help her finish dressing.

"You are Mr. Stanton's sister, I trust?"

"I am indeed, although you would never know it at the sight of us, would you?" She gave a little laugh. "And note that Nathaniel is my *older* brother. Make no mistake about that."

With a playful smile, she motioned for Cecily to turn so she could fasten the dress. Cecily held her wet hair away from her back so Miss Stanton could do the lacing.

"Here." Rebecca handed her a towel. "You may use this to dry your hair."

Cecily pressed the towel around clumps of her hair and rubbed vigorously. Once the majority of the moisture was out, her fingers forced tangles from the unruly locks. They were always hard to tame, but when they were wet, it was almost impossible. She looked around the room, hoping to find a looking glass. She drew a deep breath.

"Do not you fear, Miss Faire. We shall take good care of you while you are at Laurel Cottage," Rebecca said and smiled warmly.

6

It had taken Nathaniel little time to shed his muddy garments and dress in dry trousers, shirt, waistcoat, and coat. He ran his fingers through his wet hair and shook out the moisture, but it would not take long for it to dry.

He was actually growing accustomed to being damp. With all the rain and flooding of late, he had spent his days, and nights, trying to undo the damage that had been done. Normally at this hour of the evening he would be looking for a hot meal and a night's sleep. But this night would be different.

Mrs. Trent had a new companion. And this could only mean trouble for him. The former lady's companion had been pleasant enough, but her ability to bend Mrs. Trent's ear and set unrealistic expectations put him in more than one impossible situation.

It was most unfair of him to judge this new woman based on her position alone. Certainly she possessed several redeeming qualities and was a fine, principled person. But he had encountered Mrs. Trent's companions before, and they shared similar characteristics—they were often silly, trite women who fawned over Mrs. Trent's every whim and regarded him as the enemy.

So why should he care whom Mrs. Trent chose for her personal attendants?

Only he did care when he found one of them wandering around in the forest, bewildered, lost, and drenched.

Nathaniel made his way to the parlor to wait for the ladies. He took his customary brown chair next to the fire, picked up his worn copy of *The Farmer's Calendar,* and flipped it open to read, only to stop short when he heard the creak of the stairs and hushed voices coming from the corridor.

He lifted his gaze and fixed it on the foot of the stairs, anticipating whom he might see. How Miss Faire's presence in their home changed the course of the entire night.

With every tick of the long-case clock, his curiosity grew. For despite her purpose here, how often did one see such a beautiful woman in a place where she should not be? But now she was in his house. Under his roof. And if he knew his mother, Mrs. Trent's new lady's companion would likely be joining them for dinner. And breakfast. And tea in between.

Nathaniel held his breath as footsteps turned the wooden corner. Rebecca's soft voice echoed from the plaster walls. "Nathaniel is in the parlor. He will entertain you for a moment while I talk to Mother. Please, make yourself at ease."

Nathaniel stood as Miss Faire entered. He instantly recognized the dress she wore. It was one of Rebecca's better dresses, one she often wore to church. But it looked so different on the newcomer.

Miss Faire looked different.

Only a quarter of an hour ago she had been clad in a dark, heavy traveling garment that hung mercilessly on her small frame. She had been pale with wide, frightened eyes. Now she was quite transformed. The gown's hue of pale pink intensified the vibrancy in Miss Faire's green eyes and the blush of her cheeks.

But what surprised him most was her hair. It had looked dark when it was wet and plastered to her head. But now, as it was drying and flowing over her shoulders, the fire's light caught on auburn threads boasting copper glints, and as the strands dried, they pulled up into fiery curls that hung nearly to her waist.

He stood for a moment, transfixed. Perhaps she *was* like one of his youngest sister's woodland fairies.

He bowed, diverting his eyes so as not to stare.

She offered a hesitant smile.

"Please, Miss Faire. Do be seated." He was unsure of what to say, but he needed to fill the silence. He wished any one of his sisters were present, for their talent for talk put his to shame.

Fortunately, Miss Faire seemed quite comfortable. "If I may ask, what is it that you are reading?"

Nathaniel had almost forgotten about the book in his hand. He slid his finger in between the rough pages to mark his place. "Young's *Farmer's Calendar.*"

She shifted closer. "How very interesting."

He managed a little smile. So polite, just as he would expect from a lady's companion. He doubted she would find much of interest in a book of tillage and livestock. "Are you fond of reading, Miss Faire?"

Her expression brightened. "Indeed, I am."

He was about to ask her more, but Gus nudged Nathaniel's hand with his wet nose, begging for his master's attention. "My apologies that Gus frightened you. He is still young, and I fear he has a wild spirit."

A good-natured smile dimpled her cheek as she leaned forward to assess the pointer. "Oh, do not give it a second thought, Mr. Stanton. I confess dogs have always frightened me. I am certain Gus is of a gentle countenance. And if it were not for his awareness, I might still be out wandering around in the rain and dark."

Nathaniel shook his head, taking his seat only after she was settled in the chair opposite him. "Those public transport fellows are a difficult lot. But the driver spoke truth. We lost the main drive's bridge when the sluice to a nearby pond failed. We are in the process of rebuilding, and for the time being the carriages must enter the estate from the west drive." Nathaniel hesitated. "Had I known you were coming, we would have sent one of Willowgrove's carriages for you."

"That is very kind, but I only received the offer a few days ago. The letter from Mrs. Trent indicated that she was in need of a lady's companion as soon as possible. And, well, here I am."

"It is unfortunate that she is not here to greet you."

"I must say I am a little surprised. I was under the impression she was unwell and cared not for traveling."

"You are correct on that account. She is in poor health. She has spent the last two months in Bath taking the waters, but to my understanding they have not had the desired effect, and so they are returning to Willowgrove earlier than anticipated."

Miss Faire frowned. "They?"

Nathaniel sat back in his chair, refusing to allow his personal feelings for Mrs. Trent's entourage to color Miss Faire's perceptions. "Mrs. Trent is traveling with her nephew, the man who will inherit Willowgrove on her passing."

Miss Faire opened her mouth to ask another question, but at that moment his mother entered the room and, at the sight of the dog curled at his feet, gave a little *tsk*. "Honestly, Nathaniel, I wish you would consider my nerves and leave that beast out of doors."

Nathaniel peered down at the dog, who raised his head from the rug. "Oh really, Mother, he is not so horrific as you infer."

"Not so? And with a guest in the house?" She shook her head before turning her attention to Miss Faire. "Like his father, he is, always bringing animals indoors that belong in the barnyard. But how can I argue? Other than that flaw, my Nathaniel is as agreeable as can be."

His mother rested her hands on her hips, sighed, and nodded in the direction of a framed drawing on the plaster wall. "There, that is my late husband, Thomas Stanton, Miss Faire. Handsome man, was he not? His portrait was drawn by my Rebecca."

Miss Faire looked toward the drawing. "Yes, most handsome indeed."

Nathaniel straightened in his chair. The less said about his father, the better. For, undoubtedly, Mrs. Trent would give Miss Faire an earful on that account in the very near future.

He needed to distract his mother, otherwise she would fill Miss Faire in on every family detail before the hour was out. "What of dinner, Mother? I am as hungry as I've ever been."

He was almost relieved his two youngest sisters, Hannah and Charlotte, entered, their round faces bright with excitement over their surprise visitor.

Nathaniel remained quiet, as he so often chose to be in the busy moments of his family's life, and watched as his sisters immediately set about extracting all the details they could about their lovely guest. They quickly pulled every sort of information from her, such as that Miss Faire had been traveling all day. Yes, this was to be her first time as a companion, and no, she was not catching a chill from being out in the rain. Miss Faire did not have a pet pony, or any pet for that matter, but she was fond of kittens. He should stop them, for surely they were making her uncomfortable, but he had to admit, he was equally intent upon learning about her, especially given her new role.

He could not help but wonder on what circumstances such a lady must have fallen to take the position of a companion. Each one before her had a different story of how they fell from prosperity to more reduced conditions.

Nathaniel tried to listen as she spoke, but he was distracted by the shyness in her smile. The alertness in her eyes. Nathaniel was far too practical for romantic ideas and whims. His life was dedicated to his work. His sisters and mother had been after him for years to find a wife and settle down. But he hadn't met a woman with whom that ever felt right.

And so, once again, he would force his rationality to trump any feeling stirring within him. For Miss Faire was to be Mrs. Trent's companion. And if history served as any guide, it would only be a matter of days before Mrs. Trent began to fill Miss Faire's head with what a corrupt man Nathaniel was.

But he knew it was not his character she detested, but the secret they shared.

Cecily followed Miss Rebecca Stanton to the table where she was ushered to a chair next to Mrs. Stanton. The two younger sisters sat across from her, and Miss Stanton took the seat next to her. Mr. Stanton sat at the table's head. Candlelight filled the room, softening the space in its gentle glow.

The muscles in Cecily's shoulders eased.

The woman Cecily assumed to be their servant brought in dinner and served the family. The steam from the thick lamb stew, piping hot vegetables, and warm bread made her mouth water.

"Thank you, Bessie." Mrs. Stanton turned to Cecily. "We would have had something more substantial prepared for dinner had I known we would have company," Mrs. Stanton said, somewhat apologetically.

"This looks lovely." Cecily infused more energy into her voice than she felt. "I have not eaten much today."

She inched to the side so the woman could serve her. The informality reminded her of school and put her at ease.

"I'd wager this is not how you imagined spending your first evening in our fair village," Mrs. Stanton continued.

"No, it is not, I am afraid, but it has turned out to be a lovely evening just the same."

Mrs. Stanton smiled. "Well now, you will need to stay the night here, my dear. And you are most welcome."

Cecily really did feel welcome. She took a bite of the stew and found the flavor of the lamb and carrots delightful. She managed to take stock of the people around her in between bites. Mrs. Stanton, despite her graying hair, boasted a young smile and a bright complexion. Mr. Nathaniel Stanton was the eldest, followed by Miss Rebecca Stanton, whom Cecily learned was only one year her junior. The two younger girls, Charlotte and Hannah, seemed younger versions of their older sister with their flaxen hair and dark eyes. Cecily took another bite, and while she felt quite at home with the Stanton women, Mr. Stanton was another matter entirely. She tried to relax her jaw and take a deep breath, but was acutely aware of his every movement at the head of the table.

Mrs. Stanton bent toward her. "So, my dear, where is it exactly that you come from?"

"I was sent here from Rosemere School for Young Ladies in Darbury."

The youngest girl, Hannah, leaned forward eagerly, her dark eyes wide. "What was it like? Were there a lot of girls there?"

"Yes, when I left, there were thirty young ladies, I believe." Cecily smiled at the girl's unmasked curiosity. "Several were about your size. Shall I see if I can guess your age?"

The little girl grinned and shrank back against her chair, clearly enjoying the attention.

"Hmm . . ." Cecily put her finger to her lips. "My guess is that you are sixteen years of age."

Hannah burst into laughter at the obvious exaggeration.

Cecily held back her own amusement. "No?"

Hannah shook her head, wisps of blond hair swinging about her round face.

"Well then, I shall try again."

Cecily squinted, leaned close, and pressed her lips together. After creating a dramatic pause, she held up seven fingers. "Seven."

Hannah's mouth fell open in awe, and her eyes grew wide before she looked to her mother and then her sisters. "How did you know?"

Cecily smiled. "I have been around a great many young ladies, and I taught girls your age to sew."

The little girl eagerly jumped from her seat. "Will you teach me to sew?"

"Hannah! Be seated," scolded her mother.

But the child paid no heed. "I'll be right back!"

"Hannah!" her mother cried again, half standing from her chair. As Hannah disappeared around the corner, Mrs. Stanton sank back in her seat. "I do apologize for her manners, Miss Faire. I imagine they are quite a shock to you, but I assure you, I do endeavor to instill in her some sense of decorum."

"Nonsense, Mrs. Stanton. Children will be children. Make no mistake about it. Hannah is charming."

But what Cecily did not say was how at home the girl made her feel. Talking with children was easy. Talking with adults, not to mention a handsome man, was another thing entirely.

Rebecca returned her fork to her plate. "Where is it that you are from originally, prior to your time at Rosemere?"

Cecily hesitated before answering. The question was innocent and appropriate enough. She wiped her mouth with the linen cloth. "Before my time at Rosemere, I lived to the south of here on the outskirts of Aradelle Park in Detham."

Mr. Stanton, who had been a silent bystander to the conversation up until this point, responded so quickly that Cecily checked herself to ensure she had not said anything inappropriate. "Aradelle Park, you say?"

Cecily forced herself to meet his direct gaze. "Yes, sir. Do you know it?"

Mr. Stanton lowered his spoon and glanced at his mother, his eyes drawn together. "I do."

The tension was eased slightly when young Hannah came running back into the room, blond hair bouncing against her back, something pink and white in her hands.

"Merciful heavens, Hannah, do not run!" her mother said.

But the reprimand seemed lost on the girl, for she rounded the table and thrust the item toward Cecily with childlike vigor.

Cecily, grateful for the interruption, turned her full attention to the child. "And what have we here?"

The child hopped from foot to foot, her cheeks pink. "I made it! Rebecca helped me with the legs, but I did the rest."

Cecily took the doll from the girl and turned it over in her hand, examining the simple, uneven stitches. But she could not help but smile at Hannah's pride in her needlework and her readiness to share it. "I think it is lovely. A job well done."

Hannah gripped the arm of Cecily's chair in her excitement. "Will you teach me how to make more? Like your students?"

"Of course, dearest. Anytime you like."

Charlotte, whom Cecily judged to be about fourteen, spoke for the first time. "Hannah, Miss Faire will be very busy, just like Miss Vale was. She will be far too busy for such things."

"No, she will not. She just told me."

The child's temper was starting to flare, and her mother stepped in. "I'll have no bickering at the table or anywhere else in this home. Is that understood?"

Then, amid the chime of feminine tones, Mr. Stanton's rich baritone voice again echoed from the plaster walls and filled the space.

"So how is it, then, that you came to be Mrs. Trent's companion?" Mr. Stanton's gaze was unfaltering. His voice, steady. "Are you in some way acquainted with the Trent family?"

Heat crept up Cecily's neck. She was unsure of why these questions should make her uncomfortable. In fact, she should grow accustomed to them, for undoubtedly as she became more acquainted with the people at Willowgrove, they would make such inquiries. She could not place her finger on it, but there seemed to be something in Mr. Stanton's tone that hinted at more than mere graciousness. She returned her napkin to her lap. "No, sir. Mrs. Trent's former companion, Miss Vale, had attended Rosemere, and when she married, Mrs. Trent wrote to our headmistress for a replacement, and, well, here I am."

His drawn eyebrows and set jaw made him appear suspicious. If her thoughts weren't so muddied by the events of the day, her intuition might be more focused.

As dinner was coming to an end, the eldest Miss Stanton placed a cup of tea in front of Cecily. Cecily wrapped her fingers around the hot cup, allowing the warmth to spread through her fingers. The room, although small, exuded peace. She allowed her posture to slack ever so slightly.

But she could not completely relax.

How she had hoped, wished, prayed for a family very much like this one. As she watched the scene, a distant—although welcomed—outsider, her heart ached. As she did dozens of times each day, she thought of her sister. And the flame to find Leah grew brighter.

And even as thoughts of her sister tugged at her heart, there was another factor compounding the situation.

She cast a glance at Mr. Stanton from the corner of her eye.

Heaven help her. He grew more handsome every time Cecily looked at him.

She pressed her lips together and redirected her gaze to the delicate blue teacup in her hands.

She must keep her emotions in check.

She had no choice, for had she not once thought another man handsome? Those thoughts—and the actions associated with those thoughts—had led to her ruin.

No, she was here for a very specific purpose. Her chance at romance had passed, and besides, if he knew her history, he would likely have nothing to do with her.

7

After Rebecca took Miss Faire upstairs to retire for the evening, Nathaniel sat by the glowing fire in the parlor, still making sense of the odd turn the day had taken. The house was unusually quiet, save for the occasional snore coming from the dog by his feet.

His mother had taken up her mending and was now sitting in the chair opposite him. The years had been kind to her. It was only since his father died five years ago that strands of silver had intermixed with her flaxen hair, and wrinkles creased at the edges of her eyes and around her mouth. "I do wish you would leave that animal outside," his mother mumbled. "He smells to high heaven!"

Nathaniel smiled. Their age-old argument. He leaned over the arm of the chair to tousle the dog's fur. "He's not such a wild beast, see? He will calm down in due time. Mark my words."

His mother responded with a click of her tongue and a shake of her head. "La, you men and your hounds."

Nathaniel indulged one more pat on the dog's head and leaned back again in his chair.

He would be quite content to enjoy a slice of silence, but as usual, his mother seemed intent upon conversation. She bent to retrieve a bit of thread that had fallen and settled back in her chair. "Miss Faire. What a lovely surprise she turned out to be."

Nathaniel had wondered how long it would take for his mother to point out Miss Faire's charms. He chose not to respond; rather, he stared up at the painted beams crossing the room's low ceiling. He tried to think of something else, of how the smoke soot needed to be scrubbed from the ceiling, or how he should bring in more dry wood from their covered store.

She lifted an eyebrow. "You do not agree?"

Lately, the town seamstress, widow Mrs. Olivia Massey, had been her selection for him.

Nathaniel, however, was much more practical. His opportunity for love might come one day, but for now, he had responsibilities. Someone needed to lead their family, especially with their father gone.

He'd worked too hard. Sacrificed too much.

Nathaniel adjusted his position in the chair. "Miss Faire is to be Mrs. Trent's companion, and you know all too well Mrs. Trent's opinions of our family. I suggest you encourage Hannah and Charlotte to leave Miss Faire be."

"Oh, nonsense. Miss Faire seemed quite content with Hannah's company. Besides, she may not share Mrs. Trent's beliefs."

Nathaniel huffed. "If she wishes to keep her post, she will."

His mother said nothing, but her lips pressed together in a firm line and her countenance darkened.

Katherine Stanton did not like to speak of Mrs. Trent.

And for good reason.

His mother would often seem to pretend that Mrs. Trent did not exist and that their paths were not interwoven. But over time,

Nathaniel's frustration at her approach had given way to a more mature respect for her feelings. He would not push her.

His mother kept her eyes fixed on her sewing. "Well, regardless, we shall encounter Miss Faire about town, to be sure, just as we did Miss Vale. We might as well be civil."

He would not speak of interacting with her socially, but there was one thing their guest had said that he could not ignore. "Did you not hear Miss Faire say she was from Aradelle Park?"

His mother did not look up from her work. "To what point?"

Nathaniel frowned. His mother seemed to have forgotten the Trents' connection to Aradelle Park.

If she did not recall it, he was not about to remind her. He pulled off his boots and let them fall with a thud to the floor before leaning back in his chair and staring into the fire.

He was far from an alarmist, and yet the facts were too coincidental. Miss Faire seemed sincere and honest enough. But he had to be careful. Not just for himself, but for the well-being of his family. "Something about this entire situation seems amiss."

"For heaven's sake, Nathaniel, you are resolved to surmise the negative, whether it be appropriate or not. You grow more and more like your father every day."

The words "your father" hung in the air like stagnant fog, dampening the lightheartedness of their conversation.

She lowered her eyes.

Clearly she regretted the words.

A dozen sharp retorts blazed through his mind, but he could not say them to her. For her regret had been enough. She—and he—had both paid the price tenfold.

At one time the idea of securing his parents' approval had been all that mattered. But time and experience had hardened him. He still held stock by them, but now other things pressed for his attention. Like his three sisters. With their father dead, it was

Nathaniel's lot to provide for them and to ensure they married well. And it all was within his reach. He didn't need anything—or anyone—interfering . . . especially an attractive stranger who he feared possessed the power to disrupt the delicate balance of everything he held dear.

For his mother's sake, he would speak no more about this. But day after day, year after year, the tides of time lulled them into change. Mrs. Trent was growing older, and each day her health became more uncertain. When the will was read, everything would change. Had his father not assured him of an inheritance? Of Lockbourne House? Although it was in poor condition, it would be his own, and furthermore, it was far from Willowgrove Hall. And for that, he would continue to play the part.

Later than evening, when night had completely fallen, Cecily followed Rebecca into the bedchamber as they prepared to retire. It was cooler in the upstairs room, and with the exception of the occasional giggle echoing from Hannah and Charlotte's room across the corridor, all was quiet.

As she stepped farther into the room to place her candle on the side table, Cecily spotted her trunk on the floor next to the bed. She stood motionless, staring at the trunk to confirm that it was indeed hers. "Look!"

Rebecca peered over her shoulder as she turned toward the wardrobe. "Nathaniel must have brought it up while we were talking."

Cecily placed her candle on the table, knelt down beside the trunk, and touched the latch cautiously, as if it might fling open by its own power. Mr. Stanton had disappeared for almost an hour after dinner while the ladies conversed in the parlor. She never would have imagined that he was mending her trunk. All traces of mud on the trunk's exterior had been washed away, and the leather strap, which had torn away from the shell during the fall, was now securely fixed into place with several small nails. "It has been repaired!"

"I am sure Nathaniel fixed it when he went to tend the animals. He is always tinkering with this or that." The lilt in Rebecca's voice suggested that she thought nothing significant of the deed.

But Cecily continued to stare.

True, it was a simple gesture, but Cecily could not recall the last time a man had showed her such kindness. And now Mr. Stanton had not once but twice showed her kindness: first by opening his home to her and now by mending her trunk.

A strange flutter danced within her.

Rebecca pulled a white sleeping gown out of the chest and draped it over her arm. "Tell me, are you eager to be at Willowgrove Hall?"

Cecily rose from the trunk and sat on the bed as she considered Rebecca's question.

The question, although seemingly a simple one, was really quite complex.

Was she eager?

Or would she not be more content in her quiet attic room at Rosemere, among what was familiar and safe?

She knew the polite answer, regardless of the truth it held. "Yes, indeed. Are you well acquainted with Mrs. Trent?"

Rebecca pulled a green-and-blue quilt from the wardrobe and, with a flick of her wrists, spread it across the bed. "I have lived on Willowgrove grounds all my life, but in truth, I have only spoken with Mrs. Trent on a handful of occasions. At one time we used to see her often at church, or perhaps walking in the gardens, but she has been gone so much of late that she rarely attends. Nathaniel talks to her on a regular occasion, though."

Cecily frowned in contemplation. "Truthfully?"

"Indeed." Rebecca paused, propped her hands on her hips, and looked to the ceiling, as if considering her response. "Mrs. Trent is a very particular sort of woman. So often she is away, but when she is at Willowgrove, she keeps to herself and rarely ventures out of doors. Even when she attends church, she barely speaks to anyone with the exception of the vicar and his wife."

At this news, Cecily's chest tightened with the pang of disappointment. She came to Willowgrove with the knowledge that Mrs. Trent was not well, but even so, a small part of her had hoped for parties and diversions and, at the very least, outings to the village or walks in the gardens. On the journey from Darbury, her mind had woven plans to explore the Willowgrove grounds, just as she had explored Aradelle in her youth. Based on Rebecca's report, Cecily wondered if she would even venture out of doors at all.

Cecily stopped short of asking about Mrs. Trent's personality and decided not to linger on the disappointment. Instead, she quickly undressed and slipped into the flannel sleeping gown Rebecca had given her.

Rebecca handed her a heavy wool shawl and then moved toward the door. "Can I get you anything else before I retire?"

"Is this not your chamber?" Cecily asked, concerned that Rebecca appeared to be leaving the room. "'Twould be a shame for you not to sleep in your own bed on my account."

Rebecca paused at the door and turned to a small table, using Cecily's discarded candle to light a small candle lamp. "Pray, do not give it a second thought. I shall sleep in Mother's room at the end of the hall. Hannah and Charlotte sleep in the room directly across from this one should you require anything in the night."

Cecily could not help but wonder where Mr. Stanton slept since all the upper rooms were spoken for. She quickly rebuked herself for wondering so personal a detail about a man she barely knew.

Rebecca offered a warm smile as she paused in the doorway. "Good night, then. Pleasant dreams."

She pulled the door closed behind her, and the sound of her footsteps retreating down the wooden hallway faded. Cecily tightened her borrowed shawl around her, indulging in a shiver that seemed to shake her to her very core. She stepped to the window and looked out. The rain continued to fall in uneven waves. She squinted to make out her surroundings.

But she was met only with blackness.

Her eyes now burning with the cry for rest, Cecily pulled back the modest covers and crawled into the bed. She pressed her cheek against the rough, linen pillow. She kept her eyes fixed, unwavering, on the uncovered paned window, watching as lightning streaked across the black sky. She took a deep, slow breath and held it. The steady rhythm of rain should lull her to sleep, yet her mind was alive with the unfamiliarity around her.

She squeezed her eyes shut. The sound reminded her of that night five years ago when her life was forever changed. Even though she no longer felt heartbreak over the severed romance, not a day passed when she didn't think about Andrew and what their life would have been like. And equally as compelling, not a day passed when she did not regret the impulsiveness of her actions or the recklessness of her disregard.

She had, of course, found happiness at Rosemere, and she was likely far better off there than she had ever been at Aradelle. She had made peace with her separation from Andrew and her father.

But she still felt the separation from her twin with aching loss.

She reached up and touched the coral necklace about her neck, wondering for the millionth time if her sister missed it.

She'd been wrong to take it. For this necklace belonged to her sister as much as it did to her. One day she would return it. She wasn't sure where or how, but once she was settled at Willowgrove, she was determined to start her search.

8

Sunlight sliced through the uncovered window and pried Cecily's eyes open.

The previous night's storms had given way to a brilliant blue sky, with two fluffy white clouds visible through the window.

She sat up slowly, wincing at the pinch in her back and side. Today, the effects of riding in the jostling carriage and pulling the trunk behind her pressed upon every limb, and she stretched her sore, tired muscles, reaching her arms above her and wiggling her fingers.

In the light of morning, she finally got a good look at the room around her. White wainscoting met pale-blue walls. A small rosewood stand stood tucked between the window and the adjacent wall. On it was her candle from the previous evening, along with three books piled in a tidy stack. She stood from the bed and stepped to the books, picking up one volume. *The Romance of the Forest*. She knew the story well. She leafed through the pages and then set it down. She lifted her attention back to the view. Beyond her window was the stunning landscape of Willowgrove Hall.

Just as the family had indicated, the field bordering the cottage courtyard was indeed flooded, shining like glass in the morning stillness. She turned the latch on the window and pushed it open, allowing the cool, fresh morning air to swirl around her. It smelled clean, as it should after a rain, and its soft kiss on her cheeks invigorated her senses. The sound of a cow lowing drew her attention, and she leaned to her left. The cowhouse was on the other side of the courtyard wall. Two brown cows moved about a small pen.

Without warning, Mr. Stanton rounded the corner—tall, the sunlight highlighting his high cheekbones and black hair. His gray greatcoat emphasized how his broad shoulders tapered to his waist. At the sight, her heart lurched, then pounded. She pulled the window shut and stepped back. The last thing she wanted was to be discovered staring at a man from a window in only her nightclothes.

But it was more than that.

The memory of his intense gaze had stayed with her, tempting to awaken a part of her heart that she had determined must remain closed.

She would not allow her heart to feel such an inclination for any man ever again.

As she retreated from the window, she forced her mind to another topic. Today was the day. Her new life was spread before her, an unspoiled page, a story ready to be written. At the thought, a little wave of nerves coursed through her. Would Mrs. Trent be fond of her? Could she be a suitable companion?

As she turned toward her chest, her gaze fell on her traveling gown, draped neatly over a chair in the corner. Her fingers traced the gown's elegant velvet trimming and the scalloped hem. It was damp. Someone had washed it. Gone were the traces of mud that had marred the hem. The dress, the repair to her trunk, the meal, and the camaraderie . . . what kindness she was finding at Laurel Cottage.

Cecily only hoped she found the same reception at Willowgrove Hall.

She lifted her trunk's lid. All of the carefully packed contents had been shuffled, no longer in the orderly stacks and folds Cecily had so painstakingly prepared the night before she departed Rosemere. Although the outside had been cleaned, Mr. Stanton had left her personal belongings alone, for which she was grateful.

With a sigh, she lifted one muddy gown, then another. They were far too dirty to be worn, and now her traveling dress was clean, but wet.

As she was contemplating her dilemma, a soft knock sounded at the door.

Rebecca popped her head inside. "Oh, good, you've awakened. I've no wish to disturb you, but I thought I heard you rustling about."

Cecily could not help but notice Rebecca appeared different by the light of day. Her smooth, blond hair was parted down the middle and swept off her long neck. Her skin appeared much fairer in the white light of dawn, and blond eyebrows and eyelashes framed her dark eyes.

How dissimilar she looked from her brother.

Cecily smiled and motioned for her to enter. "Please, Miss Stanton. Do come in. Have I slept late?"

"Remember, it is not Miss Stanton. Rebecca will do." Rebecca stepped in, closed the door behind her, and sat on the bed. "The hour is about nine, but Mother suggested that we let you sleep until you rose naturally, considering your long journey. She worries so about people falling ill, and you were in that damp dress for so long! She always says that sleep is the best prevention of ailments, and it is also the best cure."

Cecily straightened from the trunk, gown still in hand. "That is most thoughtful."

As Rebecca's gaze fell on the gown, her eyebrows drew together in concern. "Heavens, is that your dress?"

Cecily nodded. "I fear so. The contents of my trunk fell out when the driver threw it from the carriage, and this is the result."

"That will not do." Rebecca rose and pulled a gown from the wardrobe. As she continued to sort through the garments, she said, "Hannah and Charlotte are anxious for you to be awake. I think they are quite taken with you."

Cecily smiled. "They are sweet. They make me feel at home. I am accustomed to having children around."

"I fear you will find no children at Willowgrove, but you are welcome at Laurel Cottage whenever you are feeling lonely. I am sure they would be most happy to oblige. Here, I will help you dress."

Cecily put the comb down beside her, looking at the gown in Rebecca's hand. "But that is your dress, is it not? I cannot trespass on your kindness yet again."

Rebecca nodded toward the trunk. "Well, you cannot meet Mrs. Trent in that gown, nor a nightdress. That would never do."

"I suppose you are right." Cecily sighed. "I noticed someone was kind enough to wash my traveling dress, though." She turned to allow Rebecca to help her with her stays.

"That would have been Bessie." Rebecca gave a little giggle, a soft, gleeful sound that reminded Cecily of the tinkling of bells. "I think she felt sorry for you, having to stay here when you were expecting to spend the night at Willowgrove. No doubt the staff at Willowgrove will have no trouble cleaning your other gowns, but she thought it would be horrible for you to have to arrive in a gown caked with mud. She would not want anyone at the main house thinking her incapable of caring for guests at Laurel Cottage. She has quite a reputation—an honorable one—and she is intent upon keeping it."

Cecily let her gaze linger on the traveling dress as Rebecca finished the lacing, trying to ignore the sudden pinch of homesickness. "The headmistress of the school gave me the gown before I left."

"I have often wondered what it would have been like to go away to school. My mother saw to my education, and now I help her with Charlotte and Hannah, but I fear I lack patience. Nathaniel, of course, was educated by our father. Here, put this on."

Cecily lowered her eyes as Rebecca helped her into the gown of green printed cotton. She was not sent to school to learn. Indeed, her education had nothing to do with her father's decision.

A wren's chirp floated into the room, almost as if beckoning her out into the fresh air. She swallowed the pang of homesickness and focused on the excitement of the day before her.

Rebecca motioned for Cecily to turn. "My brother says you must have brought the pleasant weather with you."

Cecily's heart gave the queerest jump at the reference to Mr. Stanton. She gathered her waist-length hair and held it up so Rebecca could fasten the buttons down the back. "Oh?"

"Yes, says you must be good luck, for you brought the sun." Rebecca smiled, fastening the buttons with a feather-light touch. "He has been beside himself with all of this flooding business as of late. He has a bit of responsibility on his shoulders, I fear. It has put him in quite a foul mood, but today his spirits seem much improved." She paused, and a mischievous twinkle danced in her dark eyes. "Perhaps it is you."

The silly smile on Rebecca's face conveyed to Cecily that her words were in jest, but why this schoolgirl flutter in her stomach?

Cecily reminded herself that she was unaccustomed to being around young men.

But then the memory of her past flashed in her mind's eye.

Budding romantic thoughts of any man, regardless of how innocent or fleeting, could only lead down a path paved with disappointment.

Once finished with the buttons, Rebecca assessed the gown on Cecily. "Well now, what do you think?"

Cecily looked down at the gown. It was so strange to see a patterned dress on her body. The printed muslin was pale beige with tiny green leaves and pink flowers running the length of it, and a narrow satin sash hugged her upper torso, well above her waist. The sleeves hung too low over her hands, and it was a little too big in the shoulders, but the narrow cut of the gown was very forgiving, and the sash allowed the gown to be pulled tight enough around her body that it looked like it fit. "Very pretty. I could not be more grateful."

"I am sure you are used to much finer gowns, but I hope it will do for now." Rebecca turned to gather the quilt Cecily had used. "I am sure you are anxious to be about your day. Nathaniel has already been up to Willowgrove this morning. He went before dawn, just as he always does, but he has returned to escort you."

Cecily lifted her head. "He is returning for me? I do not mean to be trouble. I am sure I can find my own way."

Rebecca flicked a hand. "Oh, tosh, do not give it another thought."

At the sound of cart wheels and a voice from the courtyard, Rebecca moved to the window, pushed it open, and looked to the courtyard below. "Why, Mr. Turner is with him!"

The words were spoken with such emphasis that Cecily grew curious. "Who is Mr. Turner?"

Rebecca turned from the window, the breeze through the open window catching her loose wisps of hair. "Mr. Turner is a Willowgrove tenant. His father died last year, and he took over his family farm, which is over the south hill. He is a great family friend. We grew up together, his family and mine." But it was what Rebecca did not say that spoke louder than her actual words, for the apples of her cheeks flushed pink, and her eyes glowed with unbridled enthusiasm.

Cecily smoothed her hand down the front of the gown, adjusted the satin sash under the laced bodice, and turned her attention to her trunk to begin packing. She pulled out a remnant piece of pink silk that the dressmaker in Darbury had given her. It would be the right size for Hannah to make something new for her doll. She set the scrap aside, found her comb, and quickly forced it through her hair. There was no mirror in the room, so Rebecca helped Cecily arrange her hair and hold it in place with her ivory comb.

Once her hair was satisfactory, Cecily returned her belongings to the trunk. She latched the clasp, grabbed the leather side handle, and attempted to pull it over the wooden floor to the door, but Rebecca stopped her.

"Leave it be. Nathaniel will fetch it. Come, get something to eat before you depart. Today will likely be a busy one for you, and I know Mother would refuse to send you away from our home hungry."

"Are you sure Mr. Stanton won't mind the delay?"

A grin crossed Rebecca's face. "My dear Miss Faire, my brother is the only man in a home with four females. I assure you, he is quite accustomed to such delays, as you put it. Come now."

Cecily followed from the narrow room, growing more curious about the lives of the family she had invaded. Feminine chatter and the clang of copper pots wafted up the steep, wooden steps, and she lifted her hem to keep from tripping as she descended.

She followed Rebecca through the main-floor hall into the dining room.

The room looked quite different in the bright light of day. It was a small but cozy room, with pale-green walls and an oak cupboard in the corner. Light flooded in through the latticed window, which acted as a frame to the landscape outside. Scents of bread and coffee teased her, reminding her how hungry she was. With all the commotion and girls moving about, she felt as if she were back at school again.

Upon their entrance, Mrs. Stanton stood, adjusted the fichu about her neck, wiped a strand of hair from her face, and then pressed her hands to her hips. "Well now, good morning to you, Miss Faire. I trust you slept well?"

"Very well, ma'am," she said with a little curtsey. "The most restful night's sleep I have had in quite a while."

Mrs. Stanton's eyes widened in animated expression. "Well, no doubt, after such a journey. I am only grateful you did not waken with an affliction after being so damp and cold." She motioned to the table. "Please. Be seated."

Hannah and Charlotte were both already seated at the table. They looked even more alike by the light of day. With blond hair, brown eyes, straight noses, and pointed chins, there could be no denying that these two were indeed sisters. Both sets of dark eyes were fixed firmly on her.

Cecily leaned close to the girls. "Hannah, how is your doll today?"

A grin graced the girl's face, and she said in a very grown-up voice, "Very well. Thank you for asking."

"Well, I found this in my trunk and thought of her." She produced the scrap of fabric she'd retrieved from her embroidery box. "I thought you might be able to make a little gown for her."

Hannah's brown eyes widened, and her mouth fell open in wonder. "It is the most beautiful thing I have ever seen!"

"It is silk," said Cecily, depositing the fabric in the girl's small hand. "All the way from India. It was given to me by a dressmaker in Darbury, but I think it needs to stay with you."

"Oh, thank you, Miss Faire!" The child was having difficulty remaining in her chair. "Mother, may I go work on it? Right now?" And without waiting for an answer, she jumped from her chair and ran from the room.

After a quick but filling breakfast of rolls, jam, and coffee,

Cecily and Rebecca were donning their bonnets when Mrs. Stanton handed Cecily a basket. "Here are a few things to make your stay more comfortable. Please consider yourself welcome to dine at Laurel Cottage whenever you are free to do so."

The sincerity in the woman's tone warmed Cecily. "Thank you, Mrs. Stanton. I am grateful for your generosity."

Rebecca opened the door, and they stepped into the courtyard.

With each passing moment, Cecily grew more excited about the idea of a new life. Already, she was certain that she had found a friend in Rebecca Stanton, and the rest of the family was endearing. She soaked in her surroundings. Everything had been so dark and hazy the night before that the property was barely visible. The scent of damp livestock and earth met her, and chickens scurried before her. All around her were signs of life. Before her stood the copse of trees she had traveled through the previous evening, and when she looked higher, just above the tree line, she could see spires jutting into the vibrant sky.

Willowgrove Hall.

She felt as if she were about to jump out of her own skin with renewed optimism.

Willowgrove Hall faded, however, as she saw Nathaniel Stanton, his posture straight, rounding the corner of the stable. Another man walked by his side, whom Cecily assumed to be Mr. Turner.

Rebecca was speaking to her about the berries that grew on the bush near the fence, and Cecily tried to concentrate on the words, but the rapid pounding of her heart divided her attention.

She recognized this emotion, this strange sensation of her pulse racing while all the other senses dulled. How her stomach knotted in certain turmoil, yet her heart felt light and giddy. She had experienced it once before . . . with Andrew Moreton. That ache had lain dormant in her for many years. And Cecily had been relieved, for those feelings were misleading. Irresponsible. And would inevitably lead to pain.

And yet she had only met Mr. Stanton the previous eve. Their interactions had been confined to a dinner and short conversation by the fire. How could her heart be swayed so swiftly?

"Do you care for raspberries, Miss Faire?"

Cecily snapped out of her thoughts, turning to her new friend. "Uh, um, yes, I do."

"Well then, you shall visit in a few months when it is late summer, for we always have more raspberries than we know what to do with. Mother makes the most delightful jam, and Bessie always makes pies."

Cecily feigned interest but snuck another glance at Mr. Stanton. He was dressed as one would expect of a steward, black breeches, tall, black boots that reached his knees, and a charcoal coat. The white neckcloth at his throat fluttered only a bit in the breeze, and the wide-brimmed hat that hid his face was a diversion from the more fashionable style, but it was more practical as the sun continued its ascent.

The other man, Rebecca's Mr. Turner, was leading a freshly shorn sheep with a rope. They were talking, and Mr. Stanton turned and pointed in the direction of the field behind her. But when he noticed them, he stopped and dropped his hand. They stood for a moment, staring at one another, before Rebecca took her arm and started walking toward the men.

Rebecca whispered, "Is he not handsome?"

Sudden alarm assaulted her. It was as if Rebecca had been reading her thoughts. "Your brother?"

"No, silly." Rebecca giggled. "Mr. Turner."

It was then she noticed Mr. Turner's line of sight fixed on Rebecca. And Rebecca returned the look with equal intensity.

The men bowed as the women approached. Mr. Stanton

removed his hat before speaking. "Miss Faire, this is Mr. Turner. He runs the farm to the immediate south of us."

Mr. Turner bowed again, his sandy hair poking out from beneath his hat, his dark eyes kind. "And what brings you to Laurel Cottage, Miss Faire?"

But before she could answer, Mr. Stanton responded for her. "She is to be Mrs. Trent's new companion."

Cecily thought his quick answer odd, and perhaps a bit forced, but then Mr. Turner's face broke into a smile. "I wish you luck, Miss Faire."

9

Rebecca and Miss Faire walked ahead, and Nathaniel followed them in a cart on the sun-dappled road that connected the steward's cottage to the rest of the Willowgrove property. Ancient ash trees and wild elderberry shrubs lined the waterlogged path, and if he kept his gaze firmly ahead, he could not see the water shimmering over the fields.

The morning had been pleasant enough. The rain had ceased, and judging by the vibrant blue sky, the day might be promising. He had enjoyed his talk with Turner. Laurel Cottage was so close to the main road that tenants would often stop by to discuss business instead of taking matters to his proper office at Willowgrove Hall. Nathaniel actually preferred it that way.

He only wished the day would not turn unpleasant.

For today, Mrs. Harriet Trent would return.

When he was a child, Mrs. Trent embodied the witches in the fairy tales his mother used to tell him. But as he matured, his fear of her morphed into disdain. Regardless of how hard his father worked, Mrs. Trent always treated him with irrational incivility, especially after Mr. Trent died. His father used to ignore Mrs. Trent's illogical behavior, and when Nathaniel would inquire about it, he would simply say, "'Tis not my place to judge her. My responsibility is to do my job to the best of my ability so that my actions might glorify my heavenly Father."

In his younger years, this sentiment had angered Nathaniel. When he had assumed the role of Willowgrove's steward five years ago, he had tried his best to meet Mrs. Trent's demanding expectations. He desired to prove that he had earned his position and did not grow into it as a result of the agreement between his father and her late husband. Over time, however, it became clear that Mrs. Trent was not judging him by his work. She would forever judge him as the living, breathing lapse of judgment her husband made those many years ago. For the sake of her own pride, she would never dismiss him, but she would do her best to make his tasks as difficult as possible.

But when he assumed his father's role, he began to ascertain why his father never angered at the woman. Even though Mrs. Trent's brashness had lessened over time, pity stirred within him. Mrs. Trent's unpleasantness stemmed from unhappiness.

Nathaniel lagged behind the women. His sister was doing a brilliant job at making their guest feel welcome. Rebecca had a gift for such things. He could not make out their words above the clatter of the cart wheels, but the soft, feminine tones floated on the breeze. His days were filled with working with tenants, overseeing tasks and staff, and handling endless letter writing and bookkeeping, so he counted this diversion in his morning routine a pleasant change.

He fixed his eyes on the back of Miss Faire. Her hair was unlike any color he had ever seen. Most of it was pinned up beneath her bonnet, but stray locks flowed from beneath and caught on the gentle wind. She was dressed in his sister's gown of beige, printed with flowers and leaves. Interesting how he never took note of the pattern before today. The high waist of the gown highlighted Miss Fair's slight figure. Her movements were graceful. Attractive.

He was curious about her. Her past. And now, if she were able to survive Mrs. Trent's scrutiny, he would, perhaps, have the opportunity to have his curiosity quelled.

But he quickly checked himself. For as much as Cecily intrigued him, it was best that he keep his distance—both physically and personally.

He almost laughed at the irony. How could it be that the very woman to snatch his attention would also be Mrs. Trent's companion?

He would fix his eyes on something else . . . something very different from the lovely Miss Faire.

He needed to focus his attentions on learning everything he could about land management and running an estate. For when he inherited Lockbourne, he would relocate and start a new life for himself—not continue to live the life of his father. Lockbourne would be a place where he would be free from secrets. Free from prejudice.

Farther down the path the grounds opened up on a wide, expansive lawn. Silas was walking along the half wall of the south garden, rake slung over his shoulder. His gait was slow, each step labored, his strain becoming more pronounced with each passing month. The past winter had been hard on him, and the early spring flood wreaked havoc on the land the man had worked for years.

Nathaniel thought back to the Silas he remembered as a boy, when the man would run carrying large logs over his shoulder and move dirt in great barrels. Now a hired boy often followed Silas, doing the majority of the heavy lifting, but the man was a wealth of knowledge.

Nathaniel slowed his cart as he approached the man. Silas appeared to have aged ten years in the last ten days. But despite the physical manifestations, the man would never complain.

"Good day, Silas."

Silas stopped and turned. "G'day, lad."

Silas was the only person to still call him lad. Even though Nathaniel now outranked him, he felt utter respect for the man who had taught him the importance of soil conservation, irrigation, and the proper approach to sowing any number of seeds. Nathaniel nodded at the sapling in Silas's hand. "What's that?"

"Mrs. Trent's nephew sent seventy-five of these. Seventy-five!" He shook his head. "He might as well have sent a thousand, for where am I to plant them? He wanted to put these in the south garden, but it is too flooded. I was going to put a couple in Mrs. Trent's rose garden to replace the willows we lost last year."

Nathaniel shrugged. "You know how particular Mrs. Trent is with the rose garden."

"Aye. But now it is about pleasing the new master, is it not?"

Nathaniel bristled. The man who was to inherit Willowgrove wanted to redesign the gardens to match the new, more fashionable symmetrical gardens. Nathaniel shifted. "He's not the new master yet. They arrived a little while ago. I will speak to him about it."

Silas nodded.

And with that, Silas continued down the path, and Nathaniel turned his attention back to the estate.

Enthusiasm quickened Cecily's steps as the chimneys of the great house jutted out of the tree line, reaching far into the late-morning sky. With the journey from Rosemere behind her, and having had a good night's rest, her curiosity and excitement were mounting.

Rebecca had looped her arm through Cecily's. She glanced to the side to see the groundskeepers watching them.

Rebecca must have noticed, too, because she whispered, "Pay them no heed. They are merely curious. Just be as you are, and everyone will adore you, just as I do. Even Mrs. Trent."

"But what did Mr. Turner mean by wishing me good luck?" Though spoken in jest, the comment seemed foreboding.

"Mrs. Trent has a reputation for being strict and particular. But please, do not let this sway you. For Miss Vale was quite fond of her and was vastly contented. So, as I said, be yourself and all will be well."

Rebecca's advice brought to mind Mrs. Sterling's words spoken the day before she left Rosemere.

Be true to yourself.

"Isn't it grand?" asked Rebecca as they turned the corner from a path that wove through a garden and Willowgrove Hall stood before them in all its grandeur. "I am so accustomed to it I fear I take its magnificence for granted."

Cecily's steps slowed in sheer awe as she beheld the structure. It was by far the finest structure she had ever seen. Even Aradelle paled in its shadow. It was a symmetrical building of gray stone, highlighted with lighter stone for the quoining. The front parapet boasted an ornately carved stone above the main entrance, which was flanked with columns. A balustrade ran the length of the home, interrupted by eight massive chimneys poking above the hipped roof. A cupola with a bright dome reached into the blue sky. Rows of paned sash windows reflected the sun's light to the grounds below, and the grand steps welcomed guests. A black carriage pulled by four matching bays was in motion, moving away from the entrance. Servants dressed in black and white scurried about.

Mrs. Sterling had indicated that Willowgrove was majestic, but Cecily never expected anything this elegant.

"So many people!" Cecily said. "I was under the impression that Mrs. Trent lived alone."

Rebecca looked toward the party on the front lawn. "I believe Nathaniel said she was traveling with her nephew, but I was hardly paying attention. It takes a great many people to run the estate, whether Mrs. Trent is home or not. Here, let's go around to the kitchen entrance. Most likely Mrs. Trent will not wish to meet you until she is settled."

Cecily drank in her surroundings as they walked the tree-lined path, floating as if in a dream. The sunlight danced in the bright leaves and cast lacy patterns on the ground. Roses lined a stone garden wall, and the breeze carried away their sweet fragrances. Optimism, bright and endless, surged within her. Here, her past could be forgiven. She was convinced.

Cecily listened to Rebecca prattle on about the grounds, pointing out Mrs. Trent's walled rose garden, the water fountain, the kitchen gardens, the cold house, and the stable block.

Cecily tried to pay attention, but she was still in awe of her surroundings. Was she really going to live here? To be a lady's companion? Surely this was the outcome her mother would have wanted for her. One her sister would be proud of.

She was eager to learn everything. See everything. In fact, she was so engrossed in the gardens she was passing that she nearly ran into the man walking toward her.

"Cecily Faire."

Cecily flinched. The voice rang as familiar and as true as her most trusted memory. She did not need to see the face, for although the timbre was deeper and the tone rougher, she would recognize the voice anywhere.

Andrew Moreton.

She ceased walking, held her breath, and kept her eyes fixed on the stone path before her.

He repeated himself. "Miss Faire, can it be?"

She slowly lifted her eyes, half fearing the image that would greet her. There he stood, leading a giant black horse by a gloved hand.

Indeed, Andrew Moreton stood confident and calm, as if they had seen each other the previous day instead of the five years it had been.

Laughter lightened his voice, the smile she remembered so vividly brightening his expression. "Are you a dream? A vision?"

Every drop of blood in her body had surely sunk to her toes. A mixture of shock and dread gripped her. What must Rebecca be thinking, now that a strange man was greeting her with such familiarity?

In the midst of her shock, she managed to find her voice and curtsey. "Mr. Moreton."

She hoped that Rebecca took no notice of how he assessed her. How his eyes lingered too long on her lips. Her gown. She ran a hand over the borrowed clothes, feeling suddenly self-conscious of the dirt that had gathered along the hem on their walk.

"I confess, Miss Faire—" He stopped short. "It is still Miss Faire, is it not? Or has some fortunate man given you his name?"

Heat rushed to her cheeks. "Yes, sir. I am Cecily Faire."

A twinkle shone in his dark eyes. "This is a most pleasant surprise. I must ask, how is it that you have come to be at Willowgrove Hall? Did you come to see me, I wonder?"

Her face flamed at the flirtation.

But how like the Andrew she remembered. In her younger days his irreverence of social customs had been exciting. Now it embarrassed her.

He was looking at her, speaking with her as if he were a casual acquaintance. She forced herself to meet his gaze, the dark, warm eyes that had been party to her dreams—and nightmares—so frequently over the past several years. "I am to be Mrs. Trent's companion."

He jerked his head to the side, his casual countenance fading. "Not Harriet Trent?"

She nodded, and at her response he laughed loudly, leaving Cecily confused. "I daresay, Miss Faire, if anyone will be able to handle my aunt, it will be you."

She smiled, but the humor he found in the situation was lost on her. "Your aunt?"

"Yes. Harriet Trent is my aunt. She is my father's sister. Perhaps you do not remember." He sobered. "I suppose those days were very long ago."

The weight of the words bore down with relentless pressure. She tried to digest each bit of information, knowing that she would want to revisit it in the quiet of solitude, but her brain seemed incapable of such a task.

From somewhere off in the distance, a soft, feminine voice called his name.

He looked in the direction of the voice and adjusted his grip on his mount's reins. "You will forgive me if I hurry off. I must join my guests."

And as quickly as he had appeared, he was gone, leaving Cecily barely able to breathe.

She would not panic. She refused to cry.

Cecily turned into the wind, allowing the crisp spring breeze to dissipate the moisture that was gathering. Gone were the beauty and the wonder of this place. Instead, the walls and trees around her seemed to close in. The pain and fear from years ago rushed her, stealing her breath.

Had she really just spoken with Andrew Moreton? Or was he a vapor, released from her past? Had he smiled at her? Engaged her in a simple conversation?

"Miss Faire?"

Cecily felt Rebecca at her shoulder. She gave a little sniff. She needed to be calm.

Rebecca's voice rose higher in pitch, as if her concern were heightening. "Miss Faire, are you all right?"

"Of course!" Cecily forced a brightness to her smile.

She'd hoped to keep her past, and her indiscretions, a secret, but they seemed intent upon chasing her from place to place. "I am surprised to see a familiar acquaintance, that is all."

"A coincidence, indeed." Rebecca looked back over toward Andrew's retreating figure, lifting a delicate hand to shield her eyes from the sun. "You had no idea he was here?"

"None."

Rebecca's brow furrowed. "Very odd. How are you acquainted with Mr. Moreton?"

"I-I . . ." Cecily stopped. This should be an easy question to answer, and yet the words were difficult to find. "My father was employed by his family's estate, Aradelle Park, many years ago. Our cottage was on the grounds. If I knew of any connection to the Trent family, I surely forgot it long ago."

Rebecca looped her arm through Cecily's once more. "Mr. Moreton's lived here for so long I had quite forgotten where he was from."

"Here? So long?"

"Yes. I can remember him being here from time to time since I was young, and he has made Willowgrove his home for the past several years, although he is rarely at home. Quite a traveler, he is. What a coincidence!"

Against her better judgment, Cecily glanced back over her shoulder to the direction he had walked.

As if reading Cecily's thoughts, Rebecca spoke. "That is Mrs. Trent, in the black gown."

Cecily's gaze brushed past the older woman to a young woman clad in a gown the color of sunflowers who, as Andrew approached, took the arm he extended. "And who is that on Mr. Moreton's arm?"

"That is his intended, Miss Pritchard. And her mother, Mrs. Pritchard, is to her left."

Intended. The word slammed her.

Cecily's heart sank like a stone plunging to the sea floor.

She was the person he was supposed to marry.

Or at least she had been in another world.

If Rebecca noticed any change in Cecily's countenance, she possessed the politeness to pretend that she did not. "Come now. Let me take you inside."

They continued toward the servants' entrance. It took every ounce of self-control not to run to Andrew. To demand answers. But she was not sure what she would ask him if given the opportunity.

She watched Andrew as he laughed and said something to the elegant, slender woman next to him. He had not seemed the least bit affected to see her. He had moved on. If only her wounded heart could follow his lead.

10

Cecily was grateful that Rebecca walked before her once the path narrowed and wound through the kitchen garden, for tears blinded her eyes so completely she was afraid that she might stumble. The pebble path and green spring grass blurred in and out of focus as she placed one foot in front of the other.

Later.

She could cry later, once she was alone. But for now, she had to be brave.

For whatever force caused Andrew to cross her path again, she must put her feelings aside. She was about to meet the new people in her life—the people she would encounter today and each day thereafter.

After making sure Rebecca's back was still to her, Cecily wiped tears away from her face, looked again into the breeze to allow the cool air to soothe her features, and drew a deep breath.

She followed Rebecca through a door into Willowgrove's kitchen—a large, bright room with high ceilings, white walls, and large, mullioned windows that stretched the height of the space. Scents of thyme and rosemary encircled her the moment she entered. Pots of copper and iron lined the walls and a large, open fireplace crossed the back wall with a smokejack above it. A long, wooden table ran the length of the room, and at it sat several young women, all dressed in gowns of gray with white aprons, chopping carrots and potatoes.

"Entering through the kitchen is not the greeting you expected, to be sure. But with all things considered, this might be more prudent. Through that door there is the larder, and then just beyond it is the butler's pantry, should you need his assistance at any point. I need to introduce you to the housekeeper, Mrs. Bratham. She is a brash sort, but is really quite a kind soul beneath the rough exterior. I believe—" Her words stopped short as she turned and looked at Cecily. Her brow creased. "Miss Faire, tell me if you are unwell." She squeezed Cecily's hand. "There are places you can rest."

Perhaps she had not concealed her hurt as much as she had hoped. Cecily forced a smile, refusing to play victim to the circumstances that had shaped her past. "I am quite well."

Besides, it was too late for retreat. Cecily was fully aware of all the eyes set upon her since entering the kitchen. She tried to recover the enthusiasm, the eagerness she had felt not even a quarter of an hour prior. She tried to remember her position and what she was here to do. She was not a member of the staff—a common servant. She was a lady's companion. She would not answer to the housekeeper or anyone else besides Mrs. Trent.

To the servants, she was likely another guest in the house, and they were surprised to see her in the kitchen. But she could not deny that she was as curious about them as they must be of her . . . if not more.

No one could deny Mrs. Bratham's identity. She entered with

such an air of authority and with such dramatic, grand movements that there could be no doubt.

Mrs. Bratham was much taller and broader than Cecily. Indeed, the top of Cecily's head barely met Mrs. Bratham's chin. She was dressed in a simple gown of black muslin with a high white fichu crossing her bodice. A white cap was settled over her dark hair, and while the lines on her face were severe, there was a subtle hint of kindness in her small, dark eyes.

"Good day, Miss Stanton." She raked Cecily with her eyes. "And whom do you have with you?"

"This is Miss Cecily Faire, Mrs. Trent's new companion."

Mrs. Bratham stopped midstep and thoroughly assessed Cecily. "Oh yes, we have been expecting you, but I must offer my sincerest apologies. We did not think you would arrive for another week." But her voice held neither enthusiasm nor disgust, the words spoken as a mere observation. "But what were you thinking to bring Miss Faire in through the kitchen? Mrs. Trent will not be pleased. Please, Miss Faire, forgive us such an oversight."

"Oh, it is quite all right," Cecily said. "I do not mind." Not wishing to see her friend scolded for bringing her in through the kitchen, Cecily added, "I asked to be shown the kitchen gardens. I am quite fond of gardening, you know."

The housekeeper cocked her head to the side and looked more closely at Cecily. "Miss Faire, you are pale. You are not ill, I hope. May I offer you some tea?"

Cecily swallowed. "No, thank you, no tea."

Mrs. Bratham turned back to Rebecca. "How is it that you are the one bringing her to me? She came by a coach, did she not?"

Cecily thought it odd that the woman would ask Rebecca about the journey and not her directly, but at the moment, her head throbbed with such severity she was grateful to not have to respond.

"A mishap brought Miss Faire to Laurel Cottage instead of

Willowgrove, but as you can see, she is here now, quite safe and sound. My brother asked me to deliver her to you directly and you would know just what to do. It will be a busy day for Mrs. Trent."

"And he is right too," Mrs. Bratham said. "It's plain wore out Mrs. Trent will be." She pivoted to face Cecily. "Now, where are your things?"

"Mr. Stanton was to see that they be delivered to where I will be staying."

"Very well. I will take you up to your room straightaway. I can't imagine that Mrs. Trent will be up to meeting you today, but one can never tell. I will get someone to introduce you to the grounds at a later point, but for now, I trust you are eager to get situated."

Rebecca turned and looked directly at Cecily. "This is when I leave you. Remember, if you need anything at all, you know where I am." She gave a shallow curtsey and left through the door she entered.

Cecily had not realized how much she had been relying on Rebecca for strength. For even though they had not known each other for a full day, a bond had formed.

Mrs. Bratham led her up a simple staircase with whitewashed walls and wooden stairs, but once through the threshold at the landing, a door gave way to the most exquisite room Cecily had ever seen.

She stepped into what seemed a fairyland, with rich tapestries hanging on vibrant papered walls featuring exotic birds and intertwined vines. The light bounced from the ceiling and marble statues. The room was beautiful, a gilded utopia with teak and mahogany furniture, vivid paintings of lush landscapes, and intricate portraits that were taller than Cecily was herself. Everywhere she looked she saw extravagance.

Cecily pressed her lips closed and stayed close to Mrs. Bratham. Surely someone like her did not belong here—a penniless, unconnected woman from a modest girls' school. And yet she was to be a companion, a friend, almost an equal, to the mistress of the estate.

Mrs. Bratham called out details as they moved through rooms and down corridors. "We just passed through the great parlor and the blue drawing room, which is Mrs. Trent's personal drawing room. I'd wager you'll be spending a great deal of time there. The chapel and chapel drawing room are through the main hall, and the steward's office and tradesmen's entrance are on the far end, past the staircase. If you should ever lose your way, remember that the house is shaped like a U, with everything centering around the main hall. If you find your way back to the main hall, you should be able to set yourself right."

Cecily tried to process it, but she had never been in such grandeur. She'd only been inside Aradelle once or twice, and never beyond the kitchen. "This is the staircase hall." Mrs. Bratham led Cecily up a broad staircase, complete with walnut tread and risers and leaves carved on the balusters. "There are other stairs at the west and north entrances and, of course, in the servants' area. But you'll find this one the most convenient for your needs."

Cecily followed Mrs. Bratham closely and would not have been able to retrace her steps if pressed. At the top of the great staircase, Mrs. Bratham waved her hand. "Down across the hall are Mrs. Trent's personal chambers, and here is where you will be staying."

They finally drew to a stop at a closed door. Mrs. Bratham turned the handle, and Cecily followed the housekeeper into the room. The woman made a full circle in an obvious assessment of its state. But the first thing that captured Cecily's attention was the broad, paned window framing a breathtaking view of Willowgrove's gardens.

"This is the gold chamber, the room that the former companion occupied. I have not spoken with Mrs. Trent on the matter. I am fairly certain that she would like you to have the same." Mrs. Bratham moved to the window and pulled the brown velvet curtain back even farther, allowing more sunlight to spill through the opening. "You should be comfortable here. The water basin is on the table. I will have one of the maids freshen the water. I believe that Clarkson, Mrs. Trent's lady's maid, had been in the habit of tending to the previous companion, so I see no reason why that would change."

Cecily only nodded, trying to absorb—and retain—everything that she heard.

"Most days Mrs. Trent will want you to dine with her, but on days she did not, Miss Vale always took her meals in her room. I have no doubt you and Mrs. Trent will settle into a routine. Mrs. Trent has always made it perfectly plain that she does not want her companion fraternizing with the rest of the house staff, so Clarkson, her lady's maid, will be available to you. I will help you as needed, but know I run a tight ship, Miss Faire. And I follow Mrs. Trent's orders by the letter. I have seen my fair share of companions come through these halls, and if you heed my advice, things should move along just fine."

Cecily nodded, taken aback by the woman's blunt expression. "Yes. Of course."

"Good." She ran her hands down the front of her gown and began to brush past her. "As I said, Mrs. Trent's chamber is down the hall, next door down. She insists on her companion being accessible. Once she is settled and ready to make your acquaintance, either Clarkson or I will escort you. In the meantime, feel free to rest and get settled. Walk around the grounds to get yourself familiar, if that suits you. I shall send up some tea and a bite to eat."

The woman took another step, then stopped. "I do wish you happiness here, Miss Faire. Perhaps a nice first step would be to go down and explore the gardens. Mrs. Trent is quite fond of the pink roses that grow in the walled garden. Oh, and welcome to Willowgrove Hall."

The older woman closed the door behind her.

Cecily hadn't realized she'd been holding her breath until the door latched, and she emptied her lungs with a swoosh. She dropped the basket she had been carrying and looked around the room. If she weren't so tired, and her heart so sore, she would be enchanted at the room's simple elegance. But the bright light, which she would normally find so charming, sliced her, and with her now-pounding headache, she sank down on the bed.

It only seemed right—only seemed poetic—to burst into tears in this moment. Every dream she had for the last three years now lay damp and deflated at her feet. Andrew wasn't still searching for her. He wasn't still missing her. He was engaged to another. And he seemed . . . happy. Indeed, tears would be preferable to the sharp ache in her heart.

She should leave. She did not belong here—not with Andrew Moreton so near. And even though Mrs. Sterling seemed so confident of her capabilities, Cecily knew the truth. She was not the sort of person suitable for a lady's companion.

But if she were to leave, where would she go? She had little money. She could not return to the school, for her past would certainly be exposed. How could she return without confessing the truth about why she could not continue at Willowgrove? She had managed to keep the secret of her indiscretion from everyone—even Mrs. Sterling—for all these years. But if she did not return to the school, she would never find a good position, not without a recommendation.

Cecily stood and looked down to the grounds, hoping yet fearing to catch a glance of Andrew. He was nowhere in sight, yet knowing that he was so close trumped every other thought.

In her wildest dreams, she could run to him. Demand to know why he never sought her. But her more mature self kept her in her room. She was an adult now. No longer could she be ruled by childish whims. For where had that gotten her? Alone and without a family. And even worse, her past decisions now left her with a black mark on her character, and even though only she and Andrew knew the extent, her past actions would haunt her until her dying day.

11

The afternoon sun was beginning its descent as Nathaniel sat behind his desk in the steward's office on Willowgrove's main floor. It was a comfortable room, wide and spacious, with dark-green walls lined with bookcases and a paneled oak ceiling. Its broad windows framed the east and south yards, and he could monitor the comings and goings of those through both the main and tradesmen's entrances. A large landscape painting, boasting hues of gray and green, hung by heavy cords above the side tables, and several large rugs covered the wooden floor.

This room was really a second home. In fact, he spent so much time here that to his right was a door that led to a small sleeping chamber, should his work keep him late or if he did not want to walk home in foul weather. So many of his childhood memories took place in this very space. Memories of watching his father meet with tenants and tradesmen, playing by the fire, or listening to his father's instruction. Nathaniel drew a deep breath. The memories of his father were still difficult, even so many years later.

From his windows, he could view the kitchen gardens and stable yard, which, like the main house, were on higher land and had remained mostly untouched by the floods. Rows of perfectly spaced greens and vegetables were beginning to break free from the land, and two kitchen maids were tending the garden. But then he noticed Rebecca weaving her way through the garden, the sunlight shining on her shoulders and bonnet, peering at his window as if she could see inside from the distance. She would often stop by to visit, bringing a message or something from home, but her eyebrows were drawn together. She disappeared through the tradesmen's entrance, and within moments, she was in his office.

Rebecca flew into the room, eyes wide, and dropped into one of the chairs in front of his desk.

"Oh, what a day this is proving to be!" she said, tugging her bonnet from her head and waving it to fan herself. "I do believe this is the hottest day we have had yet this spring!"

Nathaniel pushed some papers back away from her and leaned his elbows against his desk. His sister was always full of energy and enthusiasm for things little and great. He was eager to learn what he could about their new visitor.

"I trust you were able to get Miss Faire settled?"

"Yes. I introduced her to Mrs. Bratham. That woman can be as sour as an old goat."

He really should reprimand her. She should not be saying such things. But had he not harbored similar thoughts? While he was responsible for overseeing the male staff, Mrs. Bratham was responsible for overseeing the female staff. A task he did not envy. Even though she could be quite terse, he respected her.

"But I did not come here to tell you about Mrs. Bratham."

He pushed himself off of the desk, straightened his stack of letters. "Well then?"

She scooted to the edge of her chair. "My news is of Miss Faire."

At the name, Nathaniel tensed. But his sister knew him well. He allowed no change in his tone. Otherwise she might draw an assumption. "And what of Miss Faire would you like to tell me?"

"As we were coming down this path through the back garden, we encountered Mr. Moreton. It became clear that Miss Faire and Mr. Moreton were already acquainted. Nothing could have been plainer! For when he saw her he became quite engaged, asking her all manner of questions and speaking casually with her."

Nathaniel pressed his lips together. He had been right to be suspicious about her and her connections to Aradelle. In his experience, everything associated with Aradelle was tainted. And yet Miss Faire, by contrast, seemed sincere and innocent. Perhaps his first inclination to try to stay away from her was best. After all, what associated with Aradelle—and more specifically, Andrew Moreton—could be positive?

He picked up a letter and studied the inscription. "And what did she do?"

"Oh, Miss Faire was quite the opposite of Mr. Moreton. Quite so, indeed. She grew somber, as if she did not wish to see him at all, and then I thought she might burst into tears when I was introducing her to Mrs. Bratham. I felt quite ill at ease for her. The entire ordeal was quite unusual. Do you find it odd that Miss Faire did not mention the connection to the family last night?"

He did think it odd. For if she was connected with the family, then why did she not say as much? "She said that she came here by way of Rosemere. Perhaps it was a coincidence."

"Well, I felt sorrow on behalf of Miss Faire. I do not care for Mr. Moreton, and judging by her reaction, she shares the sentiment." His sister pushed herself up from the chair. "I must return home. I only wanted to tell you what happened, for I worry about her. I like Miss Faire very much, and it saddens me if she is uncomfortable here. Anyway, I am to help Hannah with her French before the afternoon's end. Are you going to be home for dinner tonight? Mother will want to know."

Dinner seemed so inconsequential. "I should."

"Good. I'll let her know. Good-bye." And with that, she exited, leaving Nathaniel in the comfortable silence of his study once more.

He stood and walked back toward the window and studied the grounds. Spring was becoming more evident on the trees and in the beds. Bright blooms of yellow and red were beginning to dot the landscape and cascade over the gray garden wall. But he could hardly focus on their beauty. It was odd—neither Mrs. Trent nor Mr. Moreton had been by to inquire after the damage caused by the flooding. It was a significant occurrence, and yet they'd made no mention of it.

No doubt Mrs. Trent would be recovering from the journey. It would likely be a day or two before she was pounding on his door, wanting updates on every happening since she quitted Willowgrove all those weeks ago.

But Mr. Moreton . . . it was quite unusual for him not to have at least stopped by the steward's office.

It was a charade, really. After being away for any significant length of time, Moreton would pay him a call to be briefed on what had occurred on the grounds. Nathaniel would give a short list of happenings, and then Moreton would be comfortable that he had done his duty as an estate master-to-be.

Their "arrangement" was superficial, and Nathaniel preferred it that way. The last thing he needed was anyone—even the future estate master—meddling in the way he conducted his affairs.

But as Nathaniel reached for his satchel and prepared to leave for the day, boots clicked on the marble floor outside his door. He recognized Moreton's obnoxious laugh, followed by words spoken far too loudly.

But in the end, what did it matter what Nathaniel thought of

Moreton's mannerisms? Every brick in Willowgrove's walls and every tree on its grounds would belong to Moreton in the not-so-distant future. And if Nathaniel had his way, he would be preparing his own home at Lockbourne.

Moreton did not wait for an invitation when he pushed open the steward's office door with his walking stick, slamming it back against a framed map on the wall.

"Stanton! There you are, good man."

Nathaniel straightened in his chair and let his satchel drop to the desk. "Mr. Moreton. Good to see you again. I trust your journey was pleasant."

"Oh, you know, traveling with women and how they fuss over this and that. I thought for certain we would have to delay our journey another day on account of Aunt's fits, but thankfully, we are here. Fortunate thing, not sure I could have lasted in a carriage a moment longer."

Nathaniel pushed himself back in his chair and rested his elbows on its padded arms. He did not want to drag this visit out any longer than necessary. "Did you receive my letter? About the flooding?"

"No, never received it." Moreton walked over to the fireplace and adjusted a small marble statue on the hearth. "Quite a surprise when we arrived and saw the fields. Shock to have to go in through the west gate. Couldn't be helped, I suppose. But looks like quite a mess."

Nathaniel attempted only slightly to mask his sarcasm as he repeated the words back. "A mess?"

"You know, the fields and everything."

Nathaniel's patience grew shorter by the minute. How he wanted to remind the man that he had brought the situation of the damaged sluice to Moreton and Mrs. Trent's attention last autumn, and that they did not want to apply funds to get it properly repaired. He'd voiced his concerns that the makeshift repairs Mr. Moreton had authorized would not suffice, but the man had been firm. And by such negligence, all was damaged within an hour's time. It would take months to repair.

Now it was his problem to solve. And Moreton's lack of concern heaped coals on Nathaniel's already hot nerves.

The sooner he could get this conversation over with, the better. "The masons are going to start on the bridge tomorrow. That is, if the river continues to go down. But the clouds seem to be passing. We may be able to avoid more rain."

Moreton rolled his eyes and waved a hand. "Oh yes. You know I pay little attention to such things. Whatever you think is best." He turned back to Nathaniel, his expression twisted as if he had a brilliant thought. "What do you think of the new trees for the south garden?"

Nathaniel raised an eyebrow. He recalled the saplings Silas had been carrying. "The saplings? All seventy-five of them?" He tried to keep his sarcasm at bay. "I spoke with the gardener about them this morning. The south garden is too waterlogged for new planting, so Silas was contemplating putting them in the walled garden."

Moreton seemed oblivious. "No, they are to be situated in the south garden. My intended has a fancy for pears, and these are the exact variety. We shall have an orchard. The walled garden is far too small."

At the reference to Miss Pritchard, Nathaniel scratched the back of his head and held his tongue. There was something about Andrew Moreton that he just did not trust, an unevenness about his manner that concerned him. He was a man of swift, if imprudent, decisions. As Nathaniel was contemplating his response, Moreton said, "So, what are your thoughts on the new addition to Willowgrove Hall?"

Nathaniel raised an eyebrow. "What?"

A grin slid across Moreton's face, and he pushed himself up from the chair. "Am I to believe that the ever-observant Nathaniel Stanton failed to notice the pretty new addition to our party?"

Nathaniel leaned back against the chair. "My job is to tend to the estate. It is not my business who Mrs. Trent chooses to invite."

Moreton snorted as if amused. "What a proper response."

Nathaniel looked past Moreton and down to the ground again. He had noticed more than he was prepared to admit to anyone—even himself.

Nathaniel cleared his throat. "About the bridge."

Moreton waved his hand again. "Oh, do what you must about the bloody bridge. Just get it repaired."

"And the sluice? We will have this trouble again if it is not tended to."

"Very well."

Nathaniel went down his list of other issues to discuss with the heir. The neighboring farmer's flooded fields. The draining of the gardens. The purchase of new carriage horses. But every word seemed more trite. Normally, he could ignore such ignorance. But this man was inheriting the estate that should belong to Nathaniel.

Nathaniel loved Willowgrove Hall. He had spent his entire life in service to it, caring for it and those who were employed here. But Moreton cared more for the cut of his coat and the hue of his waistcoat than the legacy that had provided for families all around the county for generations.

It sickened him.

12

Cecily sat at the small writing desk, folding and stacking the letters she had written. The afternoon had been a long one. She had not ventured from the room to the gardens, as Mrs. Bratham had suggested. Instead, she stayed in her new bedchamber. For all of its charm—the pale-yellow walls, the mahogany furniture, the vibrant lady's portrait in a gilded frame—she could focus on naught else besides the ache within her chest.

At first, she cried. Silent, lonely tears, mourning her renewed sense of the loss of her emotional and physical innocence. The sharp pang of regret and loss stabbed her. Then, when the tears subsided, she watched the goings-on outside her window, hoping—and fearing—to catch a glimpse of Andrew. But it never came to pass. Then she napped—an unsatisfying bit of sleep that left her even more tired and with a considerable throbbing in her head. When Cecily rose, the long slants of light signaled the fading day. She washed her face with the cool water in the washbasin.

She assumed that Mrs. Trent would not want to meet her since the hour had grown so late. She looked at her quill.

It had been over a year since she last attempted to write her aunt in Manchester. Either her aunt was no longer at the same address, or she had chosen not to respond. Either way, the lack of response was maddening. Even if her letters were reaching her aunt, Cecily was closer to Manchester now than she had been at Rosemere. Perhaps she could travel there herself.

A knock sounded at her door. Cecily eyed the paneled door suspiciously before rising, walking toward it, and turning the brass handle.

She had expected to see a maid. Or perhaps Mrs. Bratham. But instead, it was Mr. Stanton.

At her bedchamber door.

Their eyes met.

This was not proper. A bolt of fire flamed through her. The last thing she needed was any appearance of indiscretion.

But then she took notice—he had her trunk on his shoulder.

He adjusted the trunk before speaking. "Where shall I put this?"

She stepped back, still unsettled from seeing a man so close to where she would be sleeping. "Um, there, on the carpet, is fine."

He stepped in to put the luggage on the floor. "Of all the footmen, I couldn't locate one, so I brought it up myself. I didn't want you to have to wait any longer. My apologies for the intrusion."

"No. Not at all. This is most kind." She hesitated as he straightened from the task. "I-I did not get the chance to thank you for repairing it last night."

He nodded and looked down at the pitiful piece of luggage. "A nail had come loose, that was all. An easy repair."

"Well, I thank you just the same."

He started to bow and then looked directly at her. She grew uneasy under his scrutiny. "Are you well?"

She suddenly became aware of how she must look—of how the tears and sleep must have affected her features, of her hair pulling loose from her comb. Furthermore, it was the way he looked at her—as if he could see into her heart. Her soul. She hesitated. "Oh yes, quite well. Only tired."

"Are you certain?"

"Quite. It has been an eventful couple of days."

He rubbed his hands together. "Very well, I will bid you good night."

Mr. Stanton turned and disappeared into the shadows before she could verbalize a response.

The interaction only lasted two minutes at best, but merciful heavens, how her heart raced. Maybe it was seeing him so unexpectedly. Or perhaps that he had been so kind to her.

Mr. Stanton was a handsome man. Even when she closed her eyes she could still see his strong outline, his piercing blue eyes. A little flutter danced in her stomach.

She remembered a similar flutter from many years ago.

Odd how seeing Andrew today had made her feel ill and weak.

How time did change one's outlook.

As Cecily turned to her trunk, there was another knock at the door. She did not even have time to move from her spot before the door swung open.

There, in the cased doorway, stood a slip of a woman with thin lips and hollow cheeks. Age lines gathered around her pointed features and crinkled her dark complexion. Silver strands laced her dark, wiry hair, which was coiled tightly to her head beneath a white cap. Her face bore no emotion.

She stared at Cecily for a few moments before speaking. "I am Clarkson, Mrs. Trent's lady's maid." Her eyes glanced at the middle of the room. "I will see to you while you are here. I see you got your trunk."

"Yes, Mr. Stanton was kind enough to bring it to me."

"Mrs. Trent will see you now."

The change of topics was abrupt. Cecily jerked her head toward the door, her mouth suddenly dry as cotton. She glanced out her window, confirming that the sun was setting and the hour had grown late. "What, now?"

Clarkson opened the door wider. "She has asked for you. 'Twould be in your best interest not to keep her waiting."

Cecily brushed her hand against her hair. It had the most unfortunate tendency to be wild, and gauging by Mr. Stanton's inquiry about her health, she supposed she must look quite altered. She wiped her eyes with her hand. They felt puffy.

She could do nothing about that now.

With a sigh, Cecily lifted her candle lamp from her desk and followed the maid into the dark, windowless corridor and to the entrance to Mrs. Trent's chamber. Clarkson did not knock but pushed the door open with confidence.

Anxiety wound its way around every one of Cecily's nerves, and she smoothed her gown and then patted her hair in place. She was still in Rebecca's borrowed printed dress, and the too-long sleeves, which hadn't bothered her as much earlier in the day, now presented a problem. She reminded herself that this was the last difficult task. She'd met most of the others. She'd even encountered Andrew. Her entire range of emotions had made an appearance over the last several days. She would not let herself be intimidated now.

Despite the ache in her heart, she did have to admit that Mrs. Trent had piqued her curiosity. Like a puzzle, she had gathered clues to the old woman's personality from the people she had interacted with thus far. She was anxious to know who she would be spending her time with and what tasks would fill her days.

It was the distraction that her aching heart needed.

Clarkson proceeded and gave a quick curtsey. "Miss Faire for you, Mrs. Trent."

Cecily almost missed Mrs. Trent at first glance, for she was tucked away in the evening's gathering shadows between a window and the door to the dressing room, in a brown leather wingback chair. She was rather slight, with thin arms and a slender face, dressed in a black high-necked gown. The only relief from the dark colors came from her stark-white hair and pale skin. Upon closer inspection, the apples of her withered cheeks boasted an abundance of bright rouge.

Not sure what else to do, Cecily curtseyed and waited to be spoken to.

And waited.

The woman did not hide her assessment. She scanned Cecily from head to toe. "Step forward, child. Into the light. I cannot see you if you are lurking in the shadows."

Cecily obeyed, taking two steps forward until she was in the glow of the evening's last rays. She felt as if she were on the steps of Rosemere again, uncertain of the future course.

At this closer distance, Mrs. Trent's features became more defined. Dark, small eyes, a narrow nose set in a long face, thin lips, and skin that reminded Cecily of parchment. Her complexion, although faded and wrinkled, hinted at past beauty. The scent of mint and lavender hung in the air. The woman's posture carried with it the air of authority, her expression the air of certainty and confidence.

Neither of which Cecily possessed at the moment.

"So you are the girl Mrs. Sterling has sent me from Rosemere, eh? What is your name again?"

"Cecily Faire, ma'am."

Her eyes narrowed on Cecily. "Miss Faire. You are pale. Are you well?"

Heat rushed to Cecily's face. "Yes. Very well, thank you."

"I do hope you do not have a tendency to fall ill. I fail to accept that women have such weak constitutions as men would have us believe."

The bold statement took Cecily by surprise. "No, ma'am. I am of a sound constitution."

"Good." Mrs. Trent held a bony finger in the air, waving it for emphasis. "There are a great many number of men here at Willowgrove who would have you believe that I am weak and am nearing the grave. Ha! I ask, I may be advanced in age, but do I look as if I am at death's door?"

Cecily could feel her eyes widening. "No, ma'am. Not at all."

Mrs. Trent continued her assessment. Her pointed gaze landed on Cecily's hair. "My goodness, but your hair is bright."

Cecily bit her lip. She felt more like an animal on an auction block than someone taking part in a formal introduction.

"But you are pretty enough, I daresay." The older woman's voice cracked as she spoke. "Is your room satisfactory?"

"Yes, ma'am. Very lovely. It is by far the nicest room I have ever had."

"I am glad to hear it. The gold chamber, I trust?" But before Cecily could respond, the woman's gaze raked over Cecily's dress. "This week we will have a dressmaker come by and take your measurements for some new gowns."

Cecily would have noted that this was not her gown, but thought better of it. "That is kind."

"Clarkson, do not forget to send for Mrs. Massey, for this ensemble will never do." She turned her attention back to Cecily. "Are you acquainted with my former companion, Miss Vale?"

"Yes, ma'am. That is to say, I knew her several years ago."

"I liked her very much, but she is married now, has a husband and is far too busy for me, but then again, I suppose that is best.

Miss Vale was clever. She had a lovely reading voice and was quite attentive."

Cecily nodded. She did sincerely hope that she would be able to live up to the elevated expectation set by her predecessor.

"I know that it cannot be much fun for a young woman to be tethered to an old lady like me, but I will do my best to make sure you do not find Willowgrove too tiresome. But do know that I like quiet. I do not like to wait, and I expect you to be quick and polite. You will find me to be reasonable. Your evenings after I retire will be your own, but I expect you to be at my disposal during my waking hours. Is that clear?"

"Yes, ma'am."

Mrs. Trent reached for a cane propped against the chair and then motioned for Clarkson to come and help her stand. "Tell me, Miss Faire. What is it that you like to do to fill your hours?"

"I enjoy needlework above all, ma'am. And I am fond of reading."

"Well then, Clarkson, see to it that our Miss Faire has what she needs for her needlework, and tomorrow someone will help you find your way to the library. My husband was an avid reader, and there are enough volumes to entertain a young mind. You are welcome to any selections you should choose."

Cecily watched as Mrs. Trent stood, pretending not to notice how the woman's arm trembled as she leaned on her cane and how unsteady her legs were. "That is most kind. Thank you."

Mrs. Trent jerked her arm away from Clarkson in a manner that suggested that the lady's maid was to blame for any difficulties and hissed inaudible words before turning back to Cecily. "I trust that you and I shall get along fine. I rise early, and I retire early as well. I know you are still getting settled. Clarkson here will see to your needs, help you dress and the like, and offer any other assistance that you could need."

Cecily resisted the urge to look over at Clarkson, for even across the room she could feel the weight of the servant's gaze.

"And one last thing, perhaps the most important. As my companion, you must show complete discretion. I wish for you to limit your interactions with the servants, except for Clarkson here. They can be a meddlesome lot. It is hard to find anyone a person can wholly trust. You will also be privy to conversations that I have with my family and other business acquaintances. Whatever you should hear is not to be divulged. Are we clear on those two points?"

Cecily could not help but wonder what hush-hush business dealings a lady of Mrs. Trent's circumstances could possibly be involved in, but then she thought of Andrew. And dread washed over her. "Of course, Mrs. Trent. You have my word."

After being dismissed, Cecily returned to the gold chamber with Clarkson, who helped Cecily undress. A fire was now glowing in the fireplace, and fresh water was in her basin.

"It appears someone has been here."

Clarkson stoked the fire. "An oversight, miss. We did not expect your arrival today, so while you were speaking with Mrs. Trent, I had one of the maids set things right. I would have had it done sooner, but when I checked in on you earlier, you were asleep."

As Cecily turned, she noticed a vase of cut pink roses. Their floral scent reached her from several feet away. It was odd to have an actual servant attend to her, when before it had always been her sister, a classmate, or another teacher.

After helping her out of the gown and stays, Clarkson shook out Cecily's borrowed dress. "I shall have this washed out for you. Is there anything else you need?"

"As a matter of fact . . ." Cecily moved to the chest and opened it. She retrieved her four soiled gowns. How odd it felt to give someone her dirty things. "These took a tumble from the trunk on my journey, and I fear they are quite dirty. I am happy to help clean them. I am just not sure where I should go."

Clarkson held the gowns before her, eyes narrowed. "I will have these cleaned by morning. No need for you to concern yourself with such things anymore."

The word "anymore" struck Cecily as strange. She paused to look at Clarkson, but the aging lady's maid was busy situating the gowns over her arm. The word suggested that Cecily should not be accustomed to such help. But how could Clarkson know that?

"Shall I help you unpin your hair, miss?"

Cecily touched her hand to her hair. "No, that is not necessary."

"Very good, miss. I'll bring up something to eat."

The thought of consuming even a morsel of bread made Cecily's stomach turn. "That is not necessary. I could not eat a bite."

Clarkson eyed her as she stoked the fire in the grate. "I hope Mrs. Trent's observations weren't true. You aren't ill, are you?"

Cecily shook her head.

"Very well." The servant straightened and returned the poker to the stand. "I will be by to make sure you are awake in the morning in time for breakfast with Mrs. Trent."

As the door closed, Cecily blew out her breath and fell onto her bed against the gold-and-ivory striped silk cover. She was eager to be alone with her thoughts. After several moments she retrieved her comb from the trunk, sat next to the fire, and set about removing the pins from her hair and combing her tresses.

So she had met the woman she would be a companion to.

Met the woman to whom she would be tied for the unforeseeable future.

She had met Andrew's aunt.

Cecily often wondered what—if any—impact their thwarted plans had on Andrew. The result, for her, had changed the direction of her life. But had he received any reprimand? Did his family even know?

Well, at least for the moment, Mrs. Trent had no idea that she had any connection to the Moreton family. She was fairly certain that Andrew would not speak about their past, and she vowed the same.

The house was quiet. Even the wind was silent outside her window, and she looked to the ground below, noting that the leaves on the trees lining the near garden wall were still. She thought about what an evening would be like back at Rosemere. She had never had a room of her own. The silence, the stillness, made her uncomfortable. This time of night everyone would be busy preparing for bed. There would be happy chatter as they brushed their hair, or they would simply sit quietly, reading.

But then her thoughts went back further, to evenings when she had lived with her family. Leah. How her heart ached for her twin sister. Leah had been her first friend, her first confidante. They had comforted each other when their mother died and shielded each other from their father's wrath.

At least her allowance would permit her to save, and one day she would personally travel to Manchester and look for Leah.

Cecily turned to her trunk and pulled out the rest of her damp things. She placed what she could on the floor to dry, but when she came across her mother's coral necklace, she sat back on her heels.

She let the tears fuel her energy. Cecily rose, moved to a bureau, and put the necklace in an ornate porcelain box. She had one clue from the letter—Manchester. Mrs. Trent had forbidden her from fraternizing with the servants, but surely that didn't include the housekeeper and the steward. She would start with them.

Cecily extinguished her candle lamps and crawled into the bed, which was higher and finer than any she had ever slept in. She watched the shadows play on the canopy's fine fabric curtains until her eyes finally closed in sleep.

13

The evening sun slanted low through the budding birch trees as Nathaniel walked back to Laurel Cottage. He was eager to be free from the cares of the day and to be home among what was calm and peaceful.

At least at home he knew what to expect. With so many women under one roof, it could become quite chaotic, but it was home. As he rounded the bend, his steps slowed. An empty cart was in front of the cottage, a pony tied in place. And by it stood Turner.

Even as Nathaniel lifted his hand in greeting, he knew Turner was not here to visit him. He hadn't expected to see Turner again so quickly after their morning discussion, but the idea that had become a nagging suspicion was becoming a glaring reality.

Nathaniel first suspected Turner's intentions earlier that morning. For it was no secret that Turner was infatuated with his sister, and had been for some time. Nathaniel had sensed that it was what Turner had wanted to speak with him about earlier in the day, but when his sister and Miss Faire had exited the cottage, their conversation had ended.

This was the moment he had loathed since his father died, because as the head of the family, the responsibility now fell to him to make sure that each of his sisters married well and had a significant enough dowry.

Selfishly, he wanted none of his sisters to marry. He wanted his family to stay intact—a tight unit—and then, when he inherited Lockbourne House, they would all travel together.

But the family was changing, and time marched on. Rebecca was no longer a child, but a woman who had attracted the attention of a well-off farmer.

And she was in love.

Nathaniel drew a deep breath and adjusted the bag over his shoulder. He could hear a peal of laughter come from the cottage. A cow lowed from the cowhouse. Gus met him on the path and wove in between his legs.

As he drew closer, Turner stepped away from his cart and walked to meet Nathaniel halfway. His thinning hair fell over his wide forehead, and he adjusted the hat on his head. "Stanton! I trust your day was well."

"It was. And how is the sheep?" Nathaniel inquired after the sickly sheep Turner had with him earlier that morning.

"She will be fine, I am sure. She has spent the day in the pasture, which is a good sign. We did not have the opportunity to finish our conversation this morning, and I was hoping for a few moments of your time tonight."

Nathaniel eyed him and then nodded toward the cowhouse. "Come with me while I pen the cow."

Nathaniel had always liked Turner. He was hardworking. Earnest. Turner was but two years Nathaniel's junior, and he had fond memories of them chasing the sheep on the stony crags. The men were cut from the same cloth, really. Both of their futures were predetermined before they were born—Nathaniel to follow in his father's footsteps as the steward of Willowgrove, and Turner to continue his family's legacy as proud tenant farmers. Now, with both their fathers dead, they were coming into their birthrights.

Turner's steps fell in time with Nathaniel's. "I suppose there can be no doubt what I want to talk with you about," Turner said, leaning his arms over the stall railing as Nathaniel led the animal in.

"No, I do not suppose there could be."

Turner looked directly at Nathaniel. "I would be a good husband to her, Stanton."

"I know you would." Nathaniel was not ready to hear such words about his sister. In his mind's eye she was but a girl, with her hair in plaits and playing with dolls. But in truth, she was a woman of twenty, pretty and bright, ready to reach for her future. A future that, if she married Turner, would not involve him. For as soon as he was able, Nathaniel would move north to claim his inheritance. How often would he see his sister then?

Leaving one of them behind, even in the safe arms of a happy marriage, had not been his plan.

"I wanted to ask your permission. To propose."

Nathaniel looked down as he reached for the pitchfork. He was not a timid man, and yet he found it difficult to look his friend in the eye. "The decision is my sister's, and hers alone. If she is in agreement, then I will not stand in the way."

Turner gave a giddy laugh, more like that of a youth than a grown man. "Thank you."

"When do you intend to speak with her?"

"Tonight, if I might ask her to accompany me for a walk."

Nathaniel finished spreading the hay and leaned the pitchfork back against the wall. "I will send her out."

He finally looked Turner in the face. The man was positively giddy, his eyes shining with the brightness of unaffected optimism.

Something within Nathaniel envied Turner.

How would it be to start his own family? To have a wife? And no secrets?

"Wait here."

Nathaniel followed the path to the cottage, Gus weaving in and out of his legs. He drew a deep breath as he approached the door.

He had watched Rebecca. Watched them together.

They were better people when they were around each other. The mere company of the other brought smiles to their faces. He was happy to be bringing his sister happiness.

He stepped through the threshold. To his left, Rebecca was sitting in the parlor, her blond head bent over her sewing. Hannah sat next to her, a book in her hand, and their mother was absent.

Nathaniel removed his hat and forced his fingers through his hair. "Rebecca, there is someone outside to see you."

She lifted her face. She looked so much like their mother, with her dark eyes and round face. "Who is it?"

"Turner."

A coy smile curved her lips. She scooted to the edge of her seat, bit her lower lip, her eyes lively with enthusiasm.

"Just go."

Like a flash of summer lightning, she discarded her sewing, jumped from her chair, paused to look into the looking glass, and flew out the door.

"Can I go too?" asked Hannah, lowering her sewing to her lap.

"Uh, no."

Hannah's lips formed a pout. "Why ever not?"

"Never you mind."

Later that evening, after the proposal had been accepted, news shared, and the initial celebration behind them, Nathaniel and his mother sat by the fireside.

"The girls are abed, but I'll wager Rebecca does not sleep tonight," Nathaniel mused as a floorboard creaked above their heads.

"It is an exciting time for her," his mother said, leaning her head against the back of the rocking chair. "I imagine they will marry quickly. As they should."

Nathaniel reached his hand down to pat Gus's head. "Next it will be Charlotte's turn."

"Charlotte?" His mother gave a little shrug. "I figured the next one of my children to marry would be you."

"Me?" Nathaniel adjusted his position in the tufted chair and propped his foot up on the stool. He shook his head and rubbed his hand over the stubble on his chin. This topic of conversation came up often.

"I have no intentions of marrying," Nathaniel said. "Not now, anyway. Not for a long time."

His mother eyed him in the way that made him feel like she could read his thoughts. When she did speak, her voice was soft. "If you are waiting to marry because you are concerned for the welfare of your sisters and myself, I hope you know that we will flourish under any circumstance."

"It's not that."

"You say so, and yet I do not understand the reason for your delay." She lowered her sewing to her lap. "Mrs. Massey is a lovely woman, Nathaniel. And she is obviously quite taken with you. Nothing could be clearer. I cannot understand why you are not more interested in pursuing a relationship with her."

Nathaniel rubbed his forehead and then scratched the back of his head, thinking of the beautiful widow—the local seamstress—who had made her intentions toward him quite plain. His mother was right. She was a lovely woman. But to fall in love meant he would have to trust someone. And he was not ready to expose his family's secrets.

But that did not mean he was not ready to talk about them.

He looked over at his mother. For the past five years, he had endeavored to protect her, and his way of protecting her was by never bringing up the fact that Thomas Stanton was not his father. She was content to continue on as they had been before Nathaniel learned of the incident, and he had indulged her.

But while ignoring the facts seemed to appease his mother, it caused the wound within him to fester.

He was uncertain how best to broach the topic, but Lockbourne seemed as good a place to start as any. "Mother, you speak to me of settling down, but do not forget I plan on relocating to Lockbourne once the time has come for me to inherit. I do not think it is fair for me to court a woman and omit that critical bit of information."

Katherine Stanton jerked her head up. The firelight reflected from her hard, dark eyes. "I certainly hope you are not serious, and kindly lower your voice. What if one of your sisters should hear you say such a thing?"

He had no wish to bring his sisters into this conversation, but it was too late. "Then they would be hearing the truth, would they not?"

She pressed her lips together, and the color seemed to drain from her face right before him. For a moment he thought she might cry, but then her eyes narrowed.

He leaned forward, resting his elbows on his knees. "At some point they are going to know. They deserve to know the truth."

"And why should they?" she shot back. "What good could come from them knowing about their mother's poor choices?"

"For heaven's sake, Mother, they do not need to know all the details. But at some point do you think we should prepare them for a future at Lockbourne?"

"No, I do not," she snapped. "And I cannot believe you could be so selfish as to think of actually relocating to a place that *he* would leave you."

His heart began to race. "And why shouldn't I? At the very least, they will learn of Lockbourne. Do you think they will not wonder about that?"

"Of course not. You and your father have been trusted stewards at Willowgrove. It is not unseemly for a master to leave such a gift."

He needed to change his tactic. "Very well. Suppose we omit the girls from the discussion. What about me, Mother? Do you not think that I deserve to know the truth?"

Her face deepened to crimson. "How can you be so disloyal to your father by asking such things?"

"It is not being disloyal, Mother, to want to know the truth behind who I am." He softened his tone. "I think Father would want me to know."

She held his gaze, hard and unwavering, for several moments before easing back into the chair. She put her sewing to the side and reached for the shawl on the nearby sofa.

"Very well. What do you want to know? But I caution you. Once something is heard, it cannot be unheard."

Nathaniel's muscles tensed. Could it be that after all this time she would finally address this matter? Questions balanced in his mind, but he remained silent. Now he needed to listen.

"I was young, Nathaniel—only nineteen. My parents were both dead, and I had been in service since I was quite young. When Mrs. Trent selected me as her lady's maid, I was thrilled. Me, a lady's maid to such a well-respected gentlewoman! We became friends. She was different then, Nathaniel. Not so hardened."

Nathaniel leaned his elbows on his knees and stared at the planked floor beneath him.

His mother's voice was soft, barely above a whisper. "Mr. Trent was always very kind to me too. But over time that relationship changed. Foolish girl I was, I fell in love with him. Or I fancied myself in love, anyway. When I realized I was with child, I informed him."

Nathaniel rubbed his hand along his jawline and stared at the woven rug beneath his feet. Now that he was hearing the story, he was unsure he wanted her to continue.

She put her hand to her cheek, as if trying to recall a detail. "To this day I am unsure how Mrs. Trent learned of it, but when she found out about the baby, there was quite the commotion. She discharged me immediately, but then, much to my surprise, Mr. Trent intervened. He agreed I should leave, but he wanted to raise you as the heir. As you can imagine, Mrs. Trent would have naught to do with that. Mr. Trent concocted a plan and approached your father, who was a bachelor at the time. Mr. Trent declared his desire to have you raised on the grounds, and told your father that if he would marry me and raise you and give you his name, he would ensure his position would always be secure and that his offspring would always find employment at Willowgrove. In exchange for discretion, he provided us with this cottage. I, of course, was in no position to reject the arrangement. I had no family, no dowry, and being with child and without a positive reference, I was destined for the poorhouse. I accepted your father, with the understanding that we would never speak of it and nobody would ever be the wiser."

His mother paused, as if to signal that she had said all she was going to say on the matter, but then she drew a sharp intake of air. "At times, I would almost forget you were not Thomas's son. Our family was so happy. So complete. And I rarely encountered the Trents, except for the occasional church service. But then something would remind me. Do not think I take this lightly, or there is not a day I do not wish I had exercised more decorum."

Then the light in her eyes changed. "Despite my imprudence,

one thing I can say with absolute certainty is that you have been a blessing to me. Since your father's death, you have been the rock of our family, and I thank God daily that you are here."

Nathaniel finally smiled. He stood. "I hope I have not upset you too much, but I do thank you for sharing the story with me."

The next morning was Saturday. Cecily rose even before Clarkson came to wake her.

The last thing Cecily wanted was to oversleep on her first full day as Mrs. Trent's companion. And, if truth be told, she hadn't really fallen into a good night's sleep. Andrew weighed heavily on her mind, and ghostly dreams of herself as a child with her mother and sister had plagued her during the midnight hours.

She must have drifted off at some point, for she woke to a cheerful fire in the fireplace and fresh linen next to her washstand. She noticed her wardrobe door was slightly ajar. As she opened it, the scent of lavender met her, and her gowns were hung inside, clean and pressed.

She pulled out the blue one and held it at arm's length. The morning sun filtering around the brown drapes highlighted the fabric. Cecily marveled at it. The fabric looked like new. A small tear in the lace on the bodice had been repaired, and a small stain of stubborn ink had been removed from the sleeve.

She placed the dress on the bed and washed her face in the bowl of lukewarm water, cleaned her teeth, and sat down at the tiny writing desk. Dawn was breaking just outside of her window, spreading light on the flooded grounds. Despite the fact that the water should not be there, it was quite beautiful. A morning mist hung over the standing water, making the tranquil scene appear more like a painting than real life.

As she was enjoying the morning view, there was a tap at the door and Clarkson stepped inside.

"Oh. You are awake." The older woman's countenance seemed not to have improved since the previous evening. "Next time you wake, pull that cord and I'll come straightaway."

Cecily followed Clarkson's direction and located a velvet-covered cord next to the bed.

"I've only just woken."

Clarkson did not respond but went about straightening items in the room.

Was it something Cecily had said? Perhaps Clarkson had been close to Miss Vale and resented Cecily's presence here, but even that seemed unlikely. Whatever the reason, Cecily's hope of finding a comrade in the woman seemed improbable.

"Mrs. Trent has awoken. Says she isn't feeling well this morning and will take breakfast in her room. She wants you to take breakfast with her." Clarkson pointed her thumb at the gown Cecily had placed on the bed. "This the one you want to wear, miss?"

Clarkson was silent as she began dressing Cecily. No inquiries of how Cecily slept or if she was settling well. The maid helped Cecily into her stays and petticoat and then into her gown and laced the back.

Cecily lifted her hair so Clarkson could fasten the buttons. "I wanted to thank you for cleaning and repairing this dress. I don't think it has looked so lovely since the day I first received it. You even removed the spot of ink from the sleeve. I am most appreciative."

Clarkson's hand slowed at the compliment and then resumed the buttoning with fervor. "'Tis nothing a little juice of sorrel, lemon, and vinegar will not take care of, miss. Although it is always best to treat such stains straightaway."

When the woman had completed the task, she said, "Mrs. Trent's breakfast will be up shortly. I suggest you be quick about things."

And with that, she walked out, leaving Cecily standing in a quiet room. She tried not to be hurt by Clarkson's abruptness. At Rosemere, the servants were like family, practically on equal ground with the staff and students. Here, the sentiment toward servants seemed much different. Cecily assumed Clarkson had been at Willowgrove for quite some time. Perhaps Cecily would be wise to follow Clarkson's lead.

Cecily used the water from her washbasin to dampen her hair and then used her fingers to loosen the tangles. After pinning it up away from her neck and shoulders with a comb that Mrs. Sterling gave her many years ago, she stood back and observed herself in the looking glass.

She could not help but wonder if she would see Andrew today. No doubt he would think her much changed. She no longer looked like an adolescent. He would recognize her dimple. The hue of her eyes. But her hair was slightly darker now, not quite so coppery as it had been in her youth. Her figure had changed, and she was taller. But it was not just her appearance that was different. Her heart was not the same.

Her countenance.

Her mannerism.

And hopefully, her restraint.

A quiver coursed through her, but it was no longer one of new-found love. During the quiet hours, she had inspected her heart.

She feared seeing him, not because she feared rejection, but because he blurred her present with her past. He was a physical, constant reminder of the mistake they had made.

That *she* had made.

He knew far too much about her.

And that made him dangerous, to be sure.

She would be expected to eat her breakfast, but her stomach was tied into such knots she doubted she would be able to keep a morsel down. She tried to muster confidence, but homesickness for Rosemere overtook her. Mrs. Sterling, in her calm way, would soothe her spirits. Pray with her. It always seemed to help, but Cecily rarely prayed on her own. She would never know what to say.

She nearly jumped when the large cabinet clock in the corridor struck the hour. Cecily patted a wayward curl into place, pinched her cheeks for color, and tidied up the mess she had made. She left her room, closing the door and securing the latch behind her.

A young maid with an empty tray was leaving Mrs. Trent's bedchamber. Her face was red and she was shaking her head, oblivious to Cecily's presence. Cecily's heart began to race. She hoped that it wasn't a harbinger of her mistress's mood.

She tapped on the door, and within moments Clarkson opened it wide enough to step through.

Cecily nearly caught her breath when she entered the room. The previous day, the heavy curtains had been drawn. She had noticed few details in the dim light. But today, the curtains were pulled and several windows were open, flooding the grand space with light and cool swirls of fresh morning air. Sunlight glittered off the gilded frames on the overmantel mirror and danced on the red floral wallpaper. It shimmered off the silver tea service on the table where Mrs. Trent was seated and reflected down from an ornate chandelier.

But it was another view that stole her breath, for the window framed a majestic landscape that put the view from her bedchamber to shame with its vibrant hues of emerald green and pastel blooms. She beheld a masterfully planned garden with pathways and shapes spread before her as a maze. A long reflection pond divided the landscape into two halves. The garden ran all the way to the forest's edge, and beyond that, the moors, dressed in shades of purple and green, stretched as far as the eye could see.

Mrs. Trent motioned toward a chair. "Do be seated, child. It makes me nervous to have you up and moving about like that."

Cecily took the chair opposite of where Mrs. Trent was eating breakfast. There would be time later to explore and appreciate all the beauty around her. "I hope your sleep was restful, Mrs. Trent."

"I rarely sleep well, child, as you will soon learn. My rheumatism bothers me greatly, but all in all, a decent night." Mrs. Trent, with a shaking hand, applied jam to a roll. "Help yourself."

Not wanting to appear insolent, Cecily took one of the rolls and placed it on a plate before her. "Do you often prefer to take breakfast in your room?"

"No, not always. I find the breakfast room too warm, and my nephew will not rise this early to eat. I daresay his intended and her mother will not either. You will meet them all later. Perhaps at dinner this evening."

Cecily took a bite, trying not to react to the mention of Andrew.

"I am glad you are here," Mrs. Trent said after a pause, her voice rough. "It is nice to have company. You might consider it odd that I wrote to Mrs. Sterling for a suitable, well-bred companion. Most ladies I know have companions who are relatives or family friends. But I find selecting trustworthy companions difficult. I have been burned in the past by those I have trusted, but I have grown to rely upon Mrs. Sterling's judge of character."

Cecily nearly winced at the words "well-bred." As the daughter of a blacksmith and a seamstress, she would hardly be a typical lady's companion. But something told Cecily that Mrs. Trent was beyond worrying about societal expectations. At least, she hoped that would be the case.

"This morning I would like you to accompany me as I meet with Willowgrove's steward."

"Mr. Stanton?" Cecily blurted out before recalling his warning that it might be best to leave out the fact that she had already visited Laurel Cottage.

"Yes." Mrs. Trent's white eyebrows rose. "Are you acquainted with the man?"

"Yes, ma'am."

"Ah, well, then you must know that he is rather unpleasant." Mrs. Trent shook her head with emphatic disdain and returned her cup of tea to the table. "But nevertheless, he is my steward here, and is part of a long legacy of stewards who have served Willowgrove."

Cecily seized the opportunity to learn more of the family that had offered her such kindness. "I am surprised to hear of his shortcomings. He seemed kind."

"Oh, I suppose he would seem that way, but I have known him and his family for a very long time. If you were as well acquainted with him as I, I daresay you would think differently on the matter."

"If I may ask, how long have the Stantons served as stewards here?"

"Oh, mercy me. His father and grandfather were the stewards before young Mr. Stanton, for as long as I can remember, and they have always seen to the care of the estate and managing the servants and accounts and such. Willowgrove has never had a separate land steward or bailiff, and so the Stantons have always seen to the needs of the tenant farmers. It is a very serious undertaking."

"If you are not pleased with Mr. Stanton's work, then why not hire another?"

"I did not say I was not pleased with his work. The Stantons have contributed greatly to Willowgrove's success. I adored my husband, but his head was not one for figures, and I daresay that Mr. Stanton's father guided the estate through some very trying times. No, my esteem for his work is entirely separate from my opinion of his personality."

Cecily took another bite of brown bread, ready to let the topic pass, but Mrs. Trent continued, "Furthermore, before he died, my husband asked that I never dismiss Mr. Thomas Stanton, or his son after him, citing the service his family has performed over the years. I am a woman of my word, Miss Faire. I have complied with this request, begrudgingly at times."

Cecily wondered about the source of Mrs. Trent's disdain. Mr. Stanton had seemed quiet, distracted perhaps, but unpleasant? His manner was a bit gruff at times, but his sisters seemed quite fond of him. He was gentle with his mother. He had offered Cecily a service—even repaired her trunk.

But perchance Mrs. Trent never saw that side of her steward.

Or, more likely, she knew of a side of Mr. Stanton yet unseen.

Mrs. Trent fidgeted with the black fichu at her throat. "The flooding of the grounds must be answered for. I have not seen it this bad in decades, Miss Faire. *Decades.*" She shook her head vigorously. "And having to enter the estate through the stable entrance? Unacceptable."

Cecily listened to the older woman prattle on about the grounds. The breakfast. Her time spent taking the waters in Bath.

Cecily had never been to Bath. She had hardly been anywhere at all, but traveling did not appeal to her, especially to a city. She preferred the quiet countryside with trusted companions. The idea of throngs of strangers did little to impress her.

"And tonight we shall dine with my nephew and his acquaintances. He will only be in town a few more days, and I feel it fitting to spend a little more time with him. At my age, every visit may be the last."

Cecily winced at the mention of Andrew. But the reference to her expiry could not be ignored. "Do not say that, Mrs. Trent."

The older lady laughed. "Ah, youth always thinks such things. But you see, I am not frightened of death. I am anxious to see my husband once more, and I have little on this earth left to stay behind for."

Mrs. Trent spoke the words so calmly it was shocking.

"Have you experienced a lot of death in your life?" Mrs. Trent asked.

Cecily put down her tea, uncertain of her ability to keep it upright. She fixed her eyes on the delicate violets decorating the cup. This was a topic she rarely talked about, not even to Mrs. Sterling, who had tried to help her with the nightmares that accompanied her memories. She glanced up. Mrs. Trent's dark eyes were on her, expectant.

Cecily drew a deep breath. "Yes, ma'am. My mother died when I was but nine years old."

Mrs. Trent's expression changed. "I am sorry to hear it." She settled back in her chair and crossed her hands before her, as if preparing to hear a story. "Tell me of your family."

Cecily wished her chair would swallow her whole. Another topic she did not discuss, especially now that she knew Andrew was Mrs. Trent's nephew. She thought it best not to mention Aradelle Park by name.

"I'm afraid there isn't much to tell."

"Do you have any siblings?"

"Yes, ma'am. A sister."

"Is she older or younger than you?"

"She is older. By twelve minutes."

"Ah, a twin."

Cecily looked through the window to the broad expanse of green, wondering if the woman shared the same opinion of twins as Cecily's father. Mrs. Trent seemed relatively unshocked by the news.

"And where is your sister now?"

Cecily looked down at the bread on her plate. She did not want the woman to see her expression for fear that she'd read every emotion. Cecily's story was full of injustice and sadness, but Mrs. Trent seemed to have an opinionated nature. She would never approve of Cecily's past and upbringing . . . and Cecily needed this position.

But the one thing she would let her pride fall on was finding her sister. At the thought, she began to feel nervous. Moisture gathered on her palms, and she wiped them on her skirt.

She might as well know what the older lady thought of her plight, for without her support and understanding, finding Leah might be impossible. "I am sad to say that I do not know with certainty where my sister is."

Cecily forced herself to glance up and meet Mrs. Trent's eyes. "You do not know where she is?"

"No, ma'am."

Mrs. Trent leaned forward. "How can that be?"

Cecily picked over all of the words jumbling about in her head, trying to arrange them to best explain without giving away too much of herself. "When I was sent away to school, Leah stayed behind. And we have since lost contact."

"Why, that is preposterous!" Mrs. Trent's jowls shook as she spoke. "How on earth could you lose your sister?"

A queer sort of panic settled in her stomach. "I am not sure, really. I wrote to an old friend not long ago, and she told me she heard that Leah was in Manchester. So I was pleased to learn that Willowgrove was in such close proximity to it. I-I was hoping to go there soon and see if I can locate her."

"What, alone? That will not do, I am afraid, for I am certain not to travel there. It is a dirty, vile place." Mrs. Trent's wiry hair blew against her face as she shook her head. "Manchester is no place for a lady. Not to travel to alone. Why, the idea!"

Cecily bit her lower lip, crestfallen.

"But, if you are determined, say something to Mr. Stanton. He travels to Manchester periodically. He might be able to offer some assistance."

"Thank you, Mrs. Trent. I shall do that." The words offered her hope.

"Now, finish your breakfast. For we have much to do today."

14

Nathaniel hesitated outside of Mrs. Trent's drawing room, adjusting his neckcloth.

He had not seen the woman in nearly two months.

But still, he hesitated.

He was a man of business. Little intimidated him. But this was one task that irked him. After each of her trips, Mrs. Trent demanded an account of the estate's activities.

Mrs. Trent was a woman of strict propriety, and as such, she insisted upon limited interaction with the staff at Willowgrove. She believed all such news pertaining to the household should come directly from the steward, butler, or housekeeper and would speak to no one else on such matters.

And yet, as his fist hovered, preparing to knock on the door of the blue drawing room, he recalled the conversation he'd had with Mrs. Trent the evening his father was buried. The elderly woman had been irate over a matter he could not even recall, and in the fury of grief and the bravery of youthful courage, he informed her of how his father had told him everything. About his illegitimacy. About Mr. Trent's unfaithfulness. That his mother had been Mrs. Trent's companion. About his impending inheritance of Lockbourne. At the confrontation, her fury was unleashed, but he had stood his ground. Since that day, they never spoke of it, and yet it was the undercurrent of every interaction. At that moment they became silent enemies, both choosing to remain as civil as possible to hide secrets neither wanted exposed.

He had to admire her, on some level. For after her husband's death, Mrs. Trent assumed Mr. Trent's duties with unusual vigor, determined to learn all aspects of the estate, even wanting to meet some of the tenants and refusing any help. But whereas her husband had been a man of business and practicality, Mrs. Trent ruled with emotions.

Nathaniel knocked on the paneled door. He barely waited for a response before opening it.

Mrs. Trent jerked her head in his direction. She was dressed as she always was, in her extravagant black dress adorned with a ridiculous amount of black lace. A thick black shawl draped over her shoulders, and a jet pendant hung at her throat. But he was struck by how pale she looked, despite her customary bright rouge. Her hair, which had always had a silver luster, was now powder white.

"Mr. Stanton, there you are. We have been waiting all morning for you." Her voice sounded thick with accusation.

He gave a short bow. "Mrs. Trent."

Nathaniel nearly stopped mid-bow, however, when he noticed Miss Faire in the chair opposite Mrs. Trent. He'd expected them to be together, for Mrs. Trent was never alone when she could help it, but he should have prepared himself better for the effect the new companion would have on him.

Miss Faire was dressed in a simple, high-waisted gown of blue.

Sleeves covered her arms, and white embroidered flowers embellished the neckline and hem. The gown's pale color only served to make her hair brighter. Her eyes, more lively. His mind recalled how she appeared that first night, with her damp hair splayed wild and untethered over her shoulders. Today it was smoothed into feminine curls atop her head. Elegant. Refined.

"Mr. Stanton, Miss Faire tells me you have already met."

"Yes." Mr. Stanton gave a short bow in her direction. "Miss Faire. It's my pleasure to see you again."

Miss Faire nodded at him. The simple action stole his breath.

He was going to need to employ every inch of self-discipline to stay focused on the task at hand.

Mrs. Trent jerked her head, her eyes narrowing on Nathaniel. "I trust you and your family are well."

He shifted his weight. Must they go through this charade each time they interacted? Harriet Trent cared little for his health, and even less for that of his family. "Very well, ma'am. I trust you found Bath enjoyable."

"Tolerably."

Nathaniel cast a cautious glance toward Miss Faire, trying hard not to notice the way the sunlight caught the glimmer of her hair and her feathery eyelashes. She appeared to be as uncomfortable as he, for even though she was still, her eyes were wide and watchful. And her gaze was latched onto him.

"Be seated, Mr. Stanton. It pains my neck to look up at you in this manner. What news do you have for me? I know you must want to be about your business."

Nathaniel did as she bid. He had made a mental list of the news she typically liked to receive when she returned from her travels. "Mr. Shire died a week ago. The youngest Hardy boy fell from his horse and broke his arm."

"'Tis a shame to hear."

"And the new carriage horses are here, four of them, all matching bays. James has been working with them and says they will be ready before too much longer."

"And what of the bridge?" she said. "It was most unsuitable to be forced to go back to the west stable entrance."

"I take it you did not receive my letter."

Mrs. Trent clicked her tongue. "Bothersome having to drive around to the back gate after all these years coming up the main drive. I shudder to think what my nephew's guests thought of the inconvenience."

He cast a glance over at Miss Faire and thought he detected a hint of a smile tug at her lips. She knew the inconvenience all too well.

But this is how it always was. Mrs. Trent and her nephew could not see past the minor disruption of taking the stable drive when their tenants would suffer greatly from this incident.

He cleared his throat. "It could not be helped. I have already been in contact with an engineer in Manchester to repair the sluice. He should arrive within the week to assess the damage and formulate a plan for repairs."

"Have you spoken with my nephew yet on this matter?"

"I spoke with him yesterday."

"Then I leave the matter to you and him. Do what you must to rectify the situation."

Mrs. Trent stood, gripped her cane with her bony hand, and crossed the room to a painting.

The painting.

The painting that Nathaniel avoided looking at every time he came into this particular drawing room.

And then he waited for the condemning conversation that was sure to follow.

"I cannot help but wonder how my late husband would have

handled such a situation." Mrs. Trent's voice seemed louder, as if she were trying to prove a point. "This was my husband, Miss Faire—here, in the painting. He was a handsome man, was he not?"

Nathaniel looked down at the toes of his boots.

He could not say why she always managed to point out the painting whenever he was in the room. Perhaps it was to remind him of their secret. Or of his illegitimacy. Or of her authority.

Miss Faire stood, shook out the folds of her gown, and stepped across the plush rug toward the painting, her steps nary making a sound. She laced her fingers behind her back as she studied the portrait. "Yes, he was a very handsome man."

Nathaniel could not look at it. For it was like looking into a mirror. The blue eyes. The square jawline. The straight nose. They were all features he bore. Someone who looked too closely might notice the resemblance.

"He was the most respected man in the county," Mrs. Trent said. "So wise with ways of business. His talents on such matters were unequaled."

Miss Faire stepped even closer and rested her hand on the back of a sofa, her expression pensive as she studied the large canvas. "You must be very proud of his legacy."

Nathaniel needed to change the subject.

He knew little about the relationship between mistress and companion, but he did know one thing about Mrs. Trent: She usually took her companion into confidence.

And what would he care if Miss Faire knew his secret? A man made his own way in the world, despite his parentage. He was playing the hand he was dealt, and he was proud of his work.

But Nathaniel did care for his mother and the reputation of his sisters. For it was different for women. He could quickly overcome such a disgrace, but his sisters' chances of marrying well were dependent upon their reputations, especially since their dowries were small. He did not want anyone thinking down on his mother for her past actions.

He purposefully avoided looking at Mrs. Trent and instead turned to Miss Faire. "Tell me, Miss Faire, what do you think of secrets?"

She cut her eyes to Mrs. Trent but then looked at him, unwavering. Her cheeks flushed.

Something was hiding behind her shy expression.

Miss Faire pushed her hair from her face, a trait he was beginning to recognize as something she did when she was uncomfortable. But her answer was surprisingly bold. "I think everyone has secrets, sir, and a right to their own thoughts. It is human nature, I think."

"I do not know if I agree," Mrs. Trent shot back. She might be aging, but her tongue was as sharp as it had been when he was a boy. "Some secrets are like a noose. The more you resist, the more they strangle you."

The tension in the room expanded, pressing on him. Even after all these years he could not identify the emotion he experienced around Mrs. Trent whenever this topic—or even the reference to this topic—surfaced. He wasn't sure if it was anger. He was fairly confident it was not sadness. But the constant need to walk a fine line with the woman grew old.

Whereas he would respect her and her position just as his father had demanded, she seemed determined to try to push him to the point of breaking. Then she could despise him for something that he did, and not something that his parents had done. But his best course of action would be to stay strong and behave in the manner in which he knew to be right.

"I am growing tired, Mr. Stanton," Mrs. Trent said, returning to her chair. "You may leave now. But before you do, please escort Miss Faire to the library on your way to wherever it is you are going. She does not know where it is, and I should like her to read to me."

Cecily jerked her head up at the mention. The thought of being alone with Mr. Stanton, even for something as simple as walking to the library, sent a tremor through her.

She was not sure what had just transpired between Mrs. Trent and Mr. Stanton. With each word, the tension between them pulled harder, a battle masked behind civil, even tones.

She tried to follow their veiled dialogue and found it impossible, but after the strange conversation, she was certain of one thing.

Nathaniel Stanton had a secret.

Something that Mrs. Trent knew. Or perhaps it was Mrs. Trent who had the secret.

And that mystery made the handsome man standing before her even more intriguing.

Her mere presence in the same room with him made her head feel light and her thoughts muddled. And even as her encounter with Andrew reopened old wounds, the woman in her could not deny the attraction to Mr. Stanton.

She found her voice and turned toward Mrs. Trent. "Are you certain? I can visit the library while you are napping if you prefer company."

"No, I think not. Go now." Mrs. Trent returned to the sofa and took a few moments to settle herself. "Please select some poetry, dear. And nothing too sentimental."

Cecily complied, keeping her eyes low. She preceded Mr. Stanton to the corridor. The distinct scent of leather and sandalwood met her as she passed him, and she was grateful when she stepped in the hall to put a little more distance between them.

He closed the drawing room door and turned to her. "Have you not had a proper tour of Willowgrove, Miss Faire?"

She shrugged. "No, sir. Not as of yet. I did not mean to take you away from your duties. I fear I am becoming quite a nuisance to you, Mr. Stanton. I am sure I could have found the library. Eventually."

He held a door open as she stepped through to another sunlight-filled corridor. "I am sure you could have, but this is much easier, is it not? This is an old home. Wings have been added and demolished over the decades. Some parts of it are a bit of a maze."

She paused to take notice of a large painting of a woman holding a small child. "This is by far the largest house I have ever been in. I fear I shall have to write this down so I can commit it to memory."

"I am sure you will do just fine. Here is the main staircase. This area is called the Staircase Hall."

She immediately recognized it from both the previous day when the housekeeper took her to her chamber and when she and Mrs. Trent descended from her bedchamber to the blue drawing room earlier that morning.

"Find this and you will always be able to find your way back to the main hall. We will be going up one flight of stairs. The library is across from Mrs. Trent's chambers."

Cecily placed her hand on the varnished handrail as she ascended and could not help but wonder why, if the library was so close to their chambers, Mrs. Trent did not show her the room herself.

But before she could ask, he spoke. "Tell me, how was your first night at Willowgrove?"

She almost laughed. Her first night had been emotional. Heart-wrenching. Sleepless. "It was well."

"I am glad to hear it. I trust it was more comfortable for you than Laurel Cottage?"

She smiled. "I must say I missed the company at Laurel Cottage. How is your mother? And your sisters?"

He paused at the landing and allowed her to pass. "They are all well. In fact, Rebecca, just this past night, became engaged to Mr. Turner, the man you met in the courtyard yesterday morning."

"Oh, how delightful! Please pass along my felicitations."

"I would be happy to, but would you not prefer to do that yourself? My family would welcome you at any time." At the top of the stairs, he motioned to a door at the end of the corridor. "Here is the library."

When she stepped past him into the room, Cecily had to catch her breath. For the ceilings in the room were exceptionally tall. The curtains were drawn and the room was dark and cool. Oak bookshelves lined every wall, and the space above the shelves but below the crown molding was painted a bright shade of emerald green. The showpiece of the room was a marble chimneypiece boasting intricate caryatids flanking each side. Above the mantel was a striking painting of a young man, large enough that it might have easily been a life-size portrait. A writing desk with rich leather inlay stood in the middle of the room, a small, square table was tucked in the far corner, and two chairs sat near the fireplace.

Mr. Stanton walked to the window and shook the curtains open. Light tumbled into the room, reaching to every corner and illuminating motes in the air.

"You will have to forgive the state of the room, Miss Faire. It is rarely used and remains closed off from the house most of the time."

She could barely hear what he was saying, for she was still soaking in the sheer volume of books around her. She had only been in one library before this moment, and it had been the modest room at Rosemere. It paled in the shadow of the leather volumes here. "What a magnificent collection!"

"Mr. Trent was an avid reader, and he took great pride in his assemblage. I believe last I heard there were more than four thousand volumes, the oldest of which dates back to 1498. There is a complete catalog on that podium, if you are interested." He looked around the room, fists on his hips, as if assessing it for the first time. "I recall you mentioned you were fond of reading, so you should feel right at home here. Sadly, there have been no new additions logged since Mr. Trent's death, but I am sure you will find something to entertain yourself and Mrs. Trent."

"I am certain I will. Thank you."

He stepped past her, his scent of leather distracting her. "If I am not being too presumptuous, I will point you in the direction of books my sister has read. I often take books back and forth for her to read, and I have started putting them in the same place. She just finished reading this one."

Cecily recalled the stack of novels she saw in Rebecca's room.

He handed a volume to her. *The Tales of a Fashionable Life*. "Have you read it?"

She flipped through the pages. "No, I have not."

"Rebecca said it was amusing. There are a few other books by the same author here. And there are some older works by Byron and Wordsworth on the opposite shelf. My sister is fond of them."

She tucked the book in the crook of her arm. "And what about you, Mr. Stanton? Are you fond of them?"

He shrugged. "I have read them a bit, but I find most of my reading is occupied with much more exciting topics like husbandry and agriculture."

She laughed. "I am surprised, pleasantly so, to find that Mr. Trent was fond of such poets."

His countenance sobered. "Mr. Trent spent many hours in this room, but you will find that Mrs. Trent rarely comes in here."

"Why ever not?"

"This was her husband's personal library. I suppose the memories are too much to bear. You will learn soon enough that Mrs. Trent is particular with some things, and this is just one of them."

"Yes, I wondered why she did not show me this room herself, or, in the very least, have Clarkson show me. It is so very close. I apologize again for taking you away from your duties."

"I assure you, Miss Faire, this was much more pleasant than the other tasks I have waiting for me." His smile brought a flush to her cheeks. "I will leave you to your exploring, then. If you need anything else, I will be in the steward's office, which is just next to the north entrance. Mrs. Trent's private rooms are through that door there."

She hesitated. Had Mrs. Trent not said she should ask Mr. Stanton about Manchester?

"Before you go, I was hoping to ask you one other question."

He stopped in the doorway and raised an eyebrow. "Of course."

Suddenly, the idea of sharing her personal journey with a stranger made her arms feel weak.

"It has nothing to do with the library," she muttered, feeling the room grow warmer with each syllable, "but I was sharing a slight family matter with Mrs. Trent, and she suggested that you might be able to help me."

He stepped back into the room. "I am at your service."

"How far are we from Manchester?"

He scrunched his face, as if surprised by the question. "Manchester? Oh, probably a few hours by carriage, if the weather is fine. Why? Do you have business in Manchester?"

"I have reason to believe my sister is there."

"Reason to believe?" he repeated. "Do you not know?"

She shook her head and looked down to the plush carpet beneath her boots. "We were separated when I was sent to Rosemere, and we have lost contact. I received a letter indicating that she had taken a position as a dressmaker there. I have never been to Manchester, but Mrs. Trent said that you have business there every so often."

"I do. Granted, I do not often interact with dressmakers, and it has been some time since I was there last, but I will help however I can. What is your sister's name?"

A shiver of hope shot through her. "Leah Faire. At least, I think it is still Faire. I do not know if she has married."

"Do you have any other information about her?"

"Not much. I believe she might have stayed with my aunt, who lives—or lived—in south Manchester."

He shook his head. "That is not much to go on."

"I know, but it is all I have. I am determined to find her and would be eternally grateful for any assistance you could offer, little or great. I do hope to travel to Manchester soon to look for her myself."

His eyebrow shot up again, and he folded his arms across his chest, his expression morphing to that of amusement. "Does Mrs. Trent know about that plan as well?"

Cecily shook her head, feeling almost like a child being asked about her actions. "No, sir."

"Well, Miss Faire, I would have to advise you to stay away from Manchester. It can be a dangerous city. No place for a lady on her own."

A lady on her own.

How long would those words shock her? Being called a lady.

Well, she could keep up this charade if it helped her find her sister.

He must have noticed a change in her demeanor, for he smiled a kind smile. "But I will do my best. I will mention it when I next write to a colleague in Manchester and see if he can be of assistance. He is a man who knows everything about everyone, and if anyone knows how to go about such a search, he would." He turned to leave, but then stopped and looked at her over his shoulder. "Leah Faire. Manchester. Seamstress. Correct?"

She smiled. His manner seemed so much more carefree now

than when in the presence of Mrs. Trent. A manner that she much preferred. "Yes."

"Good."

He gave a short bow, smiled.

Cecily watched him leave the room and then stared at the space he'd just vacated. She drew a deep breath.

If she was not careful, it would be easy to romanticize Mr. Stanton.

Very easy indeed.

15

It was the moment Cecily had dreaded all day.

From the time when Mrs. Trent informed her that they would be dining with Andrew, his intended, and his intended's mother, Cecily could focus on little else. She'd been grateful that she and Mrs. Trent spent their day confined to the blue drawing room or her bedchamber, where she was in no danger of accidentally encountering Andrew. Now that the time was nigh, having been seated by Gordon, the butler, her hands trembled so that she could barely trust herself to lift her fork.

Despite her discomfort, the grandeur of the room was not lost on her. The silver serving dishes on the sideboard. The Chinese murals reaching to the molded ceilings. The flickering candlelight. She determined to appreciate the beauty around her, but in spite of her best efforts, her every thought centered on merely surviving this dinner with her dignity intact. Andrew sat directly across from her at the broad table. Beside him, Miss Pritchard. And beside her, Mrs. Pritchard.

Cecily tried not to meet his eyes. She feared what message she would find hidden there, or even worse, what he might see in her expression.

The dinner marked the first time she had seen him since their encounter on the path the previous morning. She sought him in her quiet, still moments, and yet she also wished to avoid him. And here he sat, in flesh and blood, the object of her thoughts for so long.

While he had aged, the carefree expression in his dark eyes had not changed. His laugh was still easy and light. But instead of the gangly boy she remembered, with long arms and a wiry frame, he'd grown into a man, with broad shoulders and a thicker frame.

Her ears flamed as she heard Andrew's voice mutter something to the lady beside him and then chuckle.

At the sound, another feeling was emerging.

Hurt.

Andrew seemed oblivious to her presence. She did not expect any loyalty, for Cecily's heart had long ago bid him farewell. But the fact that he never sought after her burned, and his current disinterest jabbed at her heart.

She looked to Mrs. Trent. Cecily had expected the older woman to guide the evening's conversation, something that appeared to come naturally for her. But here, in the midst of their guests, the poker-straight footman, and the butler, the outspoken woman was surprisingly reserved.

As Cecily pushed the fish on her plate with her fork, it was becoming clear: Her presence here was not so much to be a companion but a buffer.

Cecily gathered her courage and looked up at Georgiana Pritchard, the woman Andrew was going to marry. From what she had gleaned from Mrs. Trent earlier in the day, the wedding date was to be soon.

It was odd—Cecily and Miss Pritchard had never been formally introduced. She was a beautiful woman, one who *looked* like she should be a mistress of a grand estate such as Willowgrove. Her glossy, dark hair was swept up from her long neck. Pearl earrings bounced with her every movement, and an intricate amethyst pendant graced her neck. Her gown was unlike anything Cecily had ever seen. Strands of silver were woven into the gray fabric—every movement shimmered, and pearls embellished the neckline. Far different, she could not help but notice, from the simple coral necklace adorning her own throat.

Lady Pritchard and her daughter shared little resemblance, for the mother's features were much more severe. Like Mrs. Trent, Mrs. Pritchard dressed in black. Her hair was much lighter than her daughter's raven locks, but her eyes held the same haughtiness.

The table had a clear divide, for Andrew and his guests seemed to focus only on one another. Was this typical behavior for Andrew? If so, Cecily could plainly see why Mrs. Trent would be in need of a companion.

She lifted a spoon of vermicelli soup to her lips.

"Miss Faire, I must say, you do live up to your name. You are lovely."

Cecily held her spoon steady and lifted her gaze to see Miss Pritchard looking directly at her. Despite the smile, her eyes lacked warmth. They were dark. Hollow.

Cecily lowered the utensil and returned Miss Pritchard's bold gaze. For even though she had a secret that she—and certainly Andrew—wanted to keep, there was no reason for her to pretend to be shy. "Thank you, Miss Pritchard."

"It seems that we were not properly introduced."

Cecily stiffened at the obvious jab at Mrs. Trent. A fire began to simmer within her. Mrs. Trent was an old woman. Her attentions to such detail were clearly not as she was certain they had been in the past—a reason to overlook the slight impropriety. Miss Pritchard seemed resolved to point out such oversights. Cecily kept her eyes on Andrew's betrothed.

"And where are you from, Miss Faire?" Miss Pritchard said in a honeyed tone.

Cecily returned her napkin to her lap. "Most recently I was at Rosemere School for Young Ladies in Darbury."

"A ladies' school? How fascinating. And were you a pupil?"

"At one time, yes, but more recently I was a teacher."

"And what did you teach?"

"Embroidery, among other subjects."

Cecily did not need to see Andrew's face to know that her response had affected him. For the first time during the dinner, he fixed his eyes on his plate, pushing the stewed celery to the side.

When they were younger, and very much in love, Cecily had embroidered him a handkerchief with his initials. He had carried it with him always. It was a silly, romantic gesture, and in hindsight, brazen. But what about her behavior back then had not been?

Cecily doubted that Andrew would ever share such private details, and yet Miss Pritchard's tone seemed to hold a note of challenge. "And who is your family? Perhaps we have encountered them at some point."

Cecily's blood ran cold.

It had not been that difficult to share with Mrs. Trent that she did not know much about her family. But the silent judgment balanced in Miss Pritchard's words was unmistakable.

Cecily pressed her napkin to her lips before speaking. "A tragedy separated me from my family a few years ago."

Miss Pritchard's hand flew to her throat, and she looked to her mother. Either the display was in earnest or a show of false sympathy. "My condolences."

Cecily had not even realized she had glanced over to Andrew

until their eyes locked. She quickly returned her attention to Andrew's betrothed.

Miss Pritchard forced a smile and adjusted the amethyst hanging around her neck. "Well, Miss Faire, I do hope that we shall be able to get to know each other, if even just slightly, before we depart for London in a few days. We have been invited to stay with the Langleys for the next week."

Miss Pritchard spoke as if Cecily should know of the Langleys, but if it was an effort to impress Cecily with their connections, it was beyond her.

As the volume of the conversation rose above the tinkling silver, sudden pity for Mrs. Trent pricked Cecily. Andrew had asked Mrs. Trent about her day at the start of dinner, but other than that, no one spoke to her. Cecily knew what it felt like to be excluded. Mrs. Trent may be eccentric and opinionated. But she was also kind. And lonely. The day had taken a toll on the woman, for the shadows beneath her eyes were more pronounced.

Cecily reached out and put her hand on top of the older lady's. "Can I call for anything, Mrs. Trent? Perhaps a bit more soup? Or an apricot tart?"

Mrs. Trent looked toward Cecily and smiled. "I am tired. These long days are a bit much for me. I think I shall retire."

Cecily frowned and glanced through the window, where the sun had not even yet begun to set. "Are you certain?"

"Like I told you yesterday, my dear, I need my rest."

Suddenly Mrs. Trent seemed fragile. Cecily took note of her plate, which still held a complete lamb cutlet and untouched asparagus. "Surely you mean to eat something. You'll fall ill."

Mrs. Trent ignored Cecily and glared across the table at Andrew. "I shall retire now," she announced. "Miss Faire will see me to my room."

"But, Aunt, it is early." Andrew's protest came too late.

"I bid you good night."

Cecily jumped up and hurried to retrieve Mrs. Trent's cane when the older lady attempted to stand on her own. She then instructed a footman to send Clarkson to Mrs. Trent's chambers before casting an apologetic smile to Miss Pritchard and her mother. Secretly, she was grateful to be leaving the confines of the room.

Mrs. Trent moved slowly, one shaky step in front of the other, and Cecily held her arm as the two left the dining hall. She was certain she could feel the heat of gazes drilling into her back, yet she continued to keep her head high and her arm steady.

In the hall to the foyer, the air felt cooler, a welcome relief from the hot pressure they'd just escaped. Voices and laughter resumed from the dining hall. No doubt the occupants inside were eager to be free of Mrs. Trent.

The injustice of the thought sickened Cecily.

Clarkson was waiting for them in Mrs. Trent's chambers. The sun, which they had enjoyed that morning, had traveled to the west, and with the heavy brocade curtains drawn, the hour seemed later than it was.

After her first full day of trying to impress Mrs. Trent and keep her feelings in check at seeing her long-lost fiancé, Cecily was worn.

Once Clarkson finished her duties and quitted the chamber, Cecily drew a heavy, wooden chair next to the bed. "Shall I read to you?"

Mrs. Trent settled into the bed, her frame rather tiny in the sea of bedclothes and pillows. "Yes, dear."

"Any requests? I have a book of Wordsworth's poems from the library. What of that?"

Mrs. Trent's breathing sounded labored. "No. Not tonight. The Bible is on the cupboard there. Read from that, if you will."

Cecily retrieved the Bible and shifted it in her hand. She could not recall the last time she had held a Bible in her hands, much less read one. Childhood memories rushed her. Her mother had memorized several psalms and would recite them to her and Leah before bed. Her mother had insisted that Cecily memorize them too, but time had robbed her of the recollections. For some reason, her heart now yearned to remember them.

She flipped forward, then backward, through the pages. "What shall I read?"

"It makes no difference, child. Anything will do. Miss Vale used to read to me from this before bed, and I have grown quite accustomed to it. Your voice is a bit lower than hers, but I think it will suit me fine."

Cecily cleared her throat. She opened the Bible to Psalms and started to read. The words were foreign—yet oddly familiar too. She tried to read the words without hearing them, to separate herself from them, and yet their cadence struck a chord within her—the knowledge she should heed the words she was reading. She hoped for it and feared it at the same time.

Nathaniel trudged home, each step feeling heavier than the last.

Even Gus seemed abnormally slow, his gait listless.

Normally, walks home at the end of a long day were pleasant, especially this time of the year when the evenings were neither cold nor hot, but a pleasant balance of comfort. But gathering clouds to the west hinted that storms might be headed their way again. He shook his head as he thought about the bridge.

More rain was the last thing they needed.

While nobody else would likely care if the bridge's repair was delayed another week, he did.

Workers had demolished what was left of the existing stone

and timber bridge, and a dam had been constructed to restrain the flowing water so the workers could build footings. As of yet, all seemed to be going as planned. But any more rain might cause the makeshift sluice to give way, which would force them to start anew.

He rubbed the back of his neck, attempting to release the tension stored there. Mrs. Trent did not seem to care about the progress. Neither did Mr. Moreton. It should not matter to him, then.

But it did. And he knew why. His father had dedicated his life to Willowgrove. And whether it was out of respect for his father, or just a result of his teaching, he could not turn his back on what he knew was right.

His body cried for a hearty meal and bed, for the next morning would begin before the sun rose.

He turned the bend in the road and approached Laurel Cottage, and within moments he was inside. Soft laughter came down from the upper rooms.

It felt good to be home.

He called up to his sisters from the bottom of the stairs and then turned to the parlor. He sat on the worn wingback chair—which had been his father's—and removed his boots. He unfastened the fabric buttons down the front of his tailcoat and tossed it on a chair next to the fireplace. He tugged on his neckcloth to loosen it.

Suddenly, from behind him, a sweet voice sounded, so softly he was not quite sure he had actually heard it or only imagined it. "Good evening, Mr. Stanton."

He whirled around. There, in the threshold, stood Mrs. Olivia Massey. She was, as always, a vision of perfection. Her dark hair was smooth and intricately arranged, and her gown of deep plum hugged her figure with precise proportions. Her eyes were fixed on him with brazen directness.

"Mrs. Massey!" Realizing he was not properly dressed to meet with a woman, he reached for his coat. "Forgive me."

"Think nothing of it. My husband used to remove his coat in just such a manner at the end of a long day." She stepped casually into the room, her hips swaying with each step. "You were not expecting company, I daresay."

"Uh, no." He pushed his arm back through the sleeve and stuffed his stocking feet into his boots. He looked over her shoulder. He did not like the idea of being alone with her in this way. It would be too easy to give a wrong impression. "Where are my sisters?"

"Rebecca and Hannah are upstairs. I just came down to retrieve some ribbons from my trunk. We will start preparations for your sister's wedding gown soon."

He followed her gaze, and sure enough, a trunk stood open at the foot of the stairs, overflowing with fabrics and lace. He'd not even noticed it when he entered.

Trying to think of how to get her back with his sisters, he said, "Would you like me to carry that up the stairs for you? 'Twould be no trouble at all."

But she did not answer. Instead, she wove the ribbon she was holding through her fingers slowly and cocked her head to the side. "I hear there is a new addition to Willowgrove Hall."

The reference to Miss Faire pricked his senses. Why, he was not exactly sure. But he did know one thing: He did not want to discuss Miss Faire. Not with Mrs. Massey.

She stepped closer, her bright eyes locked on him like a hunter on his prey. "Mrs. Trent's maid sent a missive asking me to come by this week. It seems I shall have the privilege of dressing our new acquaintance. I understand from Clarkson that she is in dire need of new dressings."

She paused, as if waiting for him to respond. But what could he possibly add? Her gowns were the last thing he would pay attention to.

When he did not speak, she continued, "I hear she is lovely, with titian hair and skin like ivory."

She was clearly waiting for his assessment. The room seemed to grow warmer with every second.

She stepped closer. So close that the hem of her skirt swished against his leg.

Mrs. Massey was a charming woman.

But instead of flattering him, her attentions made him uncomfortable.

Mrs. Massey's husband had died two years ago of a fever. Nathaniel had been great friends with Mr. Massey, and out of duty and respect for his departed friend, he had done everything he could to help the widow begin a new life. He had helped her establish her business. Assisted with repairs to her home. And somewhere along the line, he assumed that she had misinterpreted his service for romantic intentions.

But the more she pressed, the more he digressed. How could he court a woman and keep the truth about his true identity? Perhaps it would be different if he felt any inclination toward her, but it would take a great deal of trust to share a secret he had kept so long hidden.

No. If he were ever to marry, he needed to wait until he was settled at Lockbourne.

Not before.

And not with a woman as forward as Mrs. Massey.

If Mrs. Massey noticed his growing discomfort, she did not let on. "I will be at Willowgrove the day after tomorrow to meet our lovely new friend. At least, I hope I shall be friends with her."

He looked up from the toes of his boots, met her eyes briefly, and then looked to the door behind her.

Her smooth voice was barely above a whisper. "Shall I see you at Willowgrove?"

Before he could respond, Hannah came bounding down the stairs. "Nathaniel, you're home!" She ran over and hugged his waist.

He wrapped his arm around her shoulder and knelt down to look at his sister at eye level. "And how was your day?"

"Good!" She thrust a handful of ribbon into his face. "And look, Mrs. Massey gave me these ribbons. Aren't they lovely?"

He looked at the tangle of satin and cotton strips in every color of the rainbow. "Yes, very pretty."

"I shall add them to the dress I am making with the fabric Miss Faire gave me." Hannah smiled and turned toward Mrs. Massey. "Mother wondered what was keeping you and sent me down to see if you needed any help."

Nathaniel spotted his opportunity. He reached for his hat and, without making eye contact, stepped back toward the foyer. "I will let you ladies get back to your business. Hannah, tell Mother I will be in the cowhouse."

Without waiting for a response, he stepped outside into the damp night.

Later that evening, after Mrs. Massey had quitted Laurel Cottage, Nathaniel sat with his mother in the gathering dark of night. His sisters were upstairs. Giggles and chatter wafted downstairs. He was always grateful for this time of day. A time when he could sit and be still.

But tonight he felt restless. A voice nagged at him, and yet he could not make out the words. It was . . . confusing.

Across from him, his mother's features were pointed, her frustration written in her furrowed brow and pursed lips. And he knew why. She adored Mrs. Massey, and since the day the young woman's husband died, she had pegged the widow as Nathaniel's future wife. Everyone had.

He had avoided Mrs. Massey while she was here. He didn't come in for dinner.

His actions may not be considered gentlemanly, but how much worse would it be for him to give her false hope?

Many months ago, he had been tempted by Mrs. Massey's charms. For a brief time, he thought himself enamored with the manner in which her cheek dimpled when she smiled. But then, as he grew to know her character, his emotions seemed to cool until it became evident: Mrs. Olivia Massey was not the woman he wanted to marry.

And yet the more reserved he was, the harder she pushed.

The harder everyone pushed.

He was able to consider it little more than a minor inconvenience, but for some reason, today was different.

For whether he liked it or not, he had encountered a woman who intrigued him.

Miss Faire, with her entrancing hair and radiant green eyes.

She brought with her an air of mystery, a depth of character. Ever since he left her in Mr. Trent's library earlier in the day, he had been able to think of little else. The earnest expression. Her concern for her sister. It was driving him to utter distraction. The lingering memory of her haunted him. And even now, she dominated his thoughts. They'd spoken of secrets. What secret was Miss Faire keeping? he wondered.

And what was even more frustrating—it was nonsensical. He'd spent little time in her presence, and yet from the moment he'd encountered her alone on the road, he felt an undeniable sense of connectedness.

He could not help but wonder if she felt it too.

But even if she had such an inclination, she was unreachable. Destined never to be a part of his world. For she was Mrs. Trent's companion. If history taught him anything, it would be that Mrs. Trent would have Miss Faire turned against him in a matter of days.

The thought incited frustration within him. Yet another facet to his secret. He was like a puppet on a string, tethered to Mrs. Trent's personal vendetta.

A future with Miss Faire would never be. He needed to keep his sights set on his duties at Willowgrove, his responsibilites toward his family, and his future at Lockbourne.

"You are distracted." His mother's words were more a statement than a question.

He stretched out his booted leg and expelled the air in his lungs. "No. Just tired."

She looked up from her needlework. "How were things at Willowgrove today?"

"The workers cleared much of the old bridge, but we must wait until the water levels subside before we go much further. The engineer will be here before the week's end."

"Your father would be proud of you for the way you are handling all this."

Nathaniel stared into the fire, watching the dying flames of orange and white as they popped and sizzled. His mother always did this . . . brought Thomas Stanton up in conversation. Would it ever get easier to discuss his father with his mother?

Fortunately, she changed the topic. "Mrs. Massey was lovely today."

"She always is."

"It is a shame you did not join us for dinner. She was quite disappointed that you were not present." She lowered her sewing. "I do not understand your opposition to her. She is the kindest, most affable woman I have had the privilege of knowing. Life has handed her much difficulty, and yet she exhibits naught but grace and dignity. And I do believe she is quite taken with you."

At this, Nathaniel leaned back in his chair and folded his arms across his chest. "I've no intention of marrying her or anyone else. Shall we leave it at that?"

She lifted her sewing again. "You say that now, but you will change your mind one day."

"One day, possibly. You know my reasons. I promised Father I would not—"

"Oh, stop." She pointed her finger at him. "Your father would not want you to not seize life by refusing to live it. As I told you before, he told you so you know the truth about who you are. You needed to know."

"I am not refusing to live life," he protested. "You know my reason for hesitating. It wouldn't be fair to her."

His mother shook her head. "She is taken with you, Nathaniel. Not your lineage."

"You know full well that once that will is read, I will be leaving this county. Lockbourne is far from here—far from what she knows. It isn't fair for her to not know what she is getting involved in. Besides, I cannot connect with someone I do not trust."

His mother's hand flew to her chest. "You do not trust Mrs. Massey?"

"No, I do not. I cannot satisfy you with an explanation of why, but it is an inclination. A strong one. When I meet the lady, I will know. When I inherit Lockbourne, life will change dramatically. I am in no rush to marry."

"Mrs. Trent may well live a long time."

"Well, if I meet someone else in the time being, then it is up to me to decide." He stood. He was a grown man. Fully capable of knowing his own heart.

"I just want happiness for you, Nathaniel. That is all. Do not pass up the opportunity for happiness because you are waiting for your circumstances to be ideal. They never will be."

16

Cecily did not know how long she had been asleep. But when she jerked awake, the book she had been reading to Mrs. Trent had slid from her lap and lay open on the floor. Mrs. Trent snored softly.

Cecily was surprised that she had fallen asleep. Sleep had eluded her of late. But she could not deny that the emotions of the past several days had taken a toll on her.

She must have slept for at least a couple of hours, for darkness now blanketed the chamber. Careful not to wake Mrs. Trent, Cecily extinguished all but one candle lamp, stoked the waning fire, and exited the room. A single stream of moonlight slanted through a tall casement window in the corridor and sliced across the maroon rug. Wind hinted at coming weather, and it shook the glass panes. Her candle cast eerie, bending shadows on the stone walls and the ancient tapestries hanging on them.

She'd left her book of Proverbs down in the blue drawing

room where they had spoken with Mr. Stanton. She decided to retrieve it before returning to her own chamber for the night. She lifted the hem of her skirt and headed down the stairs. The house was quiet and still, lying dormant in the night's cool stillness. Cecily turned the handle to the blue drawing room, pushed the door open, and stepped inside. Without the brightness of sunlight, the room appeared much more foreboding. The walls appeared dark. The faces on the paintings were austere and, if her mind were allowed to run rampant, frightening.

She hurried to the sofa where she had left her book.

It wasn't there.

She frowned.

She turned to look on the other side of the room. That's when she saw him, standing in the corner. Andrew.

"Merciful heavens!" Cecily hissed, drawing her breath and trying to calm her nerves at the shock of seeing a person where he should not be. "What are you doing, lurking about in the shadows? You gave me a fright!"

But he did not respond. He only looked at her, the whites of his eyes shining bright in the shadows, his expression somber, opposite of the jovial, carefree façade he had displayed during dinner just hours ago.

He stepped away from the wall, and the moonlight through the window illuminated his hair, which fell carelessly over his forehead. He looked tired. Older. The pale light caught on the crystal glass in his hand. He spoke, his voice barely above a whisper. "I looked for you."

At his words, her breathing slowed.

She tightened her grip on the candle lamp.

He straightened before taking another step toward her. "I looked for you. Everywhere."

As he drew closer, her throat began to tighten. He carried with him a sharp scent of brandy. She inched backward until the wall prevented her from moving farther.

How long had she dreamed about just one more moment alone with Andrew?

But this was not how she imagined it. Not at all.

He was different.

She was different.

She swallowed, trying to calculate the smartest course.

He probably knew the answer to so many of the questions that had plagued her over the past several years, or at least, he could point her in the right direction for the information she sought. But the look in his eyes gave her reason to pause. "Perhaps we should speak in the morning, Mr. Moreton. I fear you are under the influence of drink."

"Call me Andrew." His words slid through gritted teeth. "Can you not give me that at least? Or are we destined to interactions laced with false propriety and empty greetings?"

She was torn between her desire to comply with decorum and her yearning to hear what he had to say. Her heart had let him go long ago. But that did not change the fact that he might have answers that she needed. About her father. About her sister. "Very well. *Andrew.* But perhaps tomorrow, or another—"

"No." His sharp response silenced her. "I want to speak now. I have waited for years. I will not be put off another day."

As his words sank in, her heart pounded harder. Surely he could hear it. He'd been thinking of her?

"So, you went to a girls' school," he said casually, as if resuming a conversation in progress.

"Yes. My father took me there that night."

She was hesitant to give too much away. She had protected her secrets for too long to risk any kind of exposure—even to him.

"And where is your father now?" he asked.

"I was hoping you would be able to tell me. I have had no contact with them these five years."

Andrew shrugged. "That next day your father paid a visit to my father, and it did not go well. It resulted in your father's termination with no reference. My father was so angry he sent me to live here with my aunt. I have no idea where your father is."

"Do you know where my sister is?"

"No."

The single word sliced at her hope. She eyed him. She had not seen an intoxicated man since her father, but how vividly she could recall the signs. The red-rimmed eyes. The lackluster expression.

His words slurred into each other. "And now, here we are."

Fear gripped her. For Andrew did not like to be told no. He was a person used to getting his way. That much she could recall with pinpoint accuracy. "I should go."

He stepped toward her, touched her arm. "Don't."

But alarm kept her frozen in place. Heat radiated from his hand. "You are engaged, Andrew."

"In all actuality, are *we* not still engaged? I fail to recall either one of us calling an end to it."

She pulled her arm free. "It was broken that night. We were young. Too young for such a decision."

His voice hardened. "So, am I to believe you have no regrets? That you have not wondered how things would be different?"

She jutted her chin in the air, refusing to waver. "Our decision sent us each down different paths. I am no longer the same person I was. I daresay you are not either."

He pinned her with his stare. "It's not too late."

"Yes, it is." She sucked in a breath. "If my presence at Willowgrove is an issue for you, please say as much. I cannot afford to lose this position, Andrew."

But then a door creaked at the end of the hall. Cecily stiffened. She had felt this same way that night her father discovered their plan.

Boots clicked.

A door opened and shut.

She flinched, fearful of getting caught in a situation that could look suspect, but Andrew snapped to action. He simply locked eyes with her, put his finger to his lips, and began walking through the chamber to the great hall.

Cecily was stunned at the similarity of the past. For once again, Andrew left her to deal with an impossible situation. Yet this time she felt none of the joy in his presence that she had all those years ago. Instead, she felt dread.

As Andrew's footsteps faded, the others drew near. She was not familiar enough with the layout of the ground floor to follow Andrew. It was a maze, with doors, nooks, and corridors that led to places Cecily had not yet explored.

She gripped her candle lamp in one hand and swallowed her fear. She had done nothing wrong. She had simply encountered another person within the halls. She spied her book on the small side table. She snatched it up, pushed her shoulders back, and prepared to step out into the corridor.

But when she did, she was facing none other than Mr. Stanton.

Miss Faire looked as pale as a ghost, her eyes wide. One thing was becoming clear: She could not hide her emotions behind her facial expression. She had a white-knuckled grip on her candle lamp, a book clutched to her chest, and her cheeks flushed pink.

"Miss Faire!"

She lifted her book. "I'm afraid I left this in the blue drawing room earlier today, and since Mrs. Trent has already retired for the evening, I thought I would read."

"I've no wish to bother you. I was working in my office and heard voices." He looked over her shoulder. He really should not press this issue, but he was curious. "Was there someone else here with you, or am I imagining it?"

At this, she bit her lower lip, but her eyes remained fixed on him. "I encountered Mr. Moreton in the corridor. Surely that is whose voice you heard."

At Moreton's name, his stomach sank. He cared not for the thought of Moreton alone with Miss Faire, even for something as simple as passing in a corridor.

The candle lamp in her hand cast shadows on the hollow of her neck. She brushed a lock of hair from her face. "It seems terribly late to still be working, Mr. Stanton."

He shrugged. "I often work late. It is the benefit, I suppose, of living so close. I haven't far to go once I complete my tasks."

She drummed her fingers on the cover of her book. "Well, I shall leave you to your duties, then, sir. Good night."

Miss Faire gave a shallow curtsey.

He stepped closer to stop her. "Forgive me, Miss Faire, but during dinner at Laurel Cottage, you mentioned that you grew up on Aradelle's property."

"That is correct."

"I am curious. Were you aware that Mrs. Trent had connections at Aradelle?"

She shook her head, eyes innocent. "Do you mean Mr. Moreton?"

He nodded.

Miss Faire released a breath. "No, I did not. And if I had ever known that bit of information, I had long forgotten it. I have been away from Aradelle for many years. I had never heard the name Trent before it was mentioned to me at Rosemere. Why do you ask?"

"No particular reason. Like I said, merely curious." He smiled, trying to put her at ease, but he could not erase the words that Moreton had spoken of her the day she arrived at Willowgrove. "Were you well acquainted with the Moreton family?"

Her grip on the candle seemed to loosen, and she lowered her book to her side. "Well, my father was employed by the estate, but his interactions with the Moretons themselves were limited. He was the blacksmith there for many years."

He was surprised. The daughter of a blacksmith seemed hardly the most suitable choice for a lady's companion, of all things. And yet, what did it matter? She was withholding something from him. He could sense it. His sister's words came to mind of how upset Miss Faire had become at seeing Andrew.

He would not press her, for time had a way of making all known, as he well knew. He could not help but notice how different this interaction was from those with Mrs. Massey. Whereas he could not wait to free himself from Mrs. Massey, he could not tear himself away from Miss Faire. He nodded toward her book. "What are you reading, if I may ask?"

"It is the book of Proverbs, given to me by the headmistress at Rosemere."

He looked at the volume. "My father used to read often from Proverbs. And do you have a favorite?"

She pressed her lips together. "I am not sure I do."

Sensing her hesitation on the matter, he quickly changed the subject. "Oh, and it is fortunate I encountered you, for I wanted to tell you that I did indeed write to my colleague, Mr. McGovern, and asked for advice on how to start looking for your sister."

At this, her eyes lit up, the sight a reward in itself.

"I will be traveling to Manchester before too long, and I will make a point to follow up with him on this matter."

"Thank you, Mr. Stanton. That truly is kind of you." She offered a sheepish smile and nodded. "You and your family have been good to me since my arrival. I don't know how I can ever repay you."

"No need to repay me, Miss Faire. I am happy to be of service."

She looked down at the candle lamp, then cast a glance over her shoulder. "I must be going. Good night, Mr. Stanton. And give my best to your family."

"Good night, Miss Faire."

She brushed past him, and he pivoted to watch as she rounded the corner. The diminishing light signaled her retreat, and then he heard her delicate footsteps on the staircase.

Nathaniel had never been in love. Over the years, one or two women had captured his interest, but that had been fleeting, and never with any intensity.

But she had secrets. That fact was written in her every expression, making him consider how trustworthy she may be. But did he not have secrets of his own?

17

The rain continued through the night, and the next morning Cecily awoke with a throbbing in her temples and tightness in her neck. She'd woken once at dawn when a chambermaid came in to tend her fire and couldn't fall back asleep. She pressed her hands to her forehead and drew a deep breath. Her first thought was of Andrew. Their odd interaction in the blue drawing room left her with more questions than answers. But her second thought, of equal intensity, was of Mr. Stanton. And her heart gave a little leap. The kindness in his expression was so different from the wild uncertainty she had found in Andrew's.

A quick glance at her timepiece confirmed the hour was early. With today being the first time she attended church with Mrs. Trent, she did not want to be late.

She rose and rang for Clarkson. She poured some of the icy water from the pitcher to the bowl and washed her face and cleaned her teeth. The lady's maid came in as stoic as ever.

"Which dress will it be, miss?"

Cecily looked at the few gowns hanging in her wardrobe. They all paled in comparison to the dress that Miss Pritchard had worn at dinner. She sighed and pointed to her Sunday dress—a simple yet delicately cut gown of yellow muslin, on which she had embroidered a pattern of light-pink flowers along the neckline. "That one will do."

After helping Cecily dress, Clarkson propped her hands on her hips. "Shall I dress your hair?"

Cecily shook her head. She'd always done her own hair, and she'd been told that the curls made it difficult to arrange. "No, thank you. I can do it myself."

"As you wish. I will go wake Mrs. Trent. She does not care to be rushed on Sunday mornings. She will be ready for you in a few minutes, I am sure."

Cecily paused to view her reflection in the looking glass, then retrieved her comb and dressed her hair. Once the task was complete, she smoothed the satin piping along the bodice of her gown and adjusted a white chemisette at her neck. Moments later the sound of Mrs. Trent's high voice reached her even out in the hall, and she hurried from her chamber.

Mrs. Trent was sitting upright in bed, her sleeping cap tilted to the side, her face pale.

"Good morning, Mrs. Trent. How did you sleep?"

Mrs. Trent waved a dismissive hand in the air. "I never sleep well, child."

Cecily smiled. Each morning the woman responded with the same words.

"Never," Mrs. Trent continued. "Draw those curtains, will you?"

Cecily obeyed, pulling back the long, heavy curtains and allowing the morning's early rays to flood the space. "Would you like to get dressed and take breakfast in the breakfast room?" Cecily asked, sweeping her hair from her face.

"La," the older woman grunted. "No, we will enjoy our breakfast here, in my bedchamber. I will take dinners with them, but breakfast, no."

Cecily poured a cup of tea that had been left by one of the servants, carried it to the bed, and sat next to her. Her heart tugged at the woman's apparent frustration. "Why ever not?"

Mrs. Trent's jowls shook with emphasis. "Because they are vultures, horrid creatures, waiting for me to die so they may have Willowgrove to themselves, to do with as they please."

Cecily straightened, a little shocked by the bluntness. Yet she could not argue. The dinner the previous night had been difficult to endure. Guilt was starting to tug at her. She had a past with Andrew, and yet she kept it a secret from Mrs. Trent. The closer Cecily grew to her, the harder it would be to conceal her past. It felt as if she were lying.

She extended the teacup toward Mrs. Trent. "Here, have some tea. I will have Clarkson bring up some breakfast. Do you care for toast and fruit this morning? I, for one, say you need to stay healthy and strong for a good, long time and beat them at their own game."

The older woman laughed. "You remind me of myself when I was your age. Full of spunk. Twenty-one years of age, you say?"

"Yes, ma'am."

"So much ahead of you. So many exciting adventures to anticipate. I envy you, Miss Faire."

Cecily looked to the window, down to the carefully manicured lawns below. An older man walked along the garden wall, a rake propped over his shoulder, a bucket in his hand. "Is that the gardener?"

The older woman stretched her neck to follow Cecily's gaze. "Yes. 'Tis Silas. Been here since before I married Mr. Trent."

"He must be very skilled to have retained the position for so long."

"I suppose. But that was my husband's way." She accepted the tea with shaking hands and then kept her eyes on Silas as she watched him saunter across the lawn. "When he developed a fondness for someone, he was loyal. Loyal to a fault, I used to tell him. Once he struck a bond or promise, he would never go back on his word. It was a fault he had, and don't you say otherwise."

Cecily frowned. "I do not see how that could be a fault."

Mrs. Trent lifted the teacup to her lips before responding. "I loved my husband. Make no mistake. And would never speak ill of him. But he allowed himself to be swayed, to be taken advantage of."

Cecily stood and poured herself a cup of tea into a delicate teacup and added a lump of sugar. "I suppose I can see how that could happen."

"It *can* happen, Miss Faire, and it did." Mrs. Trent's eyes widened. "He's been gone six years now, and this estate is still darkened by such alliances."

Cecily wondered what Mrs. Trent was inferring, but thought it best not to linger on it. "Fortunately, there is always hope for fresh beginnings."

"When you reach my age, I fear hoping for change diminishes. But I imagine once I die, all will be vastly altered at Willowgrove."

Cecily was not completely sure what Mrs. Trent meant, but she did not like talking about death. It opened up too many questions. She forced a smile. "Well, I think you need to stop with all this talk of death. You are going to live a long time."

Mrs. Trent patted Cecily's hand, as if amused by the idea. "Foolish girl."

"No, in all earnestness!" Cecily said. "Come, it's early. What do you say to a walk in the garden before services?"

The older woman laughed. "My dear child, I haven't been on a walk to the gardens in months."

"Then it is time, is it not? It will be short. The clouds are clearing and the weather is fine, and we will walk down, select some fresh roses for your vase over there, and then return in a quarter of an hour. A beautiful way to greet the morning."

A flush of color tinted the woman's withered cheek. "You may need to help me."

Cecily smiled. "That is why I am here."

"I'll call for Clarkson to help me dress—"

"There is no need for that. I can—"

But the woman's sharp words cut her off. "No. Clarkson dresses me."

The woman's tone changed in an instant.

Cecily nodded. She stepped away from the wardrobe, feeling like a scolded child, and pulled the bell cord. She lowered her hands to her sides. She was quickly learning that Mrs. Trent was very particular about certain things, and her dressing routine was one of them.

Within moments Clarkson was at the door. Cecily stood by as the lady's maid quickly set the woman's stays and arranged her petticoats and gown. She adjusted her fichu just so, applied rouge and powder to her face, and dressed her hair in a chignon. She used curling tongs to create unnatural curls in front of each ear.

When Clarkson was done, she reached for a shawl and draped it around Mrs. Trent's shoulders. Cecily gathered a basket for flower clippings and cupped Mrs. Trent's elbow to begin their journey out of the bedchamber. It was then she was reminded of the extent of Mrs. Trent's afflictions. The woman had great difficulty descending the staircase, and they paused for her to rest in a chair in the great hall before venturing out of doors. The elderly woman's breathing was labored, and beads of perspiration dotted her brow. Cecily questioned the wisdom of continuing, but instead of growing discouraged, Mrs. Trent seemed to be more determined—a trait Cecily could not help but admire.

The morning's sun sliced through the shifting clouds and slanted across the expansive lawn. "I haven't been outside at this hour in so long," Mrs. Trent said.

A crisp breeze swept over the manicured grounds, bringing with it the scent of damp earth and the suggestion of more rain to come. All around them, aspens and birches were budding in vibrant shades of green and white, and despite the standing water visible on various sections of the grounds, the lawns boasted brilliant shades of emerald and jade.

"It is a beautiful time of morning." Cecily drew a deep breath. "Over the last couple of years, I have taken to walking on the moors at dawn. Of course, that was quite a different landscape, but this walk is very pleasant. Very peaceful."

"And do you plan to continue your morning walks now that you are at Willowgrove?"

"If you will join me."

Mrs. Trent laughed. "Oh, Miss Faire, I do believe you are medicine for my soul. Better than Dr. Collingswood and his elixirs and tonics."

"And who, pray tell, is Dr. Collingswood?"

"You have yet to make his acquaintance. He is my physician. He is a frequent guest at Willowgrove and shall arrive in a day or so. One of the few friends who has remained loyal to me since my husband's passing."

The women walked arm in arm in comfortable silence to a garden gate, adorned with intricately woven vines of honeysuckle. Servants were bustling about the yard, tending to their tasks, and a stable boy was leading a horse down the path.

"It pains me to see the water. Shameful. I do wish Mr. Stanton would hurry with the repairs." The older woman's voice shook. Cecily paused to soak in the beauty around her, but Mrs. Trent seemed intent upon focusing on the negative.

"I am sure he is doing his best. I would imagine such things take time."

"You are kind, Miss Faire, to give him such credit, but you will soon learn that he is not as capable as you may think. Here"—Mrs. Trent pointed to the walled garden—"let's walk in here."

The iron gate creaked and groaned with the effort as Cecily pushed against it. But once inside, Cecily nearly gasped at the sight she beheld. Hundreds of spring blooms of scarlet and violet met her in each direction she looked. They cascaded over the walls. The intoxicating scent of roses teased her, transporting her back to happy childhood times with her mother in their own modest garden.

Cecily followed Mrs. Trent farther into the garden. Mrs. Trent's steps were slow and labored, and she leaned heavily on her cane in order to reach a rose petal with her trembling hand. "My husband had this garden planted for me my first spring here. And so it continues even after his death, as enchanting as it ever was."

Cecily kept her tone light. "How thoughtful."

"Yes, he always saw to it that roses were in my rooms. Those days are long ago."

Cecily lifted the scissors from the basket they had brought with them. "Well then, we must see to it that you still enjoy them. Which roses do you fancy?"

The woman looked around her before pointing her unsteady finger in the direction of a tall, climbing bush with vibrant crimson roses just starting to bud on their stems. "Those."

Cecily clipped several roses, careful to avoid thorns and to remove excess leaves from the stems. After she had gathered enough for a bouquet, she placed them in the basket and turned. "There, that should do."

A smile tugged at Mrs. Trent's lips—sheepish and distant. It was a true glimpse into the older woman's heart.

They walked back through the garden gate to the south lawn,

and before long, Cecily spied Mr. Stanton walking across the property, toward the tradesmen's entrance. When he noticed them, he paused and tipped his hat. Cecily smiled and nodded back, but Mrs. Trent's expression, which moments before had been soft and vulnerable, became stern.

Cecily continued to watch him cross the lawn, dressed every bit as the gentleman in gray breeches tucked into black riding boots, a gray frock coat, and a beaver hat, which was quite a change from the wide-brimmed hat she had grown so accustomed to seeing him in. He seemed so young to manage such an estate, but as he paused to speak to a footman, the respect he garnered was evident.

She must have slowed her pace, for Mrs. Trent gave her arm a nudge. "Is it Mr. Stanton you are watching?" Mrs. Trent gave a little snort. "You may as well grow accustomed to his presence, for you will find that Mr. Stanton is always present, whether he is welcome or not."

Cecily held her arm steady as Mrs. Trent struggled to approach the stairs at Willowgrove's entrance. Her confidence was growing. The majority of her interactions with Mrs. Trent had been pleasant, so perhaps she could take this time to get to know her a bit more. "I still do not understand why you dislike him so. He has always seemed congenial."

At the top of the stone stairs, Mrs. Trent turned to Cecily and met her gaze directly. "I am sure that I will be the first to tell you that things—and people—are not always as they seem. You have not been at Willowgrove long, Miss Faire. There are secrets within these walls, ghosts locked behind the doors. You need not know my reasons. Just heed my words." She paused and tipped her cane in Cecily's direction. "I caution you. Do not be fooled by his dashing smile, child."

The intensity of her stare sent an immediate rush of heat to Cecily's cheeks. "I was not, er, that is, I did not intend—"

But Mrs. Trent's glare silenced her. "Do not think that I do not remember what it was like to be young. Oh yes, it was a long time ago, and I do forget a great many things. But that I do not forget." Her expression sobered. "You are a bright, beautiful young woman, Miss Faire. You are destined for things greater than the likes of a man such as Mr. Stanton. Set your sights on higher ground."

She looked out again to Mr. Stanton, who was closer to them now.

Perhaps Mrs. Trent would think differently if she knew of Cecily's own secrets, for she imagined they could rival any of those lurking within Willowgrove's halls.

As he drew closer, his profile became more focused. The breeze lifted the edge of his coat. His strong jawline was set in determination, silhouetted in the morning sun. The memory of how he looked when he stepped from the tree line haunted her. It was as if he were stepping from a fairy tale.

It was then that Mr. Stanton noticed them. His pace slowed and he gave a short bow.

Cecily nodded in return, but Mrs. Trent only took Cecily's arm and repeated herself. "Do not be swayed, Miss Faire. Mark my words, you will be disappointed." Mrs. Trent put one shaky foot in front of the other and leaned her weight against her cane. "I have known Mr. Stanton since the day he was born."

Cecily didn't know why this statement should surprise her so. She knew the family had been connected with the property for generations, but the thought of Mr. Stanton as a boy seemed odd. He was quite self-assured for one so young.

"His mother was a trusted servant of mine. She was my lady's maid, prior to Clarkson, and had been for quite some time."

Cecily took short steps to keep pace with the older woman. It didn't make sense. Had she not said that her husband had been a loyal employer, not one to part ways with trusted staff members? "But I don't understand. I thought—"

"Like Mr. Stanton said yesterday, we all have our secrets. If you are at Willowgrove Hall long enough, I am sure you will learn them, just as others have before you."

They approached the threshold to reenter Willowgrove, and Mrs. Trent lifted her hand. "Come here, Lorna. Give me your arm."

Cecily did as she was bid, but as soon as she was assured Mrs. Trent was steady, she corrected her. "Cecily."

"What?"

"My Christian name is Cecily. You called me Lorna."

Mrs. Trent's eyes narrowed and her voice heightened. "I most certainly did not!"

Not wishing to upset her, Cecily held her tongue and continued walking. But in that slight moment, something seemed amiss. The older woman's expression slipped from quiet confidence, to confusion, to almost fear. "Where is my green pendant?"

Cecily frowned. "Your green pendant?"

"Yes, now do not cross me, Lorna." The tone of her trembling voice grew almost desperate. "Where is it?"

Cecily shook her head. "I think you are mistaken, Mrs. Trent. I am Miss Faire. Cecily Faire."

"Hold your tongue, Lorna. You took it again, didn't you?"

The look in the older woman's eyes gave Cecily reason to pause. "I am sorry, Mrs. Trent. I do not know what you are speaking of."

The stood together a few moments, and then Mrs. Trent put her hand to her forehead. "Is it Sunday? What are we doing out here? We should be preparing for services."

"You are right." Cecily stepped aside to give the woman room, but could not prevent her eyebrows from drawing together in concern. This was unusual, even for Mrs. Trent's eccentric mannerisms. She looped her arm thorugh Mrs. Trent's. "Come, I will take you back upstairs, and we will prepare to depart for the church."

18

When it was time to depart for church, the clouds had gathered in the pewter sky. Cecily had been correct when she thought she detected the scent of rain earlier. Looming storm clouds replaced the morning's wispier ones, and a sharp wind swept down from the gables and cut through the thin fabric of her muslin gown.

Mrs. Trent must have noticed Cecily looking upward. "The weather changes quickly in this part of the country. You will grow accustomed to it."

Cecily wanted to remind the woman that she had lived on the moors for many years, as they had discussed at length several times, but instead, she took Mrs. Trent's arm as they descended the stone steps. Cecily did not want to upset her. Not again.

She lifted her hand to still the satin ribbons on her bonnet, and as she did, she noticed a tall man walking toward them. At first her heart clenched for fear it was Andrew, but then she breathed a sigh of relief when she realized it was only a footman.

Even though she was told that the church was not so very far from Willowgrove, they were to take the carriage. That fact alone ushered in another fear—that of sharing a carriage with Andrew, especially after their odd interaction the night before. But when a second carriage arrived, pulled by two matching bays, her tension dissipated.

Cecily and Mrs. Trent rode to the church in the second carriage. Cecily watched in earnest as the scenery quickly changed from that of flooded countryside to the bustling town of Wiltonshire. She had been at Willowgrove for several days, and now that she was growing used to her new home, her curiosity of what lay beyond was also growing.

After a short ride, the coach door unlatched and creaked open. But it was not the coachman who assisted them down, but Andrew.

He assisted Mrs. Trent first, not looking in Cecily's direction.

He saw Mrs. Trent safely to the ground, then handed her the cane. Next he extended a gloved hand to help Cecily down.

Cecily glimpsed his hand, hesitating.

A calm and easy smile was on his lips. "Good day, Miss Faire." His words were too direct. Too intimate. "I trust you slept well?"

He held her gaze, refusing to look away.

She felt dizzy. Sick. The words were difficult to form. "Very well, thank you."

Against her better judgment, she placed her gloved hand in his and stepped down. She would not look at him. As the sole of her kid boot landed on the soft earth, he squeezed her hand.

At the subtle pressure, she pulled her hand free and stepped away to Mrs. Trent.

She did not want to think about how warm his hand was—and how the touch unlocked a slew of memories, all rushing forth, demanding to be noticed.

But he was not the Andrew she once knew, she promptly reminded herself. And she was not the girl she had been.

And as the breeze brushed her face and cooled her, she caught a glimpse of him looping Miss Pritchard's arm through his own.

It disgusted her.

And now he looked adoringly at his intended, smiling and laughing.

She swallowed and put one step in front of the other. In truth, she felt pity for the beautiful Miss Pritchard. She likely was unaware of the true nature of the man she was to marry.

As they approached the church, Cecily forced the incident to the back of her mind and focused on her new surroundings. The influx of new faces intrigued her. The parish was much larger than the one in Darbury—the church, much grander. The familiar sound of bells pealed in the late-morning air. She could feel the eyes of curious parishioners and kept her face lowered. But then she noticed young Charlotte Stanton and looked past her to the other ladies of the Stanton family coming down the path.

Upon seeing Cecily, Hannah pointed at her, gave a little hop, and waved. Her sisters followed suit.

How comforting it was to see familiar faces, even those of people whom she'd known mere days. She genuinely wanted to talk with her new friends, especially Rebecca. She missed having another woman her own age to converse with.

She walked along with Mrs. Trent to the front of the church.

"Here is our pew, Miss Faire."

Remembering her purpose, she drew closer to Mrs. Trent and then helped her with her coat. "Are you warm enough?" Despite the colored light filtering through the intricate glass windows, it was cool inside the stone walls.

Cecily settled on the padded pew next to the old woman. Andrew's voice filled the space behind her, and she drew a deep breath and employed every ounce of self-control to not look in his direction.

Movement by the door captured her attention, and Mr. Stanton entered. He swept his hat from his head, his jet-black hair tousled by the motion. He shook hands with a man to his left and then headed to where his sisters and mother were seated. But on his way, he paused to greet a family. She recognized the man as Mr. Turner, but he was seated next to a pretty woman Cecily had not yet met. Mr. Stanton smiled warmly at the woman and bowed slightly. A strange flutter ached in Cecily's chest, and she looked down at her folded hands in her lap. Why should she be so affected by his smiling at a woman?

The vicar, a thin, wiry man, began speaking to the gathered congregation. Cecily attempted to focus on his words, but after several minutes, she felt movement at her shoulder. Mrs. Trent's eyes were closed, and her white head bobbed slightly with each breath she took. Cecily looked over her shoulder to see if anyone had noticed, and her eyes met Andrew's immediately. She snapped her head back around.

The service passed quickly, and when the patrons began to rise to exit the church, Cecily patted Mrs. Trent's hand. "It's time to leave, Mrs. Trent."

Mrs. Trent awoke with a start, her dark eyes wide.

Cecily helped the woman up from the pew and held her arm as they shuffled out. Mrs. Trent's movements seemed unusually slow and labored, and Cecily hoped this morning's walk hadn't taxed the woman too much.

At the door, the vicar greeted Mrs. Trent with a broad smile and clapped his hand over hers with stark familiarity.

"Mrs. Trent, how pleasant to see you back in the country. How long have you been at Willowgrove?"

"I just returned, and to a most pleasant surprise." Her voice was thin and shaky, and yet her eyes lit up with rare enthusiasm. "For here is my new companion, Miss Cecily Faire."

The elderly man turned, and a kind smile creased his cheeks. He was the sort of man of whom his age was impossible to guess. For even though small lines creased at the corners of his eyes when he smiled, his voice sounded youthful and bright. He gave a slight bow and smiled. "Welcome to our parish, Miss Faire."

Cecily gave a curtsey. "Thank you."

Sensing people behind her waiting to exit the church, she stepped out into the morning. She lifted her hand to brush the lock of hair that had pulled loose from her chignon and was blowing in the cool spring wind.

Mrs. Trent climbed into the carriage, but Cecily noticed Rebecca Stanton approaching. Cecily settled Mrs. Trent, then turned.

Rebecca's smile was kind and warm, her cheeks as rosy as the gown she wore. "How are you finding life at Willowgrove, Miss Faire?"

"Very well, thank you. Your brother informs me that congratulations are in order."

Rebecca's dark eyes lit. "Yes, thank you. I am so very pleased."

"Oh, I think it is wonderful news. I am so happy for you."

Rebecca reached out and touched Cecily's arm, her expression earnest. "Please, do stop by the cottage when you can. We would love the company."

"I should like that very much. Mrs. Trent retires early. Perhaps one day I will call in the evening."

"That would be lovely. We should look forward to it." She glanced over her shoulder at her sisters and mother speaking with another woman and then turned back to Cecily. "I must go. But do not forget your promise to call!"

She gave a slight curtsey before returning to her family, and Cecily climbed into the carriage.

"With whom were you speaking?"

Mrs. Trent's tone was cool. Cecily tensed. Rebecca's assessment of Mrs. Trent flashed in her mind. "Miss Rebecca Stanton."

"Nathaniel Stanton's half sister."

Cecily winced. *Half sister?* Cecily bit her lower lip and looked at her own gloved hands in her lap. Could Mrs. Trent be speaking the truth? Mrs. Trent's tendency to repeat herself and confuse facts gave Cecily reason to doubt.

She reminded herself that this was not her business, but so many things about her new surroundings were not what they seemed—or what she expected. She glanced out the carriage window. Rain was starting to fall, and through the raindrops, she saw Mr. Stanton. Tall. Strong. Handsome. It could be her imagination, but so many of the mysteries she encountered seemed to have something to do with him. For the sake of curiosity, she determined to keep an eye on Mr. Stanton.

19

The next day was Monday, the day Cecily had anticipated since her first evening at the estate.

Today Mrs. Olivia Massey, the local seamstress, was coming to fit her for new gowns. With the exception of the ensemble that Mrs. Sterling had given her, it had been almost a year since she had a new gown, and hers—with their subtle patches and slight discoloring—were showing their wear. In her mind, new clothes would make her transition to her new life complete.

Cecily sat at the window in Mrs. Trent's bedchamber, elbow propped on the sill, watching the grounds below. A lazy rain floated down in gusty mists and a dying fire in the grate kept the air's slight chill at bay. Behind her, Mrs. Trent napped on the chaise lounge, her breath coming in soft snores. Mrs. Massey was supposed to arrive early in the afternoon. Cecily glanced at the mantel clock . . . again. A quarter after one.

The change in activity was just what Cecily's mind needed. Most of their hours were spent in Mrs. Trent's bedchamber sipping tea and reading or in the blue drawing room below, where Cecily would embroider. She was growing desperate for diversion and for new conversations.

At breakfast, Mrs. Trent had spoken of little else besides Mrs. Massey's arrival. "She is a wonderful woman but does not have the means to keep a carriage," she had pointed out. Mrs. Trent had already shared a great deal of information about their visitor—she was clever and always brought interesting news of town life. She'd been married but a short time before her husband died, and Mrs. Trent thought she was entirely too friendly with the Stanton family.

When the sound of carriage wheels and a shout pulled her from her thoughts, Cecily's posture straightened. A black carriage approached from the back entrance.

Cecily jumped from her spot, hurried over to the sleeping woman, and tapped her shoulder. "Mrs. Trent? Mrs. Trent! Mrs. Massey is arriving."

Cecily stepped back to give the woman room and waited as she awoke.

Mrs. Trent sat up and reached for her cane with an unsteady hand, lively and happy as Cecily had ever seen her. "Oh, good."

Cecily helped her stand up and adjust her gown and patted her hair into place. "I cannot wait to make her acquaintance. After your glowing review I know I shall adore her."

"She is one of the loveliest people I know. She has made all of my dresses for years now, and before that, her mother made my gowns. She is as close as a member of the family. Well, closer than any member of the family, that is to say. Her mother was a very dear friend of mine before she died, perhaps the only other woman I counted a friend in the entire county. Mrs. Massey and her mother and I passed many a lovely afternoon sewing and talking together."

Cecily had to smile at Mrs. Trent's enthusiasm. "How fortunate to have someone whose companionship you enjoy live close by."

"Yes. Even though her mother has been dead several years now, Mrs. Massey has not forgotten her old friend. In fact, since her mother's death, we have grown closer. I quite think of her as a daughter. But let's not dwell on that. I hear her now."

The sound of a sweet and melodic voice echoed from the hall.

Cecily drew a deep breath, smiled, and waited for Mrs. Massey to enter.

Clarkson entered first, carrying two leather satchels, and hurried to put them down in Mrs. Trent's dressing room, which was just off the main bedchamber.

And then Mrs. Massey entered. She practically floated into the room.

She was every bit as breathtaking as Cecily could have imagined. In fact, Cecily was unsure if she'd ever seen anyone quite so elegant—not even Andrew's intended. Mrs. Massey's hair was the color of jet, straight and glossy, parted on the side and pulled in elegant twists and interwoven with pink ribbons on the back of her head. Her flushed cheeks highlighted her bright eyes. Even though Cecily had read in novels of ladies with violet eyes, she had never actually seen one. Even for the afternoon, her gown was elegant and flattered her small figure. The crepe fabric was the color of the bluebells in spring, embroidered with dainty white flowers and with beads of white and blue embellishing the bodice.

Mrs. Massey brushed past Cecily to get to Mrs. Trent.

"Dear Mrs. Trent!" she said. "I must say I have been looking forward to this visit since the moment your invitation arrived."

Mrs. Trent reached out to embrace the woman in a loose hug. "Dear child, you were not at church yesterday. I had a notion to send Clarkson to inquire after whether you had fallen prey to an illness."

Mrs. Massey took Mrs. Trent's hands in her own gloved ones and kissed her withered cheek. "You are so kind to concern yourself with me. I had the sniffles, nothing more." She then turned to Cecily.

Cecily straightened under the scrutiny and smoothed the blue dress she had chosen for the day, and despite the new satin sash under her bodice and a newer white fichu, she was acutely aware of its worn state, especially in comparison to Mrs. Massey's finely cut gown. She brushed her hair from her face, feeling quite like a doll on display.

She was grateful that Mrs. Massey spoke first. "And this must be the Miss Faire I have heard so much about."

Mrs. Massey strode forward confidently, as if she owned every stone in Willowgrove's walls. "Why, you are as lovely as I've heard. Look at that complexion! I daresay you will turn every head in our quiet Wiltonshire, and I am honored to be the one to make gowns for you. I shall endeavor to do your loveliness justice."

Mrs. Massey circled Cecily, placed both hands on Cecily's shoulders, ushered her into the dressing room, and pivoted her toward the looking glass. "Now, shall we tend to the task at hand?"

Cecily felt odd staring at herself in the broad mirror, and even odder that Mrs. Massey was doing the same.

Mrs. Massey tapped her fingers to her lips. "Ah, look at that stunning hair. Look at the way it glimmers when the light hits it. See?"

Mrs. Trent tapped the crimson rug with her cane. "Did Clarkson not tell you that you would think her lovely? And she will be much improved with proper attire."

Mrs. Massey paused her assessment, lifted Cecily's arm, and touched the embroidery on Cecily's sleeve. "But look at this embroidery!" She appeared shocked. "Do you not see how lovely it is, Mrs. Trent? How even the stitches are? Whoever did this?"

Cecily felt sheepish under the praise, but at the same time, proud that someone had noticed. "It is by my hand."

Mrs. Massey's hands fell to her sides and her eyes widened in apparent disbelief. "No!"

Cecily nodded, feeling heat color her cheeks. "My mother was a seamstress. She taught myself and my sister when we were both young."

"Well then," Mrs. Massey exclaimed, "that is something we have in common. I had a feeling we would be friends, and see, we share a similar passion."

Cecily warmed under the praise and grew giddy and interested as Mrs. Massey turned to pull out some fabric swatches from the bag. She held up a lovely piece of green silk. "I have heard reports that your hair was of the loveliest titian hue, and at once I knew that this would be perfect. And see? See how it makes your eyes shine like emeralds?"

Cecily was confident that no one had ever compared her eyes to emeralds before, but before she could say anything, Mrs. Massey held up a piece of coral muslin.

"Ah, lovely."

Cecily picked up a piece of rust sarcenet from the pile. "Mrs. Trent, this color would look lovely on you."

At Cecily's words, the room seemed to chill. Mrs. Trent and Mrs. Massey exchanged glances, and Mrs. Massey took the fabric swatch from Cecily and ran it through her long fingers. "Mrs. Trent only wears black now."

Cecily pressed her lips together and turned back to the looking glass. How could she have been so thoughtless? She thought of Mrs. Trent and how sad she still was over the loss of her husband. Of course she wore only black.

Mrs. Massey shifted the conversation. "I think that this peach sprigged muslin will do perfectly for the ball, perhaps with the white net overlay. I shall have to hurry if I am to have new gowns to you by next week's end."

Mrs. Trent leaned forward, the confused expression on her face matching Cecily's own confusion. "What ball? I've heard of no such plans."

Mrs. Massey tilted her head to the side, surprised. "The private ball the Turners are holding to celebrate the engagement of their son to Rebecca Stanton. I suppose it is really more of a country dance, nothing as grand as the balls you are accustomed to attending, Mrs. Trent. Still, it is quite a reason for excitement in town. Were you not aware?"

Mrs. Trent tilted her nose to the air. "Humph. Why would I be aware of that sort of celebration? I hardly concern myself with such matters."

"Come now." Mrs. Massey turned and smiled, her voice sounding almost like one would use to talk to a child. "This is Mr. Stanton's sister. The eldest. Surely after all these years you would feel a little interest. The Stantons have long been a part of Willowgrove. Certainly you must be pleased at this news."

Cecily tried to press her lips together to keep her mouth from falling open. Not since she arrived had she heard someone speak so freely to Mrs. Trent. Not even Mr. Stanton or Clarkson. But there seemed to be a bond between Mrs. Trent and Mrs. Massey, a trust.

Mrs. Trent shook her head. "You know my sentiments about the Stantons."

"Yes, but you cannot deny that this is an occasion worth celebrating. And with all of the rain and dreary days, we could use a little bit of a celebration, could we not?" She lowered the fabric in her hands. "You will not attend?"

Mrs. Trent jerked her head, her expression incredulous. "Of course I will not attend. The idea! I do not understand your softness toward the Stantons, Mrs. Massey." She then looked directly at Cecily. "Several times I have tried to advise Mrs. Massey against forming such alliances, and yet she heeds me not."

"But surely you will allow Miss Faire to attend?" Mrs. Massey said. "Imagine what a message that would portray, for the Stantons are among the most respected families here in Wiltonshire."

Mrs. Trent extended a shaky finger to touch a piece of pink

brocade lying on the bed. "Miss Faire may make her own decisions. But I, for one, cannot understand why either of you would have any interest in attending such a gathering."

Mrs. Massey raised her eyebrows in triumph and turned to Cecily. "What do you say, Miss Faire? As for me, I am of a particular situation, being unmarried and unengaged. It is entirely poor form of me to attend events alone, but I will not miss such a celebration. Will you attend with me? I know the Stanton family well, and they will not mind my extending an invitation, especially since I know they think so highly of you."

At the words "I know the Stanton family well," Cecily felt a queer jump in her stomach. But at the idea of a ball, a real ball, a thrill of excitement swept over Cecily. For years at Rosemere she had practiced dances, but she had never actually attended a ball or even danced with a man, except for George, the old caretaker at the school, whom they occasionally would talk into taking the gentleman's part for the sake of practice.

Cecily cast a glance over to Mrs. Trent for her reaction because, like it or not, it was really up to Mrs. Trent to give her permission to do such a thing.

"I can see in your expression that you want to attend." Mrs. Trent's tone remained hard.

Cecily found her courage. "It would be nice to meet some of the local people."

"Of course," cried Mrs. Massey. "And as my guest, I would make sure she associated with only respectable people. You have my word, Mrs. Trent."

Mrs. Trent waved a dismissive hand. "The decision rests with Miss Faire."

Cecily tried to ignore the scowl on Mrs. Trent's face and turned to Mrs. Massey, her hands clasped before her. "That is kind of you. I would be delighted to accept the invitation."

Mrs. Massey giggled. "We shall have a lovely time. You will see." She held the peach fabric up to Cecily's chin. "Do you care for this selection?"

Cecily looked at her reflection in the mirror. "It is beautiful."

"I am sure this will catch every young man's eye, Miss Faire." Mrs. Massey's words were soft. "But I suppose you are accustomed to that."

Cecily remained quiet, only studied her reflection.

"Never you fear, Miss Faire. I shall make it my mission to find you a suitable partner, just you wait and see."

Nathaniel heard her before he saw her.

"Mr. Stanton! Mr. Stanton!"

Most women Nathaniel knew would never dare call to a man from across the lawn.

But Mrs. Massey was not most women.

He stopped mid-track. He had been on his way to the stable and did not want to take the time to stop. But she was looking at him so intently, and after his questionable behavior the night of her visit, he felt it only polite.

"Mr. Stanton," she continued, stepping away from the carriage and walking his direction. "I was hoping we would have a moment to speak."

Nathaniel adjusted his direction and met her halfway. He gave a slight bow.

She curtseyed. "I am so excited to hear about the ball the Turners are hosting in honor of your sister's engagement. Rebecca told me of the plans for the festivities, and I have not been able to close my eyes in sleep for the excitement of it."

"Yes, we are all pleased." His words were controlled. Proper.

"I have just come from meeting Miss Faire, and my goodness, everyone is correct. She is one of the most charming ladies I have ever encountered. I have some lovely emerald silk I wish to fashion into a gown for her. I hope I did not overstep my boundaries, but I invited Miss Faire to attend the celebration as my guest. I-I hope that is all right."

She looked at him slyly from the corner of her eye.

Mrs. Massey was not a woman who was normally so forthcoming with praise, especially for another woman.

"I do not think Mrs. Trent would allow her to attend," he said. "You know how closely Mrs. Trent guards her companions."

"Oh, tosh." Mrs. Massey waved her delicate, gloved hand in the air. "I have spoken with Mrs. Trent and have already secured her permission."

Nathaniel blinked. "You did?"

Mrs. Massey nodded. "But of course! Mrs. Trent is a reasonable woman. She knows she cannot keep the girl under lock and key." She lowered her eyes and cocked her head to the side. "You shall be in attendance, am I correct?"

"Indeed."

She smiled. Her hand flew to her chest. "Well then, I shall look forward to seeing you there."

Movement over Mrs. Massey's shoulder caught Nathaniel's attention. It was Miss Faire, in her blue gown and a straw bonnet, walking toward the walled south garden.

He'd been hoping to see her. Just that morning he had received a response from his friend in Manchester. It burned in his pocket. He needed to speak with her about it and had been seeking such an opportunity all day. "May I see you to your carriage?" he asked Mrs. Massey. "I must attend to a matter of some urgency. Forgive me."

A frown tugged at her lips, but she quickly recovered. "My, you are terribly busy, Mr. Stanton." She cast a quick glance to see what had caught his attention and then turned back to him, a forced smile on her lips. "I look forward to seeing you at the ball, then."

"The pleasure will be mine."

He helped Mrs. Massey into the carriage, and once it was down the path, he jogged around the corner where Miss Faire had been.

The sun was just now peeking out from the earlier storm clouds. It felt warm on his dark coat and soaked through the wool fabric to the linen shirt beneath. How pleasant it was to finally feel warmth instead of dampness. And his spirits were brighter. At least, they became that way when he saw Miss Faire walking outside.

He caught up with her on the path to the south walled garden.

She turned as he approached, a basket nestled in the crook of her arm. A look of surprise flashed across her face. "Mr. Stanton," she exclaimed, then added a curtsey belatedly.

"Miss Faire. I hope you do not mind the interruption. I was hoping to speak with you."

"You are not interrupting, Mr. Stanton. Mrs. Trent has sent me to gather roses, that is all. She needed some rest after Mrs. Massey's visit, so she is napping now."

He nodded toward the garden. "Might I walk with you a moment?"

"Please do."

Their steps fell together in a natural cadence. A cool breeze swept from the north, fluttering the ribbons beneath Miss Faire's chin. "Mrs. Massey shared with me that you are to attend the ball to celebrate my sister's engagement."

"Yes, that is true. I do hope it is not an intrusion."

"Nothing of the like. Rebecca will be thrilled to hear of it." He hesitated. "I have some news that might be of interest to you. I have heard back from my friend, Mr. McGovern, in Manchester."

Miss Faire stopped abruptly. A vulnerability shadowed her

expression, and she lifted her hand to further shield her eyes from the sun. "What did he say?"

"I wish I had better news for you, but the name was not familiar to him."

Miss Faire's shoulders hunched slightly, and she looked down to the ground. Her bonnet brim now hid her face from him. How the thought that he had brought her any pain stabbed.

She began to walk again toward the garden gate slowly, and his steps fell in time with hers once again. He quickly added, "Do not lose heart, Miss Faire. Mr. McGovern has assured me that he will pass along the request to his colleagues and inform me if he should hear of anything. Mr. McGovern is a powerful man, one who knows how to do the impossible. I've witnessed it myself on several accounts. Have faith."

Miss Faire drew a deep breath and fixed her eyes on the iron garden door ahead. "I knew it would not be easy to find her."

He reminded himself of his plan to not get involved. But the words left his mouth, as if on their own accord. "If I may ask, how is it that you came to be separated?"

At the question, her steps again slowed.

He had overstepped his bounds.

And yet, something about the idea of her taking him into her confidence renewed him. He waited, careful to give her time to prepare her response.

"I was sent to Rosemere under unusual circumstances. I will not bore you with the details, but as a result of being there, I had limited communication with my family, most of whom were not aware of where I had gone."

Her words were so hesitant, so guarded. He could almost feel the bits of pain woven in each word. He wanted to know more. Know everything.

He stayed quiet, allowing her space to continue.

"My sister was among those who were unaware of my departure. In fact, I never even bid her farewell. By the time I was able to make contact, it was too late. She had already left Aradelle, and she left no forwarding information."

"I am sorry for it, Miss Faire. It is terrible to be separated from those we love."

Her smile was forced, but he admired her desire to remain calm. "I cannot help but think of her whenever I am around your dear sisters."

He relaxed his shoulders. For even though his sisters could try his nerves at times, he loved each of them. Very much. He could not imagine being separated from them. "Was your sister older or younger than you?"

A pretty smile lit Miss Faire's face. "We are twins. She is older than me by twelve minutes."

"A twin," he exclaimed. "How remarkable. That should make her easier to find."

"I'm not so certain. When we were young, we did resemble one another, but as we grew older, we took on our own traits. Her hair is lighter, and her eyes have brown in them. At least, that is what I recall."

She stopped when they reached the garden gate. "I do have hope, though, that she is in Manchester, and I do intend to find her."

He wondered if she was aware of how every emotion seemed to render on her face. Because even though her words boasted confidence, the slight arch of her eyebrow hinted at her timidity. Either she was as transparent as glass, or she knew exactly how to play heartstrings. "I will continue to help search for her," he hastened to add.

"Thank you, I would be most grateful."

He opened the garden gate for her. It groaned and hissed as the iron door was moved on its hinges. It would not be proper for him to accompany her inside. Walking with her along the path on the busy estate and under the bright afternoon sun was one thing. Accompanying her into the solitude of the walled garden under the canopy of ash and willow branches was another.

She stopped next to him.

He remained quiet.

"I am fond of Mrs. Trent. She is kind to me, and I enjoy our time together. But I cannot help but notice the manner in which she treats you."

At this he felt the wind leave him. Had Mrs. Trent told her of his secret?

But then Miss Faire smiled in a way that threatened to buckle his knees. "But I did want to tell you that I do not share her opinions. You and your family were kind to me, and I am most grateful."

So she did not know.

He stared at her for a moment, oddly remorseful of that fact. For the first time, he wanted someone to know about it. He didn't want to have to hide anything. Or pretend to be something he was not.

He nodded. "And you are most welcome." He spied an opportunity to steal more time with her. "I know my sisters are most anxious to see you again. And Mrs. Trent retires early. Why do you not come to Laurel Cottage one evening this week? Hannah has been beside herself wondering when you would return. She has been working on her doll's gown and is eager to show you."

"Oh, I would like to see her." She toyed absently with the brightly colored necklace about her neck.

"Then you will visit?"

"Yes, I shall look forward to it. As soon as I can."

"Good, then I will let them know." He gave a short bow, but as she turned to leave, somehow Miss Faire's finger caught on the edge of her necklace. When she turned, it broke, sending the vivid beads in all directions below.

When Miss Faire realized what happened, her face deepened to the color of the roses within the garden, and her eyes grew glassy with tears, making them shine so green they rivaled the leaves on the trees.

A cry escaped her lips. She immediately dropped to the ground and began hunting for the beads in the grass.

"Oh no. Oh no!" she whispered, her fingers trembling as she pushed them through the thick grass.

He immediately dropped to his knees beside her and began to help gather the bright-orange baubles.

Her hands were shaking now, and tears balanced in her eyelashes. "It's my mother's necklace!" She paused her task long enough to wipe her eyes with the backs of her hands.

During his every interaction with Miss Faire, she had been controlled. Poised. Now she was crumbling before him. He couldn't even begin to guess why.

As he helped her gather the beads, he groped for words to bring her solace. "I am sure your mother will understand."

She did not stop her frantic searching. "My mother is dead."

At the words, he froze. How could he be so dull! She had mentioned she was separated from her family. He did not imagine her mother was dead. "I-I apologize."

A single sob shook her shoulders. She spoke as if to herself. "I should never have taken it!"

Not knowing what else to do, he covered her hand with his. It felt warm and soft, and he squeezed it gently to stop the trembling. "Please. Stop. Just for a moment."

Her other hand stopped in midair, and she looked at his hand atop hers before lifting her eyes to meet his. Her eyes and nose were red, her chin trembled. A lock of hair fell forward.

He certainly did not know any details, but whatever story was tied to this necklace was deeply woven within her. He squeezed her hand once more before releasing it. She sat up straighter. "What are you doing?"

Nathaniel retrieved a handkerchief from his pocket. "Here," he said, spreading it open in his hand. "We can use this."

She sniffed and wiped her eyes again.

Together, they worked in silence, retrieving the small beads from the grass, the warm sun providing ample light. He was close to her, closer than he had ever been. He could sense emotion coming from her—a pain that, for whatever reason, was unleashed by the breaking of this simple strand of beads.

Her breathing eventually calmed. "I found the clasp." She sniffed, dropping a silver clasp onto the handkerchief.

He picked up the tiny piece of metal and held it up. "It appears that this part is bent. See?"

She nodded.

"Is that all of them?" he asked.

"I think so. I hope so."

A dozen questions flashed through his mind, but he decided they would be best saved for another time. He stood and extended his free hand to help her up.

She hesitated at first and then placed her hand in his and stood, oblivious to the grass markings on her skirt.

She pressed her lips together and rested her palm on her cheek. "I-I apologize. I am not sure what came over me. I must have been quite the sight."

"Think nothing of it, Miss Faire." He wrapped the handkerchief around itself to secure the beads. "Will you allow me to fix it for you?"

"Oh no. I couldn't."

The sadness in her eyes plagued him. He would do anything, say anything, to get her normal cheerfulness back. "It would be an honor."

She stared at the handkerchief for several seconds. "I would be most grateful."

He tucked the treasured beads into his breast pocket. "Consider it done."

He retrieved her basket and scissors, which had been discarded in the incident, and handed them to her.

She took the basket in her hands. He could not help but notice how they continued to tremble. "Are you certain there is nothing else I can assist you with?"

She finally smiled. "Quite certain."

He gave a short bow. But why was it so hard to leave? The longer she looked at him, the stronger her lure pulled, tightening around his heart. This feeling was new. And he was not sure what to make of it, but he knew one thing—he was becoming increasingly attached to her.

20

Cecily let the door to Mrs. Trent's bedchamber fall closed behind her, and she paused in the corridor with a sigh. She pressed her palms against her cheeks.

What a day this had been. First her girlish excitement at meeting Mrs. Massey and the anticipation of attending her first dance, followed by the panic of breaking her mother's necklace.

But what haunted her with equal frustration was how she had reacted in front of Mr. Stanton.

He must think her ridiculous.

She gave a little groan and slumped her shoulders. She had cried in front of him. And he knew nothing of the significance of the necklace, only that it had been her mother's.

No doubt he thought her a child.

Interactions with Mr. Stanton always left her feeling as if her legs were not strong enough to hold her weight, her breath insufficient to fill her lungs.

To complicate matters, by the time Cecily arrived back at the chamber, Mrs. Trent had acquired a fever. It was not yet even time for the evening meal, and the older woman was already dressed for bed, asleep. But it was not the fact that Mrs. Trent was sleeping that shot yet another shiver of alarm through Cecily. It was the old woman's appearance. Her skin, which was normally pale, was more of a gray color. Instead of being steady, her breathing came in jagged gasps, each one leaving Cecily to wonder if another breath would follow.

As Cecily was about to enter her own chamber, Clarkson turned the corner and nearly ran into Cecily.

"Pardon me, miss," Clarkson stammered. "I did not see you standing there."

Cecily seized the opportunity to learn more. Her nerves were already raw. She did not like feeling as though Mrs. Trent's health was a secret that everyone knew but her. "Forgive me for detaining you, Clarkson, but I must ask. Exactly how ill is Mrs. Trent?"

Clarkson glanced back at the door to Mrs. Trent's bedchamber and balanced the basket she was carrying on her hip with one hand. Cecily thought for a moment that Clarkson was about to brush right past her without responding, but then the lady's maid sighed and focused on her. "Several months ago, Mrs. Trent fell very ill, sick as I have ever seen a person, and she has never really recovered." She gave her head a sharp jerk. "Breaks my heart, it does. I've known Mrs. Trent most of my life, and to see her in such a state pains me to no end."

It surprised Cecily to hear Clarkson share so much. "I had no idea that you had known Mrs. Trent for so long."

"You could say we grew up together, of sorts. I was an upper house maid at her parents' house. After she married the master, she had a falling out with her lady's maid and asked if I would come wait on her. And I have been, for more than twenty years now."

Cecily masked her surprise. She knew that Clarkson had been Mrs. Trent's lady's maid for some time, but it seemed there was a stronger connection than she had suspected. No wonder she had been so insistent on Clarkson dressing her. "Is there anything at all I can do to make her more comfortable?"

Clarkson's voice was barely above a whisper. "No, what she needs now is rest. She gets overtired sometimes, and with her return from Bath, her nephew, and meeting you, I think the excitement of it all has caught up with her."

Cecily could only nod.

"Will there be anything else, Miss Faire?"

"No, Clarkson, that will be all. Thank you."

The older woman curtseyed and turned to move down the corridor, but Cecily reached out her hand in a spontaneous motion to stop the servant. "Wait, there is one more thing I was hoping to ask."

Clarkson stopped and turned, but in the corridor's shadows, it was impossible to distinguish the woman's features. Cecily snatched back her hand as if she had just touched hot coals.

Cecily had little desire to be considered a gossip, but in light of her position at Willowgrove, there were certain things she needed to know. She bit her lip, mustering her courage. "Who is Lorna?"

"Lorna?" Clarkson shot back in a hushed whisper. She stepped closer, close enough that the light through the nearby window illuminated her brown eyes, which were narrowed in pointed interest. "Where did you hear that name?"

Cecily swallowed the rising self-doubt. She was within her right to ask such a question, was she not? "Mrs. Trent has called me by that name twice now, yesterday just before we left for church and again this morning at breakfast. I am concerned."

The slanted light coming through the door highlighted the twitch of Clarkson's jaw. The lady's maid opened her mouth, hesitated, and adjusted the basket in her arms. "I-I put your clean gowns in your wardrobe."

And with that, she disappeared down the hall.

Cecily stared after her, frozen to her spot until the clicking of footsteps on the wooden floors faded. She had overstepped her boundaries. Inquired too much about something she had no right to know.

She stood alone, in a shadowed corridor, with naught but the silence for company.

She had been here several days, and still she could not grow accustomed to the silence. Her throat began to tighten, and she turned toward the gold room. Her bedchamber was pleasant, but it was silent. And lonely.

She was about to retrieve a book when she spotted the wardrobe door ajar. Inside hung the gown Rebecca had loaned her just a few days prior, clean and pressed. She opened the wardrobe door and touched the dress, an idea forming. She could stay here in her room, avoiding Andrew, feeling lonely, or she could go for a walk and return the gown.

The thought of possibly encountering Mr. Stanton again unnerved her, especially after her dramatic display by the garden gate, but she had noticed his habit to stay at Willowgrove until late in the evening. Surely she could go visit Rebecca and the rest of the Stantons and be back before he returned home for the night.

She carefully folded the gown into a small satchel she found in the bottom of her wardrobe, and she then retrieved a few more swatches of fabric from her embroidery box. She grabbed her shawl to guard against the chilly spring breeze and left her room.

She paused by Mrs. Trent's door on her way out. Cecily was always hesitant to leave the woman, even for a walk. It pained her how much Mrs. Trent did not care to be alone. But when she opened the door to check on her, Clarkson was sitting by her side, sewing. The maid looked up when Cecily entered.

Cecily whispered, "Is she sleeping well?"

Clarkson lowered her work to her side. "Yes."

"I am going for a walk, if you think it is all right to leave her for a bit."

Clarkson looked offended. "I am here. She will not be alone."

Cecily nodded, pressed her lips together, and exited the room. Voices wafted up from the floor below. Not wishing to risk encountering Andrew or one of the Pritchards, she took the servants' stairs and exited through the kitchen.

Out in the wide expanse of Willowgrove's lawns, the tension Cecily was carrying vanished. A cool wind swept down from the distance, carrying with it the lush scents of outdoors and disrupting her bonnet's satin chin ribbons and the folds of her gown. But she did not mind. The soft music of the wind danced through the budding trees, perfuming the landscape with the sweet aroma. The path to Laurel Cottage was muddy from the earlier rain, so she walked in the grass alongside the road.

She tightened her shawl about her and quickened her pace. The farther she walked, the more her confidence wavered. She could not recall the last time she had paid a visit to anyone alone. She was normally accompanied by the other girls or Mrs. Sterling. But her desire for company far outweighed her discomfort, and before she knew it, she was coming around the last bend.

Laurel Cottage came into sight. It was as charming as she remembered. Fluffy smoke puffed from two of the chimneys. A few chickens and a goose hurried across the yard. The windows were open, and curtains floated in and out on the breeze. Cecily drew a deep breath and tightened her grip on the satchel.

She walked through the courtyard. Feminine voices and laughter floated from the home, reminding her of the constant sounds at Rosemere. She made her way to the door and knocked.

Within moments the door flew open, and Hannah Stanton's small face peered through.

The child's dark eyes lit with surprise. "Miss Faire! Mother, Mother, it is Miss Faire!"

In quick succession, Charlotte joined her, and then Mrs. Stanton was at the door.

"How lovely," Mrs. Stanton exclaimed, smoothing her skirt and then her hair from beneath the white cap she wore. "We've been hoping to receive a visit from you. Please, please, do come in!"

Cecily was ushered into the home, her warm reception melting away her anxieties. Rebecca appeared and offered a friendly embrace. "You are visiting us at last!" she said, taking Cecily by the arm and leading her to the parlor.

"I do hope I am not interrupting."

Rebecca guided Cecily to one of the chairs by the fireplace and then took the seat opposite of her. "Of course not! I am so pleased you are here."

Cecily retrieved the gown from the satchel and extended it toward Rebecca. "It has been cleaned and pressed. Thank you again for your kindness in loaning it to me. I am not sure what I would have done otherwise."

Rebecca took the gown and placed it on her lap. "Of course, and you are welcome to my gowns anytime you find yourself caught in the rain. Here, do come into the parlor."

Once in the cozy room, Hannah settled at Cecily's feet next to the chair by the fire, and Charlotte sat on the sofa. At the sight of the girls, she recalled the fabric scraps she had in her satchel. She leaned toward the girls, as if to share a great secret. "I have something for you."

Hannah squeaked and clasped her hands in front of her in anticipation, her wide eyes unblinking. Charlotte leaned forward with more reserved curiosity.

Cecily reached in and pulled out the swatches of cream and peach muslin, as well as a length of silver cording and a pale-green ribbon, and extended them toward the girls.

Hannah jumped to her feet, her skirt swishing with the movement. "Charlotte, look!" she squealed, gathering the spoils as gingerly as if they might evaporate at her touch. "They are the most beautiful things I have ever seen!"

Cecily could not help but laugh at the child's dramatic acceptance. "I am so glad you enjoy them."

Charlotte took the green ribbon in her slender fingers. "This is beautiful. I think I will wear it to the engagement ball."

"Oh yes," Cecily said, turning to Rebecca. "Mrs. Massey told me of your engagement ball. It sounds as if it will be quite the event."

Rebecca scooted to the edge of her chair. "So you have heard about it, then. I do hope you will attend. I wanted to send you an invitation, but I was concerned Mrs. Trent would not approve. Please know you are most welcome."

"At first Mrs. Trent was skeptical, but Mrs. Massey was able to get her to come around. I hope that is all right."

"All right? It is more than all right! I am so pleased."

Cecily pivoted toward Rebecca. "Mrs. Massey mentioned that she has been a friend of your family's for a long time."

Rebecca nodded. "I have known Mrs. Massey since we were children. She grew up in the village. Her father died when she was a baby, and her mother was the town seamstress. But I am positive she must have told you that."

Hannah shifted her attention from the fabric in her hand back to Cecily. "Mrs. Massey is going to marry my brother one day."

Cecily jerked her attention to the child, stunned by what she had just said.

The fire grew too warm. The air too thin.

"Hannah!" Rebecca said, leaning toward the little girl, her

expression stern. "There are no such plans. Why should you say such a thing?"

A frown darkened Hannah's expression. "But I thought—"

"You thought wrong," Rebecca snapped before casting a wary glance in Cecily's direction. "I am so sorry. You know how children are."

"Think nothing of it," Cecily stammered.

But Cecily could not miss the silent exchange between Rebecca and Mrs. Stanton, who had taken her spot next to Charlotte on the sofa. After having worked so closely with children, Cecily knew how perceptive children Hannah's age could be—how they interpreted the nuances of behavior and conversation in a way many adults failed to.

And Cecily's heart fell.

Bessie, the Stantons' housemaid, brought in tea, and Mrs. Stanton rose to take the tray from her. "So, tell us, how are you getting on with Mrs. Trent?"

Grateful for the change of topic, Cecily forced a smile to her face. "All is well, I am pleased to say. Mrs. Trent and I have taken very well to each other."

"Good, I am glad to hear it, although I can hardly say that I am surprised," added Mrs. Stanton, pouring the steaming liquid into a cup and handing it to Cecily. "You are such an agreeable young woman. I find it difficult to believe that anyone could find fault with your company."

"That is very kind of you to say."

Rebecca accepted a cup of tea from her mother. "And how is Mrs. Trent? I heard reports while in town that she took ill while in Bath and has taken to her personal chamber. And yet she was at church, so I was not sure what to take as truth. I asked Nathaniel, but you know how men are about such things."

Cecily chose her words carefully, not wishing to speak out of turn. Mrs. Trent was misunderstood in the village. Nothing could be more obvious. She felt the need to protect the older woman—even from the Stantons. "Mrs. Trent is tired from her travels, I believe. I am sure after a few nights of rest she will be much recovered."

Hannah lifted the hem of Cecily's woven shawl from the edge of the sofa where it had been discarded upon her arrival. "Will you show me how to make a flower like this?"

The girl gathered the shawl in her arms and scurried over to Cecily.

Charlotte stood and walked toward them. "Hannah, Miss Faire does not have time to show you that now."

"Yes, she does!" She looked at Cecily with big eyes. "You do, do you not?"

Cecily smiled and assessed the embroidery in question. A simple stitch. "Of course I do. Fetch a needle and some thread. I can show you on the muslin I just brought."

The next hour passed in happy companionship, complete with much-needed laughter. Cecily taught Hannah and Charlotte a series of simple backstitches to form little flowers, and Rebecca and Cecily discussed their opinions on the book Cecily had seen in Rebecca's room, *The Romance of the Forest*.

The evening sky visible through the window was a painting of vibrant pinks and oranges and then faded to periwinkle and lavender hues as the sun continued its descent. Inside, the white light of afternoon had been replaced by the yellow glow of candles and the fire. Cecily had lost track of the hour. It was only when she heard footsteps outside and smelled the scent of meat and bread that she realized the lateness of the hour.

The door creaked open. "I'm home!" His tenor voice echoed through the hall.

Cecily froze. She had not intended to stay so long. She intended to only be away from Willowgrove—and Mrs. Trent—for a brief span of time. A quick glance at the clock confirmed the hour had grown later, and now Mr. Stanton was here. Heat crept up from her bodice. To her neck. She could feel her cheeks growing warm. She had not seen him since the necklace incident.

Hannah jumped to her feet and ran from the parlor. Cecily watched as she grabbed his hand and pulled him forward into the room where they all sat. "Miss Faire is here, Nathaniel!"

He removed his hat. Her heart ached at how handsome he appeared. There was a smudge of dirt on his sleeve. His hair disheveled. His cheeks unusually pink, most likely due to the increasing wind. He stared at her for a moment and a smile tugged his lips. "Miss Faire!" He bowed. "Pleasure to see you."

"Good day, Mr. Stanton." Cecily straightened the edge of her sleeve.

She wondered if he would say anything about their earlier encounter, but instead, he glanced around at the fabric strewn across the sofa and chairs. "What is going on in here?"

Hannah retrieved a scrap of fabric and reached it up to his face. "See! I am sewing flowers. So is Charlotte. Miss Faire taught us."

Mr. Stanton reached to steady the art in his sister's bouncing hands and assessed it. "Very lovely. Miss Faire, it looks as if you will make fine seamstresses of my sisters yet."

Miss Faire was the last person he had expected to see.

But oh, how it made him smile to come home and see her sitting amongst his family. So naturally. As if she belonged.

"How was your day, son?" His mother ushered him to the chair opposite Cecily.

He ducked through the doorway to the parlor, barely taking his eyes from Miss Faire. "It was pleasant enough."

Miss Faire, on the other hand, seemed to grow increasingly uncomfortable. Her cheeks were flushed. The memory of her hand beneath his by the garden gate, although fleeting, played in his mind. If he did not know better, he would think she was embarrassed by the touch.

Before he was even seated, Miss Faire jumped from her seat. "I must be going." She whirled to Rebecca. "Thank you so much for a lovely afternoon."

Rebecca jumped to her feet. "But will you not stay for supper?" She reached for Nathaniel's arm. "Nathaniel, help me convince her to stay."

"No." Miss Faire's response came quickly. "I really must be going. Mrs. Trent will be expecting me. The hour is already much later than I thought."

His mother tilted her head. "If we cannot persuade you to stay, perhaps we should be grateful that you were able to stop by, even for a short visit."

Miss Faire hugged the younger girls good-bye, donned her shawl, and within a matter of a moment, had bid her farewells and was gone.

He wanted to stop her, to come up with a reason to detain her, yet the words would not form.

When Miss Faire was out of sight, Rebecca slapped his arm. "What did you do?"

Stunned, Nathaniel drew his arm back. "Ow! What do you mean?"

Rebecca blew back some loose hairs that had fallen in her face. "We were having a very lovely visit, and then you came and ruined it."

"I did no such thing!"

"She was perfectly content until you got here. We get company so seldom. And then you arrive, and she leaves as quickly as she possibly can."

"Oh, this is ridiculous," he grumbled. "Think what you like. I did nothing wrong." He stomped toward the door and grabbed his hat. "I'll be tending to the animals."

But as he exited, he could not keep a smile from crossing his face. The surprise of seeing her in his home was enough to brighten his spirits. Night was falling, but in the distance, far down the lane, he saw Miss Faire making her way back to Willowgrove.

He tapped his pocket, then looked back at the cottage to make sure that none of his family saw him. He took off down the lane.

"Miss Faire!"

She stopped and turned. She tucked a loose piece of hair behind her ear and tightened her shawl about her. "Mr. Stanton?" Her eyebrows drew together in concern. "Is everything all right?"

"Yes, of course." He drew to a stop as he approached her. "I hope you did not leave on my account."

"Oh no. I really must get back to Mrs. Trent. She is not feeling well, and I fear I have been away much too long."

"Yes, I heard she had another setback today."

Miss Faire shifted her weight. "About earlier today, the necklace, I must explain. I—"

"You needn't explain anything." He reached into his pocket and retrieved her necklace.

"What—?" A smile spread across her face. She reached out to take the beads from him. "How did you fix it so quickly?"

At the sight of her smile, warmth spread through his chest. "The clasp had broken, but 'twas a simple fix."

"It's wonderful," she said. "Honestly, I cannot thank you enough. This necklace means a great deal to me."

He wanted to learn more, such as why she became so upset and what she meant about not taking it, but he did not want to do anything to ruin her smile. He stepped closer. "Is there nothing I can say to convince you to stay at Laurel Cottage for just a little longer?"

At this, he may have gone too far.

Her smile faded, and she fastened the necklace about her neck. "Thank you for the invitation, but I must be going."

"It is growing dark. Shall I escort you?"

"No. Please, no," she stammered. "But thank you for my necklace."

And with that, she rushed off down the path.

21

Cecily sat primly on the edge of the sofa, minding her posture, focusing intently on the embroidery project in her hands, and trying to remain as quiet and unnoticeable as possible.

For tomorrow morning, Andrew, Miss Pritchard, and Mrs. Pritchard would depart for London.

And Cecily only had to make it through one more evening in their presence.

It had been a few days since she had visited the Stantons, and the following morning Cecily awoke to find Mrs. Trent much improved. So much so that the two had been able to take an afternoon walk through the south garden again. And now, night had fallen, and Mrs. Trent not only joined her nephew and his companions for dinner, but also consented for a game of whist.

Cecily would like to think that the improvement of Mrs. Trent's countenance was some of her effect, but ever since her physician, Dr. Collingswood, had arrived the day after she took to her bed, her spirits had been much lifted. Dr. Collingswood had joined them for dinner and was participating in their game.

This had been the first dinner Cecily had shared with Andrew since her first full day at Willowgrove, but it had passed much more comfortably. For Dr. Collingswood was a pleasant character, with a jovial sense of humor and quick wit, and he managed to include all the dinner participants in the conversation.

Cecily glanced around the room. Mrs. Trent, Dr. Collingswood, and Miss and Mrs. Pritchard were seated at the gaming table. A cheery fire danced in the fireplace, glinting off the painted wallpaper and portraits that decorated the walls from plastered ceiling to wood floor. Next to Miss Pritchard's chair stood Andrew, watching his intended's plays with interest.

Cecily was content for it to be that way. For in no way was this evening as enjoyable as the time she had passed with the Stantons. Tonight, she was to be a quiet observer.

Or she hoped she would remain that way.

With Andrew departing for London in the morning, she could put that part of her life to rest for now and focus on the future. A few questions had been answered, and now that she was settling in, renewed optimism flourished within her. She was finding friends in Mrs. Massey and the Stantons. She and Mrs. Trent were growing close. And as much as she was trying to convince herself otherwise, her heart leapt at the thought of even passing Mr. Stanton in the corridor.

She scooted closer to the candle lamp for light. For but a brief moment, she let her gaze flick to the party before her, and instantly regretted it. For her gaze met with Andrew's.

Her heart lurched. She stared down at her sewing, a little disoriented as she tried to find her place again.

She heard his footsteps above the chatter of conversation, and then his shadow spread across the rug beneath her feet and on the hem of her gown.

Cecily had no choice but to look up.

Andrew motioned to the padded armchair next to her. "May I?"

Cecily's tongue seemed to grow thick. She cast a quick glance at the card players, who appeared oblivious to anything amiss. "Of course, Mr. Moreton."

He chuckled as he sat down next to her, as if he found something amusing.

But Cecily found nothing amusing about this or any of their interactions since his arrival at Willowgrove.

She fidgeted with the sewing on her lap. The past had taken a toll on her. And even though their lives had gone in different directions, a part of her wondered what toll it had taken on him. Deep down, while her heart did not feel the romantic love she had felt for him all those years ago, something buried deep within her heart could not help but care about the boy he had been.

He leaned forward, resting his elbows on his knees, his scent of leather dangerously near.

The blood roared in Cecily's ears.

He seemed calm and cool, utterly carefree.

He raised an eyebrow as he looked toward the card players in the same manner he used to as a boy. "I think we have fooled them."

But whereas his smile indicated he was attempting to make light of a difficult situation, her humor soured. "I am not sure that is something in which we should take pride."

His smile faded. "Would you have been more pleased with the alternative?"

She resumed her sewing, afraid to let her eyes linger on him, fearing her emotions might write themselves on her expression. "And by the alternative, you mean your aunt knowing about our past?" She winced as the needle pricked her hand in a careless motion.

"Of course I mean our past." His voice was so low it could barely be heard above the crackling fire, let alone the voices coming from the table. "Aunt knows I made a misstep with a young lady. She is aware, to be sure. After all, I have made my home at Willowgrove these past several years. But she knows no name. The matter has not been discussed in years."

"A misstep?" she repeated, willing the anger that flared at the casual nature of the word to subside. "Your aunt is a very perceptive woman. I would not be so quick to discredit her."

"I've no wish to discredit her."

Cecily had to hide a huff. How else could he explain his coldness toward her? His irreverence? "The past is in the past, and it shall remain that way."

"If that is how you wish it."

"Is that not how you wish it? Miss Pritchard is very lovely. I am sure you are eager to leave the past and find your future. I understand from Mrs. Trent that you are to wed in November."

"Why must you change the topic?" His eyes were latched onto her. She need not look at him to feel intensity radiating from them. "I cannot believe that you never imagine what would have happened if things had ended differently that night."

She refused to allow the conversation to go down an unproductive path. "All has happened for the best."

"The best?" He gave a laugh and slumped back in his chair. "My dear Cecily, if this is what you call the best, then at some point we both must have believed a falsehood."

She pulled an incorrect stitch. Cecily was not about to recount the tally of their sins. "I am saddened by the loss of my family, but I must believe that all works together for good. I suppose, in the end, we have received the punishment we deserve, each in our own way."

"Punishment? We may have made a few mistakes, but I do not think a punishment was necessarily deserved." He glanced toward the party before speaking. "Your punishment was out of cruelty."

"And your punishment?" The words were poignant. But she wanted to know.

"My punishment?" he repeated, straightening. "I think you know the answer to that question. Forced into the life of my father. Forced to come to terms with an existence evaluated on monetary gain. That is not what I wanted. And yet, here I am."

Cecily drew a breath. She had no desire to upset him. But somehow, knowing how he felt brought a sense of closure to the pain and uncertainty that had plagued her for years. And even though her romantic feelings had changed, he had, at first, been her friend. "And now?"

His expression grew stoic. "I will accept my role."

"But Miss Pritchard is lovely," Cecily said. "And Aradelle—"

"Miss Pritchard is an advantageous match." He hissed the words with unmasked sarcasm. "Or so Father says. The proposal may as well have come from his lips."

Her response was out of her mouth before she could check it. "That does not sound very romantic, I fear."

"Romantic?" He pressed his lips together, as if weighing the wisdom in his words. "I tried following romance once. It sent me down a path that is far more proper, but sadly leaves much to be desired."

He grew silent. She noticed he had not yet asked her about her feelings. About her plans for the future. She was glad for it. For this was his way. Had it not always been as such? Andrew was a passionate being. He displayed emotion compellingly and fully. And yet his concern lay chiefly in his emotions, and his alone. Had he ever wondered how their decision left her?

He seemed to finally notice the sewing in her hand. "What are you working on?"

She glanced up from her netting. "Sewing."

"In such low light? How the devil can you see? But I suppose it suits you. You were always fussing with this or that. I remember you sitting in the orchard, just so, sewing away."

He spoke to her with such familiarity. "And what exactly are you making?"

She refused to glance up at him. "A reticule for Miss Stanton."

"Miss Stanton?" he sneered. "Nathaniel Stanton's sister?"

"Her name is Rebecca Stanton."

He folded his arms across his chest. "I think I would reconsider taking such a familiar standing with a family such as the Stantons."

The sudden emphasis behind his words came as a surprise. She did not lift her eyes from her work. "I do not understand why you speak their name with such disdain. She and her family have been very kind to me since my arrival."

"I am sure they have." He leaned closer. "I know your trust of me is fairly nonexistent, but trust me enough to believe me when I say that the Stantons are probably not the best place to turn for company."

She did not know why the slight should irk her so. Did he prefer she keep company like him?

She glanced up at the timepiece on the mantel. The clock would soon strike the ninth hour.

Surely Mrs. Trent would tire soon.

And yet her crackling laughter pealed out, taking Cecily by surprise. She'd heard Mrs. Trent laugh so seldom that the sound was foreign to her. She thought to remind her of the hour, and yet she could hardly deny Mrs. Trent genuine enjoyment after the hours she spent sitting alone in her room.

Andrew had leaned back in his chair. He was staring at the card table, a blankness in his expression.

"When we spoke in the library the other night, I told you that we were different people in the past, and that my opinions and hopes had changed."

"I remember."

"Well then, I do have a request to make of you . . . as a friend."

"A friend?" he huffed. "Well, as a *friend*, how can I deny you?"

The gravity of his response sank within her. "I told you that my father sent me away, and now that I am out of school, I am trying to find my sister."

"Yes. You mentioned at dinner the other night you were unsure of her whereabouts."

"I have reason to believe that she may be in Manchester, but I am unsure. That is where I was hoping you could help. Will you be at Aradelle soon?"

"Yes, I will be traveling there after London."

At this, her heart began to race. How many times had she recently revisited Aradelle in her thoughts? But not the Aradelle with painful memories, but the happier memories of time spent with her mother and sister. The flame of an idea started within her. Her only contact with Aradelle since she left was the letter she'd received. But perhaps Andrew could find out more.

She lowered her sewing to her lap and cast a quick glance to Mrs. Trent. "Would you be so kind as to deliver a message for me?"

But before he could respond, a playful groan echoed from the whist table. The game had ended. Miss Pritchard had a victorious smile on her lips.

Cecily quickly turned back to Andrew. "Could you ask if anyone remembers her? Start with Mrs. Sherwin. Please?"

He smiled and stood, as Miss Pritchard was already headed their direction. His eyes locked on her. "I suppose I owe you that much." He glanced over at Miss Pritchard. "Very well. You have my word. I will find out what I am able."

22

Two weeks had passed since Andrew left Willowgrove. The days had flashed by in predictable routine.

Cecily looked forward to the time she spent with the Stantons. Several mornings a week, while Mrs. Trent slept, Cecily would spend an hour or so at Laurel Cottage teaching Hannah and Charlotte new embroidery techniques. Then, in the late afternoons, Cecily and Rebecca would take a walk. Occasionally Mr. Stanton would join them, if his duties permitted. It became the time of day Cecily anticipated most. She missed the camaraderie of people who were close to her own age, and even though they were not in the same situations, the laughter and diversion they shared was what she needed to balance the somber, albeit peaceful time spent with Mrs. Trent.

One pleasant afternoon Rebecca accompanied Cecily to the south garden to cut roses—a task that Cecily performed nearly every day. As they sat in the warm sun amid the fragrant blooms of pink, red, and white, Cecily lifted her face to the sky. "What a lovely day this has turned out to be."

Rebecca paused after cutting a thorn from a rose. "It is. How fortunate we are to have had such a break from the rain."

Cecily brought a rose close to her nose, inhaled its floral scent, and lowered it to the basket. "I am so glad you could join me for a walk today. I tried to convince Mrs. Trent that a walk out of doors was just what she needed, and yet I could not persuade her. She said that fresh roses on her side table were all the out of doors she required."

Rebecca swatted at a bug. "Is she much improved, then?"

Whether Rebecca's concern was genuine or she was asking as Cecily's friend, she was unsure, but Cecily appreciated the inquiry just the same. "I am afraid that is a difficult question to answer. There are days when she will walk the grounds with me, and then others that she cannot leave her bedchamber, not even to go to the drawing room. It is a great comfort that Dr. Collingswood has stayed on these past two weeks. He seems to be a great comfort to her."

Rebecca clipped another rose, leaving the stem long. "Well, I have heard nothing but admiration for her physician. And at least these flowers should bring her a little happiness." She dropped the rose in Cecily's basket. "Can you believe Saturday is but two days away? I can hardly believe the ball is already so near."

"Oh, that reminds me," Cecily said, rising to her feet. "Mrs. Massey delivered a couple of my gowns yesterday. Would you care to see them?"

"Oh yes, I would love to!" Rebecca returned her scissors to the basket.

"Come with me. Plus, I have a surprise for you." Cecily led the way out of the garden and up Willowgrove's steps. Once inside, she guided her guest through the main hall and staircase to the upstairs landing.

"I have never been this far into Willowgrove before," Rebecca whispered as she followed Cecily up the curved staircase. "Are you sure it is all right?"

Cecily nodded, holding the hem of her gown as she stepped upward. "Of course! You are my guest. Besides, how else will you be able to see the gown?"

As they made their way down the corridor, Cecily held her fingers to her lips and nodded toward the door. "Mrs. Trent's rooms are through there. I am sure she is sleeping. My room is through that door there."

Once inside her bedchamber, Cecily quietly shut the door behind them.

"This is beyond anything I've seen before," exclaimed Rebecca, hurrying over to the window to look at the lawn below. "I cannot even imagine waking up to this every day. I do not think I have ever been this high from the ground. Why, look! You can see the Brentle farm from here!"

Cecily went to the wardrobe and opened the door. "It is the finest room I have ever stayed in, to be sure."

Rebecca turned from the window and propped her hands on her hips, drinking in her surroundings. "Was Rosemere not elegant?"

Cecily giggled. "It was nice, but it was much smaller than Willowgrove. During the last two years, I shared a small attic room with another teacher. We were cozy, but elegant it most definitely was not."

Cecily did not miss the look of confusion that flashed across Rebecca's face. Propriety undoubtedly kept her questions at bay. She probably expected Cecily to be used to such opulent surroundings. After all, she was a lady's companion. Rebecca would be most surprised to learn of Cecily's humble beginnings.

Cecily turned her attention back to the wardrobe. A little flutter of regret shot through her. In her short time at Willowgrove, Rebecca was becoming a very dear friend. But the relationship was indeed one-sided. Rebecca generously shared all about her life—the details necessary to become truly acquainted with another—while Cecily held every detail of her own life with such guarded possessiveness that it would be quite impossible for Rebecca to really know her.

It had been much the same at Rosemere. Finding the confidence to share her hidden thoughts with anyone had been difficult. Now she was being given the opportunity for friendship. She could choose to trust her new friend with a few snippets or retreat back into solitude.

Cecily hesitated before continuing. "And before Rosemere, I lived in a small and very old cottage with only four rooms. So you can imagine what a luxury this all seems to me. My father was a blacksmith. He worked mostly for Aradelle Park and did odd jobs around the village." She turned away from the wardrobe, half expecting to see a look of shock or disapproval on Rebecca's round face, but instead, she found her friend's eyes fixed on her, intent and sincere.

"Was?" Rebecca asked. "Is he no longer a blacksmith?"

Cecily had to look away. She fidgeted with the bonnet she'd just removed. "I do not know. I have not seen or heard from him since I came to Rosemere." As soon as the words were free from her mouth, Cecily wished she could snatch them back. For her secret was starting to slip. Rebecca was a bright girl. Would she not decipher the fragments of information?

"That is terrible. What of your sister, then? You mentioned you had one. Surely you speak with her?"

Cecily shook her head. "The truth is that I have not spoken with her since before attending Rosemere. But I am looking for her. In fact, your brother is helping me." That was all she could muster. Perhaps one day she could share more. Instead of answering, Cecily turned back to the wardrobe. "But let us not linger on that. See? Here is the first gown."

She retrieved it from the wardrobe and placed it across the striped coverlet on the canopied bed.

Rebecca clasped her hands in front of her. "Why, how lovely!" She lifted the skirt of pale-plum satin and ran it through her fingers before lifting it to look at the detail more closely. "Look at this white work on the bodice, and how she carried it down the sleeves. You must be so pleased."

"I am." Cecily reached for the peach gown, careful not to catch it on the wardrobe door, and held the gown in front of her, angling herself so her reflection would show in the mirror above the mantel. It really was a stunning gown, constructed of fine satin. Small beads created a delicate floral pattern on the bodice, and a white netting overlay embellished with silver threads floated above the fabric of the skirt. The sleeves were short, and Mrs. Massey had given her white gloves to complete the ensemble. "I shall wear this to the engagement dance. Do you like it?"

Rebecca quickly discarded the plum gown, took the peach gown from Cecily, and held it at arm's length. The sun caught on the silver threads in the overlay and shimmered in the afternoon light. But then Rebecca frowned and brought the dress closer. "Oh dear. There appears to be a misstep with the stitching."

Cecily focused on the area Rebecca called out. She had noticed it too. "Yes, it puckers a bit there at the sleeve. It is very obvious when I have it on. But that should be easy to remedy. I plan to work on it tomorrow."

"I am most surprised," Rebecca said, still examining the area in question. "It is not like Mrs. Massey to overlook such an error. On most counts, she is meticulous."

Cecily took the gown back. "Fortunately, it should take no time at all to repair."

She had noticed bits of imperfections on the other gowns—a slight tear in the seam of the black bombazine gown and an uneven hem in the plum muslin. She did not wish to offend Mrs. Massey's work, but Cecily planned to make alterations to them as well. She recalled the odd words that Mrs. Massey had spoken to her at the fitting about the time that she had spent with the Stantons, not to mention how she did not think her work would be acceptable to someone as accomplished at needlework as Cecily. The words, while kind on the surface, left Cecily with the sense that she had done something to offend her new acquaintance. Despite Mrs. Massey's lavish attention to Mrs. Trent on her visits, she barely spoke to Cecily. At the final fitting, she made few alterations, despite the fact that obvious oddities existed. Cecily was not one to suffer from oversensitivity, but the cool nature of Mrs. Massey's treatment of her was impossible to ignore.

Cecily took the gown back from Rebecca and lowered it. "I cannot help but wonder if I have offended Mrs. Massey in some way."

Rebecca cocked her head to the side. "Why would you have such a notion?"

"I cannot say for certain." Cecily plopped on the bed, unsure she should share her private thoughts on Mrs. Massey. "Just a suspicion."

"Well . . ." Rebecca sat on the bed next to her, looking more like a child who had been caught saying something inappropriate than a woman about to marry. "Like I have told you before, I have known Mrs. Massey for a very long time, and I do consider her a friend. But I do not think it is a secret that she has somewhat of a fickle nature. Sometimes I think she has befriended me because she has set her cap on Nathaniel."

As if realizing what had just come from her mouth, Rebecca's eyes grew wide, and she clapped her hand over her mouth. "Oh my! I did not mean that as it sounded, for certain!"

Upon noticing her friend's uneasiness, Cecily shrugged. But the words interested her. She had wondered about a possible connection between the two, especially after Mrs. Massey's comments the first day they met and Hannah's unusual outburst. "Think nothing of it. But I could not help but wonder if there was an agreement between the two."

"An agreement? No. At least, not one that I am aware of. It is an odd relationship, really. Like I told you, I have known Mrs. Massey my entire life, as has Nathaniel, but it was not until after her husband's death that we became better acquainted. Mr. Massey and my brother were great friends, and before he died, Mr. Massey asked Nathaniel to watch out for his wife. So Nathaniel oversaw some repairs to her cottage and helped her establish her business. I think some people may have misunderstood that as romantic interest."

"And by 'some people,' do you mean Mrs. Massey?"

Rebecca gave a little smile. "I would think that if Nathaniel returned the sentiment he would have responded by now, but as it is, he is so private about such things."

"Mrs. Massey is very beautiful. I am surprised she has remained unattached."

"Mother had it in her mind that Nathaniel would one day propose to Mrs. Massey, but I think she has quite given up on it. Nathaniel is so focused on his duties. I never understood the dedication. Mrs. Trent treats him horribly, and yet he persists."

"Perhaps it is loyalty," Cecily reasoned, returning the gown to the wardrobe.

"Or perhaps it is stubbornness." A coy grin crossed Rebecca's face. "So perhaps Mrs. Massey has been offended in some way, or maybe she is merely concerned that there is a new lady's companion at Willowgrove Hall who is charming and lovely."

"Rebecca!"

Her friend shrugged. "There can be no mistake. She has had her eye on Nathaniel for quite some time. And now there may be competition—"

"Please do not say such things. Please do not." Why the words should have such an effect on her, she did not know, but she felt panic rising within her.

Rebecca shook her head as if confused. "Do you not wish to marry one day?"

Cecily pressed her lips together. Marrying would mean confessing the past. Who would want to marry her once the truth was brought to light? She had no dowry, no connections, and worst of all, had already given herself to another. "I do not know." Her words snapped. "At the moment, my main concern is reuniting with my sister."

"I certainly understand wanting to stay close to your sister. Mine are a handful at times, but I would miss them immensely if they were gone."

Cecily immediately regretted the path the conversation had taken, and her shortness of temper. Of course Rebecca would expect her to be seeking a suitable match. But after what she had been through with Andrew, she doubted she would ever have the sort of relationship with a man that Rebecca had with Mr. Turner.

But the exchange uncovered another thought. Would it even be possible for Mr. Stanton to notice her in any way other than as Mrs. Trent lady's companion? The thought both warmed and frightened her.

Cecily needed to change the subject. "Oh, I almost forgot. I have something for you."

She hurried to her writing desk, pulled open the small door underneath, and retrieved the blue reticule she had made for Rebecca. "This is for you."

Rebecca's face flushed as she noticed the silk purse in Cecily's hand. "This is for me?"

She reached out and accepted the delicate gift and traced the silver tambour work with her finger. "This is so elegant. You made it yourself?"

"Yes. I thought you might like to have it for the engagement celebration."

"Oh, Cecily!" she exclaimed, drawing her into a spontaneous hug. "This is so very kind of you! I am sure it is the finest reticule I have ever had!"

Unaccustomed to such praise, Cecily kept her eyes low. The moment, however, was not lost on Cecily, for despite the hardships she had faced, it warmed her to realize that Rebecca had become a dear friend.

23

Two days had passed since her visit with Rebecca, and the day of the engagement celebration was now upon them.

Mrs. Trent had requested to see Cecily's gown prior to her departure, so with Clarkson's assistance, she had donned the pale-peach gown. Cecily had spent a better part of the previous day repairing the side seams and further embellishing the bodice with delicate, beaded flowers and silver thread. And now Cecily was certain it was the most beautiful dress she had ever seen. She pivoted to see the back of the gown, and as she did, satin fabric shimmered in the fire's glow. A delicate netting of white floated over the skirt and sleeves, intricately embroidered with leaves and pink flowers. A white satin ribbon laced the gown down the back. She reached for the satin gloves and slid her hands inside, smoothing the soft fabric over her forearms.

The final piece of her ensemble was her mother's coral necklace. She lifted it, paying close attention to the clasp. What mixed emotions this piece of jewelry conjured. For not only was the memory of her mother and sister tied to every bead, but that of Nathaniel Stanton as well.

Cecily glanced at her timepiece. Despite the recent, inexplicable coolness from Mrs. Massey, Cecily was still planning to accompany her to the festivities. Cecily would take Willowgrove's carriage to Mrs. Massey's home, and the ladies would continue on together to the inn where the event was being held. Cecily hurried into Mrs. Trent's chamber to show her the gown. Though the old woman had grumbled about Cecily attending, she had seemed like a proud parent, eager to see her little one dressed in her finest attire.

Cecily entered Mrs. Trent's chamber, surprised to see she had already retired. Cecily moved over to the bed and sat. "I did not expect you to be abed so early."

Mrs. Trent sighed. "I do not feel well, child. Not tonight. But don't you worry. It is nothing that a good night's sleep will not resolve. Now, stand up and let me see you."

With a smile, Cecily complied. She turned a complete circle and then returned to the side of the bed. "Do you like it?"

Mrs. Trent managed a weak smile. "Mrs. Massey's work is impeccable." She reached out to touch the netting with her shaking finger. "But you are right. The silver thread did improve it. And did you allow Clarkson to dress your hair?"

"I did." Cecily reached up and gingerly patted the curls. She'd been reluctant at first, but when Clarkson was done, Cecily was surprised at the talent the lady's maid possessed. In a relatively short time, Clarkson had smoothed her stubborn curls in an intricate chignon and woven a white ribbon across the crown of her head and into the style.

Mrs. Trent adjusted her blankets around her and shook. "She is most talented. But despite that fact, I really should not allow you to go. *Tsk.* There is no telling who will be there. But it is not fair to you. I cannot keep you prisoner here forever."

"Dear Mrs. Trent, you hardly keep me prisoner." Cecily sat down next to her on the bed and took the withered hand in her own. "I enjoy the time we spend together."

Mrs. Trent managed a weak chuckle. "I would expect you to say that."

Cecily patted her hand. "Mrs. Trent, please believe me when I say I am happier here at Willowgrove than I have been in a long time."

Mrs. Trent frowned. "When would you have not been happy? But then, I suppose you haven't shared much with me about your days before you came here. Perhaps one day you will. But those conversations are best left for another day. Go now. But mind yourself. And stay close to Mrs. Massey."

A knock on the door sounded, and Clarkson poked her head into the room. "The carriage is ready and has been brought 'round, Miss Faire."

With a nod, Cecily turned her attention back to Mrs. Trent. "Are you sure there is nothing I can get you before I depart?"

"No. Go, child, enjoy yourself. And take my fan, there on the bureau. I will not have you getting overheated. People always try to cram far too many bodies into too slight of a place. No wonder women are prone to fits of fainting and dizzy spells."

Cecily could not help but smile at Mrs. Trent's generalization. "Thank you, Mrs. Trent. I am sure it will be helpful."

Cecily hurried down the dark corridor, across the landing, to the main staircase. She stepped down the stairs, out of Willowgrove's main entrance, and to the carriage. The night was fair and cool and carried the sweet scent of roses from the garden. Nightingales chirped their songs in the glow of the setting sun, and all seemed peaceful.

Then it dawned on her. She was content.

The ride to Mrs. Massey's home was a short one, just down the main road past Wiltonshire's town square. Mrs. Massey lived on the far edge of the village. As soon as the carriage drew to a stop in front of their destination, Mrs. Massey was already out of the door. The coachman assisted her into the carriage, and within moments, the dressmaker was seated comfortably across from Cecily.

"Mrs. Massey, such a pleasure to see you again," Cecily said while smiling.

"Good evening. I trust you are well?"

The carriage lurched into motion. "I am very well."

Cecily could not help but be impressed by the magnificent gown adorning Mrs. Massey. It rivaled any that Miss Pritchard had worn. Her eyes soaked in the gown of silver lutestring. It shimmered with every movement. A string of pearls adorned her throat, and delicate pearl drop earrings highlighted the angles of her face. Tiny pearls decorated the bustline of her gown, and matching gloves reached up past her elbows.

"Oh, Mrs. Massey, you look positively beautiful!" Cecily exclaimed, taking note of how the absence of color in the silvery-gray gown made her eyes appear that much more violet. "Truly stunning!"

"Thank you, dear," Mrs. Massey said, not making eye contact. "Since I had been in mourning for my dear husband, I had grown quite accustomed to wearing dark colors. As someone who shares my fondness for beautiful gowns, you must know how pleasant it is to be able to wear such fabrics again! This color is still approporiate, mind you, but lively at the same time."

"I was sorry to hear of your husband's passing. Mrs. Trent told me a little about your history. I do hope that is all right."

Mrs. Massey smiled. "Of course. I've no secret to hide. My husband and I married young. We were very much in love and were blessed with a few happy years together. But God above saw fit to take him home. Being in mourning, I did not feel it appropriate to attend any social functions. But it has been above two years. More than enough time has lapsed."

"Mrs. Trent told me your husband was a noble man."

"He was. Thank you. But alas, I did not marry for money." She gave a quick, knowing smile and looked out the window. "The past couple of years have been trying, at best. Thankfully, my mother taught me a great deal, and I have been able to support myself. That is why I believe you and I will be such good friends. We are the same type of woman, working to support ourselves without assistance."

Cecily was growing more curious about Mrs. Massey, for she seemed to be a paradox. No wonder the Stanton ladies were so fond of her, and based on Rebecca's words, slightly cautious. "Do you not have family, Mrs. Massey?"

"No." She pressed a wrinkle from her skirt. "My father died when I was an infant. My mother provided for us by making dresses and clothing of all sort, and I am fortunate to continue that today. I have no siblings, and the cousins I do have are scattered across England's south coast, not nearly close enough for a quick visit." She glanced up. "The Stantons have been kind to me since the passing of my husband. Particularly Mr. Stanton."

Cecily looked down at her gloves, fearful that her own thoughts and feelings about Mr. Stanton would be apparent. She tried to forget Rebecca's words about the dressmaker's interest in Mr. Stanton, but she could not shake them from her memory.

"I grew up here, Miss Faire. Not a mile from the Stantons' door. I am closer to Mr. Stanton's age, and even though the Misses Stantons are younger than I, I have always been quite fond of them. We are great friends."

Mrs. Massey's tone had a possessive quality, which both confused and disheartened Cecily. But since this would be the first time she would see Mr. Stanton and Mrs. Massey in each other's company, she would be able to perceive much about their relationship. Cecily knew little about Mr. Stanton's personal life other than what she had witnessed herself.

Mrs. Massey clasped her hands in front of her. "Tell me, dear, how did you find your gown?"

"Oh, I could not be more pleased. I hope you do not mind. I took the liberty of embellishing the bodice slightly."

"Oh." Mrs. Massey's face was hidden in the shadows, but Cecily thought she heard annoyance in the woman's tone. "I had almost forgotten. You are fond of embroidery as well. I do not blame you, for I cannot imagine not adding my own artistic touch to a gown I was to wear. I hope you did not alter the gown because the workmanship of the gown was not to your liking."

At the directness of the statement, dread filtered through Cecily. No, she did not think the work extremely fine, but she would never say as much. Whether it was from lack of skill or an intentional slight, she may never know. "Of course not. I just like to add my own embellishments."

Mrs. Massey did not respond. She only pointed out the window as they entered the village square. "There, that is my shop. I suppose you have not had reason to see it."

Cecily followed her direction. It was a charming little shop with two large, leaded bay windows flanking a red door. "You must be very proud of it."

"I am. Mr. Stanton was most helpful in helping me secure the spot. He was even kind enough to find funds to pay the first several months' lease. Here, we've arrived at the inn."

Every mention of Mr. Stanton felt like a blow. There could be no denying the message Mrs. Massey attempted to convey.

Cecily swallowed and looked out the opposite window. The ride had been short, for they were only going to the village. But for as long as she had been at Willowgrove, she had little reason to go to the village other than church. Mrs. Trent had no need to venture beyond the church, and Cecily would never presume to travel there on her own.

The carriage drew to a halt. Seconds seemed like hours as she waited for the coachman to open the door, and as her slippered foot landed on the road below, Cecily felt as though she had arrived in a fairyland.

Sparkling lanterns lined the walkway to the Pigeon's Rest Inn. Garlands of spring roses and honeysuckle swung over the door, and yellow light spilled from paned windows in the blue dusk. Sweet strains of flutes, violins, and laughter danced on the evening's warm wind. People, shadowed by dusk, darted to and fro.

After weeks of quiet and predictability, she grew anxious to learn more about the village she now called home. She pushed her thoughts about Mrs. Massey and Mr. Stanton to the side and focused on soaking in every detail.

As they began up the walkway, Mrs. Massey took her arm. The act of familiarity took Cecily by surprise.

Dozens of people were already inside. Cecily did not recognize most of the faces. A few she remembered from church service, but for the most part, she was in a sea of strangers. But it mattered not. For the first time in weeks she felt the cares of her daily existence fade away. She fussed with the borrowed fan looped around her wrist and flicked her hand nervously over her skirt.

Cecily had never been in the Pigeon's Rest Inn. From what she had gathered from Rebecca, the inn was mostly used by travelers. But tonight, all the tables had been pushed aside to make a clearing for dancing. All around her, roses and greenery hung from the rafters and candles hung from the ceiling. Above them, musicians were assembled in the loft, their jaunty music showering down on the dancers below. The warm air whooshed past her as the dancing couples swooshed through their steps, their laughter mingling with the music.

"Now, it is important we make the appropriate introductions," Mrs. Massey said. Cecily leaned closer to hear above the song.

"Do you see Miss Stanton?" asked Cecily, rising to the tips of her toes to see above the moving crowd, looking for Rebecca. She almost had to shout to be heard above the movement and voices. "I told her I would find her as soon as we arrived."

"All in good time, dear." Mrs. Massey flicked her own oriental fan open. "I promised Mrs. Trent I would introduce you to the necessary parties, and I intend to do just that."

Cecily dropped back down so her feet were flat. But before she could move, two tiny arms hugged her around the waist. "Miss Faire! You came!"

Cecily looked down to see young Hannah, her fair curls pulled away from her sweet face and cascading down her back.

"Dear Hannah!" Cecily leaned down to return the child's hug. "Now, stand back and let me look at you." She held the child at arm's length.

Hannah beamed. "Do you like my dress? It used to be Charlotte's, but Mother adjusted it for me."

"I adore it!" Cecily smoothed the sleeve of the child's gown. "I am particularly fond of the blue sash."

"I am too. Nathaniel got it for me. Mother says he spoils me, but how can such a pretty thing be spoiling me?"

Cecily laughed. "Well, I am sure that he thought such a pretty young lady needed a pretty blue bow. And I think he was absolutely correct."

"Hello, Hannah," Mrs. Massey interjected.

Cecily stepped back to include Mrs. Massey in the conversation. "Hannah was just telling me about her new sash."

"Lovely, child." But Mrs. Massey seemed preoccupied. "Where is your brother? Do you know?"

Hannah put her finger to the side of her face. "Um, he was over talking to Mr. Weymeir, but he's not there anymore."

Cecily could not help but smile at the child's innocent observations. As she looked in the direction Hannah pointed, she saw him.

She tried to pretend it was the heat that made her heart flutter. Her eye caught sight of his freshly shaven jaw. The manner in which the flickering light played on his spontaneous smile and emphasized the lightness of his eyes.

She yearned for him to look in her direction as much as she feared it.

She wondered if Mrs. Massey had the same reaction.

But Mrs. Massey clearly did not see him, for she instructed Hannah to tell Mrs. Stanton they had arrived and then ushered Cecily across the room—in the opposite direction.

Around the room they went. Smiling. Nodding. She met Mrs. Donnelly. The Lerens and their three daughters. Mr. Felton.

They were all welcoming, but Cecily found it odd how their expressions altered when Mrs. Trent's name was mentioned. How could it be that they all thought so poorly of her? Mrs. Trent was a bit eccentric, but these people seemed to not care for her at all.

And then Mrs. Massey led them around to Mr. Stanton.

Mr. Stanton was speaking with a young man, and Mrs. Massey joined their conversation as if she had been invited, her arm looped through Cecily's, pulling her closer. Interrupting a conversation between gentlemen in such a brazen way made Cecily uncomfortable. She shifted from foot to foot and lowered her eyes. Not wishing to appear as uncomfortable as she felt, she gathered the courage to glance up at Mr. Stanton. He was already looking at her. As their eyes met, the corner of his mouth lifted in a smile.

She listened more closely to Mrs. Massey.

"And, Miss Faire, you already know Mr. Stanton, but this is Mr. Curley. Mr. Curley runs a farm on the other side of the vale."

The men bowed in unison. Mr. Curley's bold gaze held hers. She did not have the opportunity to return the greeting, for Mrs. Massey was already speaking.

"Mr. Curley, Miss Faire has not yet had the opportunity to

dance, and I do believe that the musicians are about to take up their instruments again."

Heat flushed Cecily's face. She did not wish to be singled out. Nor did she feel confident enough in her abilities to dance.

But Mr. Curley's eagerness made refusal impossible. He stepped forward, a broad smile on his round face, giving her a glimpse of his crooked teeth. "I would be honored. Miss Faire?"

Cecily cast a nervous glance toward Mrs. Massey and forced herself not to look at Mr. Stanton. "I would be delighted."

She allowed herself to be led to the floor, to the thick sea of dancers and swishing gowns. She recognized the dance from her days at Rosemere, and that brought her a little confidence. But as she stood facing her partner, preparing for the dance to begin, she turned and saw Mrs. Massey with her arm draped through Mr. Stanton's. Cecily had to sneak an extra glance. For even though it would be breaking every rule of decorum, it almost appeared as if she were pulling him to the dance! Mr. Stanton, on the other hand, appeared uncomfortable. His expression was resolute. Almost stern.

Before she could contemplate their relationship further, the dance started and she refocused her attention on Mr. Curley.

Despite his teeth, he was not an altogether unattractive man. His light hair fell over his broad forehead, which by some might be considered too large, and light lashes framed kind, if not overeager, eyes. He had a nice, easy smile. But she knew better than to soften toward kind eyes and warm smiles.

"And where are you from, Miss Faire?" He seemed to almost shout in attempt to be heard over the music.

"I am most recently from Rosemere School in Darbury."

"Darbury? That is quite a distance. And do you find Wiltonshire to your liking?"

The music grew louder, a happy, lively tune, and yet his questions did not stop.

"I am very fond of it, yes," she managed to say between steps.

But if he noticed her need for concentration, he did not let on. "And how do you like Mrs. Trent?"

"She is a very kind woman." Cecily circled around and waited until she once again faced her partner.

"Is that so? I have heard she is quite testy."

At this, Cecily stiffened. She did not like to hear unkind things about the mistress of Willowgrove. "I have found the opposite to be true."

His expression narrowed, as if he did not believe her, but then it softened again, and he extended his gloved hand toward her for the next move.

Somehow Cecily survived the dance with no major mistakes. She only turned the wrong direction once, but it was barely noticeable against the backdrop of so many people and such loud music. As Mr. Curley led her from the floor, she felt quite proud of herself.

Mrs. Massey had been talking to Mr. Stanton during the length of the dance, and as Mr. Curley and Cecily approached them, Mrs. Massey locked eyes with Cecily. "You two looked absolutely lovely."

The music began again, and Mr. Curley turned to Mrs. Massey. "Would you care to dance, Mrs. Massey?"

A look of surprise crossed Mrs. Massey's face. "Oh, I don't think so, Mr. Curley. I—"

But his rebuttal came quickly. "Oh, you cannot refuse! You cannot ask your friend here to dance without dancing yourself."

If she was annoyed, she did not look it. "Very well." She extended her gloved hand and placed it on his waiting arm. "Thank you, Mr. Curley."

Mr. Curley led Mrs. Massey to the dance floor.

And that left Cecily alone with Mr. Stanton.

24

Nathaniel hated to dance. A silly waste of time, and yet another opportunity for his mother to try her hand at matching him with one of the local young ladies.

Even now, he sensed her watching his every interaction. Under normal circumstances, he would find any excuse not to attend such a gathering. But seeing as this event was to celebrate his sister's engagement, he could hardly refuse.

And despite his general attitude toward such events, he had come almost willingly.

For he knew Miss Faire would be in attendance. And he noticed the moment she entered.

She was a mystery—a contradiction. Beautiful and bright, yet guarded and demure.

He watched as Hannah hugged her waist and as Mrs. Massey ushered her around the space, trying to maintain focus on the conversation he was having with Mr. Curley. Her vibrant hair was swept high off of her neck, soft curls bouncing with each movement.

Her cheeks were flushed the most becoming shade of rose, and her full lips curved in an easy smile. Twice she had extended her hand in greeting, her every movement delicate and graceful. Heaven help him, he was no better than the rest of the men in the room, curious and infatuated with Mrs. Trent's new companion.

He'd noticed her discomfort at their introduction. Mrs. Massey was always brazen—quite the opposite, he'd learned, of Miss Faire's more reserved nature. He'd wanted to at least try to make her feel more at ease, but within moments, Mrs. Massey had her dancing with Mr. Curley. And as he watched them dance, her hand on his arm, Nathaniel could barely breathe.

By contrast, Mrs. Massey's presence was suffocating. She'd taken hold of his arm the moment she arrived, and try as he might, he could not free himself. But now, the tide had turned. Miss Faire was standing next to him, her soft scent of rosewater teasing him, watching the dancers swirl around the room.

He stepped closer to be heard above the music and voices. "Did you enjoy your dance, Miss Faire?"

"I did, very much." She turned away from the twirling couples to look at him. "But I am afraid I lack talent."

"On the contrary, you looked quite at ease." He had not meant for the compliment to slip so openly, but at his words, a flush of pink kissed her cheeks.

She toyed with the fan around her wrist. "Well then, I played a part well, for I have little experience dancing, really. At the school I typically took the gentleman's part, and, well, I am afraid my lack of experience will betray me."

He could not help but notice the necklace that she wore. The bright beads were entrancing against her cream skin. He nodded toward it. "Your necklace is lovely."

She touched it with the tips of her fingers and smiled up at him. "I have you to thank for it. It seems you have gotten in quite the habit of assisting me with things I manage to break. First my trunk and then my necklace."

He returned the smile. "It is my pleasure."

She rolled a bead between her forefinger and thumb. "I told you it had belonged to my mother. I have such fond memories of her wearing it to church every Sunday. Losing it would have been like losing her again. So I thank you."

He seized the opportunity to learn more. "When you dropped it, you said that you should never have taken it."

"Did I?" She adjusted the necklace again.

"Yes."

She looked out to the dancers. "The truth is my mother left this necklace to both me and my sister. When we were separated, I had the necklace. I am sure she has wondered what became of it all these years. I am so clumsy I am certain it would have been safer in her care. But one day I shall return it. I am sure she misses it, just as I would."

She offered him a smile. He could not look away from her. Her statement was simple enough, a short explanation that, on the surface, appeared to be little more than a reason behind her distraught behavior earlier. But to him, it marked something very different. It marked the first signs of her breaking down the shell of her reserve—and the start of her letting him into her world.

As the dancers widened their circles, Nathaniel moved closer to Miss Faire to make room, but once they passed, he did not return to his original position. With the soft music, the busy room, and the glint of the candlelight off her face, he quickly forgot about Mrs. Massey and the others.

They were alone. He'd been hoping for just such a moment, for in his pocket was the letter he had received from Mr. McGovern just the day prior. He had been saving it, waiting for the opportunity to give it to her.

He said nothing, just pulled it from his waistcoat and held it out to her. Her attention shifted to the note in his hand.

A tiny frown tugged at her full lips, and she tilted her head in an attempt to read the inscription. "What's this?"

"Go ahead," he said. "Take it."

She took the letter, opened it, and angled it to catch the light from the nearest candle. As she read, her eyes widened. "Is this . . ."

Her voice trailed off, yet he could see the question in her eyes. "It's a list of several of the reputable dressmakers and seamstresses in Manchester. It is not complete, but it is a start."

A little laugh escaped her lips. "Why, this is wonderful!" He thought he noticed moisture gathering in her eyes. "I don't know what to say!"

"You do not have to say a word."

"Thank you, Mr. Stanton."

"You do not have to thank me. Mr. McGovern is responsible for the list, not I."

"But you . . . you . . ." Again, her voice trailed off. "I shall write to these establishments tomorrow. You have given me renewed optimism."

Perhaps they were more alike than he expected. Both of them searching for freedom from a family situation. But whereas he was searching, reaching for his own identity, trying to free himself from family prejudices, she was doing the opposite . . . reaching for a connection.

"I hope you do not think me bold, Miss Faire. But I do wish you would let me assist you more."

Her face fell, and she made herself busy with putting the letter in her reticule. "But you have already helped me so much."

"Do you recall that first day that Mrs. Trent was back at Willowgrove? When we were speaking in the blue drawing room?"

She nodded.

"We spoke of secrets. You said that you believed that everyone had them. It was in our nature."

"Ah, so I did."

He had to force his focus, for he was mesmerized by the way the light caught the glimmer in her eyes. "There is one thing I cannot figure out about you. You have shared that you are here for employment. You hope to find your sister. But what I do not know is how you came to be separated from them in the first place."

"You are right, Mr. Stanton." She pivoted away from him slightly. "I did speak of secrets. And like most people who have something to hide, I wish to be free from it. But I believe I also said that everyone is entitled to a secret or two."

"I do not disagree." He dipped his head slightly to be nearer to her. "But I wish you would share your secret with me."

She flicked her eyes up. "Why?"

He was caught. He had let too much slip. "Because I-I . . ." He decided to change his tactic. "Because I wish to help you, that is all."

And it was a falsehood. He knew it. She probably could sense it too. But how could he tell her that she had captivated him, and he would not find rest until he knew she was happy?

"You and your family have been kind to me. But I caution you about being too interested in my past, for I am afraid you would not like what you would find there."

He raked his fingers through his hair. "That is an intriguing comment."

"I did not mean for it to be intriguing. I meant for it to be honest."

"Everyone has something in their past that is less than favorable."

The music stopped, and applause and voices filled the room, bouncing from the plaster wall and low ceiling.

Mrs. Massey and Mr. Curley were coming back to them, and

just the sight of it annoyed Nathaniel. He wanted more time with Miss Faire.

Mrs. Massey was the first to speak. "What a lovely dancer Mr. Curley is! But I am parched. Shall we go find refreshments?"

Nathaniel acted quickly. "You'll forgive me, but Miss Faire has promised me this dance."

Mrs. Massey's eyes widened. "But you do not dance, Mr. Stanton."

"I shall make an exception."

He offered his arm to Miss Faire. He forced himself to meet her gaze, afraid he might find refusal there. But instead, she smiled and placed her gloved hand atop his arm.

Nathaniel led her to the floor, not pausing to look back.

Once they were settled in their spot, Miss Faire leaned closer. "Why did you do that?"

"Because we had not yet finished our conversation."

The music started, and he bowed before her. Her eyes darted to the couples dancing around them. "I am not familiar with this dance."

"Just follow me."

She put her gloved hand in his. It had been a long time since he had danced. But when her hand touched his, he was willing to do whatever necessary to be close to her.

Miss Faire cast a nervous glance over her shoulder. "I do not think Mrs. Massey is pleased with me."

He placed his hand on the small of her back as he guided her through the next step. "Mrs. Massey is not my concern."

"I do not understand why you are asking me about my secrets, sir, for I believe you have some of your own."

She caught his eye before she turned for the next dance step. She had him cornered. For she was correct. He did have secrets. He waited for her to complete a turn around another dancer before speaking.

"I suppose you are right."

He accepted her hand as she returned from her steps. She moved very close to him. Her skirt brushed against his boot and her scent of rosewater teased him. "But how can I trust you with the secrets I may have if you cannot trust me with yours?"

Nathaniel was standing close to her, and Cecily felt as if she might faint. The movement around her. The warmth of the room. The effect of his hand on hers when it slid around her waist during the course of the dance. It took her mind back to another time.

But her growing feelings toward Mr. Stanton were quite different from the feelings she'd had for Andrew. She'd been a child then, who was looking at romance as a means of escape. Or of rescue from a life of unhappiness.

But the warmth in Mr. Stanton's eyes was different. It made her *feel* different. No longer was she seeking escape. And that freedom opened her heart and mind to an entirely different type of emotion.

She knew well the pain of disappointment. But she had survived. That survival had given her strength.

The dance ended. The musicians paused their melody, and the dancers clapped and laughed. Mr. Stanton stood too long, looking down at her.

She did not want to move. On the contrary, she wanted to continue their discussion. She did believe she could trust him. He had proven to her in many ways that he was willing to help her. She wanted to share every detail of her past. To free herself from the chains binding her. But the words would not form. Her heart had paid the price once for trusting too soon.

She looked up at him and met his pale-blue eyes. "It is not easy for me to share my past. It is not that I do not want to. It is that the words will not come."

He spoke softly. "I understand, Miss Faire. Believe me, I do." He offered her his arm and led her from the dance floor. "I am here to help you. Despite what you may think, you are not alone."

25

You are not alone.

The words rang in her head like a cadence. After she had arrived home, she had tried to sleep, but the magic of the night kept her awake.

Nathaniel Stanton.

Had she imagined it? The genuine look of concern in his eyes? Dare she even think it . . . affection?

Cecily had not spent the duration of the evening with Mrs. Massey, as she had planned. Instead, the Stantons had folded her into their family. Mrs. Massey seemed to disappear. Several times she had sought out the seamstress, only to find her deep in conversation with someone.

She had prepared herself for the realization that Mrs. Massey and Mr. Stanton might be involved romantically. Mrs. Massey had made her opinion of Mr. Stanton quite plain, and based on that information, Cecily probably should have declined Mr. Stanton's offer to dance, if only to protect Mrs. Massey's feelings. She could not have done so, however, without offending him. It became evident over the course of the evening that Mr. Stanton did not share Mrs. Massey's affections. And even though Cecily had spent most of the evening in the company of the Turner and Stanton families, Mrs. Massey's lack of conversation and pointed stares during their carriage ride home spoke volumes of the woman's annoyance with her.

She pushed the thoughts of Mrs. Massey to the back of her mind, for another memory battled them for dominance: the memory of Mr. Stanton's hand on hers.

Whatever secret he was hiding, whatever reason it was that Mrs. Trent did not care for him, no longer mattered.

No, it was not reckless disregard she was feeling. She knew well the difference. Her heart was trumping her rational side. She would be careful. Would be slow and intentional.

She wanted to jump from the bed, dress quickly, and find him—he was certain to be on the grounds somewhere. And just knowing that he was close set her imagination alive with possibilities for the future.

But instead, Cecily spent the quiet, predawn hours writing letters of inquiry to the dressmakers on the list. With each one, her heart soared with optimism. She would find her sister.

The door opened and Clarkson entered, interrupting Cecily's reverie. "You are awake. I am surprised, as late as you returned. How was last night, Miss Faire?"

Cecily stood, a bit surprised at the maid's unusual friendliness. She turned to look at her and noted the dark circles beneath her eyes. Cecily cocked her head to the side. "It was lovely, thank you for asking. How is Mrs. Trent today?"

"She woke just a few minutes ago," Clarkson said, adjusting the bed coverings. "She had a difficult night, I'm afraid."

Cecily frowned. "You should have woken me. I would have sat with her."

"No need, miss." Clarkson helped her dress in a gown of blue silk that Mrs. Massey had made. Once dressed, Clarkson stepped back, propped her hands on her hips, and assessed Cecily's gown.

She pivoted to look into the mirror. Mrs. Massey had done a splendid job on the dress, and with the adjustments she had made herself, the gown was about flawless. Her figure looked transformed when she shifted from the shapeless school gowns to a lady's wardrobe. She smiled and looked over her shoulder at the back of the dress, where the lacings down the bodice gave way to a simple bow.

She was starting to feel like a lady. But it was more than just her exterior that was changing. She picked up her comb and began to work it through the tangles.

Clarkson gathered Cecily's nightclothes and put them in the wardrobe. "I'll bring up Mrs. Trent's breakfast. You can go on in. I know she will be anxious to hear about last night."

Cecily nodded, gave Clarkson the letters she had written to post, and once her hair was pinned loosely up off of her shoulders, she slipped her feet into matching slippers and left the room.

When she entered Mrs. Trent's room, she saw no sign of the older woman.

Cecily frowned. Every morning, Mrs. Trent sat at the table beside the window. Today, the sunlight slanted over an empty seat.

"Mrs. Trent?" she called.

Silence.

She poked her head inside the dressing room adjoining the main bedchamber.

Empty.

But as she turned around, she spied the toe of a black stocking poking out from the other side of the bed. She ran to the woman's still form and dropped to her knees, gripping her shoulder. Mrs. Trent's eyes were open, but they were vacant.

"Clarkson!" she shrieked.

Cecily struggled to help the woman to a seated position. "It's going to be all right, Mrs. Trent. Let's get you into bed, and I think—"

But Mrs. Trent pulled away, swatting her hands at Cecily. But her words were sluggish. Slurred. "Stop it, Lorna! Stop your screeching."

Cecily jerked her hands back as if she had been burned. "It's Cecily. Cecily Faire."

The older woman struggled to get up, her small frame surprisingly strong.

The wild expression in Mrs. Trent's eyes alarmed Cecily. "Clarkson! Come quickly!"

"Stop that shouting, Lorna, at once!" Mrs. Trent said.

But Cecily ignored her. She was in the process of trying to help Mrs. Trent into the bed when Clarkson came bustling through the door, tray in hand.

"Whatever happened, miss?"

"Thank goodness you are here. I came in and found her on the floor. She is talking nonsense."

Clarkson dropped the tray to the table and rushed to her mistress.

Mrs. Trent's eyes were closed now, but her breathing came in labored puffs. Her skin was ghostly white. Cecily had seen her disoriented before, but never like this. Never this dramatic.

Clarkson leaned over, put the back of her hand to the older woman's forehead. "Mrs. Trent is worn out, she is." She cut her eyes to Cecily. They held nothing but a warning.

Cecily shook her head, alarmed at Clarkson's simple assessment. "No, there is something more." Her voice grew louder. "She needs her physician."

As soon as the words were out of her mouth, she remembered. Dr. Collingswood had returned to Manchester two days earlier. Panic besieged her.

Mrs. Trent was now looking past both of them, mumbling nonsensical words and shaking.

Clarkson straightened. "Very well. I will ask Mr. Stanton to send for him."

Cecily recognized the wildness in Mrs. Trent's expression. It was the look that her mother had when she had been delirious with fever those many years ago. Tears were gathering in Cecily's eyes as she immersed a linen cloth in the bedside water basin. Her own hands were trembling as she pressed the cloth against Mrs. Trent's forehead.

But Mrs. Trent would have none of it. In uncoordinated movements, the unsteady woman pulled the cloth away, her actions more like that of a sick child than an adult.

"Mrs. Trent," Cecily said, "you must leave it there."

But Mrs. Trent fixed her eyes on Cecily, the intensity of which froze Cecily to her core.

"You're not supposed to be here," Mrs. Trent hissed.

Fear trickled down Cecily's back. She lowered the linen cloth at the woman's cryptic words. "What do you mean? I'm here to help you. I'm your companion."

"But you're dead. You died."

Cecily shook her head. "I am not dead. Mrs. Trent, you don't know what you are saying."

"I know what I know. Have you come to take me? Or to haunt me?"

An eerie shiver assaulted Cecily. "You are ill, Mrs. Trent. Please, lie down."

The woman's eyes rolled closed. Beads of perspiration lined her withered forehead, and her breath came in shallow puffs.

Hurried footsteps sounded in the hall. Within moments, Clarkson, followed closely by Mr. Stanton and Mrs. Bratham, rushed into the room.

Mr. Stanton was in first, his lips pressed in a line. He pushed past the other women, practically jogging to the bed. He sat down next to her.

At the motion, Mrs. Trent's eyes flew open, and they fixed on Mr. Stanton.

"You," she seethed. Her eyes took on an anger unlike any Cecily had seen before. "You have done this. It is all because of you."

But Mr. Stanton remained controlled. "Stop now. You're unwell. You need to rest."

"Rest? Ha! I will never rest. You would like to think I am unwell. You ruined it. You ruined everything."

The inflection in her tone was cruel. Hateful. Cecily could not bring herself to make eye contact with Mr. Stanton. Instead, she stepped to the other side of the bed and sat down. She took the woman's hand in her own. "You do not mean that, Mrs. Trent. Mr. Stanton is merely trying to help."

Mrs. Trent ripped her hand from Cecily's grasp, her glare never leaving Mr. Stanton, her jowls shaking. "You'll never know what he did!"

Mr. Stanton rose from the bed and adjusted his waistcoat. His expression remained stoic. "Get some laudanum to make her comfortable. I'll send for Mr. Collingswood immediately."

A flurry of activity ensued. Clarkson adjusted Mrs. Trent's blankets. Mrs. Bratham fetched the laudanum.

Cecily stood from the bed, gripped her hands before her, and stepped toward Mr. Stanton.

The lines around his face softened, and she noticed how he glanced around, assessing the situation. His composure calmed her nerves.

He leaned in, his voice low enough that the servants could not hear. "What happened?"

"I am not sure." Cecily folded her arms across her waist. "I came in to join her for breakfast, just as I always do, and she was there, on the floor. And when I went to her, she was angry. She kept calling me Lorna."

At the mention of the name Lorna, a flash of recognition shone in his eyes. He diverted his gaze toward the window.

He knows about Lorna.

They had spoken the previous evening of secrets.

Well, she was growing weary of them. Weary of keeping them. Weary of having them kept from her. And now, emotion tugged on her as she watched Mrs. Trent grow more delirious.

"Who is Lorna?" she blurted.

He forced his fingers through his thick hair and fixed his eyes on her.

"Please, now. We talked of not keeping secrets," she reminded him. "Tell me."

He blew out the air he had been holding, propped his hands on his hips, and nodded to a small painting tucked in the corner. "There."

Cecily turned and took a few steps forward to get a better view. After all the time she had spent in this room, she had never really taken notice of this small painting. The painting was of a young girl, probably twelve or thirteen, with piercing blue eyes and long, black hair that fell over her shoulders. She was a pretty girl with high cheekbones and a pleasant smile.

Mr. Stanton's scent of sandalwood and outdoors signaled that he had drawn nearer. "That was Lorna Trent. Mrs. Trent's only daughter."

Cecily's hand flew to her mouth. She did not know why the words should surprise her so. Mrs. Trent had never spoken of children, and she had always assumed that the Trents never had any. But as she looked at the young woman in the picture, she could make out a few similar features. The arch of the eyebrow and the shape of her eyes.

"Why would she never say anything to me about her? Does she live close?"

"No. Lorna died from a fever when she was fourteen. Mrs. Trent forbade everyone from speaking about her. That is likely why you have never heard her mentioned before."

A sickening wave swept over Cecily. Poor Mrs. Trent! Cecily knew how painful it was to lose a mother. She could only imagine the pain of losing a child.

But in addition to the sorrow Cecily felt, the pang of hurt crept in. How could she not have told her something as important as having lost a child? In hindsight, there was much that Mrs. Trent had not told her. About Lorna. About her reasons for disliking Mr. Stanton so much. Had she only imagined that Mrs. Trent had taken her into her confidence? Perhaps it was Cecily's desire to have a family that made her imagine that she and Mrs. Trent had grown close.

But then again, Cecily hadn't exactly been forthcoming with her either. The thought was sobering.

She turned to find that Mr. Stanton had moved away from her and was speaking with Clarkson. His low, calm voice brought a little comfort. If her interactions with the steward had taught her anything, it was that he would know what to do and how to set things right.

Cecily returned her attention to the painting without really seeing it. The realization was becoming clearer: How could she expect others to trust her with the intricacies of their lives if she was not willing to reveal hers?

26

The next day Cecily awoke to a sliver of light sneaking through Mrs. Trent's drawn curtains. As soon as the fog of sleep faded, she lifted her head and pushed her hair from her face to look around.

Cecily had spent the night on the small sofa at the foot of Mrs. Trent's bed. The elderly woman's night had been difficult. Her fever had steadily intensified, and delirious rants plagued the midnight hours. Dr. Collingswood had arrived from Manchester late the previous evening, and he now slumbered in the adjoining dressing room.

Cecily stood. She was still in her dress from the previous day. She shook out the wrinkled skirt and stretched to wake up her sleeping muscles.

A single lantern was still burning on the stand next to Mrs. Trent's bed. Cecily extinguished it and then ducked under the velvet canopy to sit next to her. The sight alone brought a lump to Cecily's throat. Mrs. Trent's skin was as pale and colorless as the linen gown she wore. If it were not for her jagged breathing, Cecily could not be certain she was still alive. Cecily drew a breath of her own. She had not been awake five minutes, and already her emotions were heightened.

Dr. Collingswood had said it was unavoidable.

Mrs. Trent would likely not recover from this bout.

Her fever was too fervent, her heart too weak.

She tried to remember everything that Dr. Collingswood had said. He had been unwilling to give a formal diagnosis, for her symptoms were unpredictable and inconsistent. But he had said that all signs pointed to a failing heart.

Cecily held the lady's hand in her own and looked down at the protruding veins in the paper-thin skin. How sad it was, now, in the twilight of her life, that Mrs. Trent had no family to comfort her. And, in comparison, the sobering reality that if Cecily were in a similar situation, she would have no one to comfort her either. She didn't know if it was the lack of sleep, the seriousness of the occasion, or the unknown future, but tears gathered. Cecily could not help recall how she held her own mother's hand in a similar fashion, hours, nay—minutes, before she perished.

Before her mother died, Cecily had been happy. Her entire family had been. Her mother had been her father's light, and when she was gone, he became cold and bitter, the hollow shell of a man. Cecily could recall slivers of time when her father had made her laugh. When he would sweep Leah and her up in his arms and swing them around, giggling. But that was before the fever struck their village.

After her mother's death, her father retreated, allowing anger to replace grief. The target of his anger was the very things that reminded him of earlier times, and more specifically, Cecily. Her father, whose beliefs were rooted in folklore, believed the birth of twins to be bad luck—he believed one twin to be good and one to be evil. In his grief, he came to blame Cecily for his wife's death.

Leah, by nature, had always been more soft-spoken and complacent. Cecily, on the other hand, had been outspoken and, at times, defiant. Time would soften her hard edges, but the lesson came far too late.

Her mother's death had been a turning point in her family's story, a sad one.

In many ways, Mrs. Trent's passing would be another turning point for her.

Cecily had not been at Willowgrove but a couple of months. As morbid as it felt to think of such things, she would once again be alone.

On her deathbed, her mother had pleaded with both Cecily and Leah to cling to the faith they had. To seek God in all hardships. Cecily had tried, but in the innocence of youth, she thought that when her father turned her away, God did too. For if her own father no longer loved her, how could her heavenly Father? For years she wrestled with this idea, grappling with the gravity of it, until it became easiest to simply hide from God. But now she was tired of hiding. Tired of secrets. Tired of allowing fear to dictate her thoughts.

She looked at Mrs. Trent's still form. She was alone. No family. Besides herself and Clarkson, no one really loved her. Cecily had not realized it until Mr. Stanton told her about Lorna. If Cecily continued on her path, if she did not face the fears that kept her a prisoner and let others into her heart, she could end up like Mrs. Trent. Alone. Forgotten.

Cecily reached over for her book of Proverbs, which had been discarded on the bedside table days ago. She had been reading it to Mrs. Trent daily. It was a task that she tried not to focus on too much, for it brought back memories of her mother's reading. But in this moment she was longing for connectedness. Longing for a sense of peace. Perhaps Mrs. Trent was listening. Perhaps she was not. But Cecily needed to find comfort in the words as much as Mrs. Trent did.

27

Later that morning, Cecily had finished her reading and was looking out the window at the blanket of fog hugging the trees and landscape. Dr. Collingswood had bled Mrs. Trent in an attempt to release some of the infection. But the act seemed to make her more fragile. Clarkson brought up a tray with broth and weak tea and set it on the bedside table.

Clarkson's strained voice was unusually thin. "How is she?"

With a sharp intake of breath, Cecily quickly gathered herself. "It has been difficult. She has been calling out different names. But she appears to be resting now."

Clarkson rested her hand on Mrs. Trent's shoulder. "Like a ghost, she is. Look at her."

Cecily tried to mask her emotions as she watched the old lady's maid assess her mistress. Clarkson had been Mrs. Trent's personal maid for decades. For whatever Cecily was feeling, Clarkson must be feeling it exponentially.

But whatever emotion was inside Clarkson, she was hiding it well. For her stoic expression gave away little.

"You have been sitting up with her all night." Clarkson sniffed. "You need some rest."

"Thank you, but really, I prefer to stay here," Cecily said.

"Well, at least you will want to change and freshen up. I will help you change gowns."

Cecily looked down at Mrs. Trent. "Do you think she will be all right?"

"We will only be a minute."

Clarkson led the way from Mrs. Trent's chamber to Cecily's.

Her room seemed so calm. In stark contradiction to the angst occurring down the hall. Cecily's body ached to lie in her own bed. To find solace and escape in sleep. But her spirit was restless. How could she be calm when Death was knocking at Mrs. Trent's door?

When her life was about to undergo another change?

Clarkson finished the tie at the back of Cecily's dress, gathered a few items in the room, and then hesitated at the door. "Thank you for sitting up with Mrs. Trent. I know you are a comfort. Her previous companions would not have been so considerate."

Cecily turned, sensing the invisible barrier between them start to crumble. "Mrs. Trent has been nothing but kind and generous to me. I am fond of her."

"And she is fond of you. I have been in Mrs. Trent's service for more than half of my life. I am glad she is not enduring this alone."

"Mr. Stanton has informed me that she has no other family. Is there no one at all to send for to make her more comfortable?"

Clarkson shook her head. "No."

Cecily barely choked on her next words. "And what of Mr. Moreton? Surely he would come to be with his aunt at this time?"

Clarkson huffed. "Mr. Moreton? Humph. He will be here

when it is time to collect his inheritance and not a moment before." She shook out Cecily's gown and draped it over her arm. "I will get this washed. I think you should get some rest. The next few days may be difficult."

After Clarkson left, Cecily rested her hand against the cool glass and looked out of the window at the crisp morning. Gone was the water that had pooled on the landscape for so long. The fog was beginning to lift, and now vivid green hills gave way to lush forest. Skylarks swept across the azure sky, weaving in their course and disappearing from sight. The aged gardener was in the far corner of the west garden, tending to a wisteria in full bloom. Cecily could not help but wonder if he knew of their mistress's state.

She turned to look at the far window and noticed that the gate to Mrs. Trent's garden was closed. After being in Mrs. Trent's dark room for so long, a walk around the grounds was just what she needed. She combed her hair as quickly as her stubborn curls would allow and used two combs to pin it atop her head, washed her face and cleaned her teeth, stuffed her feet into her cream kid slippers, and grabbed her shawl and a basket.

She took the servants' stairs down to the back entrance and circled around the buildings to the garden. She nodded at the scullery maid gathering vegetables in the kitchen garden. The morning breeze was fresh and invigorating, and despite how good it felt to fill her lungs with clean, cool air, her heart remained heavy, her eyes still hot from tears.

The iron gate creaked as she pushed it open, and Cecily made her way to the flowers. Mrs. Trent enjoyed the abundance of roses. She may not be able to do anything to help Mrs. Trent's physical state, but perhaps these would help brighten her mental state. Cecily would fill her room with them.

Ivy claimed the garden's outer walls, obscuring the gray stone walls. The garden was immaculate—a testament to Silas's care. A statue of the Greek god Athena stood in the center of the curved path surrounded by brilliant blooms. With her next inhale, the tantalizing scent of fresh lavender met her.

She pulled the scissors from her apron pocket and moved to a bush full of lush magenta roses. She cut the stems as long as she could and used her scissors to trim the leaves and thorns. The sun felt warm on her uncovered hair and shoulders.

Bloom after bloom she trimmed and placed in her long basket. Her thoughts drifted to a great many things . . . Her friends at Rosemere. Her sister. Mr. Stanton.

She heard movement outside the wall, which was not unusual. On an estate this size, someone was always going about their duties.

She heard the gate creak.

Her heart leapt. She saw a booted foot and then a dark sleeve enter.

She held her breath. *Mr. Stanton.*

But it was not Mr. Stanton.

She was shocked to see before her Mr. Moreton.

His gaze was direct. "I was told I could find you here."

Cecily lifted her head from her task. Would her stomach always give an odd lurch whenever she encountered Andrew? She straightened and wiped her hands on her smock. "Mr. Moreton. You've returned."

"Yes. Mr. Stanton wrote to me about my aunt's condition. I felt it only right to come see her."

"Mr. Stanton?" she repeated, wondering why he had not mentioned it. Clarkson's warning played fresh in her ears. "When did you arrive?"

"Only just. I wanted to see you straightaway. I inquired after you, and one of the footmen saw you come in here."

She looked toward the gate. "I am sure your presence will be a great comfort."

An awkward silence followed. For surely they both knew her statement was a lie.

In an effort to mask the pause, she said, "Are the Pritchards with you?"

"No. They are at their home outside of London for the time being."

The sunlight filtered through the flowering trees, dappling his dark hair.

"I take it you have been at Aradelle Park, then?"

"I have."

"And did you find everything in order?" She tried to hide the eagerness in her voice. He'd promised to make inquiries on her behalf.

He smiled, an expression that made him look like the boy from years ago. "Oh, I don't need to tell you how things are. Everything is exactly as it was when you left, even after all this time. Mother is happy as long as her opium is near, and Father is happiest when I am not present."

Her shoulders slumped. Perhaps he had forgotten her request. And yet, despite her frustration, she felt sad for him. This was how his life had always been. "Those are strong words. One might mistake them for self-pity."

"Self-pity?" He laughed and straightened his green double-breasted waistcoat. "Dear Cecily, you know me far too well. You know my faults. Why should I endeavor to hide them?"

She was uncertain how to answer. "I knew you five years ago. You were a boy. Much can change with time."

He smirked and cocked his head to the side. The breeze caught his hair. "Do you find me changed?"

"I do."

He stepped forward, his eyes narrowing. "Dare I say you have changed, too, Cecily. Do not judge too harshly."

She let the rose she had been cutting fall to the basket. "I am well aware of how I have changed. And that is probably for the best."

He turned from her, a silent indication that this topic of conversation was closed. When he turned back around, a sober light shaded his eyes, and he sat on the stone bench. "How is my aunt?"

"I am afraid she is not doing well."

Andrew's expression darkened. "How so?"

Cecily clipped another rose and let it fall to the basket. "She has had several strange episodes. Often she does not know who I am, or anyone, for that matter."

He propped his foot on the bench. "That is most unfortunate."

Cecily wondered if he spoke the truth.

"I have something for you that I hope will cheer you, all the way from Aradelle." He reached in his waistcoat and pulled out a letter. "Here. It is a letter from Mrs. Sherwin."

She jerked her head and stared at the letter, half doubting its existence. She looped her basket over her arm and, with the other hand, reached for the letter.

The blood began to swoosh through Cecily's ears with all the force of the wind over the downs, drowning out the sounds of the birds chirping. The idea that she could potentially be holding the answers she sought for so long trumped all rational thought. She wanted to rip open the letter and devour the words, but she was acutely aware of how Andrew's eyes were fixed on her. For whatever words she might find penned within, she wanted to read them in solitude.

She looked up at Andrew and attempted to remember her manners. Her tongue felt thick and dry when she spoke. "And how is Mrs. Sherwin?"

"She is just as you remember her, no doubt. She was eager for news of you, though." He stepped a little closer. A smile tugged at his lips. "She was always so fond of you, if you remember. She asked if you were as lovely as ever."

She did not miss the shift of his tone. She looked down at the toes of her slippers, still damp from the dew.

He cocked his head to the side. "Are you not the least bit curious to know what my response to her was?"

She shook her head in protest. "Mr. Moreton, please, I—"

"I told her that you were every bit as lovely as the day you left. That the years had been kind. And it is true."

She looked to the gate, roses forgotten. Had she not dreamed of this moment? Hoping that he, like a knight in shining armor, would ride in and right past wrongs and save her from her prison? Although she no longer felt as if she were in a prison. She was in a place of her own choosing, and she had a clear mission.

She lifted her basket and slung it over her arm. "Please do not think me rude, Mr. Moreton, but I am anxious to read my letter. Thank you for being so kind as to speak to Mrs. Sherwin on my behalf and bring this letter to me, but I am sure you will understand that I wish to read it in private. Please excuse me."

She brushed past him and fled the garden, her steps much faster than her regular pace. She heard his voice call after her, but she fixed her eyes on the entrance to Willowgrove.

28

Cecily could not get to her chamber fast enough. It was as if the letter were burning her very fingers and the floor beneath her were shifting, slowing each step.

Five years ago, almost to the month, everything she believed to be true ceased to exist. She had considered that chapter in her life closed and dead for so long now that this letter, even more so than facing Andrew, was a strange glimpse into a world that had closed its door to her. Her footsteps echoed on the stone steps of the servants' staircase and her hands trembled.

The air was stiff and hot in the corridor outside her chamber. It hung about, as if quietly steaming, watching, waiting to see what would transpire. The discomfort it caused matched her mood. She studied the letter's inscription, feeling as if she were holding her sister's memory in her hand. Thoughts of the one person whom she truly missed choked her, the memory clutching her in its hot grasp. She fled to her window, turned the ancient handle, and pushed the leaded glass out into the late-morning air. Warm tendrils of an airy breeze pushed their way inside, but did little to relieve her. With her foot she pulled a chair closer and then sat. She slid her finger beneath the seal, pulled it free, and unfolded the letter.

The handwriting was rough and jagged. Her handwriting used to look the same, before her time at Rosemere. Each stroke held remnants of a relationship that had been far too long stale. She took a deep breath.

Cecily-girl,

News of you came like a ghost from the past. Mr. Moreton told me of your situation. I was pleased as can be to hear you are well. He was most discreet, protecting you from the wagging tongues that still plague these halls. A testament to the friendship you once shared, no doubt.

I've no call to pretend that I know what has happened with you since you left. In fact, the only news I had was that you were at a girls' school, and then news from Mr. Moreton that you were now a lady's companion.

The day you left was a sad one. He told me you knew little about what happened afterward. Had you written in the months following the event, I would have had to decline to write you. The master was in fits about it and was most cross with anyone who made mention of it. But time, as you know, heals many things.

I have missed you. All the girls have. I could update you on them all now, but what would I have to write you in the future? I would ever so much like to stay in touch now that I have found you again.

I am happy and my life is very different, and I am eager to tell you of all things, but all these things I can share with you in good time. For Mr. Moreton mentioned that you were most anxious to learn about your family, so I will keep you in suspense no longer.

I do not know any news firsthand, mind you, but you know how Aradelle Park is. News travels as quickly as a bird from one tree to another. So I shall tell you the rumors that I heard regarding your sister.

Miss Bige, as you know, was a great friend of your sister's. She reports that she went to live with your aunt in Manchester. But that was several years past, and I do not know what to believe. And then, this brings me to the difficult part of my letter. I heard a report through Cyrus Lindford, the new head groom, that your father died about a year ago in a town south of London. A letter had been sent here, looking for his relations, and sadly, no one had any information on your whereabouts or your sister's. Your father was hard on you, but I know you loved him, despite all that happened. I am truly pained for you.

I am eager for us to get reacquainted, but in light of my last bit of information, I shall save such news for another time. I hope now that we are reconnected, you will write. I am eager to know of you.

Cecily forgot to breathe, and truth be told, her eyes only skimmed over the end of the letter. As if acting on their own accord, her eyes sought out the word and clung to it.

Died.

She tried to picture her father, with his broad shoulders, hair the color of fire, so like hers, and ruddy complexion. But her recollection had grown dim.

She tried to remember the father of her youth prior to her mother's death. The laughter. The happy times. But all she could recall was the way he made her feel. Frightened. Flawed. Insignificant. Her memories of him smiling had faded, and all that remained was his angry scowl. But even as the unpleasant memories outweighed the good, her child's heart still wanted to cling to him, with the hope that her memories were incorrect.

She read the letter again.

Surely it could be a mistake. But the logic seemed sound, and hardly from someone who would tell a falsehood. After all, Mrs. Sherwin had comforted her and Leah after their mother died. She snuck them special treats from Aradelle's kitchen and even gave

Cecily a new pair of boots when hers had worn through. What reason would she have to lead her astray?

Cecily did not want it to hurt so badly.

For this was the man who sent her away. Rejected her.

But if the truth were to be told, her situation improved once she left Aradelle. In fact, she was treated better at Rosemere than her own father had treated her, and she had been given an opportunity that surpassed any she could have received had she lived out her days on Aradelle's grounds.

She felt numb.

She had been right about her sister. Where else but their aunt's house would she go? Their mother's only sister. But Cecily's grandmother had died when her mother was young, and the sisters did not stay close. Cecily could barely recall her aunt's Christian name. Perhaps it was Lucy. Or Lucille.

It was hard to tell if they were tears of agony or defeat that slipped down her cheeks and blotted the letter. While the letter had connected her with a dear friend, it had destroyed a hope that she had fought for years to keep alive.

Somehow she made it to her bed. Her last cognizant thought before succumbing to sleep was that she was now utterly alone.

Cecily splashed the icy water on her cheeks and looked at the small looking glass. Her eyes were red. Her skin, blotchy and pale. And with her hair, well, she just looked red all over.

She blotted her face with the linen towel. She could cry no more. Her heart ached. Her head pounded. But as she was about to read the letter again, someone knocked at the door.

Clarkson poked her head in. "I think you should come. Mrs. Trent is asking for you."

"How is she?"

"She is all right, for the time being. She seems lucid."

"Thank you, Clarkson." Cecily placed the letter on the top of her bureau, retrieved the basket of roses, and then hurried from her room.

When she entered Mrs. Trent's room, it was dark and warm. No sound. No movement.

She swallowed hard. Each time she came to check on the woman, she feared the worst.

But as she stepped into the room, a weak voice sounded from the bed. "Come over here, Miss Faire."

Breathing a little sigh of relief, Cecily moved to the chair next to the bed, just as she had so many times before.

"I brought you these from the garden." Cecily lifted her basket so Mrs. Trent could see the contents. "The garden is quite lovely this morning. Perhaps soon you will be well enough for a walk. The irises are starting to bloom."

"I fear my days of walking the garden are past me."

"You shouldn't say such things. You seem a bit better today, and tomorrow you shall be stronger still." Cecily placed the basket at her feet.

Mrs. Trent drew a shallow breath, loud with the effort. "How optimistic you are." A coughing fit racked her feeble body. When Cecily offered to help adjust her against the pillows, Mrs. Trent waved her away. When the coughing subsided, she added, "I fear I do not share your optimism. But I am a bit stronger today, I think. And you are here to keep me company."

After the news of her own father, Cecily's heart was heavy. Her nerves were raw. She could not watch another person die, and now, as she watched Mrs. Trent struggle, pain stabbed her. She could deny the truth, pretend that Mrs. Trent would be better after a good night's rest, but it would change nothing.

Cecily weighed the wisdom of each word before speaking. Perhaps it was selfish to burden Mrs. Trent with such an admission now for no other reason than to release herself from her own regret. "I know you are unwell, but I was hoping to speak to you regarding a matter that has been weighing quite heavily on me."

The older woman opened her eyes, but her expression remained still. "Oh?"

Cecily interlaced her fingers. "I have not been completely honest with you, and I was hoping to set things right."

Mrs. Trent shifted to adjust herself against the pillows. "I see."

The words were spilling out of Cecily's mouth before she had time to consider what she would say next. "That is to say, I am not the lady you think me to be."

Mrs. Trent remained quiet, her rheumy eyes expectant.

Cecily drew a deep breath. She felt like a child, waiting for her father's wrath after having done something wrong. "I was a student at Rosemere, but I was not sent there to become a lady, as one might presume. I was sent there as punishment. My father disowned me and left me in Mrs. Sterling's care. I have heard naught from my family since that day nearly five years ago."

Cecily kept her gaze low, waiting for a gasp of shock, but instead, Mrs. Trent reached out and covered Cecily's hand with her own.

"I have wondered what your secret was. But there is more, is there not?" Mrs. Trent drew a jagged breath, and the rustle of the bedclothes seemed unusually loud as she adjusted herself against her pillows. "So, if I may ask you, exactly how long have you known my nephew?"

Mrs. Trent's direct stare froze Cecily.

Cecily forced herself not to look away.

Bumps rose on her arms. Her pulse quickened. "I am not certain I understand your meaning."

Mrs. Trent raised her eyebrow in a knowing expression. "My dear Miss Faire, I suspect that someone your age may think me oblivious, but I am not as unobservant as you think."

Heat rushed to Cecily's cheeks, to her neck and ears. She had been lying to Mrs. Trent. Not an outward lie, true, but a lie of omission was still a falsehood. Mrs. Trent deserved the truth.

Cecily paused to muster her courage before speaking. "I have known your nephew for most of my life."

Mrs. Trent's lips curled slowly in a hint of triumph. "You see, I might be old, but I am not wholly unaware."

It was what Mrs. Trent did not say that extracted more words from Cecily, for the ensuing silence jabbed harder than any words could. "My father was a blacksmith. He was employed by Mr. Moreton at Aradelle Park for many years. He saw to the needs of the estate and the tenants. Our cottage was on the property."

"Why did you never mention this?" Her tone was patient.

Cecily selected the answer that would pass her lips with the least resistance. "Because I know you want me to be a lady. I-I was not sure you would approve of a blacksmith's daughter as your companion."

Mrs. Trent drew a labored breath. "We all come from somewhere, Miss Faire. What matters is how we take our circumstances and make them our own."

The burning truth ached for release. She looked down at her intertwined fingers. "But there is another reason I never mentioned my past connection to Aradelle Park."

She wanted the truth to be out without having to actually say the words. She had never said them to another living soul. And here she was about to say them to the one person who possessed the power to cast her away from Willowgrove if she should be so inclined. But Cecily felt that, in some inexplicable way, Mrs. Trent might actually understand.

After taking a moment to collect herself, Cecily spoke. "I have known your nephew, but our relationship went beyond that of a casual acquaintance. Our history, such as it was, is quite complicated."

Mrs. Trent angled her head against the pillow. "I know his history very well."

It was as if the words were a lead rope, guiding the conversation and pulling the words from her as one would a horse through a gate. "Mr. Moreton and I had a relationship, a romance, if you will, when I was but sixteen. It was when my father discovered our romance that I was sent to Rosemere."

There.

For better or for worse, it was out.

Cecily had hoped that by saying the words a magical peace would cloak her in its healing relief, but nothing of the sort happened. Instead, her anxiety wound tighter around her heart, squeezing it and choking the confidence from her.

She had never felt more exposed.

Every sound in the room was amplified.

The ticking of the timepiece on the mantel.

The staccato pop of the lazy afternoon fire.

Like a thief awaiting a verdict, she held her breath.

After the seconds ticked past at a maddeningly slow pace, Mrs. Trent spoke. "I thought it might be you."

At this, Cecily jerked her head up.

Mrs. Trent's expression grew distant. "I knew of my nephew's past, Miss Faire. Andrew is my brother's child, after all. When we learned of his ways, his father requested that he stay with me here at Willowgrove to remove him from the situation. Of course, I could not refuse such a request. But as it relates to you, go look in that trunk over there."

Cecily obeyed and moved to the trunk, which she had oft seen but never knew the contents. Her legs felt uncertain and her balance was slightly off. She knelt and lifted the lid. Inside, she found stacks of letters bound by satin ribbons.

Mrs. Trent's voice was growing thin. "For years I kept every letter I received. A testament to my life's story. I did notice my nephew's change in behavior after your arrival. He's always been of an affected bent, but I did think the alteration of his demeanor odd nonetheless. As I was rereading some letters, I came upon a few my sister-in-law wrote me around the time Andrew came to reside at Willowgrove. While she did not mention you by name, she did refer to the girl as being the daughter of their blacksmith by the name of Faire. From that moment on, nothing could have been plainer."

Cecily let the trunk lid close. "I do apologize, Mrs. Trent. I should have been more forthcoming. I confess I did not tell you because I was afraid of what you would think of me. I feared losing my position as your companion. But as our acquaintance grew, I did want to tell you. I wasn't sure how."

"Oh, child," Mrs. Trent said, motioning her to come back to the bedside. "We all have past indiscretions that haunt us. Life has handed me my share. More than I can count. Such a secret can be a blessing in that it preserves normalcy. But it can be a curse. You must learn to discern the difference, a lesson I myself wish I would have learned long ago."

"Now that all is confessed, I am relieved to be free of it." Cecily offered a little laugh. "Now it seems almost silly to have feared your response."

"One more thing I must discuss with you. There are secrets in these old halls, and they will live on long after I am gone. You shared with me your secret. I shall confess mine."

Cecily stiffened, a little frightened of what she might hear. "You do not have to tell me."

"Yes, I do. For you were brave enough to speak with me. I

should do the same." Mrs. Trent looked to the window, as if seeing the distant past. "I do. Otherwise it will haunt me from now into the afterlife. I am old, but I am no fool. I am dying, Miss Faire."

Cecily opened her mouth to protest, to tell her she should not say such things, but the older woman lifted her frail hand to silence her. "Please, at least give me the decency of honesty. I have known Dr. Collingswood a long time, and I recognized the look on his face." She looked to her left, at the portrait of her husband. Longing filled her eyes, a look of love and warmth that Cecily had not seen before. "It is the same expression he wore when my husband was dying."

But with a sudden sniff, Mrs. Trent snapped from her trance. "No doubt you have noticed my disdain for Nathaniel Stanton."

The mention of Mr. Stanton took Cecily by surprise. "Ma'am?"

"I have never cared for Mr. Stanton, but I suppose it can hardly be his fault."

Cecily bit her lower lip with the anticipation of what she was about to hear. "What do you mean?"

"Mr. Stanton is my husband's illegitimate son."

Cecily held her breath, unsure she had heard the words correctly. *"Illegitimate son?"*

"Now that I have told someone, it hardly seems like a secret worth keeping." It was Mrs. Trent's turn to grumble a nervous laugh of her own. "What lengths I went to in order to make sure the secret was never found out."

Cecily wished she could unhear what she'd heard. She felt like she had intruded on a place he'd not invited her.

For it meant that Mr. Stanton was not who he said he was.

Or who she thought he was.

But should that matter?

For was she no different, clinging to her own secret in desperate fear that someone might learn the truth?

The words were slow and dry as they passed Mrs. Trent's lips. "My husband was an honorable man, Miss Faire. But he was not immune to errors of judgment."

Cecily looked up at the painting, making little effort to hide her assessment. The painting was of Mr. Trent in his youth, perhaps slightly younger than Mr. Stanton. It had been moved up from the blue drawing room several days past. The man in the portrait was not smiling. Instead, his expression looked cold and austere, so different from how she saw Mr. Stanton.

"As soon as the result of his actions was evident, he wanted to claim the child for his own. But I would not allow it. He desired to bequeath the entirety of Willowgrove to the child and raise it here, as Willowgrove's heir, but I would have none of it. My husband was a strong man, Miss Faire. Do not misunderstand. I was the one person who could sway him. He would not send the child, or his mother, away, but instead allowed him to be raised by our steward. Nathaniel Stanton's mother betrayed me, and to this day, I am uncertain as to whose betrayal sliced the deepest."

Suddenly it made sense. Mrs. Trent had mentioned that Mrs. Stanton had at one point been her lady's companion. This was the source behind her scorn.

Cecily remained quiet, suspecting Mrs. Trent needed to finish her confession.

"Mr. Stanton did not know the truth about his identity until a few years ago. I daresay he has been trying as hard as I to keep the secret. My husband admitted his wrongdoings, yet he wanted to do right by the mother and child. I fought it, and it was my resistance, not the child, that tore us apart. I channeled my anger into trying to force the young Mr. Stanton to leave, but Mr. Stanton is loyal. How foolish I am for having fought it all these years."

Mrs. Trent's voice cracked, and she began to cough.

Cecily reached out and took the woman's hand in her own.

"That was so very long ago, Mrs. Trent. You cannot punish yourself now."

The words were easy to say to another. But how could she give advice that she was not willing to take herself?

Cecily studied Mrs. Trent's face, twisted with the pain of unresolved conflict. "Perhaps you would rest easier if you set things right with Mr. Stanton."

Cecily held her breath, half expecting a violent response.

The older woman looked at her husband's portrait. "Too much time has passed, I fear. Nathaniel Stanton has done nothing to me personally. But as long as I punished him, I continued to punish my husband. Mrs. Stanton as well. What a silly waste of time. When I die, life will go on. Andrew shall inherit Willowgrove, but my husband did leave property in the north to Nathaniel. He will leave Willowgrove. He will likely never think of me again. No doubt he is eager for my demise."

But Cecily had not heard anything after the words "property in the north."

Cecily drew a breath so sharp it hurt. Mr. Stanton—leave? She did not know why this should shock her so. After all, would she not leave Willowgrove eventually as well?

But Willowgrove seemed to be woven into the very fabric of who Nathaniel Stanton was. Perhaps it was not so much the shock of his leaving that bothered her as the fear of being separated from him.

She swallowed and patted Mrs. Trent's hand. "If you like, I can call for Mr. Stanton. I think you would feel much better if you could make your feelings known."

29

Later that evening, as the long shadows were creeping over the planked floors of Willowgrove's upper level, Nathaniel stood in front of Mrs. Trent's chamber door. He clenched and unclenched his fists.

When Miss Faire had come to his office earlier in the day, he'd been pleased . . . until he learned that Mrs. Trent wanted to speak with him.

Such an occasion was rarely a positive occurrence.

He was having second thoughts about agreeing to see her. But after Miss Faire's unmasked concern and insistence on the matter, he could hardly deny her.

Miss Faire's voice met his ears before he even stepped foot into Mrs. Trent's room. He was too far away to make out the words, but her voice was soft, like a lullaby.

Alas, he drew a breath.

He tapped his knuckles against the door before stepping farther into the chamber. Despite the slivers of white sunlight sneaking around the drawn curtains, the room was dark. A fire simmered in the grate at the end of the room, producing oppressive heat, and two candles were burning near the head of the bed. Miss Faire was seated in a chair next to the bed, dressed in a gown of pale green and gold. She was angled toward the candles, head bent over her sewing. Her auburn hair was swept atop her head, and the candlelight flickered on her smooth, white neck.

Pretending she did not affect him was more difficult with each passing day.

At the sound of his knock, she lifted her head. "Mr. Stanton."

He bowed and took another step in. "Is she awake?"

"No, she's been asleep all afternoon." Miss Faire stood and put the sewing on the table.

Now that he was closer to her, he observed how tired she looked. Dark circles rested beneath her eyes. Her fair skin was pale. She rubbed the back of her neck. "Are you all right, Miss Faire? Every time I pass this room, you are up here."

She smiled and rolled her head to look at him. "I do not wish to leave Mrs. Trent alone."

Nathaniel admired her dedication. But the toll must be hard on her. "Have you spoken with Dr. Collingswood recently?"

Miss Faire nodded and looked down to the ground. "Yes. He was up a few hours ago."

"Yes, he just left my office." He drew closer. "He told you, then? That we must prepare ourselves?"

He was surprised at how difficult the words were to say. Mrs. Trent had been against him his entire life, and yet she had been a constant. And slowly but surely, every constant was slipping free from his grip, setting him even further adrift.

She made no motion at the words, but stared unblinking at Mrs. Trent's form. "I refuse to believe it. We had a lovely conversation earlier. I-I think there is hope."

Miss Faire pushed the canopy back farther. As she did, a lock of hair escaped her comb and brushed her collarbone. "Mrs. Trent, you have a visitor."

When the woman did not respond, Miss Faire placed her hand on top of Mrs. Trent's and spoke a little louder. "Mrs. Trent, Mr. Stanton wishes to speak with you."

At this, Mrs. Trent stirred, and her eyes opened. She remained silent for several moments, and then, as if she just comprehended what had been said to her, she lifted her gray head. She squinted as her eyes adjusted to the faint light. "Where is he?"

"He is here." Miss Faire motioned for Nathaniel to draw near, and he obeyed.

At first, the look Mrs. Trent gave him was blank, almost indifferent. He knew her tendency toward confusion, and he regretted agreeing to the conversation. He cleared his throat. "You said you wanted to see me?"

"Sit, Nathaniel."

Mrs. Trent had never called him by his Christian name. He did not know if it was an oversight or if she was having one of her episodes, but he did not protest. Miss Faire motioned for him to take the chair next to the bed, and he complied.

Mrs. Trent's skin was as thin as parchment and white. How different she looked without her customary rouge painting her cheeks. It was then he noticed that she had his father's portrait as a young man moved from her parlor to this room. Looking more like a mirror than a painting, the blue eyes looked back at them, as if bearing witness to this moment.

Mrs. Trent followed his gaze and looked at the painting for several moments.

"I loved my husband."

Her words were low and strange, but somehow it did not seem fitting to question her here. For all her faults, that was one truth he believed. "I know you did."

"He loved me." Her head shook with every word. But then she turned her eyes on him. "I'll be blunt. I have not made life easy for you. But as you can imagine, your presence has been a constant reminder of his betrayal."

A dozen retorts went through his mind, but he remained silent.

After a long pause, she drew a weak breath and spoke again. "I have been wrong to take my pain out on you in the manner I have. And now I must atone or carry the shame of that with me to the next world."

His bitterness was dissolving to pity. "You owe me no explanation."

"I do." She met his gaze directly. "Your father loved you. He wanted to raise you in Willowgrove Hall. It was I who refused. It was to punish him. And I did—relentlessly. It is too late to ask his forgiveness. But I am asking you."

Heat crept up from his neckcloth, and he shifted in the chair. He'd decided long ago not to be affected by her. But as hard as he tried, the boy in him still clung to the hurt. He thought of his mother and the injustice she'd experienced as a result of Mrs. Trent's actions, and fresh anger cascaded over him.

But as he looked at the frail woman, lying still and sick, did any of it matter anymore?

He'd nearly forgotten about Miss Faire standing behind him until he heard her shoe scuff against the floor. "I will give you privacy."

He turned and reached out to stop her, unaware of the fact that he had touched her forearm until his hand was already there. "No, please stay."

Wordlessly, she stopped and took a chair that was against the wall. Something about her presence made him feel less alone. Less vulnerable. Stronger.

Nathaniel turned back to Mrs. Trent. Her eyes were expectant, her expression, ever controlled. "I forgive you."

I forgive you. The words echoed in the tall room. Did he really mean them? Or was he saying something to make a woman's last days easier?

Mrs. Trent seemed to ease at the words. Her graying head sank a little deeper into the pillow.

His voice sounded far too loud for the space. "You need to rest now."

She said nothing more, only closed her eyes. He rested his hands on his knees for a moment. He stood and turned. Miss Faire's eyes were latched onto him.

Unsure of how he felt about what had just happened, he said nothing to her. He needed a moment to settle his thoughts. Not only had Mrs. Trent just apologized—something Nathaniel had thought would never be possible—but Miss Faire had borne witness to it all. What was more affecting was that she now knew something about him that very few people knew.

He couldn't face her. Not yet.

But as he approached the door, he heard the soft padding of her slippers on the carpet.

"Mr. Stanton, wait."

He stopped. Any other time, he would relish a visit with Miss Faire. But at the moment, he knew not what to say.

"I did not mean to intrude on your private conversation. I would have gone, but I—"

"You did not intrude." He tried to manage a little chuckle to lighten the moment. "So there, Miss Faire, you were right. I did have a secret of my own, and now you know it."

But she did not appear amused. In fact, her eyebrows drew together in what he interpreted as concern. "Is it true, then?"

He frowned. "Is what true?"

"She said that you are to inherit another property. Are you going to leave Willowgrove?"

He shrugged. This was not a conversation he was prepared to have openly. With anyone. "I don't know. But will you not be leaving as well?"

She knitted her fingers together in front of her. "I suppose I will."

He looked at her. "My sisters know nothing about this. Any of it. I'd consider it a favor if you kept it to yourself until I can think of a way to share it with them."

He hadn't intended for his words to sound so sharp, but at the moment, he could not find a way to soften them. He lowered his eyes to avoid seeing the hurt look on her face.

"O-Of course. You have my word."

30

The next morning Cecily awoke with a start in her own chamber. The previous evening she had intended only to lie down for a moment, to rest her head and find a moment's solace to contemplate the day's many happenings. Her talk with Andrew. Her confession to Mrs. Trent. Mr. Stanton's secret. But as she opened her eyes, long shadows of an early-morning sunrise crossed the room.

Mrs. Trent!

She jumped up from the bed, still fully clothed in her gown from the previous day, and as she did, the letter from Mrs. Sherwin fell off the bed and landed on the rug.

She picked it up and smoothed it, refusing to look at any particular words in the process. So it had been real. Not a frightful dream. Not a nightmare. The angry child within her pleaded with her to crumple up the letter and hurl it into the fire that a chambermaid had started before she awoke. But she stayed calm and folded the letter.

Her father was dead. The man she had loved. Feared. Blamed. The man who had rejected her. He never forgave her. And she had not forgiven him.

It bothered her. Especially as she had just witnessed Mr. Stanton's act of forgiveness the day before.

Ignoring the fact that several locks of hair now escaped her comb and hung down her back, she quietly, reverently slid back into Mrs. Trent's room, her hands and feet still feeling numb with sleep. Her face itched from the effect of dried tears on her skin, and her eyes burned, made worse by the shards of light slipping through the cracks around the brocade curtains.

She was only half surprised to see Andrew in the room, sitting on a straight-backed chair at the side of Mrs. Trent's bed.

He looked as worn and as full of grief as anyone else at Willowgrove. Cecily gave Andrew credit. He played a convincing role. If it was indeed a role. He lifted his head when she entered. She tried to avoid eye contact, but his eyes sought hers and she could not look away.

She saw something in them. He was seventeen again. Too much history had transpired between them.

Then it hit her. Mrs. Trent had forgiven her for keeping her past with Andrew a secret. And Mr. Stanton had forgiven Mrs. Trent for years of pain.

But whom had she forgiven?

She had advised Mrs. Trent to forgive and ask for forgiveness, but had she done this herself?

Her heart still ached at the injustice she experienced at the hands of her father. And if she were honest, she still held Andrew partially responsible.

Andrew looked sad. Miserable, even. Was she doing the same thing Mrs. Trent had been doing to Mr. Stanton?

Andrew stood, poured a cup of tea, and extended it to her. "How was your letter?"

Cecily ignored the tea and pinned him with her stare. "You knew about my father."

His smile faded. He looked down at the cup.

Cecily interpreted his silence as assent. "If you knew, why did you not tell me?"

"I did not want to be the one to hurt you. Again."

"So you hid it from me?"

"Let me ask you this, Cecily." He paused, putting the cup down on the table. "Do you think that you are the only one this has been difficult on? In case you have forgotten, you were not alone that night your father took you away. I was with you, ready, waiting to leave. And forgive me for the manner in which I have handled things since your arrival. But what would you have me do?"

Unable to look at him, she fixed her eyes on the intricate pattern on the dark rug. His question burned her ears. "I would hope for the truth. From a friend."

"A friend," he repeated, the words sounding almost like a question.

"Yes."

Cecily thought about Mrs. Trent and her brave act of forgiveness. Cecily wanted to be free from that pain. She forced herself to look at Andrew, really look at him. The sandy hair. The dark eyes she had found so bewitching all those years ago. He was a symbol of so many things. And yet the anger, the fear she felt when she was with him, simply didn't seem to matter. She thought of the women who had tried so hard to teach her things throughout her life. Her mother. Mrs. Sterling. But it was Mrs. Trent, with her desperate desire for forgiveness at the end of her life, who affected her most.

"We cannot undo the past. It is as certain and finite as it can be. But we both need to find our freedom from it."

He nodded.

And in that moment, in that simple act, she could be in the same room with him, face-to-face with her past, and it was all right. And in her heart she knew—she could forgive Andrew Moreton.

31

Mrs. Trent was dead.

Tears blurred Cecily's vision.

It had happened sometime during the midnight hours, during the time when the moon cast silver light on the earth below. She'd been awoken by Clarkson's frantic cry before the sun's first rays.

It hardly caught them by surprise. Mrs. Trent's passing had been inevitable. They had known for days. Dr. Collingswood had told them as much. So why was Cecily struggling to maintain composure?

She wiped the moisture from her face. In a short time, Mrs. Trent had become the grandmother she'd always wished for.

And now, in Mrs. Trent's chamber, surrounded by her things in the morning light, her heart ached with every beat.

Mrs. Trent's still form lay on the bed. A white sheet covered her.

Dr. Collingswood, who had been absent from the room, stepped behind her.

Cecily's voice cracked as she spoke. "Was she at peace?"

"She never awoke."

Through the shrouds in her mind, Cecily tried to recall their last conversation. She attempted to breathe, but the air might as well be fire. Never had she expected to care for the woman who employed her, but somewhere between the reading and conversations, the walks in the garden, she had filled a void in Cecily's life that she did not even realize existed.

The still, stale air in the sickroom was stifling. She stepped into the corridor, grateful for its coolness. Morning light was just creeping in the windows, covering the space in shadows. With tears blinding her vision, Cecily was not even sure how she was taking one step in front of the other.

But she needed air.

She kept her tearful gaze downcast and increased her pace down the corridor. She was not looking, until she ran so hard into something that little black flecks scurried across her vision. Someone grabbed her arm, steadying her. She looked up. A fabric-covered button. White neckcloth. The scent of outdoors and sandalwood.

She looked up at the face of Mr. Stanton.

At any other time, such a misstep would be embarrassing. It would require acknowledgment or even an apology. But his face was etched with the same lines she had seen on the doctor's. His color, even for a man with tanned skin, seemed pale and wan.

She spoke without really thinking. "Mrs. Trent is dead."

Perhaps it was shocking to put it so bluntly. But if there was one thing she had learned about Mr. Stanton, it was that he cared little for pretentious etiquette.

"I know."

After several moments he released his hands from her upper arms, and she immediately missed the warmth she felt through her sleeves.

"Are you all right?" His words were low, almost a whisper. She was not sure she had ever been spoken to with such tenderness.

She tucked her loose hair behind her ears and wiped her face. She tried to speak, but the only sound she could form came out as a sob.

Then, in the coolness of the still shadows, Mr. Stanton moved closer. He reached out one arm. Then the other. Then wrapped them around her.

He pulled her tight against his chest.

This was not proper. She should pull away.

But the need to feel safe and not alone took over her senses.

At the touch of his hand, the sensation of him so close, a tear fell. Then another.

His words were soft. His lips grazed her forehead, causing the ground beneath her to spin and shift. She could not make out the words above the wild beating of her heart. But as his arms tightened around her, the warmth of him stilled her trembling.

This was a temporary sanctuary, she knew. But the part of her that she could not heal on her own prevented her from stepping back. She did not want to be alone. And more than that, she didn't want to be separated from this man who held her.

After a moment, she found her strength. "I apologize. I do not know what came over me."

"Do not apologize." His hands moved to her arms. Then they fell to his sides. "It is sad news, indeed."

But did he know how deep the sadness went? How it touched every part of her?

"She is at peace now," he said.

Cecily opened her mouth to respond when down the hall, the door to Mrs. Trent's chamber opened. Dr. Collingswood poked his head out, his wig askew. "Stanton, good, you're here. I thought I heard voices."

Mr. Stanton looked down at her, his expression tender. "The vicar is downstairs," Mr. Stanton said to her, "as are a few townspeople. If you do not feel like being alone, I know some of them wish to see you." He glanced up at the physician, then back to her. "And I need to speak with you. Privately, on a matter Mrs. Trent wished me to take up with you. Will you come by the office later?"

She nodded.

"Until then." He gave a slight bow and disappeared down the hall and into the room.

The undertaker, Mr. Giles Brookes, had been sent for. He was in Manchester, and it would be several hours before he could arrive. Already the staff had begun draping Mrs. Trent's parlor in black bombazine, although Nathaniel doubted many visitors would come to pay their respects.

Nathaniel retreated to his office, adjusting the black mourning band around his arm. Since the day he had learned of his true parentage and that he would inherit land, he had thought of little else. But he did not expect to feel so affected by it.

Melancholy washed over him. The fact that he was obtaining his birthright by the death of another made him uneasy. Her final words to him echoed in his mind.

I apologize.

He had poured his life into Willowgrove. His very soul into the daily intricacies of running an estate—both the main house and overseeing the tenants. Willowgrove was as much a part of him as the air he breathed. It ran thick in his blood, given to him by both his biological father and the father who raised him. He had friendships. Alliances. History. With the exception of Miss Faire,

Mrs. Trent was taking the truth about him to her grave. He was free now.

Or was he?

He had read the will when Mr. Trent died. It had been subtle, but clear. The wording had been carefully crafted by Mr. Trent himself and gave no indication that he was Mr. Trent's son, thereby protecting his mother and sisters. It simply left Lockbourne to his trusted steward upon his wife's death.

Now he could openly prepare to leave Willowgrove and begin a new life at Lockbourne. He had anticipated this day. He had always imagined his sisters and mother would accompany him. But now Rebecca was pledged to another. She would not be leaving. Would his mother choose to stay with her eldest daughter?

He moved to the locked trunk and removed the box containing the will. It had been housed here, untouched, since Mr. Trent's death.

Mr. Moreton would be coming to Nathaniel's office momentarily, no doubt, to confirm what everyone knew to be true . . . that he would be the new master of Willowgrove, as well as all of the land and businesses associated with it. There were other matters to tend to, such as personal gifts for the longstanding servants, items that were to be sent. But for the most part, everything would remain the same at Willowgrove, unless Moreton should choose to make changes, and all would belong to Moreton and any sons he may one day have.

The only surprise to Moreton would be that Lockbourne was coming to Nathaniel.

Nathaniel did not have to wait long, for not fifteen minutes had passed when Moreton came in the door without knocking.

If Moreton had been pretending sorrow at his aunt's passing, he knew better than for such charades with Nathaniel. He entered the steward's office clad in black, his expression stern.

Nathaniel reached for the box. "I can guess what you've come for."

Nathaniel pulled a small key from his desk, unlocked the box containing the will, and lifted the folded parchment. "Effective today, legally, you are the master of Willowgrove Hall and all that goes with it. And I congratulate you. You will find everything else in here."

Andrew took the will, gave a crooked smile, and stepped over to the light filtering through the window.

Nathaniel studied the inlay of his desk, waiting. He knew Andrew's main interest was the building and the estate itself. He doubted that he was even aware of the land to the north.

"Oh."

Nathaniel lifted his head but said nothing.

"It appears that a bit of land is being left to the steward on record and a few other things." Moreton pinned him with a pointed stare. "But I daresay you were already aware of this fact."

There was no need to hide anything. No need for pretense. For he had done nothing wrong. Undoubtedly such an inheritance might raise an eyebrow or two, but Nathaniel did not care. "Yes, I am."

Moreton lowered the will, stepped away from the window, and handed it back to Nathaniel. "It appears my uncle thought very highly of your father."

Nathaniel took the will and folded it neatly, then placed it back in the box.

"Well then, I suppose congratulations are in order. Does this mean you will be leaving Willowgrove?"

"Only once a suitable replacement can be found."

"Waiting for a replacement. That is very noble of you."

The tone with which the words were spoken irked Nathaniel.

Moreton, young and unobservant, probably had little knowledge of what it was that Nathaniel actually tended to on a daily basis. And in that moment, even though it was not recognized, Nathaniel felt pride in what he did. Most estates this size would have a house steward and a land steward. He had successfully overseen both. He would like nothing more than to leave the pretentious twit out on his ear, but he cared too much about the work he had spent his life doing. About the people who had worked alongside him. And yes, oddly enough, even about the memory of Mrs. Trent.

"I have a responsibility to Willowgrove," Nathaniel stated. "And I will see it through."

He knew Moreton to be prideful and half expected him to relieve him from his duties on the spot. But instead, the younger man pushed his fingers through his hair and nodded. "Thank you."

Moreton headed toward the door but then stopped. "Will you see that the other servants are notified of anything that may have been left to them?"

Nathaniel nodded. That would be one task he would find great pleasure in doing. "Of course."

32

Nathaniel closed the ledger and extinguished the candle on his desk. He yawned, adjusted his cravat, folded his arms over his chest, and sighed.

He dragged his hands over his face, then pushed himself back against the chair. The weight of grief pulled on him. Never had he thought he would be so affected by Mrs. Trent's passing. He wanted to go home to Laurel Cottage. Go someplace light and happy. He'd seen death before. Whether it was someone as close to him as his own father or a stranger, it was always hard.

He checked his timepiece. Again. He had asked Miss Faire to come by the office, and she hadn't. He had things he needed to give to her, provisions from Mrs. Trent. These were important, but there was another matter entirely that he needed to discuss with her.

He thought again, for the thousandth time, of their stolen moment in the corridor earlier that day. It had started out as an innocent gesture that turned into the moment that he was certain he would always look back on as a turning point. Miss Faire had been grieving. But there was something else that transpired between them in that silent corridor. He had never held a woman in his arms in such a manner. The memory of the softness of her, the tickle of her hair as she tucked her head beneath his chin, the warmth of her hand on his chest—all threatened to undo him.

And what's more, he trusted her. The realization pulsed through him, urging him, pushing him. She knew the truth about him. It did not faze her or shock her.

His plans to reestablish Lockbourne as a thriving estate had never been in doubt. And he had always planned to do it as an unmarried, untethered man. But now he knew . . . it would all be worthless without Miss Faire.

He gathered his things and tucked them in his satchel, imagining their future spreading before him. But as he reached for his hat, he saw Miss Faire from the window. She was walking to the east garden. She had changed into a gown of dark gray or black, making her skin appear even paler. Her head was uncovered, unusual for this time of day. Energy surged through him. He knew what he wanted and he needed to tell her. He flung the satchel over his shoulder, grabbed the letter and pouch given to him by Mrs. Trent, and hurried from Willowgrove's tradesmen's entrance, taking the steps two at a time. The grounds were more active than the average late afternoon. He jogged around the east drive and crossed the lawn. "Miss Faire!" he called. "Please wait."

When Miss Faire noticed him, she stopped short. The wind had pulled her hair free, and long, auburn tendrils flew about her face. The breeze tugged at the charcoal dress, highlighting her form. As he drew closer, her eyes glowed red with tears. The sight slowed him.

He stopped a few feet from her. Now that he was here, so close to her, he was not sure what to say. He glanced upward to the sky thickening with late clouds. "You should be inside. It looks like rain may be coming."

Miss Faire only nodded.

Her silence was unnerving.

"I-I saw you from the window and thought I might catch you. You never came by the office today."

"I apologize." Her voice was weak. "I had things to attend to. The hours slipped by."

He pulled the letter from his waistcoat. "I have something for you. " He pulled the letter from his coat. "Mrs. Trent wanted me to give this to you . . . in the event of her death."

Miss Faire flipped the letter and read the inscription. "This is not her writing."

"No, 'tis mine. Mrs. Trent spoke it and I captured it on paper. She did not want to ask you to do such a task, and Clarkson's hand is such that she can barely write anymore."

"May I ask what it is?"

"It is a letter of recommendation. She knew you had plans to look for your sister, but she wanted to make sure you were able to get a good post. She also wanted you to have this." He retrieved the small velvet pouch from his coat.

The coins jingled as he transferred it to her outstretched palm.

Once Miss Faire realized the pouch contained money, she shook her head and tried to give it back to him. "No. This is not necessary. I cannot take this."

"Take it, Miss Faire." He gently pushed her hand away. "It will do much better in your control than leaving it here."

She looked down at the small purse. "Mrs. Trent was a very generous woman. I am sure it will help me in my transition."

The word "transition" caught him off guard.

He licked his lips and shifted his weight.

But even as he planned what to say next, she brushed her hair from her face. "I can hardly believe she is gone."

He thought he noticed her chin tremble. How he yearned to

ease her pain. His arms ached to pull her into his embrace once again, to soothe away the day's grief.

But she jutted her chin into the air. "I wanted to tell you again how grateful I am to you and your family. Rebecca and Charlotte were by to see me earlier today. I do not know what I would have done without the kindness your family has shown me. Seeing your sisters today, however, reminded me I ache to see mine."

He leaned close to avoid being overheard by two passing stable boys. "I take it you have not heard back from any of the addresses Mr. McGovern sent you?"

She shook her head. "But I did receive a letter from an old friend indicating that Leah is in Manchester."

He did not like where this conversation was going. Manchester was hardly a place for her. She was independent, but also headstrong. Going there alone would be insanity. "You must let me help you."

"I cannot impose any longer."

"It is not an imposition."

She drew a shaky breath, her words growing more pointed. "This is something I must do on my own."

"Why must you? You need not do everything alone."

Miss Faire looked slightly offended. "I know that there have been times since my arrival that could make you doubt it, but I really am quite capable."

"Of course you are capable. No woman could be more so. It is your safety I am concerned with."

"Leah is all I have left. You must understand."

The words were out of his mouth before he could stop them. "She is not all you have."

At the words, her eyes fixed on him, her expression brimming with questions. He realized what he had let slip. He quickly backtracked. "That is to say, there is no need for you to continue alone."

She lifted the letter and the pouch in her hand. "You asked me about my past before, Mr. Stanton, and I would not tell you anything of significance. But now, especially since I know so much of your own history, I feel it only fair that you should be apprised of mine. I am not who you think I am, not exactly."

She waited for a footman to pass the far side of the yard before continuing. "I mean no disrespect, but your situation was not of your own making. You were a victim of circumstance. But I-I have made mistakes and decisions that affected my entire family, and they will haunt me until I make them right. And that starts with finding my sister."

"I know you are responsible for Mrs. Trent's apology to me. I appreciated it. I didn't realize that I needed to hear it. But you must trust me. It is your turn for people to be there for you."

How arrogant he must sound. What right did he have to know anything about her? And to his knowledge, she had never asked to know anything about him. It had all been handed to her, whether or not she had any interest. He studied her, from the twitch in her cheek to the wince of her eye. Had he gone too far?

"This has been a difficult week, one that has tried me beyond . . ." Miss Faire's words faded, and then she paused, as if selecting another direction for the conversation. "We must each of us look to the future."

He did not like her words. They sounded too much like a farewell. "No, I—"

"Please. It is best if things are left as they are."

She could not hide the sadness, the hurt in her eyes. How he wanted to grab her, to hold her until the stubbornness in her subsided, to finish what they started in the corridor.

"I am happy for you, Mr. Stanton, and wish you great success at Lockbourne."

Perhaps if he were better versed in the ways of women, he

would have known what to say to keep her there, keep her within close distance.

"This is not how you have to leave."

"Mr. Stanton, I am not the lady you suppose me to be. I cannot stay."

33

That night, rain pelted the windows. Cecily's chin shook not with grief, but with anger.

How could she have been so foolish? She had not allowed Mr. Stanton to finish his thoughts. She was so quick to push him away.

And why?

As much as she wished it weren't true, the painful reality met her. Mr. Stanton had touched her heart.

She squeezed her eyes shut and pressed her hands to her forehead, but even then she could not forget the look of compassion in Nathaniel's eyes. What had she done, turning this man away?

The memory of his arms around her, warm and strong, scared her. How, after all this time, could she turn to another? She did not know how. But how her heart ached for it! If she were to be completely honest, it was another matter that scared her. She would be forced to confess her past transgressions—that she was not a lady. That she had given herself to another many years ago.

What she had done was unforgivable. She could never keep such a secret from someone she loved, and yet her fear of his rejection was far too strong to allow her to risk exposure.

She stood up and went to the small teak box on her dressing table and retrieved the letter from Mr. McGovern. Day after day slipped by, and still she'd received no responses from the letters she had written. She could not stay here. Not any longer. Nor could she return to Rosemere. But as she opened the letter and read the fine writing, address after address, another idea burned brighter.

She had feared her father. His role in her life had been pivotal. But he was gone now, and unless Leah had married, she was likely alone . . . just like Cecily. She had to find her. She had to.

Later that night Clarkson entered her room, a tray balanced in her hands. "I have not seen you all day, Miss Faire. I brought you some herb soup."

"Thank you, Clarkson." Cecily turned from where she was sitting at her writing desk and scooted back to make room for the tray. As the scent and warmth of the soup met her, she sobered. Now, with Mrs. Trent gone, it felt pretentious to have someone bring her dinner. "I can go down to the kitchen to eat. There is no need for you to bring it to me."

"Don't say that, not a lady like you."

Cecily's laugh sounded forced, even to her own ears. "I am not a lady, Clarkson."

"You are to me." Clarkson broke form and softened her expression.

Cecily folded her arms across her chest and turned to look at the lady's maid. The past several days had broken down the invisible walls between them. They had been fighting the same fight, praying the same prayers. And now their time together would soon come to an end. "Are you going to stay on at Willowgrove?"

Clarkson plopped down on the bed next to Cecily. "I doubt the new Mrs. Moreton will be in need of a lady's maid when the time comes, and I have been doing this for so long I'm not quite fit for any other role here. But do not worry for me. I have saved me some money. Mrs. Trent was generous, so I can find a nice, quiet cottage somewhere and live out my days in peace."

"Do you have family to go to?"

"I have a sister down in London. Her daughter died last year, rest her soul, and she is looking after her grandbabies. Four of them! She could use the help. I could use the company. And you?"

Cecily shrugged. "I am not certain. But first, I am going to try to find my sister."

"A twin, right?"

"Yes, my twin." The words wrenched her. *My other half.*

"Where are you going to start looking?"

"I have received word she is in Manchester."

"Manchester can be a dark place, miss."

Cecily recalled Mr. Stanton's warning. "So I have been warned. But I am determined. I need to find her."

"And if she is not there?"

Cecily sighed. She did not want to consider failure as a possible outcome. "Then I will most likely return to Rosemere and decide my next steps."

"I have a cousin what runs an inn in south Manchester. It is not the fanciest place, certainly nothing like Mrs. Trent would have approved of, but when I stayed there, I was comfortable."

Clarkson rose, went to the desk, helped herself to a sheet of paper and Cecily's quill, and wrote something. "If your travels take you there, ask to talk to Marianne Dotten. She's my cousin. If she knows you are a friend of mine, she'll put you in her best room."

Cecily didn't hear anything after the word "friend." Did Clarkson consider her a friend?

Emotion tightened Cecily's chest. She took the slip of paper and studied the address. Was this the confirmation she needed?

Yet another push from the nest to take her further down life's journey?

Clarkson turned to leave. "You learn a lot about people in a position like mine. I have spent my life serving the needs of others. Even though I do not interact with them a lot, I watch. And I have watched you, miss. Do not allow pain—or pride—to blind you to what is right in front of you."

34

It was raining when Cecily left Willowgrove. But instead of the dark, rainy twilight of spring that had greeted her upon her arrival, it was the dark predawn of early autumn that shrouded the landscape. Instead of the hopeful thrill of optimism, weariness settled around her.

It was easiest to leave now, before the estate sprang to life. Cecily had informed no one about her plans to leave, with the exception of hinting at her plans to Clarkson. Now that she had seen to all of her duties pertaining to Mrs. Trent, it was best that she leave.

She had packed her things in the black of night with only her candle as her guide. She wrote a farewell letter to Clarkson and one to Rebecca. She wrote a letter to post to Mrs. Sterling at Rosemere, to keep her abreast of her whereabouts. But as much as her heart wanted to write final words to Mr. Stanton, propriety stopped her.

Had she failed at Willowgrove Hall? Cecily contemplated the question on the walk down the main drive—the very drive she would have walked down had Mr. Stanton and his dog not discovered her. She had done what she came to do . . . to be a companion to an ill woman and make her final days more comfortable. But in doing so, she had lost a little piece of herself.

As Cecily rounded the bend, Laurel Cottage could be seen through the trees. A light filtered through one of the back windows. He would be up by now. She could stop. Explain everything. But then, what good would it do? She could never love another without expressing the truth about her past, and he would surely reject her for it. What good would a confession do now? The pain of losing someone who adores you is nothing compared to the rejection of one who has stolen your heart. No, it was best to guard what she had left. She would find her sister.

This was the only way.

The next morning Mrs. Trent was buried in the family plot alongside her husband and daughter. A thick fog hung and swirled in the early-morning breeze. A few men had gathered for the burial, Andrew Moreton included, but beyond that the gathering was small. Nathaniel had not seen Miss Faire, but he needed to tell her that whatever was in her past, it did not matter. The only thing that mattered was the future he wanted them to share.

As soon as the burial was complete, he hurried back to Willowgrove. As he walked the great hall, a throng of people milled about.

He didn't want to talk with them.

He wanted to talk with her.

Their conversation on the lawn had not ended well, and since that time together, he'd sought her out, but she was nowhere to be found. He had not said what he had wanted to say. And now that his inheritance was nigh and he was free to make plans, he did not have the peace and excitement he had expected. His heart was no longer in it, for his heart no longer belonged to him alone.

He decided to go to his office. He made his way from the stairs through the hall, but at the back entrance of the main hall stood Clarkson.

He barely recognized her.

Instead of the gray dress she normally wore, she was dressed in a gown of black, and instead of the white cap, her head was uncovered and her graying hair pulled back at the nape of her neck. She was pale.

Her rough voice cracked as she spoke. "These are sad days, Mr. Stanton."

He nodded, still a little surprised she had sought him so boldly.

"I've only come for my last wages. Then I'll be on my way."

"You're leaving? So soon?" He turned to his office. As Mrs. Trent's personal staff, Clarkson was not under Mrs. Bratham's purview, like the rest of the female staff. This week, in the midst of all the abnormalities, he'd forgotten.

"I am no longer needed here," she said. "And I've family to go to."

"I thank you for your service to Mrs. Trent. I know it is because of you that she was so comfortable." He went to fetch the money from the locked box at the back of the room. "I am certain that if you still want to stay on at Willowgrove Hall, Mrs. Bratham will find a position for you."

"No, sir. It is best I leave. I've seen to Mrs. Trent's personal affairs, and it will be up to the new master what he will do with them."

"Where will you go?"

"To London. My sister is there."

He gathered money from the box and also pulled out a letter of recommendation that Mrs. Trent had the foresight to write. He handed it to her. "Mrs. Trent also wanted you to have this. It's a letter of recommendation. Mrs. Trent said she thought you wouldn't stay after she was gone, and it seems she was right."

Clarkson accepted the money and the letter and tucked them in her bag. And then she pulled something out. "Thought you might want to see these. I found them in Miss Faire's room this morning."

His eyes fixed on the letters. From here, he could see the black ink in delicate loops and curves. He swallowed. He took the letters from her outstretched hand. One was addressed to Clarkson. The other to Rebecca.

But Clarkson did not leave. Instead, she stood looking at him, making him wonder if there was something he was forgetting.

She finally spoke. "I have been at Willowgrove since before you were born. I remember the day with clarity."

Nathaniel stiffened. He had suspected Clarkson was aware of the truth about his parentage, but nothing had ever been said. He should stop her. She had no business speaking to him as such. But his curiosity got the better of him.

"I have watched you grow from a boy to a man. I saw the way you were treated by the Trents."

He was not sure how to react. Part of him wanted her to stop talking. But what a relief to know that another knew. He folded his arms across his chest. "I didn't realize that you knew the details."

"Of course I knew. I knew about your situation since before you were even born. I took your mother's post, after all. When I was a young girl, I worked at Mrs. Trent's family's estate. When she needed someone, she called me, and I was happy to come. I am loyal to Mrs. Trent, mind you. But I saw things. I know things. And if you are the type of man I think you are, then you are going to need one thing."

He raised an eyebrow. "And what is that?"

Clarkson produced one more slip of paper and handed it to him.

He turned it over. Scratched on the back was an address. A Manchester address.

"You might find something of interest." She tapped her gloved finger against the side of her head. "And I know you did not ask for it, but here is a little advice from an old fool who has seen too much and heard even more. Do not let your pain and regrets from the past prevent you from your future." She cracked a rare smile in his direction. "Best of luck to you, Mr. Stanton."

"Thank you for your service, Clarkson. Best of all to you as well."

She turned to leave, and he looked down at the opened letter to Clarkson in one hand. The address in the other.

Alone, in the privacy of his office, he placed the address on the table and opened the letter.

Dearest Clarkson,

My heart grieves with you. I know how difficult these past few months have been. I admire your strength and dedication, and you have become a dear friend.

By the time you read this, I will be on my way to Manchester. Thank you for the address, and I shall pass along your greetings to your cousin when I arrive. I do hope that we will meet again, but if we do not, I shall never forget my time at Willowgrove, and I shall not forget your friendship.

All the best,
Cecily Faire

35

Nathaniel had to see for himself. Once Clarkson quitted the office, he watched as she walked through the tradesmen's foyer and out Willowgrove's east door. For all the span of time he knew her, he knew very little of her. But as he watched the old lady's maid walking down the path for the last time, he felt a twinge. Clarkson had been a part of Willowgrove for as far back as his memory could reach. Whether he liked it or not, his world—and the world of those around him—had been spiraled into change he was not sure he was ready for. His heart began to beat harder, faster. Beads of perspiration dotted his brow. He had to see. He had to see for himself.

He hurried up the grand staircase and through the corridor to the gold room and knocked on the door.

No response.

He burst into the room.

It smelled of rosewater. Of her.

The curtains were pulled back. The room was flooded with

light. There was no sign of her. The bedcovers were tightly made. The armchair was pushed against the small rosewood writing table. All the contents were neatly arranged. The wardrobe door was ajar, and he opened it. Empty save two quilts and bedcoverings folded in the lower corner.

His chest began to tighten.

How could she have left? Without saying good-bye? Or at least informing him of her decision?

Nathaniel knew she felt it. The attraction. He could see it in the flush of her cheek. The shallowness of her breath. The directness of her gaze.

He was about to leave when something on the rug caught his eye. He reached down and picked it up. It was a letter. Addressed to her. He lowered it. He should not read it. But it burned his fingers. He lifted it and read.

It was a letter from someone named Mrs. Sherwin informing Miss Faire of her father's death. Of her sister's absence.

He tucked the letter in his waistcoat. He had made a mistake. He should have been more direct in making his feelings known. And now it may be too late.

He took the steps two at a time as he hurried back down to the ground floor. The space was alive with reverent whispers and visitors, but nothing seemed to matter as much as getting to his office. The thought of her in Manchester alone alarmed him.

But as his foot landed on the marble floor at the bottom of the great staircase, another woman appeared.

Mrs. Massey strode toward him, dressed from head to toe in black and shades of gray. "There you are, Mr. Stanton. I have been looking everywhere for you! Where is Miss Faire? I've searched high and low, and I cannot find her."

Miss Faire's name on Mrs. Massey's lips agitated him. He looked above her to the people in the great hall. "She has left Willowgrove."

Mrs. Massey's eyes widened. "What? Already? Without bidding us farewell?"

He propped his fists on his waist, growing frustrated. He doubted her sincerity, but did she not have a right to be here? For she had visited Willowgrove almost daily in Mrs. Trent's final days, only to be told by Collingswood that she was too weak for visitors.

Mrs. Massey's lips had turned down into a frown. "Mr. Stanton? Are you quite all right?"

He needed to maintain composure. For a little longer. "I believe she has gone to Manchester."

"Manchester? That seems odd. I am sorry to hear it." Her lashes fanned her cheeks as she looked to the ground. "I-I know you had grown quite fond of her."

Had it been that obvious? He tried to grasp at something—anything—to say. But there was a look in her eye. Mrs. Massey was always forward, but today she was acting almost timid. She fretted with the edge of her gray lace reticule, her pale skin peeking through her black gloves. She gave a little laugh and a shrug, but kept her eyes diverted. "I'd begun to think the two of you had an understanding. But perhaps I was wrong?"

"An understanding?" He shook his head. "No. No understanding."

But as he looked at the concern in Mrs. Massey's face, it hit him. She was a dressmaker. Not that far from Manchester. Might she know of any leads? And shops? At the moment he had no idea what he would do with such information, but it was worth a try. With renewed hope, he shifted. "I would like to beg your assistance, if you are willing."

She blinked at him. "Anything, Mr. Stanton."

He saw the expectation in her eyes. Now was the time for honesty. "Miss Faire and I did not have an understanding, but I must go find her."

As the meaning of the words sank in, Mrs. Massey's face reddened ever so slightly. "You mean you-you . . ."

She looked away, as if pausing to summon her courage, and offered a smile. "I will do what I can." And she hastened to add, "Out of respect for your family and the kindness you have shown me."

"Are you familiar with any dressmaking shops in Manchester?"

"Why, yes, there are several, especially with the cotton business so strong there. Why would you need to know?"

"Could I trouble you to provide me with a list of the names of the shops you know of in the area?"

Her pleasant expression seemed to fade before him. He knew her feelings for him. And he knew what he was asking her.

She opened her mouth to speak and then snapped it shut, as if selecting her words. "You do realize what message your actions will convey to Miss Faire, do you not?"

He nodded. His actions would be forward. Yet he was compelled. "I do."

She took a few steps away from him. "I won't pretend to know what course is best for you, Mr. Stanton. Only you can know that. I hope that you do not think me forward when I say this, but I am a widow, far too practical to play coy games. But I had thought—hoped—things would have ended differently."

He knew of what she was speaking. He looked down at the paper in his hand. Had Miss Faire never arrived at Willowgrove, it was entirely possible that their futures would look different. But now that he had experienced the depth of what true caring felt like, nothing else would do. "I do apologize, Mrs. Massey, if I have behaved in a way that would make you think otherwise."

She thrust her chin into the air. "Apologies are not necessary, Mr. Stanton. Indeed, we all must follow our own hearts. Isn't that so?"

She adjusted her reticule, looped it around her arm, and gave a forced little laugh. "I will give you the names you requested, Mr. Stanton."

He felt relief at her words—and a little hope. "Thank you, Mrs. Massey. I am most grateful."

He led the way to his office, where he gave her a fresh sheet of paper and a quill. She sat at his desk and began writing.

She spoke as she wrote. "You might find this an odd thing for me to say, but the more I contemplate it, the more I find this to be a very romantic situation."

He drew a sharp breath. *Romantic* was hardly the word he thought of. *Scary* and *alarming* were more accurate. But as his plans wove themselves into being, it became increasingly clear what he needed to do.

He paced as she wrote the list. When she was done, she stood and held it out to dry it. "Here, I am not sure of all the addresses, of course, but here are some names."

He took the paper from her.

She fixed her eyes on him. "Best of luck in your searching, Mr. Stanton. I wish you every happiness."

Renewed purpose flowed through his veins, awakening his sense of duty and energizing him. He would find her. He would marry her. Together they would start a life at Lockbourne. But first she must say yes.

When Nathaniel returned to Laurel Cottage, the hour was late, and Rebecca was waiting for him in his small bedchamber off the kitchen.

She had been crying. The candle's glow reflected from the tracks of tears on her cheeks. Not knowing what else to say, he removed his coat and hung it on the peg opposite of the bed. "I can't recall the last time you were in this room."

But the sadness lurking behind her dark eyes told him that she had not come here simply to check on his well-being. "Mother told me everything."

Like a large stone dropping into a pond, a sickening sensation sank within him. "Everything?"

Rebecca's expression quickly became an accusing one. "About Mr. Trent being your father. I am in shock. Utter shock. How long have you known?"

Nathaniel sat down on the chair beside his bed and propped his elbows on his knees. "Since the night before Father died."

"All this time? How could you not tell me? Do you think so little of me? It pains me that you did not take me into your confidence on something as important as this."

"Father specifically asked me to tell no one, including my sisters. I am surprised Mother told you."

"She also told me about Lockbourne. You cannot seriously consider relocating."

"I am not just considering it, Rebecca. I am going to take up residence there as soon as arrangements can be made."

"But why? Your life is here! With us!"

"That is just it, Rebecca. It is not my life. It is Father's life. Now you must be able to see it. Ever since Father told me the truth, it seems I have been living another man's life. If I stay here, my lie will continue, for I would never expose Mother, nor you and our sisters, to any kind of prejudice. But I need to find my own way now. I have lived with this burden for long enough. I can't help but wonder what my life will feel like when I am free to be me."

"So we are a burden?"

"That is not what I meant and you know it."

She sniffed. "And when were you going to tell us about this?"

"After Mrs. Trent passed. I did not expect Mother to tell you." He hesitated. "I really did want to be the one who told you. I was hoping my family would come with me to Lockbourne. That we could all start over."

Rebecca shook her head emphatically. "I am not leaving Mr. Turner."

"I am not suggesting you do."

"And I am not letting you take Mother away from me. I could not bear it."

"The decision is now Mother's. I will understand if she wants to remain."

"And what about Mrs. Massey?"

"You, of all people, with your romantic heart, must have the discernment to know that I am not at all connected with Mrs. Massey."

Rebecca lowered her eyes. "It is Miss Faire, is it not?"

"She is no longer at Willowgrove. Apparently she departed sometime during the night."

His sister nearly jumped from her seat, her face twisting in further disbelief. "What? Without saying good-bye to me? To the girls? Why would she leave so abruptly?"

He wished he knew the answer to that. He retrieved the letter that Miss Faire had written to Rebecca and handed it to her. "I'm going after her."

Rebecca winced in disbelief, as if he had just told her he was going to jump off of the Westminster Bridge. "What?"

"I believe she has gone to Manchester. And I am going to find her."

Rebecca stared at him, mouth agape. She broke the seal on the letter, unfolded it, and leaned toward the candle lamp to read it. "You are right. She says she is going to find her sister and she will write again when she is settled."

She lowered the letter. "That still does not answer why she left so suddenly."

Nathaniel cleared his throat and rested his hand on the edge of the bureau. He could guess why.

Rebecca tightened her shawl around her and placed the letter next to her. "So, am I to understand that you are following her because you have feelings for her, or have you another reason?"

He folded his arms across his chest, pausing to contemplate his answer. "I think she is looking for her family, looking for a place to belong. But I want us to be her family, and she belongs with me."

36

The carriage ride to Manchester was a short one compared to the journey from Darbury. The countryside flashed by in shades of green and brown, but Cecily barely noticed. All she could focus on was the bizarre ache in her chest.

She felt like that lost girl again, regretting past actions, hurting over losses, and fearful of what lay around the bend. But now the panic she had felt that day those many years ago was a more mature melancholy because she was leaving her heart at Willowgrove.

She had paid the driver an extra sum to deliver her to the address that Clarkson had provided. And when the coach turned off of the main road down a shadowed alley, fear began to creep in. She had always led a sheltered life. The quiet country life on Aradelle's grounds. The small, tight-knit community at Rosemere, where her comings and goings were carefully monitored. And then at Willowgrove, she rarely left Mrs. Trent's side.

But now her direction was hers alone.

She noticed immediately that everything was dirty. Smoke

and fog in strange hues of gray and brown hung in the air. The stench of rotting food and manure surrounded her. She was far from Manchester's fashionable end. This must have been what Mr. Stanton had tried to warn her about. But she could not begin to regret her decision.

As the carriage rolled to a stop in front of a narrow, two-story building, Cecily drew a sharp breath and nearly choked on the putrid scents in the air. She looked at the address on the door and then looked at Clarkson's note. The same address. She clutched her valise tightly to her chest and called on every ounce of courage she possessed. She stepped out of the carriage, trying not to notice the way her foot sank into the mushy ground below. Night was falling quickly. A lamplighter scurried past her followed by a small boy who could be no older than Hannah, covered in ash and soot. Men dressed in rough, smeared clothes eyed her, and her fear heightened.

She called up to the driver, "Will you wait here for just a moment?" She needed to buy herself time, just in case things did not go accordingly. But her voice was lost in the sounds of the city, and before she could stop him, the driver called the horses into motion.

She could feel people watching her. She lowered her eyes. She would not show fear. She lifted the hem of her skirt just enough to keep it from dragging through the muck, and when she crossed the road and approached the wooden door, she thought she would faint dead away.

She knocked on the solid wood door. At the noise, a dog started barking and voices could be heard from inside. At first, she thought no one was coming. She lifted her hand to knock again, and the door flew open.

A woman with an infant in her arms stared at her. "What do you want?"

Taken aback by the abrupt greeting, Cecily straightened her posture. "I am Cecily Faire. I am looking for Mrs. Dotten."

"I'm her."

Cecily cast a nervous glance over her shoulder at a man who was staring at her. "I-I'm looking for a room. I was told I might find one here."

The woman stepped back from the door. "Ain't got no rooms." She went to push the door closed.

Cecily stepped forward, putting her hand on the door to stop it. "Please! Please wait."

The woman opened the door again.

"I was sent here by Naomi Clarkson. She said she was your cousin, and if I told you that she sent me here, you would be able to help."

The woman narrowed her eyes on Cecily as if looking at her for the first time. She raked her tired eyes over Cecily's hair. Her pelisse. Her boots. "How do you know Naomi?"

Cecily adjusted the valise in her hands. "We were both employed at Willowgrove Hall. I needed to come to Manchester for personal reasons. Knowing I would need a place to stay, she gave me this address."

The baby on the woman's hip started to cry, and the woman started to sway. She narrowed her eyes on Cecily once more before taking a step back. "Come in, then. Best rooms are taken but there is one extra I keep for emergencies."

Relief rushed through Cecily. "Oh, thank you."

But she ignored Cecily's gratitude. In fact, Cecily hurried to keep pace with the woman who was leading her up two flights of dark, narrow stairs to a small landing. Cecily lifted her glove to her nose to avoid the scent of waste and filth.

Mrs. Dotten took a key from the top of the door's ledge, unlocked it, and pushed it open.

Stale air rushed at Cecily as the door swung open, and the day's last light filtered through the narrow window. Dust and motes swirled in the air. Cecily wanted to turn and run. Never had she stayed in such a place. But she would not complain. Outside, thunder started to growl in the distance. At least here she would be dry.

"You can stay here, but only for a few days. Got a regular boarder coming back to town that'll need this room. I'll need your pay now." She held out her dirty hand, and Cecily turned her back to the woman as she pulled money from her bodice and dropped the specified amount into the woman's hand.

"Breakfast downstairs in the morning. I suggest you get there early. This lot tends to eat fast."

And then the woman was gone.

Cecily stood for a moment, a little in shock, and stared at her surroundings. If Cecily stretched, she could almost touch opposite walls with her hands. She clutched her things close to her and looked at the bed. She wouldn't be able to sleep on that. Instead, she put her bag on the ground and sank into a simple wooden chair at a plain table.

She looked around. No candle. No fire. No anything.

She resisted the urge to cry. She pulled the list from her bodice and read down the names of the establishments. She would begin her search tomorrow and seek other lodging. She patted the pouch in her bodice to make sure her remaining money was still there. She needed to save at least enough to return to Rosemere if her search was unsuccessful.

Regret over leaving Willowgrove in such haste shrouded her. Why had she reacted so brashly? If it hadn't been for her own stubbornness, her own insecurities, things might be different. But they were not. She was so intent upon finding her sister and chasing her memories that she had not seen the people who cared for her when they were before her.

She turned to her valise and looked inside, seeking distraction. Her stomach rumbled, reminding her that she had eaten very little, and her head throbbed with the effect of the jostling carriage. As she sorted through the contents, her fingers brushed her book of Proverbs. She hesitated, thinking of Mrs. Trent and how she found comfort in Scripture at the end of the day.

In her darkest moments, Cecily had resisted praying or seeking God. She was not exactly sure why. Her persistent belief that God had abandoned her had ruled her emotions and actions. If she were honest, part of her blamed God for the series of events that had plagued her.

The memory of the people who had filled her days as of late rushed her, stealing her breath and strength. She had left on her own accord, yes, and it had been on the belief that she did not deserve to find happiness.

She lifted her book of Proverbs and opened the worn volume. Even though her aching soul cried out for relief and comfort, part of her resisted. Why, she was unsure. Perhaps it was fear that her past sins had been too great. Or fear that God simply would not answer.

She could barely make out the words in the fading light. At first she stared blankly at the pages for several moments, half fearing, half anticipating what she would find within. As she was about to close the book for the evening, a small verse that she had read for Mrs. Trent just a few days prior met her eyes: *"Yea, if thou criest after knowledge, and liftest up thy voice for understanding; if thou seekest her as silver and searchest for her as for hid treasures; then shalt thou understand the fear of the Lord, and find the knowledge of God."*

Cecily said the words aloud. "If thou criest after knowledge, if thou seekest her as silver. The knowledge of God."

Was that not the very thing that she sought? To understand God's plan? She nearly dropped the book. For that was the exact opposite of what she had done. She had reacted on impulse. She had reacted to fear. Never once did she seek wisdom. And now, here she was, alone—and frightened.

It had been a long while since she sought God in any circumstance. Had she been wrong all this time? She turned back to the window and looked to the sky. She repeated the verse aloud. And then she repeated it again. Each time the words met her ears, they reached within her, touching a part of her that had long been closed. A glimmer of hope from somewhere within her began to flicker, warming her with its weak strength. She committed the words to memory, and with every repetition, the glimmer of hope burned brighter.

The dismal fear that had overwhelmed her when she first entered the dingy room was, amazingly, starting to subside. In the midst of so many uncertainties and regrets, a spark of optimism, although weak, was enough to keep her going.

She slept that night at the table, her head cradled in her arms. But as she drifted off to sleep, she repeated the words. Perhaps she was not as alone as she had thought.

Nathaniel departed for Manchester the next morning as soon as the sun's first rays crept over the tree line. It was unlike him to leave so suddenly, and without a plan, but Miss Faire's safety trumped any other concern.

He paused on his journey only to water and rest his horse, and by the time he arrived in Manchester, he was more energized than ever. He'd spent his time en route devising a plan to carry out upon his arrival. He was fairly certain she would be staying at the address that Clarkson had given him, but he wanted to do a little investigating and gauge how difficult it would be to find Leah as well.

He'd not had an opportunity to send word to McGovern about his arrival, but he knew that his old friend would open his home, and if not, he could always stay at an inn.

Before even stopping by the McGoverns', Nathaniel—armed with the list that Mrs. Massey had provided—visited three modest dressmaker shops along his route. None of them had heard of a Leah Faire, or even anyone with the Christian name Leah.

By the time he arrived at the McGoverns', the hour had grown late. Clouds blocked out any light from the moon, and the only flickering light shone from the candle lamps lining the brick streets and firelight spilling from the nearby windows. Exhaustion pulled at him, but his mind was alive. He would not be able to rest until he found her.

"Good evening, Charles," Nathaniel said to the aged butler who opened the door.

"Why, Mr. Stanton! We were not expecting you."

"I'm here on a matter of personal business. Is Mr. McGovern available?"

"I believe he may have retired for the night, but I will see. Please come in. I will have the boy come 'round for your horse."

Nathaniel stepped inside and handed Charles his beaver hat. The night had grown damp, and he was grateful for the warmth inside his friend's home. But even as he felt his shoulders ease ever so slightly in the comfort of the quiet dwelling, finding Miss Faire was utmost in his mind. He fought the urge to go to the address at that very moment. But the night was dark now. She had probably already retired.

"Stanton!" exclaimed McGovern as he descended the steps two at a time, his silver hair askew and his coat unfastened. "What in blazes are you doing here?"

"McGovern! Good to see you." The men shook hands. "I am imposing, but I fear the circumstances require it."

"Ah, bah. You could never impose, for how can one impose on a friend! Come, let's go into my study. We'll not be disrupted there."

They settled before the fire in leather wingback chairs, and Mr. McGovern poured them each a glass of port. "So, tell me, is it business or pleasure that brings you to Manchester?" McGovern's boisterous but pleasant tone put Nathaniel at ease.

"Well, I am not certain what category the reason for my visit falls in. I will share the story with you and allow you to be the judge on that matter." Nathaniel proceeded to divulge the events of the past several weeks to McGovern: the flooding, Mrs. Trent's passing . . . And yet, for the moment, he omitted the details concerning Miss Faire.

McGovern listened to each bit of information, his bushy eyebrows furrowed in marked concern. When Nathaniel was finished, McGovern stood, moved to the sideboard, and seemed to contemplate a painting of a fox chase. "It sounds to me as if you have a great deal on your mind. All you need to do is tell me how I may be of service, and I will happily comply."

"I was hoping you would allow me to remain here, in your home, for a few days. I am here on a—uh, personal matter."

McGovern cocked a bushy eyebrow. "Personal matter? Hmm. Sounds intriguing."

Nathaniel forced his fingers through his hair. He could no longer delay the real reason for his visit. He was not one to speak of his feelings, per se, but for Miss Faire, he would. "Do you recall how I wrote to you of a woman named Miss Cecily Faire?"

McGovern pointed his pudgy index finger in the air with the recollection. "Oh yes, Mrs. Trent's companion. The young lady we assembled a list of seamstresses for."

"Yes, the very one. I have reason to believe that she is here in Manchester."

"Is that so?"

"Yes. She left abruptly after Mrs. Trent's death. Alone."

"Alone?" He jerked his head. "In Manchester? That will not do."

McGovern took a long swig of the port, then put the glass down and folded his arms. "There wouldn't be another reason why you are concerned about the young Miss Faire, would there?" A grin creased McGovern's broad face as he smoothed his sideburns.

Nathaniel tried not to smile. He rubbed his hand over the back of his neck. "Miss Faire is special to me, I'll not deny. But beyond that, I could not rest for fear of her safety. Anything beyond that remains to be seen."

"Well, I am at your service. Anything you need, Mrs. McGovern and I will supply you. Do you want a carriage?"

"No, I think I will go by horseback."

"Do you want a guide? I can get one of the chaps at the bank to help you track down the addresses. These streets can be a maze."

Nathaniel nodded. "That would be very helpful."

"And it is settled. You shall stay here while in the city. I'd be offended if you stayed anywhere else. You are always a welcome guest in my home. Grab your things. We'll have Charles get you settled."

37

Nathaniel's night at the McGoverns' passed quickly. He was used to a small bed in his tiny room at Laurel Cottage, so sleeping in the guest room felt like staying in a castle. The canopied bed and gilded furnishings reminded him of what he would find within Willowgrove's walls. But in truth, it was of little consequence the type of room he stayed in. What mattered most was finding Miss Faire. He ate a quick breakfast of ham and poached eggs, and as promised, his horse and guide were outside of the McGoverns' home, ready to take Nathaniel to every address, including the ones that Mrs. Massey had provided. Energy flowed fast and strong through him, and the hustle on the streets only pushed him to be faster and more diligent. He reasoned that Miss Faire would not be at the address Clarkson had given him until night, for no doubt Miss Faire would be doing the exact same thing he was—searching for Leah Faire. He would visit as many shops as he could and then would call on Miss Faire once night started to fall.

But as the morning gave way to afternoon, Nathaniel's

optimism began to fade. He visited shop after shop, and each time he was told that nobody knew a Leah Faire. He even tried the tailoring and milliner shops they encountered along the way. Nothing.

Late that afternoon, just as Nathaniel was about to curtail his search for the day and turn his efforts toward finding Miss Faire, he stepped into a dressmaker's shop on the edge of a more fashionable district. The room was quite small. But a broad counter that formed a U bordered the space, and two women stood at opposite ends of the counter. One of them, dressed in a bright gown of gold and green, nodded in his direction. "Good day, sir. Might I be of assistance?"

"Yes, thank you." He removed his hat.

"Is there something in particular you had in mind? We have recently received some lovely painted fabrics, all the way from India."

Nathaniel balanced his hat in his hands. "I thank you, but I am here for another matter."

The woman's eyebrows rose. "Oh?"

"Yes. I am trying to locate a seamstress. A woman by the name of Miss Leah Faire."

The lady who welcomed him exchanged glances with the woman at the other end of the counter.

That slight movement was a different response from any other he had received that day, and it gave him reason to hope.

The woman picked up a piece of ribbon and cut her eyes at the other worker again before speaking. "May I ask what business you have with Miss Faire?"

But at that very moment, a curtain separating them from another room opened, and a woman with an abundance of red curls flowing down her back pushed through, a mound of yellow fabric in her arms. She did not look up, did not look in his direction, but there could be no denying her identity.

His pulse thudded wildly in his ears.

He had found her.

She glanced up in his direction but quickly continued to the counter, where she reached into a bin of ribbons.

The woman with the green-and-gold gown spoke. "Miss Faire, might this gentleman have a moment?"

It was then that she looked up. Her cheeks were flushed, her eyes darker than *his* Miss Faire.

"Me?" Miss Faire looked at him, then cast a nervous glance toward the older woman. She deposited her materials on the counter and stepped forward. "Yes, sir?"

"I do hope you will excuse the intrusion, but are you Miss Leah Faire, with connections to Aradelle Park?"

She swallowed. Her eyes widened in what could only be interpreted as alarm. "I am."

"And do you have a sister by the name of Cecily Faire?"

At the mention of the name, all color drained from her face and her chin trembled. "Ye-Yes, sir. What— Why . . ."

"My name is Nathaniel Stanton. I am the steward at Willowgrove Hall. Your sister was my employer's companion. She shared that she was hoping to find you and that she believed you to be a dressmaker in Manchester. And while I am here, I promised her I would aid her in her search."

The color returned to Miss Faire's cheeks with vibrant intensity. "Where is she? Is she here?"

"She is here, in Manchester, looking for you."

Miss Leah Faire cast a nervous glance at her employer before reaching for a paper and quill on the counter. She scratched a note before returning it to him. "I work very late most evenings, but Sunday is my day off. This is my address. If you would be so kind as to share this with her, I would be indebted to you."

He held up his hand and motioned for her to keep her note. "I wonder if you would be agreeable to another idea."

And he told her his plan.

38

Cecily sat down in her tiny room and stared at the dancing flame on the candle before her. She had purchased one small candle when she had passed a chandler on the street, but the flame was short and the light weak.

She had started her morning so full of optimism, but it faded quickly. She had hired a carriage to take her to the addresses on the list that she had received from Mr. Stanton, but at each turn, she was met with disappointment.

She did not feel up to joining the rest of the boarders for dinner, so she had purchased a bit of salted meat and bread from the merchant on the street below. But the bread was hard and the meat turned her stomach. She pushed the food away, kicked off her boot, and rubbed her foot. She was unused to the uneven cobblestone streets, and although attractive, the boots Mrs. Massey had selected for her were hardly up to a day's worth of walking.

The noisy clanking of wheels on the cobblestone and the sounds of men shouting and laughing were incessant. The sharp cry of the fulmars swooping above joined the sounds of the city street, and she groaned and sank into her chair. How she missed Willowgrove. How she missed the friendships she had made.

Manchester was nothing like she had expected. She had fooled herself into believing that it would be much easier to locate Leah. How wrong she had been.

Mr. Stanton had been right.

She rubbed her hand over her arm where Nathaniel Stanton had touched her. Try as she might, she could not recapture the feel of it. She shivered in the cold, reached for her shawl, and pulled it over herself like a blanket.

She repeated the words she had committed to memory the previous evening. She was determined to draw strength from them, hoping to rekindle the optimism she found in them the night before. A single tear of frustration and sadness slipped down her cheek, and she impatiently wiped it away. But whereas she had not been able to find the strength to mutter a prayer the previous night, in this moment of exhaustion, she leaned her head on the table and whispered, "Oh, God, please show me what to do."

She sat in silence for several minutes, listening to the sounds of the people on the street below. She'd almost fallen asleep when a knock at her door jolted her awake.

"Just a moment!" she called as she stood from the table, shaking out the folds of her dress and moving to the door. She opened it to find Mrs. Dotten standing there, as stern-faced as ever. She broke her frown only to say, "There is a man downstairs to see you."

It was Cecily's turn to frown. "No, I don't think so. I don't know any men here."

"Asked for you by name, 'e did." Her eyes narrowed suspiciously. "I don't approve of gentlemen calling on young ladies. This is a respectable establishment, Miss Faire. Do not think for a moment that I condone men visiting women at such a' hour."

"I assure you, there is nothing improper. I am sure this is some error."

Her curiosity matched her desire to be away from the landlord's scrutiny. She brushed past her in the dark, narrow hallway.

Cecily lifted her skirts to step down a stairwell so narrow that her shoulders nearly scraped the sides. A dark, shadowed figure was in the hall. For a moment, she grew nervous. No one knew she was here.

But then a glimmer of joy sparked as she recognized the straight nose. The square jaw.

"Mr. Stanton!" she exclaimed before she could bridle her enthusiasm.

He pivoted, and at the sight of his face, his blue eyes, she felt all her composure vanish. Tears of relief, joy, and regret rushed her, blurring her vision.

He glanced over to the innkeeper, who was staring in his direction, and gave a short bow.

Cecily did not even possess the presence of mind to return the courtesy.

The woman stepped forward. "I don't approve of men calling on my female boarders," she repeated. "You have a few minutes to tend to your business, and then you must leave."

The landlord retreated down the hall, and once her footsteps vanished, Cecily could not help herself. She rushed forward to him.

"What are you doing here?" she gasped, barely able to get the words to pass her lips.

He grinned. Could it be that he was having the same feelings at seeing her again? "You departed Willowgrove before I had the opportunity to bid you a proper farewell."

She was unsure if she stepped forward first, or if he did, but in a matter of moments, the rough wool of his tailcoat sleeve brushed her arm, and then he reached around her waist and pulled her to himself. His intoxicating scent enveloped her.

Instinctively, she pressed her hands against her face to hide her tears, but he leaned his forehead very close to hers, and with his free hand he gently lowered her hands.

"There is no need to cry."

But even as he said the words, every tangled emotion from the past several weeks commandeered her rational thought, and she melted against him. He pulled her closer until no space between them remained.

His whisper was rough and sweet in her ear. "Why did you leave?"

In the haze of her emotions, she was not sure how she managed to speak. "I don't belong there."

"You belong wherever I am. Oh, Cecily, my Cecily, never leave me again."

He pressed his lips, warm and soft, against her forehead. His use of her Christian name felt natural. Right. She wasn't sure if she was still standing or if she was floating. Her fingers reached up around his collar and wrapped around his neck.

His hands traveled up her back as his fingers splayed through her loose hair. And then ever so gently he angled her face to look at him.

She chewed her lip, trying to find the words to convey what she was feeling, and yet she could only utter a few words. "There is so much you do not know about me."

His thumb rubbed her cheek as his gaze met hers. Unwavering. "You know my secret. If you ever decide to tell me yours, I will hear it when you are ready, but not before. For I have fallen in love with a woman who is kind. Loving. Compassionate. Giving. I do not care about your past. What I care about is our future. And when I think about that, the only thing that matters is that you are by my side."

She lifted her face to meet his. Had she heard him correctly? He had fallen in love with her? She thought she had known what love was before. But oh, how wrong she had been. For the burning within her heart would not subside.

He lowered his lips to meet hers, and at the touch, she surrendered and leaned fully against him. His kiss was soft, tender at first, but then deepened possessively. Passionately. There could be no denying she had found her home. And it was in his arms.

But even as her heart nearly burst with contentment and happiness, she knew: He deserved the truth.

She pulled away. A look of confusion crossed his face. "Is everything all right?"

She lowered her gaze. "I need to tell you what I could not tell you when we were at Willowgrove."

"You don't have to."

"Yes, I do."

He looked around the tiny parlor. "Very well. Tell me. But first, I want to get you out of here."

Cecily had been so lost in the moment she had almost forgotten where they were. "Where are we going?"

"I will share details with you later. Gather your things, and I will settle the tab with the proprietor."

He pressed his lips to her forehead once more, and she hurried back up the stairs. Since she had never unpacked her things in the dirty room, she grabbed her bag and was back downstairs by the time Nathaniel was finished with the landlord. He pressed his hand against the small of her back and ushered her to the awaiting carriage.

Nathaniel took Cecily's hand to help her into the carriage. It was difficult to contain his joy. He'd found her. She was safe. And what was more, she had returned his affection with equal passion. All that mattered now was getting her away from this horrid boardinghouse.

Within moments he joined her in the carriage and sat next to her on the tufted seat. He pulled the door closed behind him and wrapped his arm around her, drawing her close. She did not resist. Instead, she melted against him and rested her head on his shoulder, her hair tickling his chin.

Dusk was falling, and outside the carriage, merchants were packing up their carts and birds called to their mates. He put her hand in his. "The carriage ride is not a long one," he said as he gently ran his thumb over her long, delicate fingers.

"Where are we going?"

"Do you recall the mention of my colleague Mr. McGovern? He lives in Manchester, near the warehouse district. He has a large home. There is a room for you there."

Cecily pulled away and straightened in her seat. The fading light caught on her hair, mesmerizing him. Her green eyes were bright with moisture. But the expression on her face brought him back to the present.

"What is it?"

She sniffed and pressed her lips together before speaking. "I meant what I said about no more secrets."

He sobered. He wanted to hear what she was about to say, but he was uneasy about what she might tell him. But he could tell by the intensity in her eyes that she needed to tell him. And could he blame her? They were two people desperate for fresh beginnings.

"You once asked me how I came to be at Rosemere. I gave you an answer, but that wasn't entirely the truth." She licked her lips and wiped her eyes again with the back of her hand. "My father disowned me."

The words were surprising, and yet he remained quiet, giving her space to share her story.

"But in order to explain it more completely, I must go back further. You asked me about my connection to Aradelle. You were right in your assumptions, Nathaniel. When I was young, sixteen to be exact, I believed myself to be in love with Andrew Moreton. So much so that he asked me to run away and marry him."

Even though Nathaniel had suspected to hear those very words, they still lanced him, jabbing at the raw spots of his heart.

"My father was a harsh man, a cruel man, and I thought that marrying Andrew would take me away from that. I gave myself to Andrew—heart, mind, and body. But it was all too late, for when my father discovered our plan, he saw to it that I was separated from Andrew permanently and took me to Rosemere. I never heard from him—or Andrew—after that day. He disowned me because I shamed him. I shamed my family."

Nathaniel resisted the urge to react. He'd suspected that Moreton played a role in this, but he was unsure of how great a role. The thought of the man touching even a hair on her head sent fire through his veins. But was this not what he had been asking from her? To share with him? To confide in him? At the moment, relief that she was finally trusting him outweighed any disappointment.

A small sob choked her, and she wiped her eyes again. "I had no idea that the Moretons were at all connected with the Trents when I accepted the position as a lady's companion." Cecily gave a nervous laugh. "So you must imagine my surprise when I saw Andrew my very first day at Willowgrove. But what could I do? I have no family. No connections. I needed that position." She met his gaze, her fingers fretting with the trim on her reticule.

It was then that Nathaniel remembered the letter tucked in his waistcoat. He pulled it out and handed it to her.

"Why, this is the letter from Mrs. Sherwin!" she said, taking the letter from him. "Wherever did you find it?"

"When Clarkson told me you left, I did not want to believe it, so I went to your bedchamber to see for myself. That letter was on the floor."

She lowered the letter to her lap. "So you know what it says?"

He nodded, feeling guilty that he had read her private missive.

But she only tucked the letter in her valise by her feet. "But do you see now why it is so important that I find Leah? For she could be alone. I could not forgive myself for that."

Nathaniel pulled her close to him again. The evening shadows fell across the bridge of her nose and the fullness of her lower lip. He tucked her hair behind her ear and allowed his fingertips to linger on her cheek. "We all have a past, and it pains me that yours has been so difficult. But all that matters to me is our future."

Even in the dark he could see a flush rush to her cheek.

His heart thudded in his chest. For he knew. She was the one he could trust with his heart. He could no longer hold it in. "Marry me, Cecily Faire."

Cecily's hand flew to her mouth as she began to laugh and cry. Then she threw her arms around Nathaniel's neck. "Yes!"

Nathaniel again lost himself in the splendor of her kiss.

39

Cecily stepped out of the carriage at Mr. McGovern's house a different woman from the one she had been mere minutes ago. For the first time in years, she began to feel the weight of the chains binding her to the shame of her past slacken. For now, Mr. Stanton—her beloved Nathaniel—knew all, and accepted her in spite of her past. One day soon she would be Mrs. Cecily Stanton.

Nathaniel reached in, grabbed her valise, and then laced his fingers with hers. His smile was giddy. Contagious.

"Are you ready?"

She fairly floated to the McGoverns' door. She had never met the man, but if Nathaniel trusted him, she had nothing to be concerned with.

Nathaniel knocked on the door, and within moments a poker-straight butler appeared at the door. "Mr. Stanton, welcome back."

"Thank you. Is McGovern in?"

"He's in his study. You may go on in if you wish."

Nathaniel grabbed Cecily's hand and hurried toward the study. When the study door opened, she expected to see an older gentleman at the desk, but what she saw stole her very breath.

For sitting in the chair by the fireplace was Leah.

Despite time's paintbrush, looking at Leah was still like looking in a mirror.

Abundant joy coursed through her, infusing her with energy. Cecily could not form words. Instead, she ran to her sister and embraced her with all her might.

When they finally separated, Cecily held Leah at arm's length. Her heart, already tender from the reunion with Nathaniel, threatened to burst from her chest. "If you only knew how I have longed for this moment!" Cecily sobbed before throwing her arms around her sister once more. "How did you get here?"

Leah returned the embrace, squeezed Cecily's hands, and wiped her face with the back of her hand. "Mr. Stanton came into the shop where I work." She reached out and touched Cecily's cheek. "Oh, Cecily, I cannot believe it is you. I thought . . . I thought I would never see you again."

The sisters embraced again. Cecily could not help the giggles welling up within her. The day had been surreal, a complete transformation from hopelessness to complete joy.

Nathaniel retreated toward the door. "I will leave you two ladies to get reacquainted. I am sure you have much to discuss."

Cecily dropped her sister's hands and turned toward Nathaniel. His smile was warm. She whispered, "Thank you."

He simply nodded and closed the door behind him.

Cecily led Leah to a nearby sofa. "Tell me everything and quickly! Five years is a lot to catch up on!"

Once they were seated, Leah's expression sobered. "I cannot wait to hear all about what you have been up to, but do you know about Father?"

Cecily nodded and looked down at her fingers knitted together in her lap. "I received a letter from Mrs. Sherwin not long ago. She told me he was gone."

Leah's darker eyes filled with tears. "He would not tell me where you were. I begged and pleaded. I-I was afraid something terrible had happened to you—or that he had done something terrible to you."

"Do not be upset. He took me to a girls' school. How cruel of him not to tell you. And as you can see, I am just fine."

Leah sniffed. "When he returned that next day, and you weren't with him, I-I was so frightened."

At the sight of her sister's tears, tears welled up in Cecily's eyes. "I have often wondered what it must have been like for you."

Leah shook her head. "He was released from his position at Aradelle Park the next day, once it was clear what had happened with Mr. Moreton. We traveled to London, but Father became violent. Angry. I feared for my life. I remembered Mother talking about her sister here in Manchester. I ran away to find her. Thankfully, she took me in. I never heard from Father, but I did keep in touch with a few friends from Aradelle. That is how I learned of his death."

"And our aunt?" asked Cecily. "How is she?"

Leah shook her head. "She was so much like Mother. Kind and warm. But she died about two years ago. We had grown quite close. It was like losing Mother all over again."

Cecily had been focused on her own pain for so long that news of Leah's hardship was sobering. "I wrote to Aunt, but I never heard from her."

"I do not think she received your letters, for she helped me look for you for a long time. We eventually abandoned the search." But then Leah grabbed her hand, a smile brightening her face. "But you are here now. And we never need be separated again."

Leah and Cecily spent the rest of the evening in the McGoverns' study, talking until the wee hours of the morning. Sharing five years of dreams, secrets, fears, and tears.

Cecily lifted her hand to brush her hair away, but as she did, her fingertips grazed the coral necklace around her neck. She stiffened. There was still one thing she needed to do. She reached up and unclasped the coral necklace from around her neck. As Cecily pulled it free, Leah's eyes widened and then filled with tears. "Mother's necklace!"

"It was wrong and selfish of me to take it that night. It belongs to you too."

Leah took the necklace and held it gingerly in her fingers, as if it might break into a dozen pieces. "Oh, I thought this had been lost for good! I have often wondered what became of it."

"It has been with me, and it has been my deepest wish to return it to you."

Leah lifted her hair and pivoted so that Cecily could fasten it around her neck. When she was done, Leah turned back around and reached for Cecily's hands. "I have missed you."

Cecily squeezed her sister's hands. "Who knows why, but at least now we know we will never be apart again."

40

An early winter snow fell on Cecily's wedding day, gathering on the grounds in lacy droves. Dressed in a gown of cream satin with pale-pink flowers, Cecily turned to face her beloved in the warmth of Wiltonshire's stone church.

The years of pain and hopelessness flashed before her for but a fleeting moment, all of which now seemed to be a distant memory.

She glanced over her shoulder at the people filling the pews. Her past was again blended with her present: Her sister, Leah, was sitting two rows back, next to Rebecca Turner. Mrs. Stanton pressed a handkerchief to her eyes, and Hannah and Charlotte watched them, eyes wide. She lifted her eyes to view even farther back. The church was full of people she was just getting to know—people whom Nathaniel had known his entire life. And then, in the back pew, she saw him. Andrew Moreton, his new wife absent from the event. He was not in the Trent family pew, but in the back. A bystander.

So much hinged on that one decision she made when she was

sixteen. How much pain and anguish it had caused her. But now, as she stood next to Nathaniel, it was clear—she had to have all those experiences to get her to where she was at this moment.

Nathaniel squeezed her hand, and she looked up at him. He smiled down at her, his pale eyes bright and wide, his dark hair falling over his forehead. Her heart ached at the expression of affection in his gaze. Warmth welled up within her. He loved her. Not for what she had or had not done. Not because of where she came from or who her family was. But because of her.

He did not let her hand go. Instead, he interlaced his fingers with hers, holding it tighter.

In one week, they would leave for Lockbourne. They would start a new life together. It would be a future free of secrets. Free of loneliness.

Her time at Lockbourne was the opportunity for new beginnings; not only would she be starting her life as Mrs. Nathaniel Stanton, but Leah would be accompanying them on their new journey. And even though Rebecca and Mr. Turner were staying to run his family's farm, Mrs. Stanton and the younger girls were planning to travel north to spend the summer at Lockbourne. Cecily once felt so alone, and now she had a family to love—and that loved her.

As they waited for the vicar to begin, Nathaniel leaned over, squeezed her hand, and whispered, "Are you happy, Cecily?"

Tears misted her vision, but she did not want to cry today. Today she was experiencing a happiness she had never known. "Yes. More than I could ever imagine."

He wrapped his hand more tightly around hers.

Her future was before her, wide and boundless. She had new memories to create, ones that would fill her heart and give her hope, and they would face their future . . . together.

READING GROUP GUIDE

1. In this novel, Nathaniel was asked to keep a secret from those he loved. Do you think Nathaniel resented keeping such a secret? Have you ever had to keep a secret from your family and friends? How did it affect you?
2. If you were able to give Cecily one piece of advice, what would it be? What about Nathaniel—what words of wisdom would you share with him?
3. Throughout the course of the story, Cecily spent a great deal of time with Mrs. Trent. What life lessons do you think Cecily learned from Mrs. Trent? What do you think Mrs. Trent learned from Cecily?
4. During the Regency period, a woman was defined by her reputation. Is that still true today? How do you think Cecily's story would be different if it took place in modern-day America instead of Regency England?
5. In what ways is Cecily different at the end of the novel? In what ways is she the same? How does her perception of herself change throughout the course of the story?
6. Cecily and Andrew made a decision while they were teenagers that changed the course of both their lives. How do you think their experience shaped the adults they became?
7. What character in the novel (male or female) do you identify with the most?
8. Now it is your turn! What comes next for Nathaniel and Cecily? Does Lockbourne House flourish? Do they have children? What would you like to see happen to these characters in the future?

ACKNOWLEDGMENTS

Writing a novel is a thrilling journey, and as I think about the people who have encouraged me along the way, I feel truly blessed!

To my husband, Scott, and to my daughter—your loving support and enthusiastic encouragement motivate me to follow my dreams. Thank you for traveling this road with me!

To my parents, Ann and Wayne—through prayers and guidance, you have shown me that nothing is impossible. And to my sisters, Sally and Angie—you encourage me and cheer me on. Thank you for always being there for me!

To my agent, Tamela Hancock Murray—you are not only my agent, but my friend. Thank you for dreaming big and caring about my stories. I am beyond privileged to work with you.

To my editor, Natalie Hanemann—thank you for coming alongside me again and joining me in this adventure. You rolled up your sleeves and dove right into this story. Your astute insight inspired and challenged me, and this story is stronger because of your guidance. And to the rest of the HarperCollins Christian Publishing team, from marketing to design, from production to sales, your collective talent astounds me.

One of the best parts of being a writer is meeting and interacting with other writers. To my writing accountability partners, Carrie, Julie, and Melanie—thank you for the support, the encouragement, and the laughs! And to my writing "sister" Kim—you have been there since the beginning of my writing career—I am so grateful for you.

ABOUT THE AUTHOR

Photo by Emilie Haney of EAH Creative

SARAH E. LADD is an award-winning, bestselling author who has always loved the Regency period—the clothes, the music, the literature, and the art. A college trip to England and Scotland confirmed her interest, and she began seriously writing in 2010. Since then, she has released several novels set during the Regency era. Sarah is a graduate of Ball State University and holds degrees in public relations and marketing. She lives in Indiana with her family.

Visit Sarah online at SarahLadd.com

Instagram: @sarahladdauthor

Facebook: @SarahLaddAuthor

Twitter: @SarahLaddAuthor

Pinterest: @SarahLaddAuthor